SET IN THE SAME WORLD:

LHIND THE THIEF
A POSSE OF PRINCESSES
BAREFOOT PIRATE
THE WREN SERIES

LHIND THE SPY

Sherwood Smith

First published 2015 by Book View Café Publishing Cooperative
P.O. Box 1624
Cedar Crest, NM 87008-1624
www.bookviewcafe.com

Print edition 2016
ISBN 978-1-53987-554-3

Cover design by Dave Smeds
Cover photograph © Csaba Peterdi, Shutterstock
Interior design by Marissa Doyle

Lhind the Spy

One

I SAT DECOROUSLY ON a rock overlooking the mighty waterfall below the imperial palace of Erev-li-Erval, Thianra's practice harp on my lap. What a very fine picture I must make, thought I, my silvery hair swirling about my head (I twitched my scalp and my spine hair to really make it *fwoosh*), my tail spread picturesquely in a silvery cascade over the panels of my cherry-and-green-embroidered peach silk Hrethan drape, my hands upon the strings....

Plar-r-r-k! Pla-o-w-nk!

Flat! Not only had the strings gone out of tune, but I'd fingered wrong. Again. I could hear the music I wanted to make, hear it so clearly. But my fingers sure couldn't.

All right, then, I would hold the harp and look wistfully out over the water. Or did I just look sulky? Worse, guilty? How does someone look wistful, anyway? I tried half-shutting my eyes and letting my mouth fall slightly open, but I had a suspicion my expression resembled that of a cat who's about to be impolite on an innkeeper's best carpet.

I sighed and bent to tighten the harp strings, though a month's lessons still had me struggling impatiently with the basics. The only thing worse than my playing was my singing. Though the rest of the Hrethan lifted their voices in melodious song without much effort, maybe it was my being half-Hrethan that made me sound like a drowning bullfrog to my own ears.

Ploink. The mist rising from the frothing waters below caused a shimmering rainbow of vapors, lovely to behold, but its moisture was obviously not good for harp strings.

Coming out there was a terrible idea, I thought glumly.

Once again, I'd run away, a lifelong habit whenever I found myself in difficulties. This latest one a discussion about magic lessons that had turned into an argument. Guess who was at fault for that!

Now that my temper had cooled, I could see how my fretting about the relentless requirements of the mage instructors as well as imperial protocol added to the burden Hlanan was already bearing, because I wasn't the one about to be made heir to an empire—

Footsteps.

Ah! Hlanan had come after me! I wanted him to discover me in a soulful pose, so I pretended I did not hear. I picked up the harp, and—

That's when the black bag closed over my head.

The harp fell from my hands. I clawed at the bag as a weird sensation, as if I'd fallen into an avalanche of snow, settled heavily over my limbs.

Someone had hit me with a stone spell.

———◆◇◆———

"Thumb up, Lhind. Thumb up, not out. Your fingers are not spiders, so don't let them climb up the harp springs. One movement, from soundboard to harp, one...."

I was back in the imperial music gallery with Thianra, but a door had appeared between the windows.

"Come to me, Lhind. Come!"

Wary, distrustful of any voice whose owner I could not see, I tried to stay back but my feet and hands moved against my will. In spite of my attempts to cry out, to halt, I walked silently to the door. I opened it and found myself back in the music gallery again, only now my fingers moved deftly over the harp strings, but they were small brown hands, and I moved further away, seeing an unruly brown head bent over the harp, light brown hair short, thick and unkempt....

Thianra? I called anxiously, though I had no lips, or eyes, or ears.

She glanced up, gray-brown eyes distant, her face rounder than I remembered, the rest of her childish in form. I was seeing Thianra as a little girl?

Where's your brother Hlanan? I called, but she was oblivious, lost in her music.

She curled her feet tightly under the legs of her stool and bent to her harp again sending a ripple of beautiful sound out and out. I drifted with the music toward the sunlight streaming through the windows, and there was another door.

I drifted right through it.

And here was Hlanan, my own dear Hlanan, tallish, slender, only instead of wearing his old scribe robe of blue, he was clad in a long tunic of fine velvet in a shade close to the pale blue light of dawn, embroidery at collar and sleeves in twining vines with tiny rubies representing buds, his brown hair drawn up high on the back of his head into a golden comb with the imperial interlocking laurels.

Closer, closer...I strove with all my strength to halt, but a whisper beckoned me on, *Come, Lhind. Come to me.*

No, not until I know who you are, I cried, as pain prickled through me like red cracks in ceramic. Sound wavered in a deep, reverberating worble.

I gasped, and the strange burble rose in pitch, becoming fragments of speech. Pain ignited in every bone and muscle as my body woke. Helpless to move on my own, I sensed that I was being moved in jolts and bumps. My skin itched ferociously, as if a thousand needles pricked just below the point of pain.

The sense of pins stabbing me sharpened to a sting as the world whirled, then stilled.

Someone had dumped me onto grass. I lay flat. Motionless. The stinging receded gradually, restoring a sense of my limbs. One breath, two, three...the burbling fragments of speech rose in pitch to normal cadences.

I recognized one of those voices. Shock shuddered through me. That was Geric Lendan, Prince of the Golden Circle. Who by all rights ought to be languishing in prison, after all the nefarious things he'd done, beginning with imprisoning the mage Faryana in a diamond necklace, and ending with his hiring the pirates of the Skull Fleet to chase Hlanan and me.

I'd asked Hlanan, "Why isn't anyone arresting Prince Geric?"

"Because nothing can be proved."

"But he's the one who first stole that evil book, and bespelled Faryana, and all the rest of it. And the Mage Council has to know that. I know they still have not freed her, but if I could hear Faryana's thoughts, they can too, right?"

"They have their reasons for not talking about Faryana, or the necklace, or Geric's purpose for what he did," Hlanan had said. "As for everything else he did, he could claim hearsay."

"Hearsay? Sending the pirates after us?"

Hlanan spread his hands. "Short of the pirates turning up to testify, or to furnish a magic-sealed contract, Geric can claim he was their prisoner, or their passenger, or anything else." But before I could burst out against the sheer unfairness of Prince Geric's getting away with everything short of murder (and he'd tried that!), Hlanan said, "Remember, the mages know what he did. And are watching to see what he will do next."

Well, I thought sourly as I lay there, it looked like I was about to find out what he was going to do next. But I might not survive to talk about it.

He had threatened me with death at least a couple of times. Of course that was after I'd robbed him twice, but at least I didn't go around threatening people, or sticking them in evil spells!

"...Find out who they are. Even though she is a Hrethan, she is a liar, a thief, and could not possibly be the target of an imperial search — unless she has been robbing the Empress. I wouldn't put it past her."

Geric's voice sharpened, breaking into my self-justifying sulk.

Somewhere to the left, someone scraped steel over a whetstone, *hiss, hiss, hiss*. Farther away, a horse snorted, and a hoof thudded to the ground.

"We'd better pick up our feet. Curse it, Pandoc, where are you? What's Nath's sign for haste?"

I had to get away. But how? From long-ago habit, I remained

where I was, my breathing slow. Without moving a muscle, I gauged the direction of the voice and cautiously slitted an eyelid.

I lay under a darkening sky. My limbs were free. That was good. But my thief tools, which I had carried with me day and night since I was a sprat? Lying in my trunk back in the imperial palace, because I hadn't a need for them in the palace.

Irritation prickled painfully through me. I forced myself to keep my breathing slow and even. Escape first.

Another peek, this time with both eyes. A cluster of mostly gray-clad figures, one with thick, frizzy ash-blond hair, one with long ruddy-fair hair—Prince Geric—one dark, short curly hair, standing a few paces away at my left, on the other side of a campfire. Two of them wrung their hands.

I barely made out a line of horses beyond them. Without moving my head I could not see to my extreme right, but I heard no noise. Breeze ruffled over my face, carrying the scent of water, of pine—

Pine! Hope burned away the annoyance. If I were high enough in the mountains, and could get access to a cliff, I could transform into a bird. I was still too unfamiliar with my newly discovered ability to be able to transform without both the altitude and the sensation of falling into air, but pine grew high in the mountains west of the imperial city, and I heard nothing on my right.

I had to check.

"Now! Now means now—oh, someone let her know," Geric exclaimed impatiently as he flung himself away—facing in my direction. I quickly shut my eyes.

A tenor voice responded, "The hand-sign for urgency is—"

"We don't have time to spell it all out. I'll lead," Geric retorted. "Make the signal for following me. Fast!"

Another furtive peek as Geric shoved past the other two figures in gray. The mercenary Gray Wolves? That was even worse!

Geric's urgency meant I wasn't likely to get a better chance.

Without moving the rest of my body, I turned my head to the right. Slowly...slowly....

All I saw past tall grasses was air. A convenient cliff? My heart thudded against my ribs as I lifted my head. Easy, easy . . . the top of a shrub. Not a cliff, then, a slope of some sort. A bit farther away, the tops of a cluster of firs, and nothing beyond those.

A possible cliff perhaps fifty paces to the right. My hands and feet were free. I drew in a breath, rolled to my feet and ran.

A startled exclamation behind me tightened my neck. I stretched my legs out, laboring hard. Usually I was fast, and could leap high, but the spell still dragged at my limbs.

Pounding feet shortened the distance. Nearly stumbling in my frantic haste, I leaped over a tangled root of a fallen tree, spotted the edge of a precipice, sucked in my breath to fling myself over —

Pain jolted through me. Lightning strike?

I fell flat on my face — and the pain doubled me up, radiating in red throbs from my shoulder as the footsteps gathered around me. Hard fingers hauled me to my feet like a sack of turnips. I fought for breath.

A fresh wave of cold, slithery pain wrung through me as steel slid out of my shoulder. My knees buckled.

Two sets of hands held me up. Black spots blurred my vision. More jolting and joggling as footsteps crunched dirt around me, and various people panted from exertion, then the fingers let go and I collapsed in a heap.

When fingers probed at the muscle below my shoulder, the black spots bloomed again, threatening to take over. I gulped in breath after breath, my bones watery, and gradually defeated the black spots as the ache diminished to a hair below unbearable.

The ice-cold sense of shock eased enough to enable me to look around. Not that I wanted to, especially when the first thing I perceived was Prince Geric's intent gaze, the rosy firelight some-how leaching the color out of his face. Or maybe he had paled.

I scowled at him.

He sat back and let out a long sigh. "You'll live," he said. Was that relief?

"You just knifed me!" I croaked. "Or somebody did." I blinked up at Gray Wolf tunics. These warriors, I remembered with a sinking sensation in my already uncertain middle, had given us a hard chase after Hlanan and I stole that blood mage book from the evil Duchess of Thann and her mage.

"I pegged you on the right," Prince Geric said, pointing at my shoulder, which I discovered had been wrapped in some kind of bandage while I'd teetered on the edge of unconsciousness.

"Why?" I yelped.

His mouth twisted. "Because I heard that you can transform to a bird if you go over a cliff." His glance took in the Gray Wolves standing about in a circle. Maybe they were the very ones who had been chasing me the first time I transformed.

Don't admit to anything, I thought. Time for my own questions. "I mean, why am I here?" I croaked, still short of breath because of my quaky middle.

"You ruined my life," he began.

"So now you're going to ruin mine?"

His expression tightened with irritation, and I wondered if I had interrupted a grand speech he'd planned as he drawled, "It seems a fair enough exchange."

Planned speech it was, then. I would go along if I could learn something. "What's grabbing me exchange for?"

"For some unfathomable reason, Emperor Jardis Dhes-Andis of Sveran Djur wants you," he stated with smiling malice. "It is my privilege, and my pleasure, to oblige." He performed a mocking bow.

That's when I discovered that cold and slimy and sick as I felt, I could always drop through a trapdoor into something colder, slimier, and sicker.

I'd been cautiously touching the bandage, but dropped my hand.

"No," I said.

Prince Geric gave a short, contemptuous laugh. "In the time it takes to get to my camp, you may entertain yourself with contemplating the moral implications of your having robbed me. We would never have met again if you'd kept your sticky fingers to yourself."

In a way, that stung almost worse than his knife blade. No. Knives always hurt worse. But frustration boiled away inside me, because while ordinarily I believed him about as far as I could spit into a wind, I knew that much was true: If I had not robbed Geric of that strange bone whistle and played around with the voice communicating through it, I would not have caught the attention of the evil emperor who had given it to him.

I brooded about that as his minions began to mount up. Two hefty Gray Wolves stood guard while a horse was brought to me.

"Can you ride?" Geric asked, stepping up to the bridle. Before I could refuse, he said with a return to his old arrogance, "We can always lash you to the stirrups if you can't."

"I'll ride."

The hefties hauled me up again, and in spite of my "Ow! That hurts!" they threw me into the saddle, then mounted themselves. So much for trying to slow them down.

One of the Gray Wolves kept my reins, riding ahead and to one side. The second one rode a little behind on the opposite side, as the trail did not admit of three horses across.

Maybe a better rider than I could figure out a way to get the horse to slip them and gallop away. But I was a terrible rider—rarely on a horse—so escape was denied me. So were my thief tools, lying uselessly in that palace.

Worse, Hlanan did not know where I was. I'd stomped off, felt remorse for trying to start an argument, and then I thought of that *stupid* plan for his finding me at the waterfall, which he knew I loved visiting.

Oh, he might go looking there for me, but unless Prince Geric was as stupid as I had been for thinking my waterfall plan such a great idea, he wasn't going to leave clues lying about. The learner's harp I'd borrowed from Hlanan's sister Thianra had probably been pitched over the waterfall the moment after they waylaid me.

All right. One thing I'd learned during my lifetime on the run: There was no use in mentally beating myself up over mistakes. All my life I'd been my only ally, staying alive with no aid but my wits—and my few magical spells. Some of which Hlanan had warned me were called "greater magics," which meant I could unwittingly do all kinds of destruction.

None of those were the least use now. I didn't know the harmonic range of anyone's voice except Prince Geric's well enough for what I called Voice cast, the magic that strikes another's nerves long enough to force them to freeze in one place, or to release a hold, or even to fall senseless. I was not certain I could use it on him, even if the air wasn't so open. I'd heard him speaking rarely, and always in exactly the same tone of mockery. The emotions under it — if there were any — would be difficult for me to reach.

Mind cast, which recoiled far more dangerously onto me, was even more out of reach. And a good thing, for I had the least control over it. I was not ready to deal with the consequences of killing anyone with that mental white lightning.

I could hear animals' thoughts, and sometimes other Hrethan, I had very recently discovered. But I could not be thinking about or doing anything else, and like many of my sustained magics, it left me light-headed, sometimes dizzy.

I was already dizzy and weak.

Those were the things I could not do. What *could* I do? Watch and listen, for starters. Act weak. Being small and light-boned, and looking a lot younger than I really was, I'd found that people usually underestimated me. I put my left hand up to my right shoulder, which throbbed doubly at every jolt of the horse's hooves beneath me. I didn't have to fake those watery joints and the roil of nausea in my middle.

Next time, I decided, don't flounce away from an argument until after a good meal.

The inward retort was prompt: I shouldn't have flounced off at all.

This mental argument was even worse than the almost-argument that I'd had with Hlanan. Which would have been an argument, except that he hated arguing, and he'd gone silent. So — another lifelong habit — I'd run.

A swift glance around disclosed the jumble of fir and other trees that I recognized from the lower folds and hills below the mountains. Another cold jolt: I was not high enough after all for the transformation. If Prince Geric hadn't thrown that knife, I would have landed on rocks or hard ground. Ugh.

Another glance. They made their way up an animal trail, which meant leaving as little sign of tracks as they could. "Handing me off to Dhes-Andis." That had to mean magic, as the evil emperor was surely not waiting around on the top of a mountain. Why hadn't Geric transferred me to Dhes-Andis the moment he threw that bag over my head?

I still did not know much about transfer magic, other than that it hurt and was extremely dangerous. You had to have a specific destination firmly in mind, unless you had a transfer token, which fixed the transfer point for you. Most tokens shifted people between Destinations, that is, places with distinct tile patterns. Experienced mages didn't necessarily need the Destinations, but there was a greater danger: transfers could be warded. That meant traps waiting for you.

Safe bet that any Destination in reach of Dhes-Andis would be infested with protective (and lethal) magic. Therefore, Geric had probably been given a transfer token that bypassed the wards.

I glanced up the line as the horses lowered their heads and began plodding up a sharp incline. At the front rode Prince Geric, his reddish-blond hair bright against his midnight blue velvet.

Velvet. No one rode in velvet by choice. Geric, wearing his court clothes, which granted him access to the middle precincts of the palace, had to have been stalking me through the outer garden areas of Erev-li-Erval's palace, and after grabbing me didn't stop to change. The waterfall lay within what was called the Paths of Harmony, accessible only to the nobles visiting the imperial city.

So he had been relying on his identity as a Prince of the Golden Circle to gain access to the middle precincts, though he had to know I'd told the imperials everything I could about his nefarious activities. He had to have balanced the risk of their believing me against his exalted identity, but it was a safe bet he hadn't added to his risk by carrying anything magical that might link him to Dhes-Andis.

Yes. That made sense: If there was indeed a transfer token, it lay guarded in a camp. Therefore I had only the time between now and when we reached the camp to effect an escape—

An outrider ahead shouted something a heartbeat before a horn winded faintly somewhere below. Pursuit?

"Pick up the pace." Geric slung his rich cloak back and drawled over his shoulder. "You want to be long gone before they catch up."

"You." That suggested I was right about the transfer token—he was transferring away (with me), leaving his minions to shift for themselves. Taking more than two persons in long transfers was dangerous for reasons I did not understand. Right now I didn't need to understand. The important thing was that I'd guessed right about a transfer token waiting in a hidden place somewhere up ahead.

So. How could I slow him up? A fall from the horse? No, not only would that really, really hurt, but it wouldn't slow them long. Geric would have them to throw me over the saddle like a rolled up rug and tie me to the stirrups. Which would slow them maybe ten heartbeats.

I looked around. No cliffs. A stumble from my horse wrenched my body. My shoulder throbbed insistently, reminding me that even if a cliff materialized conveniently around the next outcropping, my diving over it would only end in a painful splat.

I shut my eyes, ready to reach with my mind for the minds of any hidden small creatures who might aid me. I did it rarely, unwilling to risk the lives of creatures whose minds I could hear and influence, unless I knew I could keep them safe.

I shut my mind against the old habit. No reaching on the mental plane!

I opened my eyes and clutched at the horse's mane to steady the woozy reaction. I was startled to find Geric riding next to me, watching narrowly. "Are you sick?"

"Why should you care?" I muttered.

"If you're sick, I've some whisky. It ought to settle your insides enough to get you to where we're going, but if you're hatching a plan, then I'm bringing out the ropes."

"Sick," I said, and debated adding in some extra weakness. No, that narrow blue gaze was already suspicious enough. "Shoulder hurts too much to do anything."

He shrugged, his little smirk igniting resentment in me. It didn't take a scry crystal or extra powers to see that he was congratulating himself on a deft knife throw.

"The empress appears to have sent out the entire Imperial Guard," Prince Geric said appreciatively, pointing out over the cliff edge with his chin. "Is that due to your perfidy or mine? What did you do in there?"

I nearly blurted, "Hlanan sent them." I forced myself to cough, covering the beginning of his name.

Prince Geric did not know that Hlanan was the imperial heir —
that is, it was fairly certain that Aranu Crown, Empress of Charas
al Kherval, was going to choose him over his three siblings. No
one except a handful of us knew that; according to imperial
tradition, imperial offspring were unrecognized and unknown
until such time as the ruler chose to formally introduce them at
court. Which could be any age from five to fifty, depending upon
their future position.

Nor did Geric know that my arrest had been faked to cover
several things that the empress was quietly investigating.

Sure enough, Geric said, "How did you get them to let you out
as far as the Paths of Harmony? The Hrethan, no doubt, using
their influence. Only they would be stupid enough to take your
word for parole!"

Much as I would have liked to annihilate him with a retort, I
forced myself to stay silent and turned my gaze to the patch of
late-autumn wildflowers nodding in the early evening breeze.

Geric gave a snort of contempt and urged his horse ahead, as I
ignored him and continued to survey the wildflowers in their
straggling grasses. They sloped upward toward a thick copse of
firs, bisected by our narrow trail. The horses plodded steadily, ears
flicking as they listened for sounds inaudible to us humans, and
the great mountains towered over us, peaks smothered by clouds.

Below stretched the gentle hills on either side of the river that
flowed to the waterfall, the imperial city of Erev-li-Erval tucked
between the river and the palisades overlooking the coastline far
below. Like ruddy ribbons, the canals gleamed in the westering
sunlight; in the center, like a crown, rose the palace.

Hlanan was there. Looking for me? The imperial schedule was
relentlessly strict. I was now late for the foregathering of court in
the fountain chamber, before the empress sat down to her evening
meal. Hlanan might have noted my absence, but I could see him
deciding to let me have time to get over my bad mood away from
the constant eyes of court. Privacy was as precious as gold to those
living in the imperial court.

I had to assume that I was on my own — as I had been all my
life — and didn't have long to figure something out, judging from
Geric's glances toward a cliff above the next turn in the trail.

The blond Gray Wolf captain raised her gloved fist, and the cavalcade came to an obedient stop. A chance for me?

Prince Geric clucked to his mount, who trotted up the trail. Geric's long cloak rippled down his back, swinging in folds on either side of the horse's hindquarters. His impatience, or tension, revealed itself in the shimmer of the fabric over tightened muscles. I strained to hear as one of the scouts said, "Outriders haven't signaled."

"They would if there was a threat, would they not?" Geric said shortly. He looked up at the sky, and at the surroundings. In the distance, the last fiery light of the sinking sun caught on something metallic, far below. The pursuit—whomever their target—had found our trail.

"Carry on," Prince Geric said. "Like as not the outriders are lounging about drinking something hot." He turned to the blond captain and began in a slow, loud, distinct voice, "You may discipline them—" Then he gave a sigh of impatience, turned to one of the others, and said, "Tell her that she can flog them for negligence later. Right now, we'll proceed with hands to weapons."

The blond captain brought her chin down in a nod that was almost a bow. She made a quick gesture, and a subdued rustle and clatter sounded up and down the line as Gray Wolves loosened swords in scabbards or tightened bowstrings and readied arrows.

Then we rode on.

Firelight beat with cheery welcome on the undersides of tree boughs in a sheltered glade with good watch points. As we approached, my neck and spine hairs lifted all the way down my back. Tension? It reminded me of how it felt to do—

"Magic," Geric snapped.

But it was too late.

A not-quite-smell somewhere between fire-weed pollen and hot metal made me sneeze violently as everyone holding a steel weapon shouted, hissed, or grunted in shock and dropped their weapons. Those with bows whirled to aim at a woman whose gray-streaked black hair I recognized: the mage who had conspired with the Duchess of Thann to gain a really, really nasty book about blood magery.

Instinctively I ducked my head, though I was on horseback.

Maybe she wouldn't recognize me. I'd been in disguise when we'd met so briefly at a tower window, when I pinched the book right out of her hands.

The air hummed briefly, and those holding bows trembled, bow strings snapping.

"The next spell," the woman lifted her voice, "will be fatal. I care nothing for your lives."

"Maita!" Prince Geric exclaimed, sliding off his horse and slinging his cloak back. I noticed he approached her cautiously, for all his bluster, and stopped well away from the woman. "You forget that I, too, studied magic. You can't strike us all dead."

"I can begin with you, Prince Geric," Maita retorted. "Where is my blood magic text?"

Prince Geric retorted, "The last I saw of it was when I gave it to my wife."

Wife? He was married?

He went on, "My understanding was *you* lost it."

The mage's heavy brows twitched together. "I did not *lose* it. The text was stolen before I could complete the first experiment." As she spoke, she glanced from him to me. "That is a Hrethan or one of the Snow Folk, isn't it? Wait." She stepped closer. "You look familiar. Why?"

I licked my lips and tried to distract her by lifting my spine hair and tail. She blinked as my hair and tail swirled around, silvery in the last fading light. I tried rapidly to put together a lie that would distract her from placing me at that tower when I grabbed that blood magic text.

But then Prince Geric said, "Meet Bird of the Snows, a Hrethan thief. Or was that name a lie, too?" He cast a scornful glance my way.

The mage scowled. "It was a little thief with honey-colored eyes who robbed me of my book! I know those eyes."

"You, too?" Prince Geric shouted with laughter. "Hrethan, this I will say, you and your sticky fingers certainly get around."

The mage sent him a scornful look in answer, and *her* fingers began to glow as she wove a couple of quick signs.

For the second time that day, a stone spell dropped me.

Two

CONSIDERING THE FACT THAT I had not eaten since a couple of pieces of fruit earlier in the previous day, my sense of monumental injustice increased when I woke up to morning light streaming in through a high window and was promptly sick.

That piece of nastiness was followed by the sensation of being pricked all over by hot needles, far worse than the previous time. The only good thing was that my wakening was unaccompanied by dreams or whatever that had been when I was recovering from Prince Geric's spell. But considering how much my entire body ached, I would rather have not wakened at all.

Still. Awake was awake, and in no place I'd chosen to be. Time to find out where, and get away. Long habit kept me still, listening for danger. Hearing nothing but the soft sough of wind, I cracked an eyelid.

In my range of vision: narrow window slit, the light splashing over the contours of gray, mossy stone curving in a smooth wall.

I risked turning my head, which pounded alarmingly. More curving wall. An iron-reinforced door.

Nearer, someone had thoughtfully left a jug of water on the warped wooden floor next to the pallet on which I lay. I sat up cautiously. When I touched the jug, a brief sense of...something...lifted my hair. Magic? It was gone in a heartbeat.

I sniffed with my magical sense as well as my nose. Smelled nothing but water.

I gulped it down, reveling in the clean, cold taste, then lay back, exhausted by that much exertion.

I'd scarcely recovered my breath when heavily-shod feet clattered on stone beyond the door, followed by the clank of keys. A lock! My hand snapped to my waist, but instead of finding the comforting shape of my thief tools, my palm scraped my hip bone under my fine-layered silk tunic.

The door swung wide, and in walked that mage, one hand held at an angle, fingers extended. A greenish glow flickered disturbingly, like slow-crawling lightning, around a stone that lay on her palm. "You woke at last," she said, glancing at the jug. So that flash I'd sensed had been some kind of warning spell to alert her when I touched the thing.

"While you were safely bound under my spell, Prince Geric traded your life for his," she said pleasantly, in the tone anyone else would say, "And good morning to you!"

I couldn't help cringing away from that greenish glow. I couldn't fight her. Though I was fast and agile, I wasn't exactly strong, even when I didn't have a wounded shoulder. Fighting for me always involved using the objects around me to cover my escape. There was no escape here. She and those glowing fingers stood squarely between me and the door, the only two objects besides me being the jug of water and the bed pallet.

"Where," she said, advancing on me, "is my text?"

"I don't know what you're talking about."

"Prince Geric warned me that you are a liar," Maita went on, still in that calm, pleasant tone. "And so I am prepared. This will let me know if you are willingly lying." She brandished the green-glowing stone on her palm. "I've never met a Hrethan before, much less a half-Hrethan. You have the legendary tail, I see." She cocked her head, scrutinizing the fuzz on my arms where my sleeve had ridden up because of the bandage.

What I think of as my fuzz is more like down, covering me from collarbones to my knees and wrists. It's very light and very short, almost not there, except as a soft covering, so I've always preferred loose clothes and no shoes.

She pointed at my arm. "And your fur is actually feathers. Does that mean you are not human? Or partially human? I have to admit I've never paid any attention to your kind before. Hrethan seem unwilling, or unable, to move in the circles of power and influence."

She paused. We stared at each other. Could anyone be so ignorant as to think that Hrethan were not human? But then I hadn't even known what Hrethan were, or that I was half-Hrethan, until relatively recently. Since then I'd discovered that there are all kinds of humans, but somehow I did not feel obliged to educate her.

She tried again. "I understand that Hrethan have natural access to some minor magics, though I am told you have no training."

"No training," I said truthfully. That threw me right back to the specifics of Hlanan's and my...not-quite-argument. I grimaced.

She uttered a complacent laugh. "Fear not! In this instance, your ignorance guarantees your comfort. I am pressed for time, but if you had been an adept, I should have been forced to ward you. As it is, you may enjoy the light and air of this chamber while I see my goal through—the goal that you, admittedly ignorantly, did your part to thwart." She paused, and when I said nothing, she went on as if I were lacking in wits, "The spell I worked so very long to obtain calls for fresh *human* blood, and I interpret that to mean untainted by any inherited magics that might ruin the spell. And so I will not deviate a jot from the required elements when I resurrect my beloved."

"What?" I yelped.

I'd figured she had to be up to something nasty, but *that* took me flat.

She gazed at me steadily, still smiling. "Have you not heard the poets sing that love conquers all?" she asked in that soft, calm, reasonable voice. "I believe it, and I mean to prove it. At least, I mean to prove that love conquers death. I have worked very long and very hard to gain the skill, the ancient language, and the means. And while I could probably sacrifice any of these fools serving me here, there is an irresistible piquancy in using the living blood of someone who has betrayed me twice over and irritated me endlessly."

She was talking about the blood mage text that I'd snatched

away from her before she and that horrible Duchess of Thann could use its magic on the Prince of Liacz. She wasn't just doing the duchess's bidding—she wanted to use that magic herself!

She smiled benignly. "Once my darling has been restored to me, we shall venture into questions about your relation to humanity and how that might aid my studies."

"I don't *know* anything," I whined. "I'm an orphan. Learned how to read a season ago. I'm no use to you."

"On the contrary," she said cheerfully. "I always need subjects for experiments. The degree to which your consent will be sought depends upon your cooperation. I will leave you with something to consider: I was able to copy out only the enchantment I need before that grasping fool of a duchess bustled me into her own pet project, in the midst of which you then broke in on us and purloined the book. While I don't consider your action a deliberate betrayal, such as Prince Geric committed, I believe you owe me a debt. You may repay it in part by telling me to whom you sold the book. Prince Geric said you were a thief, and thieves steal for gain, not for power. Who bought my text?"

"Nobody did," I said, and as she frowned at her stone in disbelief, I added before she could try any other nasty spells, "It was taken away from me, too." The stone flickered but didn't change color: I'd given that thing to Hlanan, and good riddance. "The Council of Magic got it before I could sell it."

Her eyes widened, and she drew in a long breath. "Really," she breathed. Then the skepticism was back. "I thought you were a better thief than that. We shall conduct an interview in more detail when I have leisure. I must return to setting a suitable welcome for Prince Geric."

"What?" I squawked, too astonished to hold my tongue. "You couldn't possibly think that pinch-sneak is going to try to *rescue* me?"

"Rescue? Hah, that was amusing. He intends to betray his promise to me and obtain you in order to trade you to the Emperor of Sveran Djur. That much I was able to ascertain when I broke the elementary wards around his camp and found his transfer token." She paused to chuckle softly, and the hairs down my neck and spine stirred. "Prince Geric thought himself so clever, placing a tracer spell on you before I transferred you. I pretended not to see. The surprise will be much more fun when he walks into my trap."

She glanced around the room, nodded her heavy chin at my jug, and said, "You will have to earn your meals with cooperation and information, but by all means drink all the water you like. I know how ill one feels recovering from a stone spell." She brandished a key, turned it in the lock, let herself out, and locked the door again.

I helped myself to a few more slurps and looked around more closely for means of escape.

The walls were walls. No indentations promising a secret escape. Solid door. I bent and tried to peer through the lock. It was too complicated for a peephole.

I turned my back to the door to sweep the room again. High, conical ceiling above the circle of my cell.

Circle. Tower?

I looked up at the open window. Good thing? It was not barred. Bad thing? It was out of reach. So the question was, how high a tower? My shoulder throbbed in protest at all this twisting and turning, and I reached back and gently fingered the scab under the loosened bandage that had been roughly tied over my silken tunic.

I turned my gaze back to the window. A couple of experimental jumps proved ineffective — good as I was at leaping, I needed space to run in order to gain height, and the cell only afforded a couple of paces. My gaze trailed down to the pallet. I dragged it under the window, and with a grunt, folded it in half.

No help. So I flapped it open and, groaning with effort, did my best to roll it, then upend it.

Then I pressed myself against the stone wall opposite the window, sucked in a breath, took two light steps, and, flashing hair and tail down to help my spring, leaped. My fingertips scraped the lip of the window. I landed on the rolled pallet, which promptly gave way, sending the jug teetering. I dove at it, catching it with my fingertips after half the water splashed out.

I froze, my heart pounding.

No footsteps outside.

With shaky fingers, I repositioned the pallet and breathed a few times to gather my strength. Not that I had much. I was light-headed, probably from hunger as much as magic residue. But waiting was not going to bring any improvement.

A deep breath, two steps, leap—and my fingers hooked the window ledge.

I dug my toes into the stone and worked them up until I got one elbow over the edge, then with a grunt and a lunge hoisted myself sideways through the window slit. There I rested, gasping for breath as my hip dug painfully into the sill, my hands outside, pressing on mossy stone, my feet dangling inside.

I twisted my neck, lifted my head, and clutched at the stone. Below: a long, long drop. I was not only in a tower, I was in a very tall tower atop a fortress built on the crest of a mountain.

A *high* mountain. In the distance around me, hazy purple peaks scraped the misty undersides of clouds. Far below, I glimpsed the narrow thread of a river winding around the rocky base of a sheer cliff. Clusters of hardy trees and shrubs grew alongside streams tumbling down the otherwise rocky slope. I twisted my head, gazing down the length of the stone walls, to the mountain beyond. I glimpsed what might be the supports to a bridge.

In the other direction, more air.

I rubbed my toes against the stone inside. No sense of magic. Was it possible Prince Geric had not told the magister about my ability to transform? A brief spurt of hilarity, almost gratitude, vanished as I recollected what she'd said.

Prince Geric was not looking out for my welfare. He wanted to retrieve me for Dhes-Andis. He'd surrendered me to save his skin—and gain time—but he'd clearly told her as little as possible about me. Maybe he expected to find me still under the influence of that stone spell, ready and waiting to be kidnapped again.

Those two could double-cross each other with my good will. I didn't intend to be around for either of their nefarious plans.

I twitched my shoulders again, unsure if I'd be able to transform. I didn't *know* enough!

And there I was, my not-quite-argument with Hlanan flooding back into mind.

No. I would not argue with him in my head.

So I pulled my knees up, wriggled until I sat on one haunch, pulled my bent knees through the slit, and fell backward.

Terror flashed through me, cold and hot at the same time, I whooped for breath—and the heat became light and I soared out on spread wings, one droopy and nearly impossible to manage as my clothing and the bandage tumbled away below.

I spiraled down after them. My things landed on the banks of a stream far below the variegated cliff below the castle. My right wing hurt too much to help me gain altitude, and without it, I spiraled dizzily.

Desperate, I gritted my teeth and stiffened my wings. Catching a slow current of air, I straightened out of the twirling drop, and began to drift. There was no chance I could fly and regain height, but at least I could bank and glide. Thus I spiraled around and around until I landed beside the stream. My body itched and tingled—and there I was, in my customary form again, but my right shoulder throbbed anew. A warm trickle warned me that the scab had torn away during either my transformation or my crazy flight.

I splashed into the stream and crouched into the cold water, which instantly soothed my shoulder. My kind don't feel cold much, coming (I gathered) from a world with snowy heights, but as the clouds began to thicken and drop, the air chilled. As snowflakes began to fall lazily, I reluctantly climbed out.

The wound had stopped bleeding. I hunted around for the makeshift bandage and located it hanging from a tree branch. I washed it out, then rewrapped myself as best I could before locating my peach silk drape lying on a flat rock. I shrugged into it, grateful that the Hrethan wear loose clothing to permit our spine hair and tails to be free. Even so, it hurt to move.

Now, which way would be the best escape?

Before I could take a step, a distant horn blatted insistently. I peered upward, shading my eyes against the sun, whose light glinted on helms and chain mail as warriors boiled along the castle walls and over the bridge stretching across the chasm to my right.

Something had happened. Like Prince Geric the Pig Snout walking straight into the mage's trap?

"Ha, ha," I gloated. I hoped her trap started off with sticking his head in a bag.

Then I remembered what her trap was for.

"No," I said to the drifting snowflakes. "No. No. No. *No.*"

Whatever happened to Prince Geric was richly deserved.

Including that kind of death?

Yes! He'd threatened to kill Hlanan in Fara Bay!

But he hadn't. And the trap resulted from my robbing him.

He was evil.

Because...?

I squirmed, loathing myself. I'd thrown the word "evil" around pretty much all my life, meaning "people who were mean to me." Since I'd met Hlanan and his sister Thianra, I'd been forced to see past my own immediate survival.

Compared to the sinister Dhes-Andis, Prince Geric Lendan was a dangerous irritant, but not....

I stood there writhing with exasperation and regret, impatience and guilt, until I imagined telling Hlanan about my escape. He'd smile, his face alight with joy... until I got to leaving Prince Geric to a horrible fate. And I could see that light dim.

Not that it was a glow as in magic, but oh, when he smiled he lifted his chin and his brown eyes widened and the light reflected in his steady brown gaze. Or was I being weak to plan my movements as a result of liking his smile? The thought felt like itchwort under the skin.

Flames of Rue! This was stupid, I thought in disgust as my own gaze ranged over the rocky palisade. While I'd been arguing with myself, I'd already spotted a possible way back up, mostly under the bridge. I was fairly certain the sentries wouldn't spot me.

All right. I'd go and see if Geric was in a trap. *Then* I'd gloat!

And following a good long gloat, if he was tied up and I was free, maybe force him to agree to let me alone if I could get him out?

Yes. Now *that* made sense. I had to find something to eat anyway. It didn't look like this rocky, barren land was going to afford me much more than water.

I bent to cup my hands and drank enough to slosh in my

middle. Then I sighed, put my hand to a granite outcropping covered with tiny lichen, tucked my toes into a hole left by some burrowing animal, and began to toil my way back up to the castle.

I could only use my right arm to steady myself, and it hurt like blazes every time I stretched it upward, but my legs were perfectly fine, and I was a good climber. Midway up it became a challenge to stay out of sight.

I spotted a pair of sentries crossing the bridge. I'd expected to find myself weeks of travel away from the safety of Erev-li-Erval, maybe even on another con-tinent. But those sun-faded violet-edged tunics made of undyed brown-wool were immediately familiar. I leaned perilously out, and caught the briefest glimpse of the front of one woman's tunic: it was embroidered with the many-branched tree of the empire.

This fortress was one of the empress's border watches!

The realization was so dizzying I actually clutched to a gnarled hedge root, my eyes squeezed tight. Mage—blood magic—empress—

Was everything I'd been told a lie after all?

No. I steadied myself: Hlanan had never lied to me, and he had said the Mage Council had that book. Then I recollected Maita's deep breath of surprise. She had not known about the book's surrender to the Council, I was convinced of that much.

I already knew that not all the empire's nobles were to be trusted. Prince Geric being my prime example.

I crept sideways along the small bird caves that pockmarked the cliff below the castle walls as the snow steadily thickened. My hands began to tingle from gripping icy rock.

When I reached a slightly bigger cave, I squeezed in to catch my breath and rest my throbbing hands. My shoulder ached as if it had been stabbed repeatedly.

Time to move. My fuzz fluffed out beneath my thin layers of silk, keeping me from freezing as I clambered the rest of the way to the base of the castle.

Here I discovered a narrow ledge impossible to see from below.

I did not know how long before a patrol would make its way along that narrow path. Trusting to my silvery-blue hair and tail and my pale peach silk to obscure me in the falling snow, I hopped down the path, scanning for a way up.

Ah. Withered tree roots had worked into cracks in the stone: a ladder for the likes of me. A quick scramble, and I perched low between the battlements of a wall, my toes squidging in thick moss, as I peered down into what had to be a private court, surrounded on three sides by buildings. This court featured four enormous oaks crammed into cracked, broken pots: imperial oaks, which would explain why they hadn't been uprooted. Two seemed stunted, their root balls foiled by the vast pots, but the two trees nearest the wall had broken through and extended rootlings to work into the stone.

Voices echoed sharply up the stones. I made out a cluster of figures on the other side of the court, their sand-colored tunics nearly obscured by the falling snow. I already knew from a lifetime of stealing to survive that eavesdropping seldom pays off, but when it does, it's always worth it.

I glanced around. Of course. The trees! It was simple for me to hop into the branches, though they afforded no covering foliage. But if I were quiet enough, no one would think to look up.

I moved cautiously from branch to branch, and as I neared, the confusion of voices resolved into words.

"...but not that."

A voice clearer than the rest, "Do *you* want to register a complaint with *her*?"

Silence, except for the soft hush of the snow and the shuffle of feet. A sword clanked as someone looked about furtively, her helmet turning quickly from side to side. The helmed guard next to her made a motion toward his lips with his gloved hand. "Then let's continue our patrol, as ordered. We don't know what she's doing up there."

Someone else, an older voice muttered, "And word is bound to get out. I don't want to be interrogated by the Ravens."

Ravens! That, I'd learned, was the nickname for the Imperial Guard, who wore black battle gear and who never talked except to convey orders directly from the empress, as they spoke with her Voice. Everyone gave way before them, even the nobles.

The crowd of guards dispersed. I turned on my branch and

surveyed the massive wall at my right. Windows lit here and there, golden and ruddy, indicating fireplaces and lamps, and blue-white where glow globes had been ignited by magic.

I lifted my gaze to the tower at the precipice end of the building, squinting past the golden glow from the lower windows that briefly lit snowflakes to tiny geometric patterns of fire before they dimmed again to the dull white of ash as they vanished below.

The building and the tower had been built of older stone than the end of the castle I had already toiled my way along—unlike these neatly hewn and finished stones, those of the older section appeared misshapen, covered with ancient ivy.

I craned my neck back, and there above me jutted a window that had not been pulled shut.

I followed it with my eyes to a tree branch near enough for me to leap to the ledge. A scramble, a swing from branch to branch (ouch!), a grunt of effort, and I crouched on the window ledge.

I peered around, stood cautiously, felt beyond the inset, and there was the ivy. I tested it. No give.

I swung myself out and up, favoring my right side. Then, using ivy and ancient rock, I climbed up. And *up*.

Because of the ivy, I couldn't see very far overhead, and I did not want to look down. My right arm throbbed so badly that I knew a transformation would at best break a crashing fall to the rocks. I hoped.

It began to seem as if I were going to keep climbing into the clouds when a whispering, a rhythmic scrape, and a cough reached me. The cough sounded familiar.

I slowed my climb, feeling with my fingertips ahead before the next boost.

An acrid, rotting coppery scent drifted slowly on the air, causing my spine hair to lift, readying me to flee. One more spurt of effort, and my fingers found a slimy, mossy window ledge.

My stomach churned in spite of its emptiness, my heart thundering. Wary of causing the ivy to rustle, I eased slowly...slowly.... Damping my hair flat against my back, I pulled my chin up to the ledge and peered into a round room, not barren as mine had been.

Visible first, three tall, unlit candles. Though no flame burned on any of them, they glowed faintly with an eerie greenish light that made my skin crawl.

I knew what that was! A deadly, horrible shren square, not complete. Hlanan had made one for me once, before we'd sorted ourselves out. No magic could get past the square once it was sealed, except that done by the controlling mage, and no one else's magic could affect anything inside the square.

Three candles. That meant she had to be putting the magic onto the fourth one at this very moment.

Impelled by a gut-gnawing fire of urgency, I hauled myself up a little farther, and peered down inside.

Two long tables had been set in the center of the room, with a small table off to one side, its bare top slanted. To hold a book? Or a blood spell? My spine crawled when I spotted the huge bowl with arcane carvings all around it, set on a shelf below the lectern.

Two figures lay on tables with arms and legs outstretched, bound by faintly glowing chains.

On one table, ruddy blond hair spilled over the edge as Prince Geric uselessly ground his wrists back and forth in the shackles.

And on the other table, lying still and pale?

"*Hlanan?*" I squeaked in disbelief.

Three

CHAINS RATTLED AS HLANAN started. He struggled to twist his head up and to the side. "Lhind! You're free!"

"Yes," I said, surprised he wouldn't assume I would do everything I could to escape.

"Why...what are you doing in that window? Is there a tower above us?"

"No, the one I was in is at the other end of the castle. She wants to experiment with Hrethan blood, and I wasn't about to stay around for that. As for what I'm doing here, she said she had laid a trap for the Prince of Stinkers over there." I raised my voice. "So I came to gloat!" No reaction from Geric. "How did you get here?" I asked more normally.

"I led the search for you, and found Geric a short while after you were taken away. Lhind, you've got to flee. Find the search party and tell them what's happened."

He knew I wasn't about to go tramping into these impossibly high mountains. He wanted me to take wing.

"I can't," I said, glaring at Geric, to discover he wasn't looking my way. But he lay so still I was sure he was listening. "Or I could, but it would take me a couple of months to walk out of these mountains. Even if I knew which direction Erev-li-Erval lay in."

Hlanan twisted even more, his face a grimace of anxious pain. "What happened?"

"That rat-spawned pebble-wit over there threw a knife at me."

Hlanan's head jerked the other way, causing another unmusical rattling of the chains, which glowed greenish when he moved. "You didn't tell me that."

Prince Geric drawled, "Are we going to chat all day about who did what? I guess we are. Maita can join in when she gets here, any moment now."

Hlanan let out a sharp breath, then said, "Lhind. She's making a shren—"

"I remember what that is," I cut in. "Do you know a spell to stop her?"

"Not like this," Hlanan said, as he wriggled against the heavy chains. "But...ah. Still there. I have your...your wallet. Back pocket. I thought, if I found you...." His voice trailed off.

My heart gave a great ba*dump* of joy. "You came to rescue me," I realized at last, grinning in delight. How charming was that? And how could anyone not love a man who brings a person her thief tools, just in case?

I squeezed the rest of the way through the window, glad that few castle-builders seem to think it necessary to put bars in high windows. I dropped to the tile floor and approached the two tables. Hlanan and Prince Geric had been tightly chained down by their outstretched limbs, their jackets yanked apart and shirts ripped open, baring their chests.

"Don't touch the chains," Hlanan murmured.

I paused for half a heartbeat to scowl at Geric, who had turned his head. He stared back, mouth twisted in a wry smile. I wormed my fingers under Hlanan's back, struggling to get past the jacket and tunic to the long pocket below the waistband of his trousers.

"They didn't search you?" I whispered.

"They were ordered to remove only magical paraphernalia from us. Disdained taking what they thought was a money-bag," he whispered back, smiling in spite of a puffy bruise on his lip.

I winced, my knuckles pressing painfully on the table. Hlanan's breathed hissed with his effort to arch his back, as he was stretched out fairly tightly.

But it was enough. My forefinger touched the familiar stitching along the outside of my tool bag, then my second finger, and a short time later I clutched my most faithful companion to me, hugging it in relief.

"You've got to get out of here," Hlanan murmured. "She will be back with the fourth candle at any moment."

I opened the bag and dug for my lock pick as I inspected the chains for the lock.

Hlanan's face pressed into the side of the table. "No!" he said. "You can't touch the chains. There's a ward on them. I can feel it."

"So that's what that glow is. Can you tell me how to break it?"

"Take too long," he said hoarsely. "Only her key will work. Get yourself free."

"What about you?"

Before he could speak, the clatter of footsteps and gear and voices echoed up from far below. Someone had begun the long climb. That could only be bad.

I looked at Hlanan, whose face had blanched. "Get away," he said.

"First," I retorted, my fingers plunged into my bag, "let's give them a little lock trouble, eh?"

"With what?" That was Prince Geric.

"With this." I pulled up what I'd sought: a diamond.

His head thumped back. "No doubt you took that from me."

"Yes," I said. "And I hate to lose it now, but...." I sprang to the door. It was a familiar lock, an ancient one, sturdy iron but very simple, with a lock access on the inside as well as the outside, which meant this tower had not always been a prison. It was also a mage retreat, which might explain that skin-prickling sense of magic in the air.

My fingers trembled, and my heart knocked against my ribs, but I clung fiercely to logic. Whoever was coming was not racing up the stairs. If I worked fast....

There wasn't much I didn't know about locks. I'd had that knowledge slapped and cuffed into me early in my life, and I'd kept my fingers nimble over the years since. Using my tools, I got the diamond nicely wedged at the top of the mechanism. Iron, meet diamond. Nobody would be opening that door.

Then I turned around, uncertain of my next step.

That's when noise echoed from below: a roar, thumping, horns blaring from tower to tower, and a deep voice bellowing from somewhere outside, "Attack at the gate!"

"Ah," Prince Geric said. "That will be Nath."

Nath—I'd heard that name before. An image in memory: a shaggy gray head, captain of the Gray Wolves.

I looked down at Hlanan, still straining ineffectually against the chains. Another glance at Geric, to thoroughly enjoy the sight of the handsome, debonair prince disheveled and filthy, stretched out helplessly. But there was no more time for gloating, because Hlanan was just as helpless.

I leaped to the back of Hlanan's table, careful to keep my toes from encountering those chains at each corner of the table, and from there to the high window.

A squeeze, a scramble, and I was out.

As I spidered my way down through the ivy again, the noise of a concentrated attack increased: from the sound, the Gray Wolves were trying to batter the gate, with a hiss and a clatter of arrows shot into the main courtyard to harry the imperial border guards.

I didn't think even the Gray Wolves, formidable as they were, could breech a gigantic castle.

But their attack might interrupt that mage enough for me to...what?

When at last I reached the join of the tower to the sentry wall overlooking the courtyard with the trees, I perched between two weather-beaten battlements, my toes curling under me. Cold usually did not bother me, as long as I didn't get wet. As snow melted underfoot, my bare feet ached, though not nearly with the maddening insistence of my throbbing shoulder.

What now? Free Hlanan, of course. But I had to think it out. No more wading in without a plan. So. That mage was somewhere inside, finishing up the last candle. There was no breaking a shren square if she got all four candles up, therefore I had to keep her from completing it.

That meant a distraction.

You'd think a battle would take care of that, but Maita wasn't anywhere in sight. Maybe she relied on her guards to handle battle. Magic was her concern.

Therefore my distraction had better be magical.

My problem? I had only my personal magic. I was not nearly

strong enough for mind thrust, even if I had her at hand. It was nearly as dangerous to me as it would be to her, especially in my present shape. Same with voice cast.

All I had the strength to command was illusory magic, which was easy but didn't actually do anything except make images. Again, when feeling very strong, I could pull at air and sound enough for brief noises or buffets of wind that felt like an effect, but that extra effort lay beyond me now.

What kind of visual illusion would be of use?

Of course! What would be more threatening than the appearance of other mages?

My empty stomach cramped again, and my head wobbled on my neck, feeling as if it might float away. I steadied myself against one of the bare tree branches, drew in some deep breaths, and then formed two, three...four...five illusions, sacrificing detail for distance as I planted them on each of the surrounding cliffs and outcroppings, plain to be seen. They had blurry ovals for faces, but each wore the distinctive robes of the Mage Council, which I had seen in the imperial city: forest green, with rank symbols embroidered in gold along the sleeves.

I did not know what those symbols meant, but I didn't need to. I didn't even have to reproduce them with accuracy. My illusion gave them a golden glint.

Then I sat back to steady my buzzing head as I waited for the effect.

It wasn't long in coming. A horn tooted a frantic signal different from the earlier one, and not five heartbeats after, a young runner raced inside—to report, I hoped.

Another effort: I gave three of the figures a greenish glow, which I trusted would look like magic being woven.

Within a short time, there she was, surrounded by armed guards. I did not wait to see where she would go: it was enough that she wasn't inside.

Three leaps, and I landed in the courtyard. I ghosted from tree trunk to tree trunk, but no one was looking inside the court. All their attention stayed on the gates and on my fine illusions looking so sinister and mysterious on the mountains surrounding the castle cliff.

The door stood open. I sped inside, sniffing inwardly for that prickly, hot metal almost-smell of heavy magical efforts. It was easy to find, testifying to the intensity of her labors. I discovered the hall upstairs empty of guards. Three locked doors stopped me long enough for my trembling fingers to pick them, and I reached her magic chambers.

In the middle stood the last tall candle, glowing faintly with greenish magic. Papers and books lay all around.

I was afraid of magical wards, a concept I barely understood. I didn't know how to make any. But there was always physical damage. I had learned that wards against water and fire were the toughest to make.

Twin candles burned on either side of a lectern. Afraid to touch anything, I ripped a bit of silk from my hem, twisted it together, and held the end to one of the candles. When the silk caught fire, I flung the twist at one of the candles, knocking it over in my haste.

It fell to the floor, the twist with it: the wick smoked, then flared. Cautiously I extended my fingers over the candle, but felt nothing magical. The lectern I did not trust, but the candles seemed to be just candles.

I poked the candle. Nothing happened to me, so I picked it up and touched it to the paper on the lectern. When that began to darken and curl in a satisfying way, I touched my flame to the book behind it, and then I hopped around the room, setting fire to anything that would burn. Some of the flames snuffed out immediately, raising a faint, nasty stench. None of them burned well.

But I knew a fire spell. Dhes-Andis had taught it to me. That memory was seared into my brain.

My illusions would not hold up very long. I had to trust to her distractions and her probable exhaustion to keep her from figuring that out. I wanted her to waste time and effort throwing magical wards and spells at my pretend mages. It would take half a heartbeat to dispel illusions. If she even bothered. Illusions could do nothing. They were merely trickery with light and air.

Summoning the last of my strength, I pulled flame from that place beyond time and space, then staggered back, falling down painfully. All around me books, scrolls, paper, wood, whooshed up in a spectacular sheet of flame.

Thrilled—and a little horrified—I gasped, frightened laughter bubbling through me as I backed away. Flames wreathed up the lectern, reflecting off what I had not seen before, the metal gleam of a ring of keys sitting along the very top.

Maita had rushed out without grabbing them, probably to keep her hands free for spell-casting.

I stretched a finger over them, almost touching, though the heat by now had become withering, causing my hair to bind tightly together, my scalp and my spine twitching.

I felt no magic itch, so I touched a key. Nothing.

As a thief, I had learned that keys were always useful, so I grabbed them all and backtracked rapidly past that tall candle, which glistened in the blaze, its contours puckering as it began to melt.

I plunged my hand into my tool bag for another stolen gem, worked it into the lock and shut the door, leaving the gem to fall into place, I hoped. I dared not wait to find out if it was successful.

I sped down the hall, passing a stairway. At the top of it I heard frantic voices. Guards, outside the cell where Hlanan and Prince Nasty were imprisoned?

I tried doors along that side of the building, and at last found an open one. I dashed through a room that looked like someone's bed chamber, and to the window, which I threw open. I peered out, relieved that I had guessed right. Below, a sheer drop. To either side, ancient ivy.

I stashed the keys in my tool bag, shoved it down my front, and once again slipped out a window, firmly gripped the ivy, and pulled myself up. By now that blasted wound was bleeding sluggishly down my back, tickling horribly in my fuzz. No help for it.

An endless time (during which I heard four horn signals, a great shout, a terrible crash) later, I popped through the window at last and dropped to the floor. I swayed and caught myself against the table, my knuckles nearly brushing a chain.

"Awk." I snatched my hand back. Reminded of the keys, I pulled forth my tool kit, as Hlanan said hoarsely, "I smell smoke."

"Diversion," I said smugly. "A good one! Now, what do you think these might be for?"

Outside the door, the muffled voices paused, then someone shouted something and rattled impatiently at the lock.

"No, I tell you, something's stuck in there," came a louder voice.

The door reverberated as someone kicked it.

Hlanan tried to lift his head, and I obligingly held the ring of three keys over his face. His forehead cleared. "Good job, Lhind: the one with the three teeth will undo our locks."

"Wait, what about the wards?"

"The key is the key to the enchantment," Prince Geric drawled. "You'll appreciate the visual pun?"

Ignoring him, I hunted over all those long lengths of interlocked metal and at last found the binding lock under the table, well out of reach of Hlanan's reach. The key caused a greenish spark when I touched it to the lock. I dropped the key, then noticed that the sinister glow over the chains had vanished.

I unlocked the chain and threw the lock down. The chains hissed and rumbled as they snaked to the floor in loops and piles.

That same voice outside shouted, "What's going on in there?"

I smothered the urge to yell, "As if we'd tell you!"

Hlanan struggled impatiently as I leaped to the smaller locks and undid them one by one. Then he sat up, rubbing at his bruised, torn flesh where he'd fought against the shackles.

"Can you get out the window?" I said doubtfully, glancing at the locked door. That diamond, I knew, was wedged in tightly.

"Keys, please?" he responded, sliding off the table. He staggered against it, and I wondered how he was ever going to climb down that ivy.

"Why?" I asked.

His lips pressed in a line as he glanced at Prince Geric, whose mocking gaze was turned our way.

"Let him stay there," I said as my first move in bargaining. First I had to get him scared.

"Lhind," Hlanan sighed.

"He was going to send me to Dhes-Andis!"

"He can't do that now."

"Certainly not—if we leave him right there," I retorted.

But as I spoke, Hlanan took the keys from my fingers, and bent to hunt for the locks chaining Geric to that table.

"I was *going* to," I muttered.

He gave me a puzzled look. "Lhind, we cannot leave someone to Maita Boniree's blood magic."

"She won't be able to do it now," I gloated.

Hlanan's lips parted, then he gave his head a slight shake. "Tell me later. We must get out of here." To Geric, he said, "Magister Boniree will be after us immediately. Continue the truce?"

"Yes," Geric said.

Hlanan grunted as he bent and fumbled at the lock. A click, two clicks, and again the chains roared as they fell all around.

Hlanan and I both turned toward the door, expecting a response, to hear nothing.

Nothing?

"They've gone?" I asked, as if Hlanan knew any more than I did.

He looked blankly back at me, and I sprang to the door and dropped down to peer beneath it. There was only the thinnest bit of space between door and floor. I wedged one eye as best I could, squashing my nose...and saw nothing.

"No one's out there," I said.

"Went to report," Geric said, sitting up and rubbing his raw wrists.

"Or were summoned to the battle," Hlanan offered.

I was already busy with my lock picks. Getting that diamond out should have been easy, but my fingers were slippery and trembled. When at last the stone fell onto my palm, I breathed in relief—and Geric reached over my head to pinch it off my palm, saying caustically, "I'll take that back now."

I scowled at him, though I had several more of his gems still in the bag. But he did not need to know that.

"Magic transfer?" I asked Hlanan, wanting to get away so badly I would even endure that horrifying wrench again.

But to my surprise, they both shook their heads, Geric wincing as if he had a headache. I knew Hlanan had a headache by the way he squinted, his forehead tight.

"Unless you know far more magic than I, transfer would be a very bad idea," Geric said, watching Hlanan, who sighed as he thumbed his temples.

To me, Geric said, "First thing she did was ward us against transfer."

He did not wait for a response but laid his hand to the door latch, then eased it open.

No one lurked beyond. Noise echoed up from somewhere.

"Which way, Lhind?" Hlanan murmured.

I started down the hall, thinking, what next? The lower floor ought to be full of enemies. No, empire guards. It was difficult to know what to think, because they were supposed to be on our side!

If they were trying to keep us in, they were enemies.

So, how to get out. How about the same way I got in? Hlanan and the Pompous Prince would be useless at tower climbing, but surely they could manage those tree branches, then over the wall to the ledge, which was on the opposite side of the castle from the action.

The thought became the deed—and I still didn't like thinking about that horrible journey. As soon as we reached my open window, I could see the cold hit them. Prince Geric had done up his shirt and tunic again. Hlanan hadn't bothered. Back when he was a chained galley slave, he had become so inured to physical discomfort that he ignored his body when con-centrating on something else—like running for his life.

I looked at that sharply etched collarbone and the rise and fall of his chest in the V, and thought, he hasn't been eating well, though surrounded by wealth and comfort. I reached to support him, but he gave his head a minute shake as Geric scowled at the tree branches a short leap away. Of course. We were supposed to be scribe and imperial prisoner, as far as Geric was concerned.

Hlanan hastily did up the front of his clothes as I pushed past both of them, hopped into the broad stone window sill, and then to a tree branch. "See? Easy," I whispered.

"If you have a tail," Geric muttered.

He was right. Where I could leap, they had to swing, not easy at all in the cold.

But they managed, and we made it to the wall. Then came the hideous climb down. Even with me feeling my way first to show them where to put hands and feet, both of them had bleeding, numb hands by halfway down, and they dropped the last distance.

Then came the miserable trip along the ledge as the snow steadily increased.

After that, we made our way half-blind up the hill toward indistinct shapes until a Gray Wolf, posted on the outskirts of their numbers to watch for a sneak attack from the defenders, spotted us.

After that things became a little easier: a little, because we couldn't see well. The cold was fierce even for me, or maybe it was exhaustion, and finally I fell onto my hands and knees in a drift of snow. Behind me somewhere Geric shouted hoarsely, his voice muffled by the thickening curtain of white. I crouched down, looking wildly for danger.

"Come, Lhind." Hlanan bent over me, hands outstretched.

I scrambled to my feet. A Gray Wolf appeared, leading a horse. Hlanan mounted, then pulled me up behind him. Prince Geric leaped onto another horse.

The rumble of hooves indicated the Gray Wolves closing around us. Good? Bad? My head ached, and my poor stomach, neglected for what felt like a thousand years, wrung plaintively.

But we did not ride far. No one could see any better than I could. Swiftly approaching hoofbeats indicated that a scout had gone ahead. I peered past Geric's bare head to where the blond Gray Wolf captain gestured with her gloved hand, and Geric raised his fist, then pointed back at her.

Our cavalcade followed her down a path into a valley, which sheltered us somewhat from the building storm.

A short time later we dismounted under a rock outcropping, and the horses were taken away.

"Pandoc," Geric yelled as he dismounted. He motioned impatiently at the curly-haired scout.

I stayed close to Hlanan's side, and as far out of Geric's reach as I could. I did not want to run out into the snow, but at the first sign of any grabbing on his part, I'd flit. Better floundering around in snow than a quick trip to the Evil Emperor.

The blond Gray Wolf captain shook back her ash-pale hair, which hung about her face in curly locks, and turned her palm over as she jerked her chin at a couple of the others. They moved to set about making a fire.

I followed Hlanan past busy gray-cowled bodies into what we discovered was an old cave. Firewood had been neatly stacked along the curving rock wall, next to barrels and jars. Of course. This close to the castle, it was probably a scout outpost, for occasions exactly like this.

"We dare not stay long," I said, peering past Hlanan's shoulder. "I don't know which is a worse threat, Geric or those imperial warriors."

"The imperial warriors," Hlanan said in an under voice, "should not be a threat at all." Reminding me again that they were supposed to be under the command of Aranu Crown.

That sparked questions.

I knew better than to ask. Instead I glanced at Geric, his cheekbones ruddy with anger as he spoke low-voiced to the Gray Wolf scout, Pandoc. The scout chopped and twirled his fingers, tapping his palms, his other wrist, his forearms, and making other signs as the blond Gray Wolf observed, head bent, expression blank.

"How did you find me?" I asked in an under-voice, while that was going on.

Hlanan said, "A courier saw a cloak-wrapped bundle in human shape laid over the back of a horse when riding into the capital. He got suspicious and reported it. They sent a message to the outer perimeter, who spotted you being taken into the mountains. They followed at a distance. By the time I got their message and transferred to them, you were gone. But they saw signs of a hastily concealed trail—starting from the remains of a lute lying on a rock below the falls."

"And so you came after me, but how did you end up captured with Geric Lendan—oh, wait. You said truce. That means you—" I smiled at him, utterly charmed. "You meant to rescue me!"

"Before we both walked into her trap," Hlanan said wryly.

"But you meant to! I've never had anybody want to rescue me before," I whispered, loving him all over again.

I'd been watching Prince Geric as the blond captain talked to Pandoc with her fingers. Geric listened to Pandoc, who translated her fast signs. Then he glanced my way, and I tried to hide my grin, but too late. Abruptly Geric pushed past her. She dropped her hands, her face unchanging.

I sidestepped around Hlanan to his other side, plunging one hand into my tool bag, though I had no weapons in it. My fingers closed around my lock pick, then loosened. If I tried to threaten Prince Geric with death by lock pick, he would just laugh.

Geric said, "What are you gloating about? Yes, Maita Boniree got my transfer token, but that only means our journey is postponed."

"Ended," I retorted promptly.

He gave me a lip-curled glance, and turned to Hlanan, who gazed back with an expression of extreme reserve. My heart squeezed behind my ribs. That expression meant that he was very, very angry.

"We'll eat, then discuss our egress," the Prince of Poltroons said, clearly assuming that Hlanan was no threat. He jerked his elegant chin toward the curtain of snow falling beyond the outcropping, flurries dancing at a slant, which indicated an icy wind propelling them. "Ordinarily I would trust to the weather to slow her up, but I know not what weaponry she has stored in the form of magical spells."

"She doesn't have any," I announced smugly.

Hlanan and Geric both gave me sharp looks.

"At least, if her spells were piled in that room with the big candles. It's all ash now. I set it on fire."

I was looking at Hlanan as I spoke, expecting an echo of my triumph. I was surprised — dismayed — to see horror lengthen his face, before his expression shuttered.

"Now *that* was well thought of, thief," Geric drawled.

As he spoke, the sizzle of dried meat in nut oil wafted greasily through the cave. My stomach lurched, and I stepped back, but then I saw a couple of the Gray Wolves setting flat round travel breads on the ring of stones circling the fire, and laying out dried apricots, figs, and a big wedge of bright orange cheese. Food that I could eat!

In short order we sat on flat stones arranged in a ring outside the fire pit, the Gray Wolves' woolen tunics gently steaming and smelling like wet hound. I gobbled down my share of the cheese and the figs, then chewed determinedly on the tough apricots as a sense of well-being suffused me. Even my shoulder hurt a little less.

Geric carried his plate in his hand as he strolled to the cave entrance to talk to his Gray Wolf captains in low voices, Pandoc fluttering and tapping fingers in signs. The blond captain's head made minute jerks as her focus turned back and forth between Geric and the scout.

I turned to Hlanan, to discover him watching them, a frown of puzzlement tightening his brow. Then he shut his eyes, gave his head a shake, and looked away—to find me standing there. A horse clopped a foot, and someone coughed in the distance before he spoke. "I wish you hadn't used that fire spell, Lhind. It's dark magic—so dangerous."

I contained my impatience. Magic was magic, or so I'd thought until I met those Mage Council magisters with their serious faces and their obvious distrust. And their refusal to teach me anything but the most useless fundamentals. "I know," I said to sidestep what could turn into another argument. "But I did not use it for a bad purpose. I did it to save you! You're not mad at me?"

"Of course not. I understand why you did it, but see, now the evidence of her betrayal is gone."

"So? We *saw* her! Heard her! *You* heard her!"

"I am just a scribe," he reminded me gently. "Until the empress decides otherwise. Any accusation must be accompanied by proof. The Mage Council won't take my word against an established magister."

Reminding me he wasn't yet confirmed as heir. And that imperial children could be passed over altogether for a cousin if the ruler was displeased enough.

Aranu Crown expected her children to follow the law.

I grimaced. "Burning that stuff seemed the right thing to do." I remembered our last encounter with that evil book and added,

"You set fire to the duchess's stuff when we escaped her."

"But I saved the evidence of her treachery first. Remember? It was that sheaf of papers I asked the king of Liacz's nephew to take to his uncle. In any case, the Duchess of Thann was not a mage betraying her oaths." He must have seen my disappointment, for he murmured softly, quickly, "Lhind, I don't mean to disparage your gallant rescue —"

"Never mind that," I said, my disappointment all the sharper. "There has to be *some* way to convince the empress —"

"Convince the empress of what?"

Geric had slithered up as sneakily as a snake.

I glared at him, secretly glad I had a perfectly unexceptionable answer right at hand. It was even true! "That she's got a stinker of a mage using blood magic right on her border," I said. "If we can get a message to the Ravens, surely the empress will drop on Maita like a load of stone, and we won't have to skulk around in this stinky cave hiding from her."

My reason seemed perfectly reasonable to me, but Geric's blue gaze flickered on the word "empress" in a way that made it clear that he did not like the trend of the conversation at all.

But he only smiled. "You seem eager to return to the empress's custody. Was her imperial majesty's prison that pleasant? But of course, you were permitted to walk the Paths of Harmony. Oh, to be Hrethan. It seems one can get away with anything, if one is possessed of fur and a tail."

"It's not fur," I muttered, brushing my fingers over the wrist of my hurt arm. "It's feathers." I gulped air, getting that vertigo feeling of swinging between lies and truth. When in doubt, answer questions with questions. "Do you have a better idea?"

"I do," he said, his gaze shifting to Hlanan. "As soon as this snow lifts, Maita will have the entire garrison out searching for us, armed with a lot of lies about enemies of the empire, no doubt. She will expect us to run toward Erev-li-Erval and the protection of the Ravens, so I suggest we ride west."

"West!" I snorted — away from Erev-li-Erval. "Hah!"

They ignored me, each eyeing the other. "There is no reason to ride west," Hlanan said in that neutral tone of reserve.

Geric's smirk broadened — he had no idea how angry Hlanan

was. "Oh, but there is," Geric drawled. "If you still carry your admittedly incomprehensible regard for your friend Prince Ilyan Rajanas of Alezand."

"Because?" Hlanan asked.

"The reason why," Geric said, "I am at this moment constrained to act as Jardis Dhes-Andis's errand runner—" He made a dismissive gesture in my direction. "Is because my late wife hired out the greater part of my Gray Wolves to him to watch the Idaron Pass."

"Late wife," Hlanan repeated. "*You* married the Duchess of Thann?"

Prince Geric's mouth twisted. "You may congratulate and commiserate. On second thought, don't waste your breath."

"And so," Hlanan observed, still in that neutral tone, "it was not you who contracted the Gray Wolves to be sent to the Idaron Pass?"

I remembered that dramatic notch in the mountains on the western side of the continent. Directly below that pass lay Alezand, full of Gray Wolves.

"It was not I. Unfortunately, my late and dear wife withheld certain crucial dealings from her, ah, nuptial confidences. Shortly before our wedding, she made a pact with Dhes-Andis, her part being to send the Gray Wolves to the Pass," Geric said impatiently. "I do not owe you any explanation of my own movements, but my own dealings with Dhes-Andis were separate from hers."

"She got the book from you," Hlanan observed, still in a neutral voice. "Was it her bride gift?"

Geric flushed, and lifted a shoulder sharply. "The book is gone. It's immaterial now. Surely even you, sitting in your scribe tower somewhere, have heard that Dhes-Andis plans an invasion. I know not if that will be this month, this year, or this decade. He has not seen fit to share his imperial strategy with me. But when I asked him after my wife's execution in Liacz to release the Gray Wolves from her pact, he said he would, if I brought him this thief."

He made another dismissive gesture in my direction. "I still do not know why he wants this tiresome Hrethan. Maybe he collects them. The important point is that I want the Gray Wolves back, not wasted in the front lines leading the charge if he does intend to invade Alezand come spring."

A cold, sick feeling harrowed my bones, but I struggled not to show it. "I don't believe anything you say."

"I don't care what you believe," Geric retorted. "You did get me out of Maita's tower, so there is the information. Call it a trade. And ignore it as you will." He turned to Hlanan. "We are riding west. Do what you want when we get there, scribe."

Four

AND SO, AS SOON as the snow began to lift, we forced our way out of the caves, the animals up to their chests in drifts. Heads down, they toiled grimly into the diminishing storm, driven on so that the last of the wind and snow would disguise our tracks.

I was wild to talk to Hlanan alone, but we rode surrounded by Gray Wolves. Geric wasn't letting us out of sight.

The Gray Wolf outriders had managed to scout ahead successfully enough to lead us down into relatively sheltered valleys, enabling us to reach the eastern slope of the mountain. We stopped when the animals needed it, sharing out cold trail food as some of the Gray Wolves stomped off in a group to do their sword practice, and others rested against nighttime guard duty.

My portion of the trail food was cheese as hard and tasty as old wood, and bread like stone. As I chewed grimly, I couldn't help but reflect on the old days when I went hungry, scrounging for food much like this and considering myself lucky.

Comfort sure spoils a person fast.

We reached flatter country before nightfall. We set up camp, Geric keeping Hlanan close by as he blabbed away about imperial politics. I didn't know any of the names he brought up, so I daydreamed, but I couldn't help noticing that when Geric got in the mood for these conversations, he monopolized Hlanan, riding at a distance from the Gray Wolves, except for the deaf one.

Did that mean he didn't trust them? Yet another question I

couldn't answer. I contained my impatience as we settled down for the night.

As always, I made certain that my mind was well warded by a strong mental wall before I dared to fall asleep. Hlanan had taught me that—and it had worked to keep Dhes-Andis from finding me in the mental realm.

But my dreams wandered anywhere they willed, and I shivered in terror as a storm-dark cloud muttering with thunder advanced on me, flashes of green lightning searching every shadow and cranny—

And there was the Blue Lady, walking through the shadows, banishing them with brushes of her hands. I recognized the graceful loops of her clothes as a Hrethan drape.

Was the Blue Lady my mother or an illusion? And if real, had she really abandoned me? Every time I tried to see her face....

I woke up.

The faint blue of dawn outlined the west. Geric's footsteps crunched dirt as he moved about, a scarcely discernible shadow figure. He gave me a boot in the side. "Up and ready to ride, thief."

I reached for a rock to throw at his retreating figure, but Hlanan caught my hand. I sighed and straightened my drape as he got up and brushed his clothes off. Pandoc lent him a comb to drag through his tousled hair. Geric watched as Hlanan returned the comb, neither exchanging more words beyond "Thanks" and "Your horse is with Thusim" from the other as he chucked the comb into a saddlebag.

Someone passed cold bread around as we mounted up.

Geric took the lead. Nobles train early in riding, especially those who like fast sports like point-to-point races. From the way he watched Hlanan from time to time I couldn't tell if he expected him to ride away or to fall off. Or maybe it was a silent contest, but if so, Hlanan seemed oblivious; when I caught sight of his profile, he seemed absorbed, as though his thoughts reached ahead down the trail.

The horses, bred for speed as well as endurance, appeared to enjoy the pace. They didn't seem to mind the intermittent snow, constant low clouds, and cold fog.

With nothing to look at but gloomy indistinct shapes around us and mud below, I watched the company, distracted by Geric's stink-eye glances at Hlanan, and finally by the blond woman I overheard addressed as Captain Nath, and once, Oflan.

Until now I'd regarded the Gray Wolves as an interchangeable parcel of villains, but that was when I was running from them. Now that I was among them, I noticed things as they went about their routines of perimeter guard, sword practice, and camp making and breaking.

Like the fact that the Gray Wolves, when responding to an order from Geric, called him "Your Grace." Ordinarily I paid no more attention to titles than I did to politics or court fashions. But I did know that princes and princesses usually went by "Your Highness," something I'd gained a great deal of private amusement from when observing that short, snotty princess Kressanthe, a few months back, being addressed as "Your Highness" by a fellow who towered at least three heads above her. Was anyone ever tempted to call her "Your Lowness?" I certainly would have, had I not been a couple fingers shorter than she was.

Anyway, "Your Grace" belonged to the likes of dukes and duchesses. So was this kind of a covert insult? I sure hoped so.

But they obeyed his commands promptly, and that included deaf Captain Nath, whom Geric completely ignored, except when he beckoned one of the orderlies or Pandoc the scout to convey an order to her in hand-sign, which he clearly did not know.

Hand languages varied from kingdom to kingdom, sometimes from city to city, or even strata within a city. For instance, I'd once been part of a gang of thieves led by an old codger who didn't hear. Their hand language had been comprised mostly of quick finger taps, meanings changing depending on what was tapped: either palm, forearm, chest, chin.

In another city in Keprima, I'd stumbled across a scribe school made up almost entirely of deaf people. These scribes were well trained and highly regarded, hired exclusively by powerful people who found it convenient to employ scribes who could not hear their conversations.

I didn't know if their employers realized how much the scribes learned from lips. My only concern had been to hide in their attic that winter—I'd been very small—and sneak down to lift food. They couldn't hear me, but they were very quick with other senses, and I'd been discovered by smell.

I'd remembered that later, when using smell to keep nosy people at a distance.

Anyway, as that day stretched into two, then three, rather than letting my mind inside its mental wall carom uselessly between unanswerable questions, I began watching the brief exchanges between Oflan and the other Gray Wolves, wondering if I might recognize some of the signals. One of the talents I'd been born with, that I had never questioned, was the ability to understand any language once I'd heard it.

After a few days, I began to perceive the meanings in the hand-signals. Words appeared to be organized differently, but the meanings behind them had all the variations and subtlety of any other kind of language, spoken or written. For added sarcasm or joke, you added expression!

At night, my dreams rambled in the usual mishmash. That was a relief, tired as I was, and still healing. Though I wouldn't have said I dreaded the appearance of the Blue Lady (mother or not) in my dreams, I always woke with an unsettled feeling of longing, or as if I'd missed something important.

But those dreams rarely occurred when I was anywhere in the lowlands.

Four days in, a storm caught up with us. Before it struck, the scouts returned at the gallop to report an abandoned courier way-station on an old road.

We reached it barely in time, and during the resulting disorganized swarm, I sidled up to Hlanan.

"Do you really believe him?" I muttered.

Hlanan cast a quick look to the side, where Pandoc, the curly-haired scout, stood between Oflan and the impatient prince, alternately talking and signing.

"The situation in Idaron Pass is so potent a danger, I believe I need to be there to see it myself."

"But what about that rotter Maita?" I asked, hopping from foot to foot in my pent-up desire to witness the full wrath of Aranu Crown falling on that mage with all the force of imperial justice.

"Where's your magical notecase thing, for sending messages?"

"Maita got it when she captured and searched us. She'll have to wait."

"But she tried to kill us! She tried to kill *you!* She might be trying that spell again, right now!"

Hlanan cast me a brief smile, then checked on Geric, who stood with Pandoc and Oflan Nath, the latter looking tight-lipped as the prince talked low-voiced with lazy gestures eastward.

"Thanks to your efforts, Maita will not get far in her experiments," Hlanan reminded me.

"But what if she made copies of that blood spell?"

He sighed. "Lhind, I want to see justice, too. I hate thinking about how long this traitor has been practicing dark magic of a kind strictly forbidden, right on our border, while trusted by the Mage Council and the empress both. But what I want and what the empire needs are not always the same." He rubbed the scabs on his wrists where his efforts to escape the chains had scored his flesh.

"How do you *know* what the empire needs?" I whispered fiercely.

"I don't. For certain. But assembling a category of needs in order of priority is a lesson we all learned young—in fact, it was this lesson that decided my sister against the heirship, though our mother wanted it for her. For Thianra, music must always be first."

"You should come first in this horrid situation," I retorted. "That mage tried to kill you, and she's flapping around free as a bird."

"Lhind." He laughed on an exhaled breath.

"Flames of Rue!" I burst out. "It seems to me that the only one who gets to decide what an empire needs is the empress! Otherwise, everyone is either guessing what they think she thinks the empire needs, or sneaking around, doing what they want."

"Lhind—"

"What does 'the good of the empire' really mean, anyway?"

"That those living under the symbol of the twined laurels have the freedom to safely live as they choose."

"Doesn't that mean your safety, too? And I can see you drawing breath to answer, but if you try on some piffling stinkrot about how great power brings great risk, I'm going to crown you with a bucket of fish guts. Because I don't see how you have *any* power. But I've seen you risking your life aplenty."

He looked at me, lips parted, brows lifted, but before he could answer the slush-slush of boots in the mud caused us to fall silent.

"You aren't actually listening to her lies, are you, scribe?" Geric said, indicating me with a dismissive wave of his hand. And when Hlanan turned away, Geric laughed, snapping a pair of riding gloves against his palm as he eyed me. "As for you, spare your breath and your efforts. You are going to Idaron Pass, at which time I will find a way to return you to Dhes-Andis. I believe he's well-equipped enough to handle even a slippery thief. After which I will consider myself quits on all scores."

He walked away, his long, neatly combed hair lifting in the rising breeze. I scowled after him, longing to fling mud at his head. I stayed my hand, having learnt to bide my time. Did he really believe I couldn't escape any time I wanted to?

Two reasons why I hadn't. One, I wasn't about to abandon Hlanan, and two, I had nowhere to go.

I turned my head to find Hlanan regarding me, his expression impossible to interpret—a pucker of his high brow, a tentative smile at the corners of his mouth. That kissable mouth.

I forced out my ire in a sharp breath. "I feel like we're talking in the same words, but not the same language. Or maybe the other way around."

Hlanan's smile turned rueful. "Then we should keep trying to find the right words, should we not?"

Somehow that made me feel better. "Yes. That's right."

The squelch of horse hooves in mud distracted us both. It was time to ride.

Each day I woke with less pain in my shoulder. But each day also brought us lower, so though I knew I could get away, there would be no convenient flying.

Gradually I became aware of a sense of someone's scrutiny, but whenever I checked on Geric, he was either far ahead, or talking to someone else. A quick sweep of the Gray Wolves was equally fruitless. Maybe it was a result of my watching everyone else, I decided, and went back to brooding.

My pout broke briefly at midday when we paused to change to the remounts and to pass around some trail biscuits stuffed with cheese. Hlanan walked a little way, gazing intently to the west, before he was joined by Geric.

I turned to see what he looked at, surprised to discover an undulating purple line of distant mountains revealed in the clear, cold wind chasing the last of the storm away to the north. A distinct notch bisected the mountains midway along: the Idaron Pass.

We had left behind the meadows, marshes, and occasional woods of the plain and entered gently rolling farmland, stubble rows brown against the mud, thick evergreen hedgerows of juniper marking borders.

We had already come halfway.

I felt somewhat better when we mounted up again, though I couldn't say why. Maybe it was the prospect of an end to this ride.

Later that day, a new storm nearly sneaked up on us from behind. A fitful wind bringing the sharp scent of juniper, and the horses' ears flicking back and forth, were the first warnings. For the first time we urged the horses up to a canter in hopes of reaching some kind of shelter before the storm broke.

We'd barely established the new rhythm when we met Pandoc and his partner riding from the other direction.

"This way, Your Grace," Pandoc shouted, waving a gloved hand over his shoulder.

The animals galloped the remainder of the short distance to where the scouts had taken over the biggest building in a tiny village. It looked like a market, with stalls for people to bring their goods to sell. The family who owned the place stood against the back wall, eyes wide as they watched the Gray Wolves swarm in, weapons clanking, their wool-gray tunics smelling like wet dog.

In quick, well-trained order a bunch of the Wolves saw to the horses, another bunch set about making camp, and the third went out to establish a guard perimeter.

I found Hlanan and grumbled, "I hope snail-faced Geric isn't going to slay them outright after taking over this household."

Hlanan's smile flickered. "We are well into Namas Ilan—which is again an imperial protectorate. The householders will be given full value, never fear." So if Prince Geric Lendan did not want gossip racing ahead of him, he must abide by the empire's laws of travel.

As Hlanan straightened cramped limbs and looked about him, I caught sight of the white-bearded head of the household holding up stiff fingers as one of the Gray Wolves counted coins carefully into his other palm.

The householder gave a satisfied nod and waved at his family, who promptly dispersed, leaving us to fend for ourselves.

I now knew roughly where we were: we had indeed started from the Anadhan Mountains, somewhere south of Erev-li-Erval, and descended into the Unclaimed Lands west of Namas Ilan. Now we rode across the kingdom belonging to one of Rajanas's sort-of allies, as Namas Ilan had lately been changing governments the way courtiers changed their dress.

Apparently the Gray Wolves had also negotiated for basic supplies. I watched hungrily as the young man in charge of the cookery carefully pressed some withered olives to a hot sheet of metal laid over the open stove fire, then tossed rounds of corn meal with sweet pepper, purple shallots, and shaved garlic mixed in. When one side had browned, he flipped them and dropped crumbled dark-yellow cheese onto them to melt into bubbling deliciousness.

I retired with my share as he turned to the meat being cranked over a spit. By the time my corn cakes had cooled enough for me to eat, we all sat in a rough circle around the fire, Prince Geric and Hlanan on the same bench. Not out of any friendship—a single glance at the sharp angles of their shoulders, the tautness of their bodies made that clear—but the prince was obviously not letting Hlanan out of his sight, and Hlanan had his own reasons for complying.

Sitting opposite, thoroughly ignored by all, I contemplated them. Strange that I could compare them feature by feature, and though Prince Geric was hand-some by most human standards, the sight of his silky copper-colored hair, the graceful line from shoulder to slim waist, and thence straight to his elegantly booted heel, the blue of his eyes above the cut of his cheek-bones left me completely unmoved, while an errant strand of plain brown hair against Hlanan's collarbones hollowed my heart and weakened my knees, and the sound of his breathing made me want to press up against him.

How could it be love if we didn't understand one another? The songs all said that desire hit like a boulder smashing on one's head. That had never happened to me with Hlanan. When I first met him, I found him plain to look at and annoying in his curiosity and determined fairness and friendliness.

The desire to draw close had been so gradual that I had not noticed it until I stood face to face with Hlanan after we took that evil book from the Duchess of Thann, and suddenly I wanted to kiss him.

My reverie broke at the noise of a new arrival, a scout with a message. Some of the Gray Wolves went to check on the animals, and others to lay out bedrolls. Hlanan was finally alone. I slunk up next to him.

"Do you think Geric loved the horrible Morith?" I asked Hlanan in a whisper.

Geric stood on the opposite side of the big room, one foot propped on one of the benches that had been shifted against the walls to make space for all of us, as he bent over a small sheet of paper and read by the light of a flickering candle.

Hlanan gave a soft, surprised laugh, then lifted his head to cast a glance toward Geric before turning to me. "Whatever made you think of that?"

I shrugged. "Trying to figure out why she and Geric would marry. I mean, I know she was very attractive, especially to young fellows," I added hastily, recollecting that Hlanan himself, during his student days, had been one of her victims. She had courted and flattered him, then tried to inveigle him into translating that same evil book. "But he's old enough to know better, surely."

Hlanan said, "There are as many reasons to marry as there are marriages, I expect. And you must consider that when power, rank, and wealth number among the reasons, love and affection might be held much lower in importance."

Geric threw the paper into the fire then turned our way before

I could move. So I sat where I was as he lounged his way toward us. "Plotting?"

"Yes," I said.

"Give it up," he said. "And cease your short-sightedness. Jardis Dhes-Andis lives in a fabulous palace. Surely he would not put himself to all this trouble just to fling you into some dungeon. He could as easily arrange for that to happen here. Have you ever considered that you might enjoy the visit?"

"I would rather pinch-bugs crawled into my trousers," I retorted. "No, into *your* trousers."

"It is a shame," he drawled, "that your discourse so ill-matches your appearance."

"The shame is all yours," I snapped back, even less interested in his opinion of my manners than in his appreciation of my looks.

He laughed, as he always did, and moved away—but within earshot. I had to shut up.

The rest of the afternoon passed without incident. Once again Geric involved Hlanan in gossip about imperial affairs. I stayed near the window, watching the storm, and again felt that unsettling sense that someone watched me. It persisted, though I saw nothing but rain out the window. So I moved away.

In the stir later on, as the night patrol got ready to go, while the hapless patrollers stuck with guarding the place stamped and shed water and got their meal, Hlanan smoothly slid between them all. Geric was busy talk/signing with Oflan Nath and Pandoc.

Hlanan came to me. Maybe that sense of being watched was due to him trying to watch over me, as I did for him. That comforting thought sustained me for about three heartbeats. And then:

"I need you to escape," Hlanan said softly.

Five

"ME? AND LEAVE YOU?" I said, dismayed.

His soundless laugh warmed my cheek. "I adore you for being worried, but I assure you, I can look out for myself." The plain little ring on his finger glinted as he glanced away, and I recollected that indeed he had unexpected resources.

"I can do that, but where would I go?" I pressed against his shoulder, and his arm slid around my back. "And don't say back to Erev-li-Erval," I whispered fiercely. "I wouldn't dare show up there and report that I left you a prisoner."

"The empress would understand," he said in an undertone.

I snorted. "I don't care what the empress thinks of me," I said, pulling back a little so I could see him. "It's your sister I wouldn't want to face."

His lips parted, then he shook his head a little, blinked, and looked down earnestly into my face. "I told you I must see the situation at the Pass myself. Will you get away and warn Rajanas? I didn't trust Geric's words, but the scout's return earlier convinces me that he told the truth, at least as he sees it."

I was about to protest, "Will that nettle-tongued Rajanas believe me?" Then I reconsidered. Rajanas and I started out heartily despising one another. Well, the heartiness was perhaps mine. Even at our worst he had never been much of an enemy. I believed he would at least give me a listen, which was more than I could say for certain arrogant, evil princes.

"I'll do it," I said. "It'll give me great pleasure to escape under their noses." My only regret would be that I couldn't gloat in Prince Geric's face when he discovered that I was gone.

He pressed a kiss to my forehead and at a sound from outside, slipped away.

As I retired to the opposite corner to sleep, I thought about how strange it was that all my life I had drifted along, seldom thinking past the next meal, the next hole I might sleep in. And I had been content that way, but now I was impatient to go because I had a destination. A purpose.

Purpose, was that what everyone else but me had?

It had felt so good to have a purpose when we'd hunted that evil book down. Since the book had vanished from our lives, I'd stayed in Erev-li-Erval with the intention of being with Hlanan as much as I could, and when I couldn't, meeting the Hrethan and learning something about magic. The Hrethan had been elusive — everybody insisting they had little to do with political boundaries and governments — and the rudimentary magic lessons frustrating. Nothing I ever did was right, no matter how hard I tried, but they had all insisted that I must master the basics before learning anything else. The stifling court routine had increased my sense of futility; only Thianra's and Hlanan's company had kept me there.

Now I had a purpose again, I thought happily, as the wind screamed around the rafters overhead, and the candles in the lanterns lengthened and streamed. I'd get some rest, get a good meal inside me, and I'd be off.

Before dawn, the guards changed their shift, the night patrol coming in to settle down and the early morning bunch going out to check the sky, warm up their muscles, then set about seeing to the animals so that they'd be ready when everyone else rose to travel.

The night patrol settled fast, wanting to snatch some sleep before our departure. I hoped I would not have to use up my precious pack of liref, which was stronger than sleepweed. I could throw a handful of the ground herb into the room, but to put this many people out would take it all, not to mention my risk of breathing it in myself.

I waited until the breathing around me settled into deep

rhythms. Relief! Before moving a muscle, I wove an illusion around the corner I'd chosen. I deepened the shadows, taking care to leave a vague form where I'd lain.

Still weaving shadows, I rose to my feet. There is no invisibility, or really any way to cloak yourself with illusions. They are trickery with light and air. I counted upon my silent movements, and on everyone else either being asleep or busy getting their morning started as I eased along the back wall.

Geric had a private alcove. Everyone else slept or occupied themselves quietly: the duty guards stoked the fire and one brought pails of water to set to boil. As long as I moved slowly, the room would stay shadowy and still on the periphery of their vision, so long as nothing brought their attention away from the fire.

A last glance at Hlanan, whose face was partially covered, his eyelashes resting on his cheek as he breathed softly. My heart squeezed, and I turned away, five steps — six — and slipped into the kitchen. The back door stood open, the guard having had a pail in each hand so he couldn't shut the door.

Cold air flowed in as I flowed noiselessly out.

From there, it was easy enough to use the snow prints already made until I got away from the building. Elsewhere in the village people were also up and about, swiftly churning up the new-fallen snow.

I spotted a pair of child-sized mocs drying on a shelf, and nipped them. My bare feet could deal with a certain amount of very cold weather, but I had a long walk ahead of me. I needed shoes.

I hoped the family I stole from would press Geric for payment.

Once I'd reached relative safety downstream, hidden by one of the ubiquitous juniper borders, I sat on a rock to try on my new shoes. They were much too wide and a bit too long, but I pulled the cords tight. I'd have to find some stockings to pad them out and keep them from rubbing.

Or so I thought for the first little ways along the road. I enjoyed the crisp chuff of my feet in the snow, the sparkle of my breath on the air, and the deep blue shadows on the junipers winding away in graceful curves toward a distant river, now a metal-gray gleam.

But very soon I remembered the problem inherent in newly-stolen shoes: the sides began rubbing the sides of my feet where the tender skin had chafed raw.

Finally I found myself a sheltered spot under some evergreens and eased the shoes off, then stared in dismay at the pinkish smears on the sides of my feet and my toes. The cold had partially numbed the pain.

I scowled at the shoes, wondering if I ought to try tying them to the bottoms of my feet or just go barefoot and get used to the cold, when I became aware of the muffled thud of multiple footsteps beyond the trees.

I snatched up the shoes and using my free hand and my tail, swept the snow where I'd been sitting, though there was no smoothing it completely. I hoped it obscured the distinctive prints as I took two great leaps and ducked down behind a fallen log.

I need not have bothered.

A rider appeared, leading a remount. I took one look at the low hat, the sweeping cape, and the heavy sword in the saddle sheath and ducked back down, readying myself to spring away as the hooves clopped straight at me.

In one move I popped up, twisted, and sprinted for the woods downslope. The horse leaped the log and cantered two rhythmic strides, easily heading me off.

I turned, sucked in a breath to leap into the nearest tree — something whistled oddly behind me — and I fell flat on my face in the snow, my legs bound painfully by wooden balls connected by supple rope. I tried uselessly to worm free, then rolled over, ready to scratch and bite — and stared up at a cowled face with frizzy blond hair spilling out.

Captain Oflan Nath of the Gray Wolves grinned down at me. She let out a laugh and vaulted easily from the saddle.

As she approached, I readied my fists. She clapped her gloved hands together in the general gesture of peace, then held her palms up toward me.

I scowled at her, and though I knew she couldn't hear me, I could not forbear exclaiming, "Let me go! I did nothing to you!"

To my surprise, she tapped two fingers on the other palm, then jerked her head at the horse, who waited in well-trained obedience beyond her, nosing the drifts for anything green that might have survived the snowfall. The remount waited a couple paces away, ears flicking.

I looked from the horses back to her as she squatted down, palms still out toward me, and when I didn't move she bent to unbind that thing from my legs.

As she straightened up, she looped the thing up expertly and hooked it over her saddle, then regarded me as I stood and brushed snow off my grimy, once-fine silk drape, now unwashed for days. One side of her mouth curled up, and she clapped lightly. I jumped and the horses' ears flicked as she pointed at me, at the distant mountains, and then spelled out A-L-E-Z-A-N-D on her palm.

In other words, she knew where I was going.

The question was, did she intend to stop me?

"How did you know?" I asked, shook my head, then wrung my hands, wondering how to convey it.

But she gave a soundless laugh, then tapped her lips, clapped her hands together and opened them like a book. *I read lips.*

I wondered if Geric knew that—and I remembered his impatience, his demanding an interpreter when he needed to convey an order. Though I would happily believe any villainy of him, I didn't think him stupid enough to talk freely around Oflan Nath as if he thought *she* was stupid. That meant no one had told him that she could read lips. Even if it would have made communication with "his grace, the duke" easier.

"Did Prince Geric order you to take me there?" I asked, snaking my hand beneath my grimy tunic toward my thief tools, and my bag of liref.

She held up a finger, then signed, *Duke's-orders-to-fetch-you.*

"To fetch me," I repeated, my fingers closing on the bag.

She touched her mouth, then made the duke sign: *His-words. Fetch-Hrethan-thief.*

She gave me a slow smile. *I-obey-orders. You-fetched. Now-we-ride. Alezand.*

"Geric *wants* us to ride to Alezand?" I asked, thoroughly confused.

Her smile widened to a quick grin. *No-orders-beyond-fetch. I-ask-*

not.

An astonishing idea bloomed. "He doesn't know we're going to Rajanas? He thinks you are going to pinch me off the road and take me back to him!"

She brought her chin down in a nod. Then she swept her hand toward her horse. *Come. I-teach-you-ride.*

That was accompanied by an ironic glance at the saddle.

I gazed back warily. This surprise seemed too good to believe.

On the other hand, there I stood, my toes numbing, my belly empty, with a very long walk ahead of me.

All right. I wouldn't get far riding on my own. In the past I'd only managed to stay on because I could sense the horse's thoughts, and now I did not dare even use that. So far I'd bounced along like froth on a boiling pot, clutching at the horse's mane — at least we'd ridden slowly.

I wavered.

Oflan frowned down at my feet and the pink stains in the slush. Then she turned her back, strode to her saddle bag, dug into it, and pitched something at me.

I caught it and looked down at a pair of thick, soft knit socks.

That decided me.

She pulled me up to sit in front of her.

I wasn't going to be trusted alone on the second horse until her strong hands had pushed and pulled me into sitting properly. It felt strange at first. She yanked on my shoulders, shoved my hips, and punched insistently at my thigh here, my arm there — but at some point I found myself anchored down, and though I'd always been able to sense how to stay on a horse in a way that was acceptable to the animal, for the very first time I was actually comfortable in the sense that I fit. Further, I could sense through the shift of the horse's muscles the animal equivalent of, "Ah, that's more like it, you silly two-legged feather-ball!"

By then Oflan had left the road entirely, following a pattern in the landscape that I could not perceive. The snow began to melt as Big Moon set in the south and the bright sun rose, leaving pools of slush that we navigated around. She chose higher ground strewn with shale until she found a way down to the river's edge, where we left no prints.

We proceeded at a steady pace as the sun climbed its arc, following the winding river. She stayed away from the occasional villages built along the water. I kept my ears alert, knowing that she couldn't hear, but it wasn't long before I discovered that the sounds that alerted me matched the sights that alerted her: sudden bursts of birds, the run of a small brown fox, our horses twitching ears and raising noses to sniff the wind.

As we turned with the river and the sun climbed steadily, my awareness underwent another of those shifts in orientation. Now I knew my location: we were cutting across the bottom of the kingdom of Namas Ilan, away from where the river drained into a big lake.

No sooner did I recognize that we had to be nearing the border into Alezand than noises on the bluff above caught my attention. Oflan had already reined the horse under the shade of a tangle of pine trees, through whose thin green-fuzzed branches we caught sight of the flash of sky blue.

Those blue tabard-tunics belonged to Alezand's Blue Guard! We could hail them — maybe send a message with them!

I turned my head, but Oflan had already kneed the horse into surging up the bank to the bluff. We emerged onto the muddy road as the last of the riders vanished into what appeared to be a small trade town.

Great, I thought, as my empty stomach complained. Maybe we could catch up with them there, and in the course of finding them at a meal, get one of our own.

At the river edge crowded three big houses for wares, and around a square sat about a dozen stores and houses with two inns across from one another, pennants and guild flags belonging to prominent patrons decorating the eaves. A small town, but from the looks of the decorative iron scrollwork, the good slate roofs and the brightly colored shutters at the windows, a prosperous town.

I mentally rehearsed the message to be sent to Rajanas as I peered past winter-bare fruit trees in expectation of seeing the Blue

Guard squad reining in at one or other of the inns.

Oflan stiffened behind me, and the horse checked its gait. "Something wrong?" I said to the air as she tapped my arm and pointed past my nearly-healed shoulder.

Part of the squad peeled off down the slope toward the nearest warehouse. The two riders paused, doing something between them — then one whirled something overhead and flung it up high to crash through a window. From inside flames began to flicker and glow.

"Fire!" I squawked.

Oflan, of course, couldn't hear me. But she'd seen. We began to gallop down the road into town, and arrived as the patrol fanned out in three groups of two.

As villagers streamed toward the fire, yelling for buckets and barrels, Oflan rode straight toward the warriors in blue. The first group had drawn their swords and stepped up either side of the door to an inn when we arrived, the horse sliding, kicking up clots of mud. I clutched its mane, desperate not to be thrown off; when the animal stopped, prancing nervously, sides heaving and head tossing, I saw the reins hanging loose.

Oflan, a sword in one hand, a long knife in the other, charged the blue-clad Alezand Guards.

Not expecting attack from behind, they faltered and whirled. Oflan cut one down with a sword strike to the knee, and broke the forearm of the second.

A bellow from behind caused the two pairs who had spread out to attack to change direction — they were about to get reinforcements. They ran toward us as, from a distance, someone howled, "Fire!"

Oflan glanced over her shoulder at me, her reproachful expression clearly saying, *Are you going to sit there or help?*

Attack Rajanas's Guards, who we were riding to warn? They had started the fire, after all. She didn't wait for me to explain my confusion, but hopped over the fallen two and plunged inside. The doorway now narrowed the field of attack.

I glanced around. I was no good with weapons. Even if I had known much about sword-fighting, my heaviest blow would be a tickle to, for instance, that gray-haired woman leading the four reinforcements. Built like a barrel of solid bone and muscle, she would run me right down. And again, too wide a space and too many people around me prevented me from using liref to put them all into a snooze without knocking myself out as well.

My gaze fell on those balls connected to the rope. I plucked the looped implement from its saddle hook, then frowned. How did Oflan throw them? I was about to put them back when Oflan swept a hand out.

I leaped off the horse and slung the loop over her palm. She shook out the balls as she stepped back out onto the porch. She whirled them expertly over her head until they whistled in the air, then cast them at the leading runner.

He fell with a crash, tripping the second one. Oflan fought the two remaining, her arms a whirl of motion. I ducked back and forth, dithering until I caught sight of the two who had started the fire. They'd gained entrance from the back of the inn, and now they shoved and struck their way through the panicking customers, swords at the ready.

My gaze swept the inn counter. Ah! A bowl of colored game markers. I leaped to the counter, grabbed the bowl, and slung the markers in a bouncing, ticking tide, watching in satisfaction as the first guard's boot slid out from under him. He crashed to his back as the second one's feet scrabbled desperately—his arms wheeled—and he, too, slammed down, skidding head-first into the counter directly below me.

As he cursed and groped about for his fallen sword, I noticed the beer keg perched next to me, balanced halfway off the counter so that the spigot was clear. It would only take a push. I sat down and put my feet against it—

"No," someone howled. "*Not* the harvest dark!"

An innkeeper thrust past a circle of gawking customers and closed his arms around the keg. Five paces away, Oflan still held the doorway, fighting against the new arrivals. A splintering crash turned heads as Oflan smashed a chair over a man's back.

The brawny woman shouted, "Retreat!"

"Cover me," the guard below me said as he scrambled to his feet, swinging his sword in a lethal circle. One of his friends tried to approach, slipped on the still-rolling markers, and shot out the front door face first, cursing loudly.

"Get out of here!" the brawny woman bawled, and followed her own advice, the last two limping behind her.

In the midst of smashed furniture, Oflan straightened slowly, wiping blood from her chin and looking down at one of the fallen guards.

"Alezand!" the innkeeper exclaimed, pointing at the black device on the guard's blue tabard-tunic.

"Alezand's Blues, attacking us! We must send a message off to the guild chiefs at once, and protest this outrage," a skinny old fellow in a worn scribe robe proclaimed in a voice quivering with anger.

Their language — the voices — "They're not from Alezand," I said, realizing what Oflan seemed to have noticed at the outset.

"What?" the female innkeeper exclaimed, then snorted. "This looks like Alezand Blue to me." She dug her toe into the side of the fallen guard, who groaned.

"Right you are, Evit." And to me, "This is Alezand's device, plain as plain," the male innkeeper stated, with another wave of that big hand downward at the blue tunic with the black device.

"But they didn't speak in Allendi," I said. "The Alezand people all speak Allendi. Or maybe the imperial tongue."

Everyone looked at one another, as in the distance we could hear the villagers fighting the warehouse fire. "I didn't understand 'em," a man said as he righted a three-legged stool. "Thought it was hot words."

I shook my head. "Both of them spoke Faran."

"Nothing good *ever* comes out of Forfar!"

"Ugh, Farans!"

Everyone looked disgusted. "Faran!" the innkeeper exhaled the word like a curse, and rubbed his grizzled chin. "Everyone knows you can hire *them* to do anything, long's you pay enough. Then they'll turn right around and rob you. Leave you for dead." He spat to the side, and then after a low-browed thought, spat again on the backside of the moaning guard.

"Why would the Prince of Alezand hire such?" the female innkeeper asked, bending to pick up a fallen chair.

The inn folk stood in a rough semi-circle, so that Oflan could easily see each face. She signed, *Not-from-Alezand. Speak Faran.*

So she could lip read Faran as well as Elras. Seeing non-comprehension from the inn folk, I translated, then added to Oflan, "What do you mean?"

Alezand-make-weapons. Equip-guard. These-here-mercenaries-from-Forfar. False-guise.

She finished with a contemptuous gesture toward the weapons left behind. I spotted a curved sword with a nick in the blade, a thin-bladed noble's weapon—probably stolen, judging by the aristocratic device worked into the handle—and a cutlass. "You're right," I said, and then, "That woman, she's going to warn whoever sent them."

No-help. We-ride-Imbradi, referring to Alezand's capital. *Take-him.* Another contemptuous gesture toward the supine mercenary.

"You want to take him along?" I asked.

The female innkeeper had been wiping her hands slowly down her apron as she frowned, not quite looking at us. But at that, she lifted her head, and nodded vigorously. "Good idea! You do that."

"Yes," the innkeeper said heartily, striding behind the counter. "Take him off with you. We'll send you with anything you like, in thanks for your timely rescue."

It was abundantly clear that the sooner they were rid of us, the happier they'd be. I noticed that most of the puzzled looks were coming my way, as if they couldn't fit Hrethan with this scene. They glanced at Oflan's distinctive Gray Wolf cowled tunic, then as quickly looked away.

Horses, Oflan signed to me, and I sighed inwardly, accepting my new post as interpreter.

With the full cooperation of the inn folk, we soon arranged for extra horses and received a satisfyingly bulging pack of good things to eat. Oflan and the innkeeper lifted the unconscious guard over the saddle of one horse and tied his wrists and ankles to the stirrups, then we left the village.

Oflan apparently had decided that I could be trusted with my own horse, and I took charge of the food as she led the prisoner-burdened horse and the remounts.

The entire population of the inn—and those villagers not busy stamping out the last of the warehouse fire—watched us until we were safely out of sight.

I waited until I could catch Oflan's eye, then said, "We're following the road now? What about Geric?"

Go-west. We-go-southwest.

I thought about this, and when next I caught her eye as she scanned high, low, in all directions, I asked, "So he will not chase us, is that what you are saying?"

Her expression tightened again, but she brought her chin down in a short nod and pointed stiff fingers to the western heights, purple in the hazy sun.

I knew she was dangerous, and I did not want to seem to be baiting her, but I struggled mentally as the day wore on. When we stopped to water the horses and change the saddles to the remounts, something she did as easily as if they were featherbeds, I said, "I have a question."

She thrust our water flasks into my hands and pointed to the stream we'd stopped beside. I obediently went to shake the stale drops out and sink the flasks down deeply enough not to catch stray bits of old grass floating along the surface.

I lugged them back, and she bent down to dribble water between the dry lips of the prisoner. He cursed her, but drank. She had let him lie where he fell, his wrists and ankles still bound; when she reached to pick him up again, he stiffened and did his best to fight.

She smacked him open-handed. He fell down, the bruised side of his head turned up, thin bits of dried blood darkening his red hair. It was a miracle he hadn't cracked his head. He must have had a fierce headache, but he still cursed her when she hauled him up by his armpits and then with a grunt flung him over the saddle again, and lashed him to the stirrups.

I hung the flasks to the saddles and, at a gesture from her, scrambled up onto the new horse. It took a moment or two to adjust myself to this horse's mind and manner, especially as I was sore in all those muscles I had learned to use so recently.

So I was silent as we started down the road toward a wickerwork of barren trees, the hills of the border striped with long golden shadows as the sun began dropping westward.

When I glanced Oflan's way, she opened her palm, fingers

curled: *Question?*

She could read lips, but the line between her brows suggested to me for the first time that she might have as bad a headache as the prisoner, or very nearly. She showed no signs of it, except that she moved with the care of someone conserving strength.

I knew enough hand-sign by now. *Go-against-orders?*

No. A definite shake of her head. *Outside-orders.* And after a time, in which the only sounds were raucous birds quarreling in the tall treetops to the right and the chuckle of a small waterfall in the stream by the road, she signed, *Betray-no-oath.*

Surprised, I forgot my intention and exclaimed, "You made an oath to *Prince Geric?*"

"Hey, you canker-blown maggots," the prisoner called in Faran. "You have made the last mistake of your lives."

Oflan had been keeping him in her vision, her lip curled. Then she winced, thumbing her temples. Yes, she had a headache. She signed, *He-duke-Thann. My-oath-to-Thann.*

She clearly thought that explained everything, but questions bloomed so fast in my mind I felt like they'd fly out my ears. My hair lifted in reaction, and I sucked in a breath to smooth it again, with no luck. All my bad experiences with Geric (admittedly in part caused by my robbing him, but still!) came out in pent-up outrage. "Surely you don't trust him?"

"What's that you're saying?" the prisoner snarled.

We ignored him as I wrestled with the idea, then came enlightenment. *Thann-your-home,* I signed. *You-loyal-home?*

I was quite proud of what I thought a profound insight. The idea of home was as novel as the concept of loyalty. But my question only caused her to look away, her jaw so tight I could see a vein ticking in her neck, and she repeated the signs for oath and Thann, slapping the backs of her fingers against her palm for emphasis.

I knew I was missing something here, but now was not the time to explore that, any more than it was for me to indulge in slandering Prince Geric as he so richly deserved. We had enough to deal with right before us.

Six

WE CAMPED AT SUNDOWN. She might not have heard our prisoner cursing and insulting us, but she must have got the gist of what he was saying as she loosened the ties to his stirrups, because once again she let him slide off and fall to the ground with a splat.

She gave him water but said as I fetched the fresh food, *He-lives. Enough.*

Good thinking. Maybe he'd be less trouble on an empty belly. But even so, I soon discovered that, tired as I was, when you have a prisoner, you have to set up guard duty. We divided the night between us, but even so it seemed the longest night in the history of the world.

When dawn finally arrived, it brought low clouds. As Oflan took care of the animals I looked at my filthy clothes, and snapped my tail and hair in a mostly futile effort to rid myself of grit.

Oflan and I shared out the cold, stale bread and cheese, our every bite watched by the prisoner. She allowed him two mouthfuls of water. His one unswollen eye was red and angry, but he made only a perfunctory resistance as Oflan threw him onto a horse and we mounted up.

We'd chosen a spot out of the wind, under what would have been the shelter of a spreading oak if the oak had had any leaves. We'd reached a plateau of low, undulating hills that stretched upward toward the mountains into which Rajanas's capital, Imbradi, had been built.

The rising wind was cold and wet, the low clouds promising sleet. I braced myself for a miserable ride—and then heard thundering hooves coming at us from over the next rise.

I shouted—of course, Oflan couldn't hear me—but she was already making sure her weapons were at hand, as the horses' ears twitched forward.

There was nowhere for us to go. We slowed our horses as over the rise trotted a patrol in the blue of the Alezand Guard.

"There they are!" a voice—speaking Allendi—carried on the wind.

At a sign from the leader, the patrol split efficiently to circle us.

Oflan flung her reins under her knee and drew weapons as we were surrounded, but when the captain, a hard-faced young man with a hawk nose and big ears, bawled out in Allendi, "Halt! Put down your weapons!" I waved at Oflan, pointing frantically at them, shouting in Elras, the most widely used tongue in the empire: "They are real Blues, they are real Blues!"

She sheathed her weapons at once.

I rehearsed the quickest words, but then surprise turned to dismay when the captain said curtly, his throat knuckle bobbing, "Disarm and bind the prisoners." And then, eyeing our prisoner, in a different voice, "Your captain and wing?"

"Thieves," he croaked. "Those two are murderers and thieves."

"No we're not," I yelled, and bit back the absurd impulse to add, *Well, she's not a thief, anyway.* "He's a Faran mercenary."

The Allendi captain eyed me. Then our prisoner. Then Oflan, surrounded by a circle of armed and ready Blues, and sighed. "A Hrethan, a Gray Wolf, and... whatever you are." His voice soured when he came to the prisoner. "We're here to investigate the attacks on the border by persons unknown, wearing our garb." And then a really mean look Oflan's way. "We thought they were the Gray Wolves in disguise."

He waved a hand. "Bind them all. Someone above me will sort them out."

They searched Oflan, took away her weapons, and then tied her hands. She endured this with a tight face and angry eyes. "All right, get back on the horse."

When she didn't respond, the searcher drew in breath to shout, but I said, "She's deaf."

"Oh." He grimaced. "I don't know hand-sign." He stepped in front of Oflan, pointed at the horse and saddle, saying loudly and exaggeratedly, "Get. Up."

She mounted easily—a step and vault—as if her hands hadn't been bound. I could see how impressed the Blues were by how several circled in close, as if she were about to pull out an invisible sword and attack them all.

As for me, the searcher assigned to me was a young woman around my own age (whatever that might be), who eyed my grimy clothes with a crimp of disgust in her upper lip. I lifted my hair, clouding it around my head, and swished my tail back and forth, hoping to distract her from the bulge of my thief tools on one side under my drape. It worked. Or maybe, seeing no weapons and discounting me as any kind of threat, she whirled her hand toward another horse. She didn't bother tying my hands.

So I mounted, taking care that my bag of thief tools stayed flat under my thigh; the long fluttering panels of my drape helped.

We set out at a fast pace, which didn't abate until we spotted the city beyond the next hill. Before we got much farther we encountered another patrol. A pause for a quick exchange (followed by all heads turning to give us a crown-to-heel scan), to refresh the animals, and we were off again.

When we reached the city gates, we were waved through, again with all eyes taking us in as we passed up the clean, winding streets. On either side close-built houses of stone or brick looked ready for winter, the window boxes gone, and thick square-paned glass in the windows under those steeply slanted roofs.

As before, the street widened until it gave onto a park, at the other end of which was Rajanas' marble palace. Oflan rode with her chin high, the only sign of emotion a little red under her strongly etched cheek-bones. Her ash-pale hair bounced softly at each hoof beat.

We rode around to the back of the palace. Somebody had obviously gone ahead, because armed guards awaited us in the courtyard. Stable hands ran out to take charge of the sweaty horses as our patrol dismounted. Tired horses plodded one way, tired patrollers another. Accompanied by Captain Big Ears and this new set of guards, we were taken in the back way of the palace I remembered so well, though I'd spent less than half a day in it all told.

Here again were the whitewashed walls and clay tile floors. I listened to the tramp of feet and the heavy breathings around me, fighting the instinct to run. Mentally making a wager whether we were headed for the toff floors or the dungeon, I sidled glances around for possible escape routes.

This city was not nearly high enough for me to try my transformation, but that was only the newest of my tricks. I was plenty good at climbing and running. Indeed, that was how I'd made my first escape after Geric had taken this city from the inside.

Recollecting this bolstered my never-very-strong courage as our escort clattered their way up some broad stairs and herded us into a plain chamber, where military types stood in a circle around a figure in black and spring green.

The circle opened, revealing Rajanas himself, pale eyes in a brown face framed by long black hair, a thin mustache his only affectation. It framed a sardonic mouth that quirked appreciatively when he saw me.

"And so we meet again, thief," he said, but not nastily. In fact, I think he was trying not to laugh at my grimy self and bare feet.

But all traces of humor vanished, and there was the Rajanas I remembered when he took in Oflan. "A Gray Wolf," he drawled.

Her eyes narrowed.

I said, "I don't know if she can read lips in Allendi."

Rajanas glanced my way, brows lifted. Then he frowned at his hands and tentatively signed *Name. Go* – then something I couldn't understand, and he shook his head and dropped his hands.

To me he said, "I knew a little hand-sign when I was small, but I taught it to Hlanan on the galley so we could talk without being overheard, and we made up our own words. Now I can't remember which were genuine and which ours." He gave Oflan a grim look, then said to me, "So you've joined the Gray Wolves, is that it? Are they the ones running up and down the border, setting fires and attacking harvest barns, dressed as my Blues?"

"No!" I yelped. "You got one of those in your prison. We

stopped one of the attacks, and grabbed him to find out who they were. That was after we rode here to tell you about the coming attack."

The words "coming attack" caused them all to stiffen to alertness, hands going to sword hilts as if Dhes-Andis and his minions were about to crash in through the window.

I'd rehearsed what to say. Out it all came in a stream, with several stops and back-fills because I remembered that Rajanas knew nothing about Maita or what had happened to that terrible book.

He listened without interrupting or even betraying much reaction, until I got to, "And Geric married the Duchess of Thann, I don't know why, but she must have done it to get the book, but now *he's* in command of the Gray Wolves."

On the word "duchess" his brows shot upward again. "Very interesting. Very."

"And he's on his way, right now. With Hlanan."

"With Hlanan? As a hostage?"

"Not sure." I wrung my hands, remembered that Rajanas knew who Hlanan really was, and so I stuck my hands in my armpits. "The thing I am sure is, Hlanan wants to get a look at the Pass himself."

"Ah. Assuming this is not one of your embroideries, he's riding in the guise of a hostage. That sounds more like Hlanan," Rajanas said with a grim smile.

Then he addressed one of the waiting equerries. "Find me an interpreter." And when the equerry had saluted and vanished through the door, Rajanas said to me, "I expect you can communicate with her, but you'll recollect the last time I saw you was after you'd managed to set fire to several pirate ships—and that was after revealing that you were in mental communication with Dhes-Andis. And *that* was after you'd made it plain that lying had been your first defense during a life on the run. At this point in our acquaintance I'm hesitant to mount a defensive strategy based on your word. Especially with an army in the Pass, at best waiting for spring and at worst, waiting for who knows what signal. Which conceivably could be conveyed through you."

Annoyance flared through me. But at least he was telling me

instead of throwing me in a dungeon. So I said, "I guess I can't convince you I hate Dhes-Andis worse than poison, and if he begged and pleaded for me to accept the empress's crown, I would run to another continent."

Rajanas snorted.

I sighed. "If you're not going to throw me behind bars, might I visit that splendid bath of yours?"

The grim line of his mouth eased. "You certainly may. Take your time. I have two prisoners to interrogate, beginning with the one you so thoughtfully brought us." He nicked his chin at Oflan and said to the waiting guards, "Bring her down to the garrison when she's done."

Before I'd drawn three breaths I was being led in one direction and Oflan taken in another, with such haste that I had a feeling Rajanas did not want me talking in sign to her. As a muscular servant in sky blue and black livery led me up the marble staircase, I remembered his "you so thoughtfully." That was mighty ambiguous. Did he really think that that red-haired prisoner was *our* disguised mercenary?

I had to fight the impulse to turn right around and yell that I could have made up a better story than *that!* I grumped to myself on the long walk, but my bad mood vanished when I reached the wonderful bath I'd seen on my first visit, an enormous pool heated by magic, in a tiled room of blue and gold and brown. One thing for sure, rich people really understood comfort, I thought happily as I wriggled free of my clothes and dived in.

I swam to the end where the fountain continually poured fresh water in. Soap of various kinds waited in little dishes. I helped myself, thoroughly enjoying a good scrub.

At length, curiosity about what was happening impelled me to climb out. In the far room I found a towel waiting and spied a cleaning frame. I put my clothes through it, and so dirty was the outfit that the cleaning magic flared in green-blue sparkles all over the peach silk.

I fluffed my hair and tail until they were barely damp, rubbed my fuzz until it was soft and fluffy again, then shrugged into my drape. I put through the stolen shoes, which didn't look much better after being cleaned, they were so old and worn, and Oflan's stockings. I put my thief tools into one of my hidden pockets, picked up the shoes and socks, and opened the door.

The tall steward waited directly outside. Threat? Not threat? He led me down the hall to a small chamber, where waited a tray of fruit tarts, cheeses, fresh bread, snap-beans, carrots, and a delicious dish of spiced cabbage. Whatever else was going on, Rajanas—or someone—had remembered that my kind don't eat meat.

Taking that as a hopeful sign, I said to the silent steward, "Are you hungry? You may as well join me."

He gave his head a shake. "I don't eat on duty," he said.

Duty. A reminder I was under guard. It didn't seem I was going to get anything out of him, so I concentrated on my meal.

I was choosing between a last plum-cake and a berry-tartlet when Rajanas appeared as abruptly as he'd gone off, still trailing equerries. "Done?" he asked me, and without waiting for an answer, said, "Good. Let's ride."

The words were an invitation, but the tone was an order that everybody obeyed, perforce sweeping me along.

Rajanas whirled around so fast his long hair swung between his shoulder blades. He'd found time to change out of those sky-blue silk clothes into the sturdy black I was used to seeing him in. His battle tunic hit the doorjamb, then with a long stride he shot out the door, issuing a stream of orders as he walked.

I trotted to catch up—accidentally leaving the shoes and stockings along with the empty plate. At three points I spotted possible escape routes, but my sense of danger was far outweighed by curiosity. And the danger didn't feel personal.

"Where's Oflan?" I asked, when the last equerry bolted down a passageway with her new orders. "Not in your dungeon, I hope."

"Riding with us." Rajanas cast a glance my way. "Your red-haired friend is staying behind in the dungeon. Needless to say, his story contradicts everything the two of you said. Giving me three potential liars."

"I'm not lying," I said hotly. Then saw in his compressed lips the urge to laugh. "I know, I know, so says the liar," I added hastily, rolling my eyes. "You can save the speeches."

"First time your lies have caught up with you?"

"I never stayed anywhere long enough for it to matter," I said, glowering.

He grinned. "The first statement I'll believe without condition."

I hissed out my breath, hopping again to keep up with his long strides. "I'd forgotten how annoying you are."

"May I return the compliment?" He sketched a mocking bow as we turned a corner, the air in this new passage smelling of horses and hay. "But this I will say, thief, life when you are around is never boring."

I could have retorted that life around him was never restful. We dashed down to the stable, where equerries had mounts waiting. A dozen Blues mounted up along with us, and in a few heartbeats we set out at a fast pace through the gates of the palace and toward the far gates of the city. Rajanas led, and the others formed alongside us, Oflan riding before me. I was at the end, the least important, or the least threatening.

We slowed when we got past the walls with their alert sentries, and proceeded at a pace that Rajanas probably considered boringly sedate, though my entire body jounced at each trot and I felt like a corn kernel popping on a hot skillet.

I caught Oflan's eye once. Her mouth quirked downward in a way that reminded me of my riding lessons, and I tried to grip the horse once again. That only hurt more. A glance at the others revealed them rising a little in the stirrups. Great. My feet didn't reach the stirrups, something no one had paid attention to, as I'd curled my feet up under my rump on either side, as usual, my tail switching from side to side.

This was going to be one long, miserable ride, I thought in resignation, as we slowed again on a steep road leading up toward thick pine forest. But at least I had my thief tools. From the emptiness of Oflan's belt and the lack of hilts sticking up from her boots, it seemed likely that they'd taken away all her weapons.

The sun finally began slanting down, and after a couple thousand years Rajanas called a halt by a cataract that spilled into a pool.

People led the animals to water, then fixed them with loose rein to lip at the grass and rest, as an equerry passed trail food from hand to hand.

My nose caught the scent of spiced dry meat of some sort, and I sighed, reminding myself that at least I'd had that excellent meal that morning—then a round golden thing spun through the air toward me from Rajanas's hand.

I caught it without thinking and discovered a hard-crusted roll into which someone had stuffed greens and cheese. I was going to thank him, but he'd already turned away and stood near Oflan, head bent, as the interpreter asked questions in sign and she answered.

As I ate I watched the horses, all of whose ears had flicked in one direction. Some forest animal? I shut my eyes to listen to their minds—then remembered I did not dare open that mental wall.

Rajanas's voice distracted me as he said to the interpreter, "If she can be believed. We might send her first, with an escort. I'll ask for volunteers, as the Gray Wolves might very well take her safety signal as a sign to shoot—"

"Your Highness!"

Rajanas broke off, head lifted at the sound of hoof-beats in a rapid rhythm.

A scout rode up, halting in a spray of kicked up mud.

"Attack! They're—" His voice broke off when an arrow sprouted in his shoulder, and he fell from his frightened horse.

That was the signal to close the trap.

Gray Wolf archers emerged from behind trees and shrubbery on the far side of the pool at our left, and sword-wielding nasties thundered down from the steep pine-shrouded slope to our right. Though my military awareness was about as good as my riding— which was to say, terrible—even I saw at once that we had ridden straight into ambush.

Rajanas sent a nasty look Oflan's way as I stashed my half-eaten roll hastily in my pocket.

Oflan paid no attention to him. She gazed upslope and then, in a fast motion, produced a knife from somewhere in her clothes and threw it straight into the gap between armor and vambrace in the lead attacker. The man spun, his steps faltering, and the attacker following behind cracked into him. They both fell into the shrubbery.

Rajanas's expression changed as Oflan made violent signs in the direction of the interpreter as she calmed her horse with her knees.

"Says they're not hers," the interpreter called.

Rajanas pulled his saddle sword and rode next to her, but instead of attacking, he tossed the sword to her hilt first.

She caught it with the same ease I'd caught my roll. I could see the unspoken choice: attack Rajanas, who was ready, or...

She whirled the horse and plunged toward the attackers a horse length ahead of Rajanas, who raised a fist for his people to form up in a drilled line.

Leaving me sitting unsteadily atop my horse, who sidled nervously, ears flat. The mount probably wanted direction from me, but I had no idea how to give it — I tried to send calming thoughts, but that was about as successful as my skill at riding.

But! I glanced around. This time I had better luck projecting my intent to the horse through muscle movement. It cooperatively sidestepped a few paces as I got my feet under me on the saddle. I leaped up, catching a pine branch with one hand. A flick of my tail and a swing, and I was in the tree, which was full of pinecones that had not yet dropped.

I might not be any good wielding steel weapons, but I had excellent aim. I leaped and swung my way until I landed on a branch above the shooters hidden on the opposite side of the pond, and began plucking pinecones and pitching them directly into their faces.

Arrows arced satisfyingly in all directions before they figured out where the attack was coming from, then arrows zipped and hissed around me as I pressed myself flat against the bole of a tree.

I risked a glance at Rajanas and Oflan leading their line uphill into descending attackers. Even I could see that fighting uphill was much tougher, but it was equally apparent that the enemy wasn't well organized, or maybe they weren't used to fighting together. There was nothing of that well-drilled rhythm of Rajanas's Blue Guard, or what you'd expect from the Gray Wolves...but even so, what could a dozen or so do against forty or fifty?

They were going down fighting. Sickness roiled inside me. What could I do? Illusion? But if the illusory warriors didn't attack, they'd know. Fog? I could pull vapor from that stream, but by the time I could build it into fog, the honor guard, Rajanas, and Oflan might be dead—

A horn blared in the distance. Heads turned. Arms tightened.

Through the trees, mud splashing high, thundered forest green-clad warriors, at their head a familiar gray-haired figure who did not look like a grandmother now: Kuraf!

They hit the line of attackers from the back, scattering them like pins in a game of bowls. The ones on the other side of the pond shot a few arrows. Clack! Clack! Clack! Up went shields— and the shooters began to melt away, then came howls and cries from the trees as group of Kuraf's warriors enclosed *them*.

It was all over. As Kuraf's people rounded up prisoners and collected weapons, I swung down and made my way to where Rajanas stood talking to a gangling blond boy of about fourteen. "Nill!"

He turned my way, and grinned. "Lhind! Was that you, throwing those pinecones?"

Rajanas drawled, "I'd forgotten how inventive you can be in a fight, thief. Nice distraction. You would have bought us half a dozen more heartbeats of life if Kuraf hadn't come along."

"What happened?" I asked, turning from him to Nill.

The boy's smile vanished. "We were at the dividing line where our scouts and the Blue Guard scouts each do their outer perimeter rounds. We might not have found the dead scouts if one of our people hadn't taken a back trail down through a valley to visit her family. Sent up the alarm. Gran mustered those of us in hearing."

I remembered being told that Kuraf had been the head of the Blue Guard in the days before Rajanas got his throne back. She was supposed to be retired now, but what that really meant was, she headed a well-trained force of warriors who lived in tree platforms, their main task to watch the Ildaran Pass.

"We've got a lot to talk about," she said, coming up to the group and ruffling Nill's blond hair.

Rajanas cast me an ironic look. "We do."

Seven

KURAF SAT CROSS-LEGGED on the other side of the campfire, the firelight glinting among the white hairs in her coronet of braids. As she had the first time I met her, she listened to me all the way through.

I noticed that the interpreter signed everything for Oflan, which I took to mean that her status had changed, at least a little, after her skilled defense during the attack.

Everybody seemed to accept that the attackers were not Gray Wolves, any more than that red-haired fellow had been one of the Blues.

So some other group was doing its best to discredit the Blues beyond the border, and to keep them and the Gray Wolves at each other's throats. I watched from a distance as they talked, the interpreter busy turning from Oflan to the others.

There were still armed guards around, but it wasn't clear whether they were there to keep her from doing anything or to protect us from another attack.

Oflan sat across from Rajanas, her closed-off expression almost a twin to his: eyes narrowed as she flicked glances from face to face.

At the end of my recitation, Kuraf said, "Even if I hadn't been able to corroborate certain details, Kee spoke well of Lhind."

I smiled, remembering Kuraf's granddaughter, my travel partner to Fara Bay. Kee had begun despising me for my thievish ways, but by the end of our adventures together, we'd become friends. "Where is she? Doing well, I hope?"

"She's my courier over the mountains," Kuraf said, leaning forward to take one of the cabbage rolls cooked in peanut oil that silent equerries offered.

I could smell meat in them and grimaced, but a short time later Nill appeared, grinning as he approached me. "Gran said to bring you this." In the shallow dish lay a heap of fat, dark purple barkleberries, three kinds of freshly shelled nuts, and two young carrots. I took it happily.

Kuraf ate two bites, then said to Rajanas, "I suspect my last message to you might have gone astray as well. We'll search." Her head dropped briefly; her couriers were all trained by her, and many of them, I suspected, were from her own family.

Then she straightened and tipped her chin at Oflan. "What Lhind says corroborates some facts I made no sense of until now. I've little regard for Jendo Nath outside of a healthy respect for a dangerous enemy. Because that's how I regard the Gray Wolves."

She spoke clearly and slowly, pausing between each sentence so that the interpreter could sign to Oflan, whom she watched.

"But I will say this. For someone about to drop a war on us, he's been mighty slow to attack, though he knows pretty well where our main lookout points are. What's more, he hasn't been hiding any of his people from us. We know where all the Wolves are. And yes, none of yon miscreants number among 'em."

Twice Oflan dipped her chin slightly but otherwise sat very still, her hands on her knees.

They passed on to more local news, full of names and places I didn't recognize. After eating I relaxed against my rock, comfortable, warm, full, and so tired that I closed my eyes. I drifted into a light sleep, waking at a stir of motion around me. A glance revealed nothing more dire than Oflan being escorted to a far tent, and so I closed my eyes again, curling up in a ball.

Maybe they thought I was asleep. Maybe they didn't care if I heard. As soon as Oflan was gone, Kuraf said in Allendi, "Now we can talk frankly."

Those words banished sleepiness. Out of habit I lay still, eyes closed. I'd saved myself from extra grief too many times to give up the habit of eavesdropping.

"It's still bad up there?" Rajanas added.

"Very bad," Kuraf said. "Even with winter coming on, I don't see how it can get worse. It's *been* winter up there. No sign of autumn. The good part is that the heavy snows have trapped that army of hirelings up there more effectively than we ever could. The bad news is that they, and the Gray Wolves, and our own watchers, might well have starved to death but for your arrangements for running supplies. I've never in my life seen the like. You said you'd tell me when we met why this is."

Rajanas said in a dry voice, "It seems we have our thief to thank for that."

I nearly bolted out of my skin. Biting back an explanation, I lay scarcely breathing.

"The magister who came to make certain the enchantment binding our border was broken explained it: that weather magic out in the ocean was the cause. The thief wielded it without knowing the consequences. Dhes-Andis gave her the means, motivation unknown."

"Can't be for anyone's advantage but his."

"That's what the mages felt, I gather. So. I take it you did what I requested?"

"With every delivery of basic stores." Kuraf chuck-led. "And they were basic. My own people are doing well, but that army has to be very, very hungry. No one fights well when hungry. And each delivery came with messages about how they were abandoned, worthless hirelings, forgotten. The latest word is, they are a hair's-breadth from fighting each other. So that killing border magic, it's gone? Not returning? I lost two good runners to it, chased by a pack of bandits. Who also lost their lives, but I am still angry over the loss of Ruska and Mec."

"Even Dhes-Andis, the mages insisted, cannot sustain that broad an enchantment without proximity, once they removed the markers the magic was bound to. There will be no repeat, they assured me, unless he or a pet mage is physically present to lay them, and they have their own warning wards laid down."

"I don't know if I'd call that good news or bad news."

"Here's my understanding. Using magic for purposes of war

rarely works twice, once the spell is broken. Mages on either side of any conflict invent wards against a second use of that spell. And magic always has to be specific. That much I learned from Hlanan."

Kuraf said, "Then we'll call it good news."

"The best news would be that Dhes-Andis and his mages stay put in Sveran Djur," Rajanas retorted, from the rustling sounds rising to his feet. "Let's get some rest. Hard riding ahead. We'll discuss the logistics of our search in the morning."

I finally fell asleep, and though every night, without fail, I made certain my mind was firmly locked inside my mental walls, uneasy dreams pestered me through the long hours of dark. I'd wake and scoff at myself for inventing fears, but the idea of Dhes-Andis anywhere on this side of the world frightened me the way nothing ever had so far.

Dawn arrived with a thin, bitterly cold rain, nicely matching my gritty eyelids and bitter mood. The entire camp seemed to be in a grump as cold food was passed out and the animals readied for travel. Groups of riders peeled off, apparently to search for Hlanan and his party. They were to spread out over the entire slope.

My silk was disagreeably damp, but I fluffed out my fuzz beneath the drape and flexed my hair so that it spread around me like a cloak. Droplets beaded up on the outside, which I could shed now and then by a ripple or two.

I had to make certain not to flick my hair because water would fly off much the same way as when a wet dog shakes. The first time I did it, curses and angry looks directed at me caused me to be more circumspect. I did not dare tell them that I was warm and comfortable in spite of my damp clothes. Though I was not fully Hrethan, the half I'd inherited was made for this kind of weather.

As the animals began plodding up a trail under soughing pines, I wondered how high we might go. Maybe I could fly again!

It was the thought of flight that caused me to look skyward now and then. The rain began to let up, but the clouds sailed on, thick as ever, and as the air be-came colder, the thin rain turned to light snow. About midday my attention was caught by a swift-moving white dot sifting through the lacework of gentle snow, discernible against the blue-gray clouds.

White? The only white bird I knew of that size was Hlanan's aidlar friend, Tir. But Tir had been left in the royal city before this mess had begun.

Also, Tir had exasperated me by homing on my thoughts. Oh. Wait. The bird would not be able to do that since I'd learned to shut out others' minds.

The idea of opening that mental door caused my fuzz to ruffle up in fear, my palms dampening. I threw back my head, found the bird again, braced — opened the door. Tir?

Lhind!

I shut the door fast. "Tir!" I shouted.

Ahead in the column, Rajanas reined up. "Where?"

I raised my hand uselessly as an eagle-sized white bird crashed through the high branches of a tree, sending down a shower of powder. Tir lit on a tree stump nearby, turning one great ruby eye this way then that. It flapped long white wings and squawked, "Lhind! Come!"

"That's Hlanan's aidlar," Rajanas said. "We will follow it."

And so that's what we did.

Tir lit off in almost the opposite direction we'd been traveling in. We turned the horses and plunged into a valley, crossed a half-frozen stream, then up and down another slope. When Tir floated high above a wooded area, circling around, Rajanas signaled with his gloved hand, and his guards began to spread out. Kuraf's group flanked us as we descended through the grove of barren silvery-brown trees.

By the time Rajanas rode out onto a promontory overlooking what in a warmer season would be a long, sloping meadow, where we saw the long tracks of Hlanan, Prince Geric, and their collection of Gray Wolves riding head-drooping horses.

In well-trained fashion, as Rajanas watched from above, the rest of his Imbradi Blues rode out of the surrounding brush and woods to surround Hlanan's party.

Who halted, looking up. My heart filled with happiness the

moment I spied Hlanan in their midst, though he looked cold and tired, his nose dull red. Prince Geric, riding next to him, somehow managed to retain his elegance—red highlighting his fine cheekbones—as he threw back his head at an arrogant angle.

When he spied Oflan, he flushed, but otherwise gave no sign that he now understood how far outside his orders she had gone.

Rajanas bowed from the saddle, every line of his body expressive of irony in a distinctly courtly manner, a reminder that he could assume it when he wanted. Or maybe when he had to; his conversation, the way he saw the world, and his habits marked him as a warrior.

From the back of his own horse, Prince Geric bowed in precise mirror image, making me wonder from whom Rajanas had learned those courtly manners. These two obviously had more history than I knew.

Beyond Rajanas, in the second row flanking him, I glimpsed Oflan, sitting between two burly guards. Frizzy strands of pale hair lifted on the wind and her customarily impassive expression altered to a sardonic smile as she gazed down at Prince Geric, but then her gaze shifted.

My head whipped around and I spotted Pandoc, the curly-haired Gray Wolf, busy signing rapidly—too rapidly for me to gather anything but the gist of his report. And it was a report, stating that the Duke of Thann intended to gather the rest of the company and return home to Thann.

When he paused, gazing up, I realized that Oflan must be responding and turned my head, but I missed her response, and *then* I realized that I was missing the spoken conversation.

"...We join our two parties," Rajanas was saying.

Without waiting for Geric's response, he made a casual gesture with his hand, and the Blues advanced steadily until the two parties merged.

Tir circled around overhead, ruby eyes gleaming in the weak light as the bird watched us all. I was afraid to open that mental "door" again, though Tir communicated much more easily mind to mind than squawking out human words one or two at a time.

Hlanan rode by me, his gaze searching my face. I smiled and he smiled back, but Geric stuck to his side as the Guards separated out the Gray Wolves.

At the same time an equally burly "honor guard" of Blues surrounded Prince Geric. "There is no need for you to go thus out of your way," he said to Rajanas. "I know we are beyond your border."

If that was a hint that Rajanas had no right to inter-fere with Geric, it went by like a spent arrow. Rajanas said, "On the contrary. I believe our paths lie together, and there is strength in numbers, is there not?"

Geric frowned at him, glanced narrow-eyed my way, then spoke to Rajanas in Imperial Court Elras —

As I said before, for some reason I still did not comprehend, I could understand any language I heard, and that included the general courtly speech such as that Hlanan and Geric and the rest of them had been raised to speak. Imperial Court Elras was what I thought of as Elras for snobs. It was the same language everyone else in the empire used, but reverted to old-fashioned verbs, forms of address, and terms as old-fashioned as formal court wear (what they call High Court Array), dating back to when the empire first became an empire.

"The Prince of the Golden Circle would give his highness of Alezand to understand that the miscreant thief will have uttered falsehoods," Geric said.

Did he think I didn't understand? I writhed with annoyance at his implication that I'd lied about his villainy!

"The Prince of Alezand," Rajanas drawled, "would convey to his highness the Prince of the Golden circle that such an eventuality might have been anticipated. And it is his desire to convey a conviction that to proceed as planned is perceived as timely." A stylized gesture skyward with a gloved hand, fingers spread, thumb pressed to his palm as the little finger turned upward.

Was there a little irony in that last bit? Geric flushed, or it could have been the weather reddening his princely skin. Anyway, I gave up trying to comprehend the subtleties of courtly jabber. It was not like I'd ever have to use it.

Scarcely had I thought that when uncertainty, even guilt followed, and I glanced at Hlanan, tense and still, wearing that non-expression that I'd privately begun calling his Heir Face. I wondered if he would look like that as an emperor.

Emperor.

Until then I had not put much thought into what the future might bring if Hlanan and I were still together. I'd spent my autumn weeks alternately delighting in his presence and ignoring court ritual as much as I could, as I beetled about trying to learn magic (useless) and music (equally useless, but much more fun because Thianra and I talked a lot).

Hlanan's focus wasn't on me. His tension eased as Rajanas lifted his voice. "Let us proceed to the Pass." Impatience sizzled through me as I waited for the Blues to sort everyone out the way they'd been commanded.

I wanted to ride with Hlanan, but not if that would cause a lot of nosy questions. We were done there, I hoped. Time to leave the lot of them.

Under gently drifting flakes of snow, we drew slowly into a long column as we headed up a narrow path. Rajanas had singled Hlanan out, which caused me to drop back, sighing to myself as Tir swooped and glided overhead.

The aidlar seemed to be looking intently at me. When I tipped my head back, Tir dipped down close enough for me to see the patterns of feathers along its head and neck, and squawked, "Follow Lhind!"

I gaped. That was Tir I'd sensed from time to time, during that awful ride with Prince Geric, while my shoulder was healing?

Tir flapped and shrilled, "Mind! Talk!"

"No," I said. Aware of attention zooming my way, I didn't dare say why.

Tir gave a long shriek and arrowed up into the sky, then vanished against the clouds. I stared in dismay, hoping Hlanan wouldn't be upset that I seemed to have angered the bird enough to cause it to decamp. The temptation to open the mental door and call Tir back was strong, but far stronger was my fear of finding Dhes-Andis standing right outside.

Still, the guilt lingered as I watched those ahead of me and tried to get rein on the galloping tangle of emotions. The path wound sharply around a striated slant of rock, topped by white bedecked firs.

I caught sight of Geric, who had summarily motioned to Pandoc, probably to hear what Oflan had reported. He listened for a short time, then kicked his horse ahead, leaving Pandoc to rejoin the other Gray Wolves being guarded by the biggest contingent of Blues. I didn't hear a word, of course, but one thing was clear. Prince Geric was not pleased at Oflan's explanation for exceeding orders.

Geric reined his horse to ride alongside Rajanas. Though I couldn't hear them, I saw Hlanan brush snow off one sleeve in two quick gestures, then Rajanas flick the fingers of his right hand as though chasing a fly from his chin.

The gestures were so quick, so subtle, I might have missed them had I not remembered what Rajanas had told me. Of course any code made up by galley slaves would have to be subtle. No overseer was going to tolerate complicated hand signs.

Maybe I'd even seen the two communicating aboard Rajanas's yacht the previous summer and hadn't recognized what was going on.

At any rate, before they vanished beyond a clump of pines Geric continued talking to Rajanas in a way that suggested that he hadn't seen the signs either.

Let him blab, I thought. At least we were done with him.

Impatience surged through me again as I waited for a chance to talk to Hlanan. That didn't happen until Rajanas gave the signal to camp. As the Blues divided up, some staying with the not-quite-prisoner Gray Wolves, some helping Kuraf's forest green rangers in setting up the tents carried on the remounts, and a few riding off to secure a perimeter, I sidled up to Hlanan.

"Ready to leave now?" I asked in the language of Thesreve, which I hoped the busybodies nearby didn't understand. "We're done with Geric and his villainy, aren't we?"

And watched his smile fade to the Heir Face. "Of course you want to go," he said. "Geric has been painfully obvious with his threats against you."

"I can take care of myself," I said, impatient, longing, and most of all conflicted. "Though the easiest way is to get as much distance between him and me that I can. Aren't you done, now that Rajanas is going to the Pass to deal with the rest of the Gray Wolves? There's still Maita and her treachery."

Hlanan said, "I used Ilyan's notecase to report as soon as we combined parties. If I were to guess, the Mage Council is investigating at this moment. If anyone can find proof, they will."

I'd completely missed seeing him send his message, which I ought to have taken as a reminder that he was very skilled at maneuvering. But I was too intent on my own matters. "You don't trust Rajanas to deal with this mess?" I asked. "Or is there something else? If you don't want to tell me, well, I understand. Rajanas has reminded me plenty about how untrustworthy I am."

"Lhind," Hlanan said softly.

I sighed. "All right, that was sulk," I admitted.

For answer he smiled briefly, and we regarded one another. I could sense in his silence, his air of question, that his uncertainty matched my own. The truth was, neither of us knew how to manage a relationship. He'd been very careful after the Duchess of Thann trampled all over his heart in an effort to trick him into doing something evil, avoiding the closeness that would lead to emotional entanglement and the confession inevitable after that. And as for me? Except one very brief foray, I'd never managed *any* kind of relationship. My best defense had been my artistically cultivated stench to keep people at a distance, and if they noticed me anyway my second defense had always been to run.

But emotional entanglement had sneaked up unawares on us both.

So here we were on the brink of another not-quite-argument of the sort that had sent me flouncing off to the cascade with that borrowed harp.

"You could return to the safety of Erev-li-Erval," he began in a tentative voice, but so slowly that it was clear he knew it was no answer. Then his expression shuttered again. "You are not happy there."

"I'm not happy with magic lessons that don't make any sense," I whispered, sidling looks around. "You know I'm not used to rules, and finicky manners, and changing my clothes a lot. It's all too new, but if you are there...." No, that sounded whiny. I sighed, and looked again. Luckily no one was the least interested in us, or my sneaky peeks probably would have acted like honey to bugs, irresistible to ignore.

I turned back in time to catch a brimming look of not-quite-suppressed laughter. Then he sobered. "Until I met you, I never considered the qualities of freedom," he murmured. "You have thought yourself free all your life, but it was conditional, lived on the run lest you be caught and your secrets discovered. My freedom has always been conditional as well, my first priority always duty."

He sidestepped Nill helping a Blue carrying a tent to be pitched near where we stood. Nill was chattering away, paying us no mind, but we still retreated behind a just-erected tent and walked side by side to the edge of the woods. Then Hlanan said, "I am unused to choices that include my own heart's desire. And I think it is the same for you?"

"Yes." Some of the knot inside me loosened. "Yes. I never had to think about another person. I never wanted to. I still don't know what is to happen to us. As an us. Does that make sense?"

"It does to me," he said on an exhale, and I knew from his tone that he had been worrying at the same questions in a parallel fashion.

Somehow that made me feel better overall.

He touched the top of my hand, his thumb circling in a gentle caress. "Shall we talk further once we reach the Pass? But please be vigilant. If you need to run, do. Geric is still determined to use you as a bargaining counter with Dhes-Andis, I believe."

"I'm not afraid of him grabbing me with all these others around."

Hlanan glanced away, as if listening for the sound of Geric's voice. "He's desperate, if not about that, then about something."

"He's a knothole," I said promptly.

"Desperate people are dangerous," Hlanan replied.

The sound of horse hooves arriving at a fast clip caused a stir in the camp. A snow-dusted scout arrived, leaning down to speak to Rajanas.

Geric appeared from a tent, his lounging step not disguising the stiffness of anger in his shoulders and the way he held his head.

Hlanan trod toward Rajanas and Kuraf as one who had the right. I, aware of my lack of status—except as a target—slipped around the back of the nearest tents, where I could listen but stay out of sight.

Not that there was any need. Rajanas looked around, lifted his voice, and said, "We've located the Gray Wolf main camp. We should reach them in two days."

Eight

NO USE IN DESCRIBING that trip. Two days uphill into increas-ingly high-piled snow? Of course it was miserable, especially as I was convinced that during any other season it might have been a pleasant afternoon journey.

There's also no use in describing all the folderol that Geric offered, promised, hinted, and insinuated during the first day's ride. He never quite brought himself to threaten Rajanas, who listened with his usual lack of affect but never agreed to anything.

I didn't think about it at the time, but I was getting a lesson in how courtiers of Erev-li-Erval negotiate.

In court, everybody is supposed to appear refined, true emo-tions hidden behind those cool, urbane countenances. You don't sweat at court. A belch would be a calamity. Any sign of emotion becomes a weapon used by the rest, or at least entertainment.

When we camped that night, Geric withdrew to his tent (he insisted on his own), while Oflan sat with Kuraf, Hlanan, and Rajanas around the fire before the command tent. Pandoc sat with them as interpreter, but I noticed that Rajanas and Hlanan were both getting more adept at signing.

The second day Geric rode alone, ignoring everyone. Again when we camped he made it clear he preferred his own company, but as I passed behind the group while looking for Nill, I saw Geric watching the same group around the campfire. His gaze was too intent to be idle.

Glad it wasn't aimed at me, I thought nothing more of it as Nill appeared and offered to share their hoarded hot cider.

The third day we reached the Gray Wolves. They'd gathered in the center of their permanent campsite, aware that they were surrounded by Rajanas's Blue Guard. I guess the scouts and outriders of both Rajanas's and the Gray Wolves hadn't bothered being stealthy, so our arrival was no surprise.

Jendo Nath, Oflan's father and the chief of the Wolves, was a man with gray hair and a small, pointy beard. I'd first encountered him when he was chasing Hlanan and me on orders of Duchess Morith.

Chief Nath noticed Hlanan and me at the same time we saw him. His eyes narrowed, his gloved hand moving to his sword hilt. Then he shifted his gaze to his daughter, who was busy signing.

Rajanas halted, lifted his voice, and said so all could hear, "I have studied the history of Thann." He glanced at Geric once, but he was talking to the Gray Wolves, Pandoc hastily signing to Oflan. "Your history parallels ours. No surprise. These duchies and principalities at this end of the valley share some characteristics. One of 'em is the right to challenge."

Geric's head turned sharply.

Rajanas grinned at him. "You know that. You once flung in my teeth how uncouth my ancestors were, my great-grandfather having challenged the previous prince. And won. Therefore, as you are now the Duke of Thann, I challenge you for the oath of the Gray Wolves. If I win, your company will swear oath to Alezand."

Geric paled with anger. But he didn't let any of it out. "I had not foreseen this treachery," he said smoothly, softly.

"Your treachery," Rajanas replied, "is expedience to some. And to others, justice." He turned to Chief Nath. "You were lied to by Duchess Morith. Hlanan the Scribe was not, and never has been, any threat to Thann. Neither has this Hrethan."

A sudden wave in my direction caused me to instinctively duck.

"If you like, you may put your questions to them both before we go any farther. But my challenge stands."

The silence after these words was so complete that I heard the soft chuff of snow falling from a tree several paces away, and further down the path, the snort of a horse on the picket line.

Jendo Nath took us all in, then inclined his head to Geric before speaking. "It is customary," he said slowly, "to allow a night to pass before challenges are accepted."

"As you wish," Rajanas said. "We will camp on this slope here. The sentries will permit you to pass the inner perimeter, with an equerry accompanying, if you want to parley."

Chief Nath bowed slightly again. Geric crossed the distance to him in two strides — forgetting to lounge — and began talking to him in a low voice. They vanished into the Gray Wolf camp.

As Rajanas's and Kuraf's people set up camp for the night I chose a tree to sleep in. As I made a nest of soft pine boughs on a broad branch, I mentally rehearsed all the things I'd say to any questions Chief Nath might put, complete to opinions about the Gray Wolves, Prince Geric, and the late and very unlamented Duchess Morith of Thann.

But Chief Nath had no interest in talking to me or anyone in our camp. I could see the glow of their fires rising above the sharp silhouettes of their brush and rock-reinforced tents. The only traveler between our camp and theirs was Oflan Nath, accompanied by a couple of burly Blues.

She returned a short time later, still under guard. Rajanas offered her a plate of food (the Gray Wolves having little to eat over on their side, due to Kuraf's people having cut off their supplies) and she sat on a rock, her interpreter nearby. Pandoc joined her as well, accompanied by a young Alezand guard.

Despite the weird situation — not quite enemies, but certainly not friends — the atmosphere between the Gray Wolves and the Alezand Blues was surprisingly easy. I watched from afar as they chattered with voices and hands about travel, weather, and similar subjects. Rajanas kept up a constant conversation in sign, sometimes laughing at Oflan's puzzled glances; she occasionally huffed a silent laugh at some of his signs, as did Hlanan.

Geric stayed out of the conversation. He sat near the fire, silent and watchful. I was careful to keep myself on opposite sides of the camp from him.

When the orderlies brought around something hot to drink, I drifted to Hlanan's side, and gloated, "Look at Geric. He's sulking!"

Hlanan gave his head a slight shake. "He's listening."

I scoffed at that, because the conversation was not worth listening to, but next day I got a rude surprise, along with most of the others when the principals met in the clearing between the two camps, scrupulously swept free of snow by the Blues.

Rajanas said to Geric, "I await your decision."

"What do you offer if you lose?"

Rajanas lifted a hand. "Since I'd be dead, take what you want of mine. If you can hold it!"

A shift and a mutter among the listening Blues made it clear what they thought of that.

Geric smiled. "I accept," he said. "A fight to the death. But as the challenged, I choose my champion."

People turned their attention from him to Chief Nath, who stepped forward, hand to his sword. Some eyed the big, burly Gray Wolf at his shoulder.

Geric's smile widened, then he said, "I choose *her*." He pointed to Oflan. "To the death."

The watchers whispered as next to me Hlanan drew in a hissing breath. I looked from Rajanas, who had stilled, to Oflan, who watched Pandoc. Back and forth, as the import sank in: one of the two would not walk away alive.

Hlanan's stricken expression, the tense silence—something was missing.

"What is it?" I breathed.

"Ilyan likes her. Geric must have seen—" Hlanan broke off, his expression sickened.

Liked? As in...I blinked, unable to wrap my mind around the idea of Rajanas and romance. Or Oflan, for that matter.

Oflan shook off her coat, unloosed her sword, and took her time in passing a cloth over it so that it shone with blue-white light.

Then she paced out into the center of the space and took up a fighting stance.

Rajanas had also shed his coat. I'd never been able to read his expression. He always looked threatening to me, even when he was amused. But I'd never seen him furious. He was furious now.

Neither spoke. He raised his weapon. She raised hers and took a step forward. She whirled her sword up and down so that the tip lay flat against her palm.

And as Rajanas halted his first strike a hair's breadth from her head, she deliberately knelt down, laid the sword in the snow, and bent her neck to await his blow.

Once again a silence so profound the soft padding of an animal running on the slope above us carried distinctly, and the soughing of the dawn breeze in the evergreens below.

No one moved, neither Blues nor Gray Wolves.

"Get up, you brainless fool." Geric's low voice carried on the icy, still air, venomous and strained. "If you don't get up I'll kill you myself. Nath, take her place!"

Chief Nath moved as if released from a spell.

With deliberate movements, he stepped up to Geric and stopped within a couple of paces. He bowed, hands together. "Your Grace, I deem you foresworn."

"What?"

"By threatening your champion, you break oath. As chieftain of the Gray Wolves I accept our defeat, and if the Prince of Alezand will accept it, offer my vow thither."

"You *idiot!*" Geric's voice rose. "That was nothing—mere hyperbole—what about Thann?"

The man looked old for a lengthy pause, then raised his head. "The Thann I swore oath to protect is gone, all but in name. I began to suspect the true intent of the duchess's orders, and I am now satisfied that my suspicions were true."

"It is not your place to question those you swore oath to!" Geric turned from one to another, eyes wide. "This is nothing but excuse for the basest treachery—"

His rapier hissed out of its sheath and he lunged at Rajanas, who whirled to meet him. Oflan swiftly rose and got out of the way.

Geric had clearly been well trained in dueling form. He looked like a prince in a tapestry, and he certainly wasn't lacking in courage, but ignorant as I am, I saw immediately the difference between dueling, which tries to make an art of violence, and fighting.

Not that Rajanas was brutal. He didn't have to be. It was clear that he had had a whole lot more experience with steel than Geric ever had. He knew what strike was coming next, how to defend against it, and within four clashes and clangs he pinked Geric's arm.

Geric's blue eyes widened, and I guess all that boiling rage he'd been holding in like a good courtier exploded, because he went wild and kept madly trying to kill Rajanas.

Three deliberate pinks he got in return, but Geric was too enraged to notice. Then Rajanas's own intent changed, and in a fast flurry he drove his sword deep into Geric's right shoulder. Geric staggered when he yanked it free, and when he yelled something incoherent and snatched the blade with his left hand from his useless right, Rajanas didn't wait, but flashed his point down and jabbed it hard into Geric's knee.

Geric gasped, then crumpled to his good knee, then fainted, face down in the snow.

Rajanas said, "Take him off to his tent. He'll live."

Hlanan's breath whooshed out as Chief Nath turned to his Gray Wolves. "We have been used as mercenaries and murderers, all in the name of protecting Thann. I no longer know what truth is, but for me, I must turn away from everything I once knew, or become what I cannot respect. My oath to the Duke of Thann I deem dissolved. I release you all from your oaths to me to do as you will."

He stepped up to Oflan. "Come, daughter. You have been granted mercy. You are free to choose your path." His other hand sketched signs in the air as he spoke.

Oflan turned to Rajanas, signing: *You-no-kill? Have-I-no-honor?*

Rajanas paused in the act of cleaning his blade, and faced her. "It was not that at all. I don't waste good people on someone else's whim. Tell her," he said to Pandoc. "I don't want to get that wrong."

Then Rajanas sheathed his sword and lifted his voice, turning in a slow circle. "Those who stay with us, we have an army to unroot from the Idaron Pass. Anyone who wants to choose another path, you've a day to get beyond my border."

Nine

"HE'LL LIVE," RAJANAS HAD said, but for the next day and a half it wasn't all that clear.

Geric's own fast reflexive twist had caused Rajanas's sword to cut more deeply into his right shoulder on its way out. And the stab in his knee rendered him unable to stand on that leg.

The strangest thing of all? None of the Gray Wolves would go near him, after they approached Rajanas and — overseen by their captain — each made new oaths.

While that was going on, Rajanas repeating the same words over and over as the long line of Gray Wolves approached him and formally laid their weapons at his feet, Hlanan and Kuraf's healer muscled Geric to his tent.

They bound up his wounds and wrestled him into another of his fine tunics that wasn't particolored with his blood. By the time this had been done, and he'd roused from his faint and drunk some steeped lister-blossom leaves, the last few Gray Wolves finished, picked up their weapons again, and proceeded in a brooding silence to break their months-long campsite.

It didn't take them long to pack. Soon everybody was ready to ride.

"We're taking him with us?" I asked, pointing to ashen-faced Geric being eased up into the saddle of a horse.

I'd asked Hlanan, but Rajanas heard, and half-turned. "You'd have us leave him lying in the snow?"

"Yes," I said promptly. "Which he'd do to me if he hadn't wanted to make me Dhes-Andis's prisoner. Only he wouldn't have left me alive."

Rajanas laughed. "For a thief and a liar, you are probably the most forthright of our merry band. No, he comes along."

I sniffed. "At least he gets a turn to find out what riding with a hole in your shoulder feels like." I rubbed my own shoulder, which twinged faintly. I had to admit that his wounds were spectacularly worse than mine, but then everything was his fault.

A quick glance at Hlanan revealed how little he liked the entire conversation. But he didn't say anything to either of us as Rajanas turned away to issue a command about how the Wolves and the Blues were to ride, and then beckoned to Chief Nath and Oflan.

The Gray Wolves had plenty to report about their months in the mountain above the Pass, apparently. Through that long day, half of which we were snowed on, different ones were beckoned forward to share their experiences as Rajanas and Kuraf listened.

I didn't hear any of it. This was not my battle. My own thoughts were entirely taken up with Hlanan's lack of expression. It surprised me how important it was to see his smile.

Weakness or strength? I was so unused to caring what anyone thought of me! Two seasons ago, I had been proud of the excellent stench that I had carefully cultivated, which kept the world well beyond arm's reach.

Geric rode directly in front of me, his head lolling to the side occasionally, before he'd make an effort that I could almost feel and lift it again. He didn't say a word, either on that long, tedious journey or afterward when we camped, and patrols went out in pairs—half Blues, half Gray Wolves.

When I understood that Rajanas didn't like the fact that they had yet to encounter a party of Dhes-Andis's mercenary army, I thought: he really wants a fight that much?

The next day, as clouds rolled in for another snow storm, the answer became clear when we rode into what had obviously been a long-time outpost.

Rajanas walked all around, looking at everything.

"They've retreated," Hlanan said finally and turned to Kuraf.

"Your plan worked."

"It's too easy," Rajanas said. He pointed. "Those huts don't look recently abandoned."

"How can you tell?" Hlanan said. "The lack of footprints is to be expected with recent snowfall."

Rajanas ran his thumb along the line of his mustache, frowning. "The weather has been inside and out of those huts. And there's no sign of an armory."

"They brought their weapons up, then took them away again."

Rajanas shook his head. "Kuraf, you know what I'm looking for, don't you? Why don't you send out some fast scouts? Armed—in case—but I'm beginning to wonder if they'll find anything. We'll set up right here, early as it is in the day. Snow is on the way. These huts will suffice."

Kuraf sighed. "I'll send my best scouts, but Your Highness, this is dangerous weather. Could take them weeks. And they might be mired...."

As soon as the word to camp had been spoken, the two forest rangers in charge of Geric had helped him down from his horse and took him into one of the huts. Rude as these were, at least they'd keep off the impending weather.

The huts were completely empty inside, cold and wet. Rajanas was right. The only smell was of mildewing wood, no lingering wood smoke, food, or people smells.

Geric was soon stretched out on a camp bed, his hairline sweaty in spite of the cold. He said nothing when the equerries piled an old blanket on him.

He didn't speak until Rajanas entered the hut, bending his head to get through the narrow door. "What do you know about this?" he addressed Geric.

The angry prince twisted his cracked lips, then said in a whisper, "The plan was to take Alezand. I'd hold it. Command the supply line from behind. Dhes-Andis ventures north into Namas Ilan. And eventually he'd take that fool, Liacz, to the north, and use his resources to move against Charas al Kherval."

"Leaving you an independent king here in Alezand?" Rajanas asked wryly.

Landless Prince Geric didn't answer.

Rajanas sat on a camp stool, hands on his knees. "If we ration the supplies we can hold out up here a few weeks. We'll wait for the scouts' report." And then, "Geric, you and I have never had any meeting of minds. But you have to see that it is likely you've been a dupe?"

Geric turned his face away, his sweat-tangled hair falling to hide it.

Rajanas sighed and got up. "This is bad," he said in a low voice to Kuraf, hand tapping and twisting in hand sign for Oflan, who stood next to her father in the door of the hut. "But we have to know...."

"Have to know what?" I asked Hlanan, as soon as I'd slipped past them, Hlanan having moved outside to make room for the others. "Why do we stay here?"

He said, "We have to know where that army is, if it isn't here."

I sighed. "That is important for the empress?"

"Yes."

"Even though we're practically on the other side of the continent?"

Hlanan's brown gaze searched my own face. The Heir Look kept me from descrying his emotions, except the obvious: this situation, dire as it was, kept him here because it was important to him.

"Come, Lhind," he said, and we walked a ways away from the churned up mud to a place where the snow lay smooth.

He knelt down, and with his gloved finger sketched out a shape. "Here's the continent. The Anadhan Mountains all down the east here protect Charas, the central kingdom of the empire."

"Charas al Kherval," I said. "I know that. 'Kherval' is a fancy, old fashioned word for a group. Now it means empire."

"The empire protects the polities in the Kherval with magic and if necessary militarily." His voice dropped out of long habit, though we were alone. "My older brother Justeon believes that military might is the greatest protection."

"I remember that," I said. "You're drawing a map, and I even know pretty much what is on it, thanks to being chased around in summer." And some of my own chases when young, but I didn't mention them. "The big kingdom of Liacz here in the north, not part of the empire. Somewhere south, the two parts of what once was Ilan."

"North-central, and south," Hlanan said, drawing some smaller mountains, then adding T. I. for Teranir Ilan and south of that, N. I. for Namas Ilan. Below that, Alezand to the southwest, and below that, Keprima, which I knew from my own experience had as many problems as Namas Ilan had had. "And over here to Keprima's east, the duchy of Thann, one of this cluster of small duchies and principalities—Tolsk, Finn, Berel and so forth. Thann being the wealthiest of them, because of its mines."

I had crouched down to watch. I ground my chin on my knees, waiting for his point.

"Shifting west again, the Kertean mountain range we stand in right now, forming the western border for Alezand, Namas Ilan, and abutting into Liacz, which stretches east and west of the mountains. Then, on the other side of the Kerteans, south of western Liacz—"

"I know, the coastal countries. Like Forfar, run by a bunch of pirate lovers. I know you and Rajanas were sold into galley slavery out of Fara Bay, and that you can do anything there if you are rich enough, and even then, there's treachery. I've heard terrible things about Forfar since I was little. So?"

"So Dhes-Andis brought an army through there, mercenaries probably hired from the Faran govern-ment—whichever corrupt lord is manipulating the old king now—or they came in from somewhere else and the Farans were paid to look the other way. The im-portant point is that the army was brought up to the Idaron Pass—where we stand—in order to come through this pass to take Alezand. If they succeed in killing Ilyan Rajanas, Kuraf, and all these people, be-cause you know they would defend their land to the last, then they slaughter their way eastward across the continent to attack Charas, the heart of the empire. Probably while a huge fleet of Djuran ships attack from the water."

"Is that for certain? That's terrible," I said, thinking of Thianra peacefully making music in Erev-li-Erval. She was trained to defend herself, but she hated warfare.

Hlanan sighed, watching his breath freeze and fall. "The imperial navy guards the entire coast very closely."

"Don't you have another brother in the navy?"

"Yes, though Bracan is a captain, not a fleet commander." Hlanan's brief smile was the one that lit his face when he mentioned Thianra. Then he was serious again. "The important thing for me to find out is the location of this army, do you see? If they aren't here after all, or anymore, where are they? Armies don't melt into the ground."

"Magic, of course," I said. "They could be anywhere! Dhes-Andis is a powerful mage, that much we all know. Maybe he gave them all transfer tokens, or something."

Hlanan shook his head. "Magic transfer...oh, think of it as burning the air when one transfers from one place to another. It isn't like that, but it's easier to think of magic with metaphors."

We use metaphors to begin with, the teacher had said to me, during one of those hated lessons. Impatience pulsed through me, and deeper, the uneasy stirrings of guilt.

To avoid thinking about that, I said, "All right, so transfer magic is like fire. Only it doesn't feel like you're on fire. It feels like you've been pulled apart and squashed back together by a giant hand. It hurts."

"It does," he said. "But for our purpose, think of fire. Two people transferring burn the air that much more, sparking magical fire between the two transport points. Any more than four, and the next person who goes through...burns up."

"Ugh."

"This is why mages at Destinations have to be careful. It's why you pay more if it is not a scheduled transfer. And it's not a matter of letting it cool down, like a pan of corn cakes taken out of the oven. Too many transfers can ruin a Destination for months, years, even centuries. So no, powerful as Dhes-Andis is, even he cannot waft armies hither and yon by magic. Not unless they go sedately one at a time, and you can be certain that the Destination mages keep track of patterns of transfer from a distance."

"In short, if it was that easy he would have done it ages ago," I finished. "I see."

Hlanan sat back on his heels, tipping his head as he looked down at the map. "Several possibilities, and all mean different things—" He lifted his head. "Was that Geric?"

"I didn't hear anything," I lied, though a muffled noise, maybe a groan had come from somewhere behind us. "Hlanan, why are you taking care of him? Rajanas will make his equerries do that, since I guess he doesn't want to...." I wiggled my forefinger in the air, too squeamish to say *kill him off.*

Hlanan blinked as a snowflake dropped on his eyelash. He glanced up at the white sky overhead as snow began to fall. Then he faced me. "If I look at the world through Geric's eyes, his life is compounded by betrayal. Raised as a prince to royal expectations, to discover that the empress has decreed that the Golden Circle is no more. Disappeared for years to be taught dark magic, and coached to connive with style, to court with pretty lies, then sent back to — well, I can see that you are not going to sympathize."

I snorted hard enough to make my nose hurt. "I am never going to feel the least pity for somebody born to privilege who finds he doesn't get any after all. What *is* royalty anyway, except a kind of illusion without magic? We're *all* just a bunch of humans with our clothes off, only I've got fuzz!"

He laughed as I'd expected, but said, "I do pity those raised to privilege, because they aren't taught how to make a meaningful life any other way. That's why I will always be grateful to my mother for the way I was raised. If she decides to choose one of my brothers as heir, I can make a meaningful life for myself as a scribe. Or as a mage, though that means years more of study. And I'm not a good student. I like being out in the world too much."

He thumbed more snowflakes away from his eyes. My middle hollowed out at the sight of his eyelashes on his cheeks, the tiny veins in his eyelids, the hint of laughter at the corners of his mouth.

He was such a good person. As for me?

I shied away from *that* thought.

"Anyway," Hlanan said, "Maybe Geric can learn something in our talk. And I can learn something from him."

"Such as what Dhes-Andis has told him?"

"Yes, and when. And how. We do not know how they are connected, only that they are."

An idea hit me then. But I wasn't going to mention it because I had no idea if it would work, and I was still embarrassed, even uneasy, about what was so new to me. So I said, "I think I did hear Geric just now."

Hlanan rose to his feet, brushing clumped snow off his knees. "He's probably thirsty again. He's been drinking a lot of water, with that fever."

He went off and I looked around. Evergreen woods in one direction, rocky screes in another, a chasm in a third, beyond which lay the narrow, twisted valley of the Pass. To either side, great peaks rose high above our heads—and we were very high.

High enough? I climbed up the scree, hopping easily from stone to stone. It felt good to leap again, springing high into the air. Oh, yes! On each spring that light sensation buoyed my middle. I recognized it now for what it was: in another form, I could fly.

So I climbed until I was well beyond the sight of the camp or the guards, then shed my clothes and thief tool bag. I hid them under a rock, stayed long enough to mark the place in memory, and swung my arm. It was healed enough for flying.

So I stepped to the edge of the cliff, and sprang into the air.

Flash! I took wing.

For a time I reveled in the joy of flight, circling spires and diving down so that the tops of the tall firs whispered beneath my belly feathers. But the pit of my right wing pulled enough to remind me that I wasn't completely healed.

So I flapped up into a climb, searching for eddies of wind to aid me—and caught sight of a patch of white against the white.

"Lhind!" A faint cry in the heavy air. But I knew that voice.

"Tir!"

Tir angled, riding a current I hadn't felt; I lifted until I felt the air streaming under me, and matched pace.

And then we had...not a conversation in human words. Nor was it quite the same as talking in the mental realm with Faryana, the Hrethan mage imprisoned within that diamond necklace, or with Dhes-Andis. I didn't have a sense of the mental plane. That is, my inner door was still shut.

But in my bird form I could understand Tir, and respond in kind. Indeed, I squawked and creeled—I know that isn't really a word, but it's so close to the sound—bird language being so very different than hu-man. The way dog language only has sounds as emphasis. The real communication is all through the complexity of scents, which humans blunder through obliviously.

I told Tir what I was about. The aidlar responded with pleasure at my intent. I learned that Tir had been watching over Hlanan and me ever since I'd first reached the imperial city, at the behest of the Hrethan.

Why? I asked.

The answer can't be put into words, and I still refused to open the door to the mental plane to share images. But I gained the sense that the Hrethan wished to know who we were. It's the "whoness" I can't explain. But it meant more than our names.

While I struggled with this communication we flew up slopes where the air aided us, and circled in a wide spiral with a slow wind pattern. I not only learned a great deal about flying, but I came to two astonishing realizations: that Tir, the aidlar, was kin to Hrethan, and that my bird form was aidlar. I laughed inside as I soared high. Were my honey-brown eyes ruby, too? But Tir didn't perceive color the same way I did, or at least eye colors were irrelevant.

With Tir's aid, I learned to sense how the snow clouds above me weighed down in an instinctive warning. The snow would soon thicken, and that would be dangerous even for birds.

We flew high in a great circle, looking down. There was the camp. No one looked up. They looked like ants below me, busily swarming around making a muddy mess of footprints.

From there we flew outward. Even though snow had fallen, it did not obliterate completely the trail made by numerous humans trampling the ground.

Circling and flying up the drafts, we located five such trails, which combined into two, and then an enormous one, winding down and down and away....

Down—the heaviness warned me that I was losing the heights that supported whatever magic caused my transformation.

Ride the high currents, Tir admonished. *Your form flies not in low, heavy air.*

I knew that! Frightened, I adjusted my wings to glide on a slow current that brought up the smells of ground and mulch into the air, and I studied the complicated line of mountains falling southward into hills, and beyond, vast plains bisected by the silver ribbon of the river.

Was that distant river south of Keprima — had I flown that far? From Tir no answer. To Tir, the land was the land. Human boundaries lay solely in our minds.

In the extremity of distance, movement in a dark line along that river, where once for a day I had traveled with Hlanan, his sister, and Rajanas....

It was time to return.

My right wing gradually tightened into ache as I climbed upward into the sky. Tir exclaimed that I was hurt, and when I favored my right wing, the aidlar flew in a way that helped push a bit of air under my right side.

Even so, I was losing the battle to stay aloft. Snow fell faster; there were fewer currents to afford me a breather. I began to fear I would have to drop and make my way somehow on foot when Tir screeched to *lift, lift — see?* I had been completely lost, flying where Tir flew. Below me I spotted the striated rock of the Pass, and above that, the familiar rocks of my scree.

I plummeted down, less a glide than a drop, and landed hard.

The transformation thumped into my chest like an invisible fist. Out snapped my legs and arms, heavy as stone, my tail feathers now a snow-sodden tail. My Hrethan tail looks like hair, but it's actually long feathers that I can lift and wave, which helps my balance — but all those tiny feathers had caught snow, as had my hair, which is a mane all down my back and spine. I felt as if a couch had landed on my back.

Utterly exhausted, I dropped into sleep without knowing it.

And there on the heights, I dreamed.

I was back on board the ship, tossing on the rising waves as Dhes-Andis taunted me.

Come, my child, whispered a sweet female voice, clearer than ever. But I didn't trust what had to be another ruse. I didn't trust anything.

My mind cowered into itself as distorted memories battered me mercilessly: branches whipping my face, my breath searing my throat, a howling mob, a figure writhing in a fire...fire...streaming in glowing orange rivers through the endless sky as my own voice shrieked, "NO SPELLS! NO SPELLS!"

Come, my child. Do not linger in fear. Here on the heights we are strong. Lift the veil that divides our minds. There is much I can teach you, but the dream realm is chancy.

No! HE is waiting there! You are trying to trick me!

Still I fought, but there was no turning over, or waking up, because my body was frozen. Untethered, my mind drifted closer to the deepest memory of all: finding myself tumbling to unknown ground. Alone with shock, pain, bewilderment.

The Blue Lady floated down above me, wind rippling slowly through her moon-pale draperies, and she held out her hands.

Memories: those hands clasping me warmly when I was very small. All around me a fierce, hot wind rose, but I kept my eyes on the tender gaze of the Blue Lady as I held out my dream hands — and again heard a voice, clear as a silver bell, familiar all my life as a fragmented whisper: *Lift the veil, my darling daughter.*

No!

Another door, as memory fragments: the feel of sand on my feet, the howl of the wind as I ran, and always, always, the caw and screech and twitter of birds, as here one dropped an apple into my lap, and there another a spray of sweet grapes.

When I was cold, warm little bodies settled on me, soft as down, tiny hearts beating a comforting rhythm. Each sensation flowered into forgotten memory.

I can't, I cried. *He'll get me.*

Reach for me, she replied, and here was the clearest vision yet. I knew her face, blue as a morning summer sky, blue eyes, not slanted like mine, but round like a bird's, midnight blue hair floating slowly about her head in soothing ripples.

Come, my daughter. You shall learn how to permit entry to only those you wish. I will teach you, she said, her arms open.

I sailed toward her, but I had no hands to reach, no lips to kiss her.

I have tried to reach you again and again, my heart.

So has he, I cried over the slow, deep bawl, as if some sea creature as large as an island bellowed deep undersea.

I have tried to send you aid as I could, through your dreams, and through our kin among the avians. But I cannot teach you unless we can meet mind to mind.

You're alive? Why did you leave me? Where's my father?

I shouted the word *Why? Why? Why?* in the dream as the strange bawl intensified to a rising, falling burble.

Meet my mind —

Her words blended with the terrifying memory of Dhes-Andis's mental voice, so friendly, so amused, so ready to offer me any magic spells I wished to learn. This is another ruse, I thought, and far below in memory I wailed in desolation, alone, abandoned and afraid.

And she was gone.

Ten

THE DREAM DISSIPATED, LEAVING me lying in the snow, panting as if I'd been running. I ached in every muscle, bone, and nerve. I rolled over and squirmed on the rocks to shed the packed snow clotting my fuzz and hair, then groped wearily for my clothes.

The snow fell in a steady curtain past which I could scarcely see. Faint golden lights dancing about unevenly in the distance resolved into a patrol carrying lanterns as they walked a perimeter around the camp. The sun had set. Tir and I had flown through the entire day.

The snow glowed dimly blue, dissolving into shadows when I reached the huts.

Ruddy light and the smell of toasted nut bread assailed my nostrils when I walked in.

Heads turned, and Rajanas said, "I thought you'd taken yourself off."

Kuraf spoke from deep in a muffler, "You're only wearing that silk. Do you not feel the cold, child?"

"I'm cold," I said, sinking wearily onto a pile of blankets airing near the fire. "Where is Hlanan?"

"Getting soup down Geric Lendan's throat," Rajanas said, one hand signing.

Oflan sat on the opposite side of the fire, fingers clasping a mug whose contents steamed gently.

The bread I'd smelled lay on a tray, which had been set on a camp stool. I felt too leaden to dash in and swipe some. I gazed hungrily at the pile, my limbs not wanting to move. My right arm throbbed dully.

Kuraf nodded at Nill. "Get the Hrethan something to eat."

I hadn't realized how worn I was until I got a few bites into the bread. Warmth spread through me, not banishing the aches, but enabling me to bear them, and to become a little more aware of my surroundings.

Kuraf and Captain Nath and Rajanas bent over a grubby, much folded map that lay on a makeshift table as they discussed how to divide up their scouts. When I left, they were putting forward ideas for provisioning said scouts.

I finished the bread, forced myself to my feet, and found Hlanan at the hut where Prince Geric lay, deeply asleep.

Even though his breathing soughed slowly, and his eyes moved beyond his eyelids, I didn't trust him. So I drew Hlanan near the door, in spite of the cold, and in idiomatic Thesreve, I told him about my flight and what I'd seen.

Before I got to the end, he took me by the shoulders. "Lhind," he exclaimed in Elras. "Do you realize what you've done? Have you told Ilyan?"

"No." I grimaced, trying to put my reluctance into words. "My secret...." I began, then stopped, looking away. But the candlelight playing over Geric's filthy reddish hair served as a reminder: Geric knew I could turn into a bird. The Gray Wolves knew.

That secret was no longer any kind of a secret.

"Come on," Hlanan said, and took my hand.

Somehow it was easier to hear him tell it to Rajanas, Kuraf, Oflan, and Chief Nath, rather than my trying to find the words. I was still too worn out to comprehend the consequences until I saw their faces change. Not just their faces. They turned around and faced our way, exhibiting several different kinds of astonishment, as Pandoc signed for Oflan.

Rajanas thumped his hands onto his knees. "You will never cease to catch me by surprise, thief," he said, shaking his head. "Do you realize you just saved us weeks, maybe months of rough work?"

"Of peril," Kuraf said, as the wind keened around the spires on the cliff above us.

"And all to discover that your plan worked," Hlanan said.

Rajanas slowly shook his head. "It's too easy."

Kuraf sighed. "All those messages. For nothing."

Hlanan said, "I don't understand. You were successful in dividing them, or surely they would still be here?"

"I think this supposed invasion is a feint," Rajanas said slowly. "To see how we respond." A noise at the door caused him to look up sharply, hand going to the knife at his side as Kuraf reached for her own weapon, then both slowly sank back again.

Prince Geric leaned in the doorway, the knuckles of his hand white as he held himself up. At his side stood one of the forest rangers.

"Thann," he said hoarsely, his face blanched paler than it had been right after that sword fight. "They're on their way to Thann," he whispered, long-jawed and shocked with betrayal.

Rajanas looked at him impatiently, then he struck his hand on his knee. "I never thought of that. Gray Wolves are here," he said, waving an arm wide. "The garrison in Thann is empty, eh?"

"Only two troops," Geric said hoarsely. "Left. Guard city."

"Go back to bed." Rajanas nicked his chin at one of the waiting equerries. "No one is going anywhere right now. We've a blizzard moving in, you might have noticed."

"Have to go back," Geric retorted, without much force.

"Not today. Nobody is moving today, including that army. Get some sleep. We'll put you on the road soon as we can clear a path."

The big equerry took Geric's arm, and led him away.

"Hah." Rajanas shook his head. "That's a twist I hadn't foreseen."

Kuraf sighed. "He's been going on about treachery, but nothing we've done holds a candle to *that*." She glanced reflectively at the window, then turned to Rajanas. "Do you really want to send him to Thann?"

"What else is there to do with him?" Rajanas retorted.

Hlanan said, "I'll take him."

Rajanas grinned. "See that he gets there, eh?" His smile vanished. "Leaving the question, why would he return there at all?

Yes, his former ally Dhes-Andis seems to have conveniently got Lendan out of the way—he and the Gray Wolves both—so he has a ready garrison for his army in Thann, but so what? The Lendans have never held so much as a vegetable plot in Thann."

"It seems to have become his home," Hlanan said.

Rajanas humphed. "He and Morith a love match, is that what you're suggesting? Impossible. He never does anything without an eye to gain, and the only thing she ever loved was power."

"I don't know." Hlanan sighed. "He's more difficult to understand than I once thought. Something is driving him hard. I'm sure of it."

"The aristocrat's affront at being crossed," Rajanas stated, as though he weren't a prince. But then a good part of his life he had not lived like one.

As equerries came in, bringing a tray of travel mugs wafting a heady aroma, I sank tiredly beside Kuraf on a rude bench.

The equerries passed out the hot, spicy crackle berry punch. I had never tasted it before—they brewed it from dried berries and carefully hoarded Summer Island spice—and I reflected on how much I had missed while living hand-to-mouth so long. Crackle berries could be found everywhere, but that spice was costly.

Kuraf spoke up after a reflective silence. "Prince Geric appears to be invested in Thann. Whether emotionally or materially might make a difference in his intent."

Rajanas uttered a soft grunt as he set his mug aside. "Which he won't tell us. Anyway, it's not my decision to make, but on reflection it seems to me a bad idea to send Geric to the same place a loose army seems to be headed."

"If they are Dhes-Andis's hirelings," Hlanan said soberly, "they are not likely to take any orders from Geric. And I will be with him."

Rajanas lifted a shoulder. "I admit I like the idea of someone keeping an eye on him, but I don't see why it has to be you. I've any number of trusty equerries I can send, who will see him straight there and report any double-dealings."

"He won't talk to equerries," Hlanan said. "I think he'll talk to me."

"What use is anything he says? We know now what Dhes-

Andis promised him, but that plan is clearly in the wind."

"You forget that for a time Dhes-Andis taught him magic. Geric believes, anyway, that Dhes-Andis considered giving him power and position before he was distracted by his discovery of Lhind's existence."

All eyes turned my way and instinctively I ducked. Rajanas's lip curled, but it was not in contempt so much as his particular kind of dry humor.

"Magic." He exhaled the word like an expletive. "Forgot that. Right." As the muffled chuff-chuff of a patrol passed by the door, he paused, then said, "I'll give you whatever you need. The sooner you get him out of here the better for the Wolves. They're morose enough."

Kuraf shook her head slowly. "They just lost their home."

"Not all," Rajanas said. "Maybe half, according to Jendo Nath. I don't see why he'd lie about it. It's he, on orders, who recruited outside of Thann for the duchess when she began swelling their numbers. The duchess had convinced him that Thann was going to be invaded. By us, actually, through Keprima." Another of those wry looks as he struck his chest and then pointed at Kuraf. "And some of his Gray Wolfe recruits are Faran."

"Faran!" Now it was Kuraf's turn to make a word into an expletive. "Then they're not better than those rats we dealt with down-mountain. Just better trained."

Rajanas waved a hand. "Oflan's mother was Faran, I learned a day or two ago. Oflan spent her early years there, before her mother was murdered. Most of the Faran Gray Wolves are her relations. She doesn't seem any happier about the corruption in Forfar than we are."

He lounged to his feet. "Which brings me back to my point." He tipped his head toward the window. "What to do with them. All that binds them to me is their sense of honor. And a fast-eroding sense of self-worth. They don't give a spit for Alezand. They need meaningful orders. Oflan wants to take them into Forfar to clean the place up. I can't think of a better mission."

Kuraf had been looking sour, but at this she rubbed her jaw. "My task protecting the pass would be worlds easier if I didn't have to deal with Faran bandits and other scum. But it almost sounds too easy."

Rajanas laughed. "For us, the easiest way to clean up our back door I ever heard of. For them it won't be easy at all. No, I want to give her her chance." His voice was reflective. Then he turned Hlanan's way. "Order what you want. Get Lendan out of here."

———❦———

I followed Hlanan out, figuring the snow was so heavy we would be no more than two vague figures in the darkness. "What's to keep Geric from going back to Thann by magic?" I asked. "I know he's at least a beginning mage."

"I searched him while getting him bandaged," Hlanan said. "He was not carrying a transfer token."

"Couldn't he transfer without one?"

"Not as weak as he is. Also, he has to suspect that the Destination in Thann has been compromised. If an army really is on the way, that means scouts rode ahead. A mage is bound to be with them."

"I still think you need to search his stuff."

We reached the hut that had been assigned to Hlanan. It was empty, a fire built in the center. The ruddy light shone on his grimace. "I hate doing that."

"I have no problem with it," I stated. "I'll do it right now. I don't care if he watches or not."

Hlanan scratched his head, making a wild mess of his brown hair. He looked around the ugly hut as if something in those barren slats held hidden meaning, then faced me. "All right, let's do it together. We need to know if he has any objects with magic on them. But Lhind, don't rob him. He's lost enough."

"Seems to me he was robbing people courtier style, trying to get Alezand and all that, but I won't," I said. "I still have some of his gems from the first time I robbed him."

"You wouldn't consider returning them?" Hlanan asked as we faced each other across the fire. "He's lost so much."

"Because he's a villain!" I threw my hands out wide. "I might be a thief, but I never joined up with Dhes-Andis to learn evil magic, or plotted against other people, or tried to kill anyone."

When he gazed down at the fire with a troubled expression, I said, "I can't believe you're sympathizing with him. It's like you forgot all the rotten stuff he's done."

"I am beginning to believe that half of that was desperation, and a part of the rest was the result of his being lied to. But you're right about his intent. Well. Let's get this unpleasantness over with."

We walked back out, bending into the wind. Geric's was the next hut over, but it felt like a long trek. The guards let us in, where we found the prince asleep. Really asleep; his face, smoothed in deep slumber, looked younger than he ever had awake. The bitter smell of willow bark lay heavy in the air as I stepped near, looking suspiciously down.

My dream still lay in the back of my mind, stirring up unsettling thoughts, foremost my wondering if he'd had a mother who loved him. His sarcasm and arrogance and angry threats left me utterly unmoved: they were the rantings and actions of a villain. I didn't have to give villains a second thought beyond avoiding them. But that shock in his face when he leaned in the doorway whispering *Thann* had revealed emotions I would have thought alien to him.

A soft noise recalled me as Hlanan opened the first of the saddle bags containing the prince's gear.

I hopped to the second one and got to work.

Where I might have flung things around, Hlanan was methodical, repacking everything exactly as he found it. I copied his movements, though I found it very tempting to help myself to a fine silk sash and a carved comb. Not that I have ever used a comb. One fwoosh and my hair settles into instant order. I just thought it was pretty.

He did have a book of spells. Hlanan looked through it thoroughly then replaced it, which surprised me. Clearly whatever was written in that book wasn't the sort of magical spells Hlanan thought dangerous.

Otherwise none of the prince's jewels or brooches bore the revealing tingle of magic. By the time I had finished the last bag (because he had a lot of expensive stuff) Hlanan had already left. As I shoved everything back into the velvet jewelry pouches, I found myself surprised, then gratified, that Hlanan hadn't waited to watch me replace it. I'd expected him to—*I* would have stayed behind to watch me! But that was the very first thing I'd realized about him: he expected the best of everyone. Including me.

Geric never stirred during this search. I left empty-handed, and because it was snowing heavily, instead of retreating to a tree to sleep I picked the hut where they'd stored the horse feed to keep it dry.

I curled up on a feed bag, slept, and if I dreamed it vanished in memory before I woke.

Eleven

IT SNOWED TWO DAYS before the sun came out. Tir returned with the clear sky, swooping down to sail into the window of Hlanan's hut.

Before I could take five steps, Tir shot out again and flew off. I watched, my emotions veering between relief and a kind of disappointment that Tir had not even tried to approach me. Relief won out.

I still refused to open my mental wall to anyone while awake. Whatever that was in the dream would stay in the dream. In the light of day the experience evanesced into non-reality. It was merely me wishing to see that smile, to feel those arms, to hear those gentle words.

The fourth morning Tir returned a second time.

Hlanan oversaw the packing of his and Geric's belongings. I didn't have any, of course, but the prince made up for it. He had enough baggage for three people.

Nill bounded up with the thrilling news that Kuraf had assigned him to come with us, to see to Prince Geric's bandages and manage for him. "My first mission alone, and I'm not yet sixteen," he said, chortling and rubbing his hands—as if this were to be fun, instead of a slog down the long, treacherous mountain roads with an arrogant, cranky prince.

"Tir will find inns for us," Hlanan said to me as Nill dashed away to tell his friends among the rangers. "We're only taking a remount for each of us so there is no room for tents, food, and fodder. Better not risk sleeping outside in winter."

"I hope the first inn is close by," I said doubtfully, following Hlanan's glance at Geric, who stood outside his hut looking awful. "It took us days and days to get up here, and I don't remember seeing any inns at all."

"That's because we came up back roads. And we could not use magic to clear the paths," Hlanan replied. "Now that we know there are no enemy scouts lurking on cliffs or in trees we can clear the snow with magic. And in any case going downhill is always faster."

"There's magic to clear roads?"

"I think you'll enjoy this spell," he replied with a flashing smile.

He was right. As soon as Geric was mounted we set off down the southward road so as not to waste daylight. As soon as we reached the untouched snowfall obscuring the road, Hlanan demonstrated, muttering and sliding his open palm in a scooping motion. The spell shot a burst of wind under the snow, sending it flying upward in a spectacular spray of white that bared the road underneath. It was not even muddy, but cold and iron-hard.

"Do it again!" I exclaimed.

Hlanan laughed. "It'll have to be repeated all the way down the mountain. Would you like to help me? It's considered a fairly elementary wind spell, one of the first ones we learned as students."

"Back to magic lessons," I said, my joy vanishing.

He gave his head a shake. "I've been thinking. I'd like to try an experiment, but we'll wait a bit. Just listen to the spell a few times and watch my hand."

Geric's two personal servants had vanished by the second night after the two parties joined. I suspect Rajanas's people had let them slip through the lines to be well rid of them. So it was only the four of us who began riding slowly down the mountain that morning.

Under a bright blue sky Hlanan repeated the wind spell over and over, causing jets of snow to explode in sparkling white clouds upward to either side. I listened to the words and watched his gesture as it guided the wind drawn from above and sent it scouring along the path under the snow.

I began to perceive that the best jets of air skimmed in a straight line at the level of the ground. It was a bit like skipping stones over water, aiming straight and true. His first few tries were not always consistent; one drove into the ground, kicking up clots of mud in a spectacular explosion, but clearing only the space around the hole his wind dug, and another skimmed too high, furrowing the top of the snow but leaving an icy blanket underneath, treacherous to the horses' footing.

He soon got it right every time. I wriggled my shoulders, trying to emulate his gesture as I listened to the blurred words.

Gradually we drew ahead of the other two, who proceeded at a slow gait. When we rounded a bend out of earshot of Nill and Prince Geric, Hlanan said, "I think I know why you have trouble with the fundamentals of magic."

"Because I learned to read so late. Or I'm stupid," I said, the old resentment back again. After all that effort in the magic classes, sitting among children, I'd still been the worst student. Though everyone had been nice—perhaps because they'd been nice—it still rankled.

"Lhind. You're not stupid. You know you're not stupid. One of the first things you ever said to me was that you were not a fool." His voice dropped a note. "I am no real mage, as you know, but I wonder if the Mage Council made an error insisting on your learning the fundamentals." He gave me his funny, wistful smile. "I think I've figured out why the magic classes frustrated you, and it has nothing to do with when you learned to read."

Now I was listening.

"You remember being taught that the basic words are not actually magic in themselves?"

"Of course. They are meant to guide the mind in shaping the spell. I did *listen*," I said. "It's just when I tried the simplest spells, the ones those ten-year-olds found so easy, mine went wild," I finished, bitter again.

"I don't understand why the instructors didn't see what I see." He looked away with a troubled expression and flexed his gloved hands. "But I think your own innate abilities are interfering. What is meant as an aid is more of a hindrance to you."

"But they said Hrethan learn magic the same way, and don't we have the same innate abilities? Back in magic school I saw a half-Hrethan in a class ahead of me, though he didn't talk to me either time."

"White hair a lighter shade than yours?"

"Yes."

"That's Ashah. He's blind, so if no one introduced you he wouldn't know you're Hrethan."

"Oh." I frowned, then said, "Nobody older talked to me. I thought it was because I'm a bad student, for whatever reasons."

"The Mage Council said that Aranu Crown requested them to give you time to adjust to the life in Erev-li-Erval."

I thought about that, then said, "You mean she wanted to see how the thief was going to behave?"

He gave his head a shake. "You would have to ask her what she meant. The words I was given were those I just spoke to you."

"All right," I said, struggling against the impulse to start another argument. He was right. Only Aranu Crown could explain the meaning of her words. I resented a situation I didn't understand, didn't trust, that made me feel foolish at times. I did not resent *him*—so it was not fair to make him the target of my resentment of someone else because he was right here before me. "Back to magic lessons. The nonsense words were a hindrance. Yes, indeed they were. Nothing *ever* worked. No matter how carefully I tried."

He brought his chin down in a sharp nod. "Then try this. You heard me repeat the spell. You saw the gestures. Let the words flow through your mind and your hand shape the wind as you draw on your own magic."

"Oh, like—" *Dhes-Andis's fire spell*, I was about to exclaim. But I stopped myself, knowing how much that would upset him.

So I said quickly, to cover the lapse, "Like this?"

His magical spell slipped through my mind as I swooped my hand, scooping wind down and through—and staggered back as an icy blast slashed through the snow in a straight line as if a gigantic hand had loosed an invisible arrow the size of a tree.

I'd pulled far too much magic, my straight arrow of air

clearing the straight section of road before us, but then plowing in juddering furrows up the side of the hill beyond where the road had turned.

We stood in silence as the violently churned-up clots of snow dropped down again with soft plops and thuds.

"I keep forgetting," Hlanan said finally, "how...." He trailed off.

"How what? Can't all the Hrethan do that? I'm only half Hrethan. They have to be better at magic than I am if it's inborn, right?" I lifted my hair and swirled it around my head, my tail waving from side to side. "I simply pulled too much magic into the wind, or too much wind into the magic. And it's not like I can keep doing that. It's like leaping. I can jump up to a rooftop, but I can't *keep* doing it. I get tired like anyone else. Can all Hrethan keep at it endlessly?"

"I don't really know," he said quickly, dropping his voice as the others rounded the corner behind us. "They don't actually talk much about their skills any more than they speak of their own internal, oh, ranks, you might call it. Though they have no titles, at least as we understand them, nor do they claim ownership of land. They say that the color of their...their feathers and their skin has no particular meaning—that the blue corresponds to the Summer Islands Hrethan—but there are some who think that color might correspond with inherited potential for magic."

"But I'm half. My hair's silver. I don't even have blue eyes. My skin under my fuzz is almost as brown as yours." I didn't want to talk about the Blue Lady.

"But talent can be inherited by all peoples—"

Clop, clop: the others caught up, and we fell silent.

"Wow!" Nill exclaimed. "What happened up that knoll?"

"Practice," I said, as Geric lifted his head, and surveyed the deep score up the hill with the piles of snow to either side. But he didn't say anything.

My next try was better controlled, and after that Hlanan and I traded off clearing the road as we descended to a plateau with relatively warmer, drier air, and less snow.

By then the extravagant shadows cast by the mountains against the slopes had seeped upward toward the peaks, pooling the cold blue air of impending dark. I was ready to snap a tongue of mage-fire, but I resisted. I still had trouble controlling the fire spell, and I did not want to recall Hlanan to the subject of learning magic and Dhes-Andis's spells. He had not only a tenacious memory but a way of connecting things. With all my being I refused any kind of connection to Dhes-Andis—all the stronger because of how very close I had come to letting him beguile me.

I had never told anyone about that.

Hlanan peered anxiously around every bend, relaxing only when we spotted the cheerful golden glow of a village on either side of a river poised above a fall. We found the inn in the center of the loose circle of round-roofed houses. No surprise that during hard winter we found it nearly empty, save for some travelers caught by the blizzard.

Hlanan talked to the innkeeper, then turned Geric's way. One-handed, the prince tossed his coin purse. Hlanan caught it, paid, and we were soon settled in the little parlor of a suite at one corner of the house.

Nill brought in the prince's bags then ran out to oversee the care of the horses, and to hover around watching the food being prepared. He followed the innkeeper's son—same age as Nill—with steaming trays.

Nill ate enough for three. Geric picked at his food, then retired, never having spoken a word. Nill remained with us, the firelight reflecting in his wide eyes. He loved staying at an inn, loved being responsible—loved everything, asking a stream of questions until it was clear that he would stay up all night talking if we let him.

Since Geric had plenty of money, and the inn charged winter prices, that is, cheap, we each got our own room. Once everyone was settled Hlanan came to mine, tired and smiling. I too was tired—but that vanished when I opened my door and found him there. After all this time pretending we were barely acquainted it was so *good* to be finally alone with him!

I don't know which of us grabbed the other first, but ah, even though we were grimy from the day's travel, mud-splashed and disheveled, our kisses burned as sweetly and as brightly as our very first.

But he didn't stay long. "We need our rest," he said presently.

"We ought to start early."

"Stay," was my response. "It's been ages since we've been just the two of us. Prince Geric is a courtier. 'Early' for him is no doubt mid-afternoon. And that's when he's well."

Hlanan laughed against my neck, and I swirled my hair around him to keep him there. "You traveled with him down the mountain from Maita Boniree's castle. He knows what early means, and in spite of his wounds he is anxious to get back to Thann. We need to stay alert on the road."

That was true. Who knew what Dhes-Andes would throw at us next? "All right," I grumped, freeing him.

"We'll meet tomorrow night, soon as everyone is settled," Hlanan said. He grabbed my shoulders and kissed me hard, then quietly slipped out.

I opened my window wide, and that night I dreamed of the Blue Lady, but she remained in the distance, wavering as if seen through water, the way she had when I dreamed about her as a youngster. I woke with the old sense of loss, grumpy at the sound of urgent knocking on the door.

"There looks like weather on the way," Hlanan said. "Let us get as far as we can before it arrives."

Since I had no gear beyond my thief tools, which I slept with, I simply stepped through the cleaning frame and followed him out to the parlor where porridge, cream, honey, and hot biscuits awaited us.

I found Geric and Nill already there. The prince never even looked up at our entrance.

Nill inhaled his meal in a way that reminded me of my days among a group of young thieves, and departed, a biscuit in hand, to see to the horses.

We left soon after, with Tir circling overhead.

And so the next few days went. I helped clear the road, which Hlanan expressed frequent appreciation for. He watched continuously: Geric's ability to stay on the horse, the horizon, the road behind us. A couple of times I caught him pressing his hand absently against his side, where his inner pocket was sewn, but of course there was no magical notecase there. Maita had stolen his as well as Hlanan's.

That gesture and his quiet determination to get us as far and fast as possible began to raise questions in my mind. I had no interest in Thann, armies, or empires. But Hlanan clearly did.

I'd expected Geric to be the one to urge speed. Oh, not at first. Those days we traveled down the mountain he could scarcely sit on the horse, though he was proud enough to try to hide how much it hurt him. It was no surprise that he was always the first to retire and the last to waken.

But as the days stretched into a week and he clearly regained a modicum of strength, he remained silent, and Nill began riding with me. This was nice, as I enjoyed Nill, but that effectively ended private talk with Hlanan.

"This is so wonderful," Nill exclaimed, looking with obvious delight at the uniformly white landscape sculpted into softness over hills and valleys. Dull brown and gray barren trees broke the ubiquitous white, and in the distance far to the south—glimpsed when we topped hills—lay the winding ice-glinting ribbon of the river.

"What do you find wonderful about it?" I asked.

"My own mission! Travel, every day different. Kee's had a dozen missions and didn't she gloat, the first time! It's *finally* my turn."

"Every day has been pretty much the same," I said, laughing.

"But we meet new people every day! And these trees here, did you notice how the hickories and all those oaks only grow on the sun-facing slopes, but the shaded slopes grow the evergreens? On the heights, we don't see a lot of these." He swept a hand at a hedgerow. His enthusiasm was fun to see.

"So you don't mind tending Prince Scowl?"

Nill's grin twisted into a rueful grimace. "I guess I'd be the same if I had a bunch of holes in me. And all the rest of it. At least he doesn't throw things at my head, the way Gran says the old king did." He shrugged. "Most nobles, she says, are stinkers. You learn to live around them, unless they're like *our* prince."

I had no interest in talking about Rajanas. "What's it like, having a sister?"

Another grimace, a shrug, then a reluctant, "Oh, Kee's all right. She's not like some I could mention. But they always used to say,

Why don't you keep your bedding neat like Kee does, or *Kee is always at the practice targets. You're old enough to have her good habits.* If she ever did anything wrong, it would be easier." He shrugged again. "I can't help being lazy." He waved a hand, dismissing the topic. "Gran said I was not to bother you, but we're days away from the rest. So what's it like being a thief? Is it fun?"

It was my turn to grimace. "It's only fun when you rob someone you really hate." I jerked my thumb over my shoulder at Geric, and Nill snickered. "But I can't tell you how much trouble *that* has got me into. As for the rest, well, it's exciting, because you don't want to get caught. Everybody hates you, and you have to keep moving."

Nill said, "I hadn't thought of that. Of course if you have friends, like Gran did under the bad old king, it doesn't sound so bad. Though she hates questions about that time, and if you ask, you get a lecture about how terrible thieving is. Even when you're starving."

"I guess if you have the forest to hide in you are all right," I said. "But I can tell you this, if you have friends and get comfortable in a city you get caught sooner."

He grimaced again. "I think I'd rather run stealth raids on the others in training. At least if you get caught you just get laughed at."

"Tell me about your training," I said, and Nill happily whiled away the afternoon with stories about his life as a ranger. Naturally he bragged at first—trying to impress me—but then he told stories about his grandmother's life when she and Rajanas recovered the principality.

And so it went for a few days as we rode steadily lower from mountains to hills to hillocks, and finally reached the river. Here inns would be easy to find, but Tir remained with us, appearing now and again high overhead.

The aidlar did not speak to me again.

———◈———

One morning I woke to the sound of sleet. When I opened the door of the tiny attic room at the inn we'd stopped at, I found

Hlanan halfway down the stairs on the landing, peering out the window with an intensity that he seldom revealed.

"What's wrong?" I asked.

He started, and flushed as he turned to face me. "We're grounded." He turned out his hands. "I don't think Prince Geric would do well out in this weather."

I sat on the stairs, my chin on my knees. "About Geric," I said, pinching my nose. "Who at the moment is lurking at the other end of this inn so he can't possibly hear us. Hlanan, why are we even here?"

His eyebrows shot upward. "You heard that discussion. You were there."

"I heard all these reasons why *he* wants to go, and you said you'd take him because you were going to get him to talk. He hasn't said anything, and it's you who frets at our slowness. Why you? Why not send Nill alone to help him? Much as I loathe Geric, I don't think he's going to attack Nill."

Instead of answering immediately, Hlanan ran up the stairs, and gestured for me to follow into my closet of a room. There was scarcely enough space for two and it was cold in there—I'd asked for a room with no fireplace, and ended up with a servants' chamber.

We stood less than an arm's length apart, close enough that I could hear his breathing and see his heartbeat tic in a vein at his temple, partially obscured by the soft fall of an errant lock of brown hair.

We were alone. Why does meeting someone's eyes have such a strong physical effect? It's not like anything touches, but there it was, that blossom of warmth in my middle. I ached to pull him to me, but I sensed a tension in him that put an invisible barrier between us.

He sighed sharply, and dropped his gaze to his hands. "You know I had to report everything that had occurred. It is my duty."

"Of course," I said, wondering why he'd state the obvious. I'd seen him march off with Rajanas's notecase, paper, pen, and ink, before we left.

"And so...I want to get to Thann first. To resolve the conflict. If I can."

"You *can't* think Geric will help you! And even if he could, isn't that army commanded by Dhes-Andis from afar? I mean, through whoever his sub-commanders are?"

"I am counting on Geric telling me about Thann. He's been there more recently than I. The more I know, the better chance I have of coming up with something by the time the army commanders reach it."

Muffled voices sounded faintly through the age-warped door.

He lifted his head, then opened the door and ran lightly downstairs. I sat where I was, mulling the quick words, that tension he had tried to mask. Something was still missing.

Later—we left the moment the sky began to clear—I watched Geric narrowly. Surely he had to be part of whatever Hlanan had not told me.

I was—as usual—completely wrong.

But I didn't begin to figure that out until a week later, after an almost headlong journey along the river road, when we passed a crossroads and found ourselves surrounded by armed warriors.

Twelve

THEY WORE THE GRAY and purple of imperial warriors. Or they were disguised as imperial warriors. Considering how many disguised people with pointy weapons I'd run into of late, I didn't trust anything I saw.

They surrounded us with the seemingly effortless skill that comes of very long training, separating off Geric from the rest of us. Geric paled, but straightened his shoulders and head with a semblance of his old arrogance.

"My greetings, Scribe Vosaga. We are here to escort His Highness safely to Erev-li-Erval," shouted a helmed man whose gold twined laurels at one shoulder indicated a captain. He seemed familiar, though I was certain I'd never spoken to him, and he certainly knew Hlanan, having greeted him by name. He appeared to be about thirty-five, with the splendid build of the lifetime warrior, and sat tall in the saddle.

He spoke with the accent heard all over the noble levels of the capital. He couldn't possibly be a disguised mercenary. Could he? I turned to Hlanan—to encounter his Heir Face.

Geric said, "There is no necessity. I am returning to my holding."

"On the contrary," returned this captain with the ease of one noble to another. "I can see from here that the reports are true, Your Highness. You are far from well."

Hlanan spoke up. "There are three of us to see to His

Highness's needs, Captain Dalcasta. We require no escort."

Captain Dalcasta's smile widened, his genial voice carrying easily across the churned-up snow. "Come along, Scribe Vosaga, we can discuss these affairs more comfortably elsewhere. Your Highness, will you do us the honor of accompanying us?" The words were spoken as a request, but it was plainly an order.

Hlanan's mouth tightened, but he said nothing more as the warriors fell in on either side of us, and away we rode.

At the nearest crossroads we turned inland from the frozen river, skirting a market town. A square, four-towered castle dominated the town from a hilltop. The tallest tower, overlooking the river, sported a flagpole. Limp in the cold breeze flew Rajanas's blue and black banner, with the imperial purple and gold flag hanging above it. So we'd reached the border of Alezand.

And there were Blues on duty. The way they deferred to Captain Dalcasta and his company made it clear who was the biggest bowwow in the kennel. As we drew up in the courtyard, the captain dismounted while calling out a string of orders that sent everyone, his own people and the Blues, scurrying every which way.

"... And lock up the Hrethan thief wherever convenient. Scribe, wait upon me in the commander's office." He lifted a casual hand toward the tallest tower.

I glared at this casual dismissal, instantly hating him, but he never so much as glanced at me. I obediently followed the four armed guards who surrounded me, doing my best to look meek and small. Sure enough, they gave me only the most cursory search outside the door to the first room that locked. It was not a prison cell — no bars — so two heartbeats after the door closed and a key rattled in the lock I sprang to the window, eased it open, and once again murmured my illusion spell as I spidered up the rough wall to the sentry walk.

The pair of guards walking the walls passed by, talking in low voices about how much their chow would be lessened thanks to the newcomers. As soon as they passed, I eased over the crenellation and ghost-footed with painful care to the tower with the flag pole where again I finger-toed my way up the side of the wall, grateful for ancient stones not quite fitted flush.

When I heard the captain's amused, tolerant voice, I halted below a window. It was shut against the cold but the glass only muffled sound.

I nearly fell off the wall from shock when Hlanan said, "And I am glad to see you, too, Justeon, but I don't understand why Mother sent you."

Mother? So this Captain Dalcasta had to be the military half-brother! In public he'd only be known by the rank he had earned.

"Hlanan. Get your head out of the clouds. Because the army that *you* reported marches eastward across Keprima! Nice work, by the way. The diplomats are busy wielding innuendo and veiled threat between here and Keprima's capital. As of last night, we still don't know what type of bribe could get Keprima to turn a blind eye to an army tromping through the countryside, or if the motivation is fear. But this army has to be getting their supplies from somewhere, eh?"

Hlanan said, "Justeon, I told Mother that I would handle this situation on my own. Will you lend me your notecase so I can write to her?"

Justeon uttered a comfortable, indulgent laugh. "Hlanan, you never cease to amaze me! Look at you here with no vestige of support. You didn't even manage to hold onto your notecase."

"That is because of the traitor mage Maita Boniree."

"I know. Very nice work, that, by the way. The mages are humming all around her former hive. Though I overheard some sharp words about the idiot who managed to burn up all the evidence. Lost control of a magical fire, very distinctive spell. I trust that wasn't you. It sounds more like something your wretched thief would try. I heard plenty about her, ha ha!"

"There should be something else to present as evidence of Magister Boniree's betrayal of her oath."

"Yes. As it happens the grisly remains of her failed experiments. Good thing you didn't set the entire castle afire, eh? Anyroad, they are quite pleased with you. Go home and bask in your earned glory. Leave the military situation to me. You *do* recognize that this is a military situation, little brother?" His tone was so kindly that I ground my teeth, longing to pitch him into the nearest pig pen head first.

"That's just it. I want to resolve this situation if I can, without bloodshed," Hlanan said.

Justeon gave a short bark of laughter, but whatever he was going to say he abandoned at a rap on the door. "Enter!"

"His Highness insisted upon an interview," said an equerry, before Geric pushed past.

"Prince Geric." Justeon rose to his feet and bowed. "You will not mind speaking before the scribe here? I gather you've been traveling in his company."

Geric ignored the question. "I desire to return to Thann, which is now my holding."

"Your Highness, you have my profound respect for your dedication, but permit me to observe that you are in no case for such travel. I will send you to Erev-li-Erval via transfer where you may have your wounds seen to in royal comfort."

"I intend to return to Thann," Geric stated in his suavest drawl. "May I remind you that though the Golden Circle is soon to cease, thanks to the decree of Aranu Crown, it does still exist, with all privileges of rank appertaining?"

My fingers slipped and I clutched the rock in a death grip. There was no flying here—I could feel the weight of the lowlands pressing on me. If I fell, landing on that stone courtyard would probably hurt a whole lot.

Carefully, slowly, I retraced my motions, renewing the illusion and pausing when sentries walked by. I didn't relax until I reached that room again.

And just in time. I'd scarcely rubbed the ache out of my fingers and toes before keys clattered in the lock. I sprang to sit at the table nearby, slouching in what I hoped was a posture that looked as if I'd never moved. But my fine acting was wasted on the equerry who barely glanced at me before setting a bowl and a stoneware jug on the side table, then locking the door again.

I gulped down the water. The bowl contained good Keprima long-grained rice boiled with vegetables and topped with crumbled cheese. I inhaled that, too.

Scarcely had I finished when the door unlocked again—and here was Hlanan. "Oh, good," he said, relieved. "I hoped you hadn't done a flit."

"I did," I said. "That is, I got out, and climbed up to your tower to ear in. 'Wretched thief.' That brother of yours is —"

"Later," he murmured. "Geric wants to leave. I told him we'd meet at the stable."

"Shall I sneak over the wall?"

He smiled and shook his head. "We are not being constrained here. We'll talk on the road."

To my surprise, that's what happened. None of the empress's company were in sight. The Blues helped us so assiduously, down to providing an extra pack of excellent fodder for the horses, that even I could see a message in their helpfulness. The only thing I wasn't certain of was the message: either "We are on your side" or "Don't let the door hit your heels."

I expected Hlanan to call a stop once we got out of sight of the castle, but we moved at a trot through the quiet town. When we got to the road beyond — cleared by magic by someone else — it was Geric who whistled his mount into a gallop, ours following.

When the horses tired, we slowed to a less breakneck pace. Now that I wasn't clutching the mane (despite those lessons from Oflan Nath, my old bad habits still persisted), I could look around at the gently undulating landscape in its hundreds of shades of white, silver, soft gray, and pale blue.

Brittle, frozen reeds and weeds and bow-shouldered willows with clumps of hibernating shrubs jutted from the icy riverbank like angry pen strokes. I forced my mental wall to strengthen, though I longed to spread my awareness out to catch the playful otters in their winter cozes, the little salamanders deep underground, and all the other creatures of water, land, and edge. It would have kept me from remembering that somewhere out beyond where the slate-gray sky met the ground moved that army.

Obviously we had to get to Thann first. Then what?

I resigned myself to a wait as the air got steadily colder, a nasty wind rising. Even Nill looked subdued, his head bent over his horse's neck and his knit hat pulled almost down to his eyes.

The cold caused my fuzz to fluff and my spine to stiffen my hair into a kind of cloak around me, rippling in the wind. As long as I didn't get wet I'd be all right, but some day I was going to have to get some more clothes.

We rode until the color began fading from the land. The sun had been invisible since midday. Hlanan looked anxious, and the animals had slowed to a walk, but Geric was the one who insisted irritably that we keep going, until he swayed in the saddle and nearly dumped himself into the ice forming across the top of the snow.

Hlanan took over at that point. As hooves crackled at each step, he turned us around to the riverside village we'd recently passed.

It was a bit larger than most of the tiny places we'd passed, being built where the river forked. Soon we sat by a fire, our clothes steaming gently. Even I was glad of the warmth.

Once we got hot food and drink into us, Geric seemed to revive.

I said, "Why are we running so fast?"

Geric raised his head as Hlanan said calmly, "We want to reach Thann first."

I sighed. "Won't the empire warriors be a good thing if that army is coming? Why don't you want them with us?"

Geric glared out of eyes circled with dark, bruised-looking flesh, the contrast making the blue of his irises look feverish, almost mad. "Because, you Hrethan twit, Thann is an independent duchy. It has struggled and connived and negotiated successfully to remain independent for four centuries. But if yon empire flunkey takes it over with the excuse of warding an army, how soon do you think we will be able to evict them?"

I glared back at him, remembering what some of that conniving consisted of. His beautiful duchess Morith had hired out assassins to fund her plot to make herself queen of Namas Ilan. "So I'm a Hrethan, and I guess they don't understand land politics any more than I do. That much we have in common. But! I *do* remember how much your duchess lied to her own people. And they weren't the only ones she lied to," I added meaningfully.

A pause, during which some bird high overhead squawked, answered by Tir.

Then, "If Thann is to swear allegiance to the Kherval," Geric said in a tired voice, "it is better if we do it on our own terms. And no one wants their city, or land, to become a battleground."

I opened my mouth to ask how he thought he was going to stop them, but caught Hlanan's eye. He gave a tiny shake of his head.

Geric sat there looking like he barely possessed the strength to fall into bed, so I relented. Baiting him was much more fun when he was strong enough to tromp around flinging threats and insults right and left for me to laugh at.

We parted after agreeing that unless we woke to a blizzard, we would be gone at first light. Nill went off to help Geric with his bandages and then to check on the horses, as some inns had better stable help than others. I used this opportunity to get Hlanan alone.

As soon as the door was shut, I took his hands — a gesture that still felt off-balance, tentative. Two seasons ago I never would have dared touch someone I liked. It hurt too much. Then came Hlanan, and for a time, whenever we were alone we couldn't keep ourselves apart.

But that was at the imperial palace. It hurt now when he pressed my hands, then let me go, his gaze distant. Clearly no hugging or kissing was going to happen, not with him in this strange, nervy mood. "Lhind, ask your questions, but then I want to look at the innkeeper's maps. I promised I'd be back down, and I don't want to risk making him wait too long before he puts them away and retires."

"Why do you have to look at the maps at all? Don't we follow the river upstream? One of its branches comes down out of Thann, right?"

"Yes, but the river branches meander all over. If there is a straighter road to Thann, I intend to find it."

"Why?" I asked. "I don't see why we should interfere. Your brother made it real clear what he thought of your help."

"Please. I know we're alone, but please don't get into the habit of calling him anything but by his earned title. You know our situation."

"*Captain Dalcasta* commands a lot of military people. Isn't that what you want if you've got an invading army on the loose?"

"No!" He took a turn around the small chamber, which looked pretty much like all the ones we'd stayed in so far. "No," he said again more quietly, but his gaze met mine, wide and intense. "Don't you see? If Justeon has his way there will be a fine battle, which he is almost bound to win. If his reinforcements get here in time. He goes back to Erev-li-Erval a hero wearing his triumphant laurels, confidently expecting the empress to make him heir."

I stared in shock.

"And she might," Hlanan said softly, making another turn. "She just might. Nothing is set until she decides so."

"So...this is a contest between you and him?" I stared at Hlanan in disbelief.

"Yes—" He met my gaze, then his own expression changed to dismay and he reddened to the ears. "No! That is, not in a personal sense. As if we were rivals in a contest or a duel."

He took another turn as he threw his head back. "My first thought is of lives. There has to be a way to *avoid* a war. I don't have military training, but I've spent time around people who do, and those who lust for war are few—that is, among those who have to actually wage it. Commanders who sit in palaces and send others to their deaths are more common."

"Is Captain Dalcasta one of those?"

"Yes. No. Oh, I believe he's willing to risk his personal safety. Though he would not lead from the front, because you see nothing except the next weapon coming at you from the front. He thinks about strategy and tactics in abstract terms, and will find some hill from which he can see the most because he needs to see the battle in the abstract."

Hlanan whirled and began pacing the other way. "When battle is distant—abstract—it is easier to pay the price in lives. Everything I've read of our ancestors' private records convinces me of that. He sees my position as weak. I see his as oblivious to the real cost, but I believe we both mean to do well by the Kherval. Does that make more sense?"

"Yes," I said, and under my breath, "But I still think he's a strutting peacock."

Hlanan had gone on talking as he paced. "Lhind, I have to find a way to avoid a war altogether. Or I'm not good enough to become an emperor no matter who else wants to be one. Do you see that?" He stopped and faced me, hands out wide. "*That's* the contest. Not a squabble with my brother, who thinks his way is the right way."

"I think you're setting yourself up for an impossible task," I said slowly.

"But that's what ruling *is*, in essence. Good ruling! Thinking out solutions at a level that involves principalities and groups and armies and conflicting interests. Persuading people in power to think of the welfare of all. You *make* the impossible possible!" He swooped on his bag and dug out a pen, an inkwell, and his battered old magic book.

As I watched he balanced the pen on the inkwell, stuck the nib end under the edge of the book, and pressed his smallest finger on the pen so that the book lifted.

Then he smiled sideways at me. "One finger lifts the heavy object with the right tools in the right place. The emperor, one person, sways the body of the Kherval for the good of all. That is who I must be. Or I may as well return to being a scribe, and writing about others' efforts."

———◆———

When I came downstairs the next morning, I found Nill and Hlanan sitting at a small table in the common room. No bustle, no peering anxiously at the window lest the weather change.

"What's happened?" I asked.

"Prince Geric," Hlanan said, "appears to have become strong enough to endure a transfer. He's gone."

The words *Good riddance!* began to shape my lips, but his distressed expression caused me to swallow my real reaction. "What do we do now?"

Hlanan sighed. "Enjoy a good breakfast?"

Nill uttered a whoop. "I'll go order it." He dashed a few steps, then halted so fast he nearly fell into the closed door. Putting a hand out to stop himself, he asked over his shoulder, "Ah, did he take the coin purse?"

Hlanan smiled as he removed a much-thinned bag from his inner pocket.

Nill was gone a heartbeat later, his footsteps diminishing

down the stairs.

"So we're not going to Thann?" I asked.

"We'll eat a leisurely breakfast and see if he returns. Or sends a message."

"But we don't have one of those notecases."

"Oh, there are ways to send messages if you know enough magic. He does. It's troublesome. Think of it as a transfer of a thing, not a person. The Destination still has to be precise...." Hlanan's voice drifted, and he abandoned a lesson in something he knew I had no interest in. "I think I failed him," he admitted finally. "That was my first gamble."

"*You* failed *him?* Aside from the absolute backwardness of that, from what I saw, how could you fail him? He never spoke until that day we were surrounded by Captain Dalcasta's company."

Hlanan sighed. "He and I talked. Late into the night sometimes. It started before we left the Pass, the first subject being how Morith had effectively used us both."

I grimaced. "So he didn't talk around me."

"And that's why I didn't tell you. Most of what he said was bitterness over the many people who have betrayed him. And they did," he added in that reflective tone, the one that had first caught my heart. "Beginning with his own parents, neither of whom wanted charge of him until he could get to an age to be of political use. Sending him away to be trained in what I gather was a fairly brutal school. He wouldn't talk about that."

Hlanan shrugged. "He wouldn't talk about where or when he met Dhes-Andis, either. So...we argued. Political strategy, magical strategy, ethics. Nothing I could build upon for the present purpose, but I had hopes...." He shook his head and whispered something under his breath.

I only caught one word, and I pounced. "Hlanan, you are not a failure."

"I said I probably have failed my second task, as well."

"It's an impossible task!"

"Anything is possible unless one fails," he said gently. "And having failed makes me a failure."

This time I did walk up and put my arms around him. His breath hitched in that little way I loved, so I wound my hair around us both and imagined us floating on air currents high in the sky where the air intoxicates, and the light bathes the world in warmth. He stood taut within that circle, so taut he was on the verge of trembling, but gradually he forced himself to relax, muscle by muscle, until he rested his cheek against the top of my head.

"How do you do that?" he whispered, his breath stirring my hair. I lifted it and swept it over his face in a caress, and I felt a tremor of laughter run through him. "Do what?" I said. "I'm holding you."

"You—" He abandoned whatever he'd been about to say as noise came from below: a hasty arrival.

It could have been anyone. The inn was not empty, and mornings in these places bustled with comers and goers. But we sprang apart, and Hlanan reached for the door a moment before it opened.

Prince Geric Lendan stood with his hands braced in the door frame, his face gray with expended effort, fury and even a trace of horror distending his gaze. Or perhaps that was the effect of transfer magic, especially twice in a day?

"The scouts have begun arriving ahead of the commanders," he said hoarsely. "Thann has no defense. The army is two weeks from arrival, strung out along the road."

Thirteen

"WHAT ARE YOU GOING to do?" Hlanan asked.

"Nothing." Geric's gaze shifted away. "There is nothing more I can do. I'll have to make a life as best I can. And I shall." He lifted his chin in an echo of the old Prince Geric dressed in velvet and gems, riding arrogantly at the head of an entourage.

"My last act was to ward our Destination. They will have to come in the conventional way. That was the only respite I could give Thann." He turned his shoulder, then turned back. "Half the servants were packing up their belongings, including my own people. Those born there are holding on, but the invaders, I am afraid, are going to find a mostly empty castle."

He walked out, shutting the door behind him. His footsteps diminished down the warped boards of the narrow hall.

Hlanan flexed his hands, looked at me, at the door, then breathed deeply with an air of decision. "If I'm right, we are only three days outside of Thann."

"No!" I yelped.

"This is my chance." Hlanan peered earnestly into my face, his gaze shifting between my eyes. His entire manner radiated conviction, determination, longing—so ardent the room seemed too small to contain him. "Stay here if you feel you should. I certainly understand."

I stepped closer, within touching distance; my arms ached to grab him and hold him there against doing anything crazy. I put my hands behind my back and gripped my fingers tight. "Hlanan. What can you do against an invading army?"

"You can't be suggesting I ought to leave those people to the mercies of either force?"

"I don't know." I twisted my hands. "I hate this situation. Everything feels wrong. Even you can't do anything against *an entire army*. And Geric said those servants are free to go."

"How free is it, really, to be driven out with no destination, no preparation, perhaps scant resources? This is why people stay when trouble comes, in hopes it passes over them. Those are the people owed protection. Not the wealthy, the strong...."

Hlanan looked from me to the window, as if he could see those people in Thann. "But didn't you hear him? The invaders aren't united. The army is piecemeal, strung out...." He turned, his thin shoulders set with decision. "Lhind, I can see you don't agree, and so I'll repeat, stay here. Or go free. There is nothing to stop you from doing what you feel is right for you."

But what about *us?* I wanted to ask. I couldn't force the words out. He was on a quest to save an empire—and I wasn't even certain there could be an *us*, except maybe when he had a free moment now and then. Assuming he survived whatever he was about to do.

Again I had to face the inescapable fact that if he did become heir to the empire, that *us* was always, always, always going to be defined as him, me, and an imperial crown.

Or should I put it this way: him, an imperial crown, and me?

And yet there was nowhere in the world I wanted to be but by his side. "Is there anything I can do to help?" I asked.

And watched the joy brighten his expression for one giddy heartbeat. Then came the doubt. "Are you certain? *I'm* not certain about anything except that I mean to go forward until I cannot any longer."

"What is it you want to do?" I asked. "I know you're not going to challenge all these various commanders to duels, the way Rajanas did up in the mountains."

"That only worked because the Gray Wolves needed it to. Anyway, for us mortal combat to decide political questions was outlawed when the Kherval was formed."

"Too bad," I said. "Not about you," I amended quickly. "Seems to me there would be fewer wars if the commanders all had to fight each other instead of ordering their minions to do all the hard work."

His smile was distracted. "Anyway, I don't think I'd need to even if I could. Look, they have recently spent two miserable seasons starving in the Pass and being shot at by the Rangers. Then they're given orders for this long march, and if I'm right, even more strict orders not to go marauding across Keprima lest they bring down that kingdom against them. If Geric's words are correct, they are anything but unified. Mercenaries seldom are. So I'll talk to their scouts, who might carry my words back to their captains," he said. "Or I'll talk to their captains and go from there. But first we have to get in."

"In disguise?" I asked.

"In disguise?" Hlanan repeated.

"Sure. You've always been in disguise. Oh, not like I used to be. But Geric thinks you're a scribe. Isn't that a disguise?"

"I *am* a scribe. But I see what you mean," Hlanan said slowly. "I hadn't thought of that, but maybe...."

"He also said the servants are stampeding." *Smart people*, I thought, then cleared my throat. "So...if we assume a disguise we can look around. See what's what. I'm certainly going to need a disguise," I said. "Hrethans probably aren't found much in Thann."

Hlanan laughed, full of excitement now that he had a plan. "Let's see what we can scare up before we go. Perhaps Nill will aid us."

"Are we taking Nill?"

Hlanan shook his head. "Kuraf would be very angry if we took him into Thann. Also, he will have to take responsibility for Ilyan's horses. They must get back to Imbradi. We'll hire mounts. If Tir is still here, we can rely on the aidlar to find us the swiftest way to Thann."

And so it went. Nill was sharply disappointed not to be going on what he thought would be a fun spy mission, but he took Hlanan's refusal well, as he felt equally responsible for the horses.

He dug in his pack and pulled out an old scarf, then he gave me his knit hat. He also gave me his extra tunic, trousers, and shoes, all so old and worn it was clear they had been handed down among several of his older relations. They were large on me, but that was a relief as it felt terrible to confine my tail again after a long stretch of freedom. Same with my hair.

Hlanan shook his head when I offered to raid the stable to find some choice stenches to further disguise us. "We want to go unnoticed," he said, laughing for the first time in far too long. "Not announce ourselves a day's march downwind!"

I didn't argue. Strange, how fast you can get used to some things. Like being clean.

He divided the last of Geric's purse between Nill and us, and we parted, Nill thrilled with the prospect of a solo mission.

"Geric didn't ask for his money back," I said as we walked the hired horses down the flagged path to the frozen stream below the inn. "Wasn't that all he had?"

"Maybe he was too proud," Hlanan said. "I admit I don't understand a lot of his motivations."

I concentrated on walking in shoes again after having gone barefoot during our days of riding. The shoes were like boats on my feet, slipping in the slushy snow. "I don't either. Here's what I do know: I don't trust him. So I'm glad we're going in disguise."

"Where's Tir?" Hlanan asked as we reached the road and mounted up.

I searched the sky, fully expecting the familiar white dot to move against the clouds, but the aidlar was nowhere in sight.

"Tir will no doubt catch up with us. As well I studied the innkeeper's map," Hlanan said, a worried furrow between his brows. "I think I know the landmarks to watch for. Let's go!"

I'm not going to describe that ride. It was miserable. But we made it in three and a half days despite two snow storms, during which we traded off clearing the road by magic until we were both sodden with exhaustion.

We changed horses a couple times, treating them better than we treated ourselves. I watched the sky, tempted strongly to reach mentally, but I never could bring myself to do it. Tir did not show up, though we both searched the skies frequently, even when at last we reached the rocky hills of Thann.

The independent dukes of Thann had constructed their principal city on the highest hill—called a mountain by the people there, though not nearly reaching the soaring heights of either of the continental ranges—with its impressive wall.

We rode cautiously on drooping horses, but saw no signs of any army.

"We'll be ready for anything," Hlanan said as we approached the open gates. "You are adept at escape."

I was about to remind him that we were far too low for me to transform to a bird, but then I understood his tone: he was trying to reassure himself. I didn't want him thinking he had to send me away for my own good, and anyway, I thought to myself, I'd always been able to eel out of danger. If you're a thief you have to be.

Sure enough, he went on in that low voice as if arguing inside his head, "And I can always transfer home in defeat." His thumb rubbed the little ring winking on his finger.

"What about Maita's magic against your transfer?"

"I felt that break about the time we reached the abandoned camp. My guess is, not long after she was arrested by the Mage Guild. I never told Geric, but he obviously must have felt it too; another thing I've never been able to discover is how much magic he's been taught."

"All right," I said, but underneath my drape, as we rode under the abandoned gate, my fingers dug into my bag of liref. The first sign that we had ridden into a rat's nest of villains, they would receive a face full of sleep-weed.

But no one stopped us. We found the stable by the smell and surprised a knot of stable hands, mostly young, playing a gambling game.

"Who are you?" one said rudely.

"I hope you're the new cook," another commented, and the first one changed expression from scowl to interest so fast I tried not to laugh.

Who could resist a hint like that? Not I! "We are indeed," I said, and Hlanan sighed.

"We'll take the beasts," the second one offered, a big blond fellow who looked like he really enjoyed his meals. "Go right in. Everyone else is," he added in a low voice.

They glanced around furtively as if afraid of being overheard.

The stable opened to a hallway. I began trying doors.

Hlanan said, "Cooks? I was thinking we could be runners if we had to claim a post."

"But you were once a pastry apprentice. Don't you remember making those delicious tartlets for the Gray Wolves before we pinched the blood magic book?"

"That was pastry making. And tartlets are about all I know how to make, save for nut cakes."

"But it's *cooking*. How hard can it be, cooking other foods? Especially if there's someone around who actually knows what they are doing, so they can tell us what to chop and where to boil it?" As I spoke I finally found a door that opened, but it was no bigger than a closet. One side was even lined with old trunks. I sprang to open the first.

"What are you doing?" Hlanan asked.

"Seeing if there is anything, uh—" *valuable*. "Useful."

"Remember we have to carry anything we find. And explain it if the residents see us with it."

"This trunk's full of old curtains. And that one's tablecloths." I let the trunk lids drop, sending a cloud of dust into the air.

"How about doing some scouting?" Hlanan suggested.

We moved cautiously into a hallway. My instinct was to hide because when I sneaked into a place it was to rob it. Hlanan's intent was different. He paid no attention to tempting rooms, but walked on in search of....

"A servant," he breathed as he spotted a thin man in livery dashing past us down a perpendicular hall. "He'll know something."

When the fellow caught sight of us, his round face changed from distraught to relief. "Are you the new cook? Where have you been?"

Hlanan and I looked at each other. His lips parted.

I said, "Yes!" And when the fellow goggled at me, I added

hastily, "Assistant cook, that's me!" He clearly took me for an apprentice.

Hlanan took a step, drawing attention his way. "Where are the kitchens?"

"Down here." The liveried man changed direction, his long legs striding so fast I had to run to keep up. "You know we've been effectively invaded. The duke promised he'd send for help and the first help we need, if we don't get the Gray Wolves back to defend us, is a cook! These newcomers said if we give them no trouble they won't trouble us. But what do they want? Nothing less than a banquet to greet the rest of the captains they said are coming in *today*."

"A banquet?" I said at the same moment Hlanan repeated, "The rest of the captains?"

"Tonight!" He threw up his hands. "And half — more — of the household vanished. I can't blame them, except the ones who took anything that wasn't too heavy to carry."

"You are the steward?" Hlanan asked as we rattled down a flight of stairs.

"I am now," the fellow responded with a rueful smile. "Nevic declared he was retiring when the new duke turned up and told us the duchess was dead." His tone didn't indicate any grief. "I was Nevic-Steward's assistant."

"Your name?" Hlanan asked.

"Well, I think you might go right ahead and call me Nevic-Steward. Everything is bucket-bottom up! The name has gone with the post ever so long. So I'll try it on, promoting myself, you might say, though there's scarce any staff left to call me that. Here we are."

He conducted us into an enormous kitchen. I breathed deeply, as I always do on entering kitchens. It seemed strange to walk right into one. In my thieving past I'd always sneaked in, my gaze scanning for the quickest path between foods I could lift and a door or window. I didn't know what to do with myself as the steward waved at a redheaded woman on the far side. "The cooks are here!"

The woman clapped her hands. "Oh, finally! We might act-ually live until tomorrow." She sounded more excited than scared.

She whisked herself out of the kitchen by that opposite door, sending back enticing smells that hinted of cold rooms with spices and flour and good things to eat.

My stomach rumbled. Hlanan and I had spent the last of Geric's coins on the horses, skimping meals for ourselves. *After all, they have to do all the running,* he'd said, and though I didn't dare listen to animals' thoughts, I had done so often enough in the past to agree with him, if with regret for my own yawning hunger. But hunger was my oldest companion, she and her sister fear.

The redheaded woman stumped back in leading a string of red-haired children of various sizes. "I'm Faura. Rolard-Cook left us with a cold-room full of prepared dishes, but those are all gone now and here's these invaders wanting a banquet tonight! I've called in my young'uns. Put them to work," she said, indicating a lanky youth of about eighteen or so. "This here's Fam." She pointed at younger boy with darker hair and fewer freckles. "Frandi." And last a short, sturdy girl with the brightest red hair of all. "This here's Deni."

Hlanan greeted each, then said, "Where are the aprons?"

Fam pointed out the servants' linen closet, which was full of table cloths, drying and polishing towels, aprons, and on a separate shelf the somewhat worn red hats of pastry makers and the yellow of cooks. Rolard, whoever he was, had neglected to take the badge of his office.

Maybe he was only hiding until the invaders left. Smart man, I thought as we helped ourselves to large aprons and yellow hats, me pulling mine over Nill's knit cap. My head was boiling under all that, but I'd endured simmering summers in thicker disguises than two hats, I reminded myself. Discomfort? Flames of Rue! I'd let myself get spoiled with a couple months of palace life.

"We'll make a line," Hlanan said to the redheads in an assured voice.

In a short time he had us working in an orderly fashion around a long prep table, measuring, mixing, buttering pans, and using the magic sparker to ignite the Fire Sticks under the brick ovens. As soon as they were all busy he said to me in the language of Thesreve, "You remember how to lay out tarts?"

"Sure, but—"

"We're out of time. I'm slipping out to see whose flags hang on the towers. If I know any of them, that's where I'll start."

Before I could put tongue to the thousand questions that crowded my mind he was gone. I had about two heartbeats to think myself safe—laying tarts on trays, folding in the mixtures and sprinkling the topping was easy—when Faura approached with a heavy step and confronted me.

Large and imposing, she frowned down at me as if she could reach in and pull kitchen wisdom out through my ears. "Where's the cook?"

"He's—"

"Inventory of course," she answered herself, but then gave me a worried scowl as she wiped a damp strand of hair off her forehead. "We put the meats to the spit, for that's simple enough, but what dishes are to go with them? Those foreign pigs have eaten up everything Rolard left prepared."

I hesitated, then thought, how hard could this be? We only needed to look busy until Hlanan did whatever it was he was going to do. "Rice, of course," I said, trying to sound authoritative. We'd seen enough rice terraces alongside the river before the road climbed up into these hills—and I remembered stealing from the spicy rice dishes when I'd lived in the attic above the Keprima scribes.

"Rice! Good. That ought to fill them up! The bags are through there," she said and bustled away, bawling at the skinny blond boy at the spits to stop gawking and tend to his job.

I headed for the dry goods chamber, which was cool, buzzing faintly with magic to ward dampness. Sacks full of rice sat right at hand. What now?

I hunted up a bowl from the stacked dishes in the room across, then slipped back to dip the bowl into the rice, letting the cool grains run through my fingers.

All right, let's be practical, I decided as I filled the bowl. This much was about as much as I ate. Add a handful or two for a grown man and then figure one bowlful for each eater.

I stuck my head into the main room and shouted at Faura, "How many of them are there?"

"Six so far, and each has an equerry. They said to expect five more."

Twenty bowls of rice, with an extra or two. But how was I to get to wherever it was to be cooked, and what was it cooked in? I strutted back into the kitchen, trying with all my might to looked assured. I stopped stout little Deni of the bright hair. "Put twenty bowls of rice into a cook pot," I said, handing her the bowl.

She gave me a wide-eyed look, but scampered off.

The trays of tarts had gone into the ovens, causing aromas to waft through the warm air. My stomach growled like ten mountain cats. I prowled the next room, which turned out to be stacked full of dishes, from fine porcelain to thick, unpainted clay.

"Here we be," Deni said breathlessly as she waved at a pot hanging from its iron arm perpendicular to a fire. The magic sparker hung on a hook. She took it down, bent to the stones beneath the pot, tapped the two sticks lying crosswise and flames shot up, the sparker glowing greenish blue. She hung it back up as the prickle of magic flashed over me like the touch of ant feet.

I marched to the pot, rubbed my hands down my apron, and with Deni standing there watching as if I were about to cast an important spell I picked up the waiting wooden spoon and stirred the rice, then swung the pot over the fire.

Deni was still watching.

I did some more stirring, this way, then that way. What was she waiting for?

What was I waiting for?

"Spices," I muttered to myself.

"No liquid?" Deni asked.

The rice was already beginning to smell singed.

"Of course," I said, striving to sound like I knew what I was doing. "Where I come from we warm the rice first."

"Oh! Shall I fetch water?"

"Yes, thank you."

I swung the pot back out again and gave the rice a brisk stir. Not burned, though some of the grains at the bottom had begun to turn a gold color. Phew! Where was Hlanan?

Deni returned lugging a bucket balanced against her thighs, her skinny shoulders tucked up under her ears. I took the bucket from her, hefted it with difficulty, and poured the water into the rice, jumped back from the steam, then poured in the rest. I wondered if that was enough — then her brother Frandi appeared carrying another bucket, so obviously they expected me to use that. I poured it in. And when Deni reappeared with a third bucket, I put that in too.

Now the cook pot was nearly brimming with water, a few rice grains floating around the top. Clearly no more water could fit in, so I said, trying to sound authoritative, "Good. That'll do. Now for the spices." And I marched away.

Ceramic jars filled every shelf in the spice room. The heady smell nearly made me sneeze. I breathed in slowly as I walked along the walls. This set of shelves here had sweet-smelling spices. That one, savory ones. I took down jars and peered into them, sniffing to find the delectable golden color I remembered from that seasoned rice I'd loved.

I found two golden spices, one more pungent than the other. They both smelled very different from what I remembered, but maybe the smell changed after the rice cooked. A baked apple certainly smelled differently than one still hanging on the tree, I reasoned, and I tapped out generous portions of both into a bowl. Then I went around adding in anything that smelled good.

When I was done, I carried the heaping bowl to my pot and threw in the spices. I was busy stirring them when Hlanan appeared, trailing a distinct scent of liquor.

"There you are," I exclaimed.

"I was right," he whispered. "They are nearly at one another's throats! What's that you've got there?"

"Rice." I scooped some rice from the bottom and lifted the stirring spoon. It came up with clots of spice.

"Oh, good thought," Hlanan said, turning his eyes obediently toward it, but I could tell he wasn't seeing the rice, the spoon, the pot, or even the fire. "Prince Banufel of Forfar is about to gallop off, find his followers, and decamp."

"How did you manage that?"

"By acting drunk."

"Acting?" I repeated, sniffing again. He reeked of whiskey.

"On my way out I took a wrong turn and found myself in the cold room where they keep the ale, beer, and other wood-casked liquors. And there was the prince's equerry, helping himself to what has to have been his third or fourth mug. He assumed I was someone else's equerry and invited me to join him. There were wooden cups hanging on the wall for measure, so I took one and helped myself. As he drank he complained and rambled. Most of what I had in my cup went down my front."

"Did you learn any secrets?"

"No, but I did learn that my guess was right. There's growing trouble between the factions. One commander was killed, another nearly so in squabbles up in the Pass. And it's worsened as they trudged cross country under mad orders. What mad orders?"

He paused then shook his head. "I'll have to find that out. I couldn't be too inquisitive lest he get suspicious. He was already angry. So when he started repeating the prince's put-upon whines about how everyone gets favored over the Farans, there is a conspiracy against them, and so on, all I did was nod my head."

"Sounds like he did all the questioning."

"And the answering." Hlanan flashed his rare grin. "So then he asked me what I knew and I rambled on, dropping ominous hints left and right how I'd heard there were secret meetings and how everyone said there were covert orders, and he leaped up and yelled, *That's just what the prince says! Everyone is talking, but not to us!* He then went straight from there to the conclusion that the others were conspiring to stick the Farans in the front lines of any coming battle, and I whined back, I don't know anything."

"So there are already rumors spreading, or did you invent some to spread?"

"I didn't invent anything. Didn't have to. All the gossip coming out of Forfar agrees on one thing: the prince is a coward. He likes violence, but only in the form of attacking from behind. Or watching from a position of safety. Probably why his name turns up somewhere behind all the conspiracies in that benighted kingdom. My guess is he joined this attack because he got caught one time too many."

"And Forfar got too hot for him?" I grimaced, remembering squalid Fara Bay.

"Judging by the sick look in the equerry's face, and the speed with which he raced off to tell the prince, I trust there might be one less mercenary commander before long. But the rest will not be so easy."

I wiped my sweaty face. A sense of headiness, almost but not quite dizziness passed through me, almost a hum. Heat? "Magic," I said.

Hlanan paused, frowning. "I felt that too. Can't be transfer magic, if Geric told the truth about wards. And I believe that from him," Hlanan whispered, thumbing his eyes then blinking rapidly. "I better go. There's one more commander down there who I know about, a renegade Thesrevan duke stripped of his title for murder. If I can get him to believe that Thesreve is about to catch up with him..." He started away, stopped short, then turned. "Will you be all right?"

"This is really easy. Even kind of fun." I waved at my cook pot.

His answer was a brilliant smile below those tired eyes, and he was off.

Fourteen

MY RICE HAD BEGUN to bubble nicely in a rolling boil, so I stirred it again, wondering what else I ought to do to it. It seemed very soupy. Of course. Vegetables!

I walked into the preparation part of the kitchen to find an argument going. Three red heads turned quickly my way. Faura crossed her arms over her formidable front. "This cook, he seems to want to be everywhere but in his kitchen," she said disapprovingly. "I think he's a tippler! Don't deny it. I smelt it."

I bit down so hard on a laugh that my ears nearly popped. But before I could speak, lanky Fam threw up his hands. "Who c-c-cares? He c-c-c-an be d-drunk as a duh-duke. Don't c-c-care. 'slong's we p-p-put food down for these th-th-f-for...invaders."

Faura said, "True." She turned her scowl on me. "We all want to wake up alive come morning. But none of us know kitchen work." She thumped her hand to her breastbone. "I'm the linens mistress. Fam here was third footman. The young'uns are runners. But we know what dishes used to be set out in the old days, and cheese pies was one. I think we ought to serve cheese pies, and we've left-over crust makings on account of using the last of the fresh apples and berries for the tartlets."

"D-d-duchess used to say. Ch-ch-cheese p-p-pies is for old p-p-people. Servants," Fam stated, with the intense concentration of someone who had repeated his point and was going to repeat it again. "These f-f-f-oreigners. W-w-ill w-w-want m-m-meats."

"We don't have more meats dressed."

"So we put what we have into other dishes to stretch 'em out," Deni chirped.

All turned to me expectantly, as if I knew the answer.

"Cheese pies are served in the Liacz army," I lied desperately.

Faura's scowl lessened to perplexity. "Well if warriors up north eat 'em, stands to reason these here warriors will eat 'em as well. Cheese pies it is, then. So tell us what to do."

"Do?" I repeated, thinking: put cheese in the crust and bake it?

"I think the tomatoes go on the bottom, then the onions, then the sweet-basil, and then the cheese," Frandi said, his throat-knuckle bobbing. "But Ma insists the onions go at the bottom."

"Onions, tomatoes, cheese," I said, trying to sound authoritative.

"And the sweet-basil?"

"Why, between the layers."

All faces cleared, and I breathed in relief.

"Do we do anything to the onions first?" Deni asked doubtfully.

"Cut them up," I said.

She eyed me with a frown that made her look more than ever like a miniature of her mother but went off to fetch onions, and I followed, hoping to find vegetables where the onions were kept. I should have known that winter was unlikely to furnish fresh vegetables short of the ones that last longer in the cool, dry room — the onions, cabbages large and small, and suchlike.

Deni took down a big jug with tomatoes preserved in something, and went off to the table where Frandi was setting out pie pans.

I returned and stared doubtfully at the cabbages. I didn't remember any cabbage in that seasoned rice dish I'd liked so much. But there had been tasty little red things whose name I had never learnt. Things the color of currants, or crackle berries. Almost as soon as I thought that, my gaze landed on big glass jars full of preserved crackle berries, and I thought, why not? Crackle berries were delicious when I picked them off hedgerows and ornamental shrub fences late in summer, and a beautiful deep red color. I was certain that the seasoned rice had not contained crackle berries, but why not try them in this dish? Rice was tasty, crackle berries were tasty, so...put them together.

I slopped a heaping load out of the jug into a big mixing bowl, noting that they were rather glutinous thus preserved, the smell a heady combination of liquor and berries, then lugged the container back to the fireplace and tossed the berries into the boiling rice. A good stir—and purple streaks began spreading through the watery rice mix, which had turned a startling color somewhere between gold and green.

Cooking seemed the simplest thing in the world. Why had I never tried it? Because nobody wants thieves in the kitchen, of course. I recollected distinctly being grateful for cabbage heels to gnaw when I was especially hungry, and thought back with wistful craving to the tender, delicately spiced cabbage I'd eaten in Imbradi.

Halfway back to the cold room that hair-prickling sensation of magic hummed through me again and I shivered. When my spine and neck hair stiffened I snatched at my yellow cook hat and knit cap to keep my hair from lifting in a cloud and inadvertently hurling them across the kitchen.

Magic was Hlanan's affair, I thought grumpily, reminded of my total failure at magic lessons. Maybe he was right about the why of it, and maybe he was just being kind, but whatever was going on, he was the best one to deal with it.

Hlanan returned, retying the apron around him, and pulling on the treasured yellow hat of a cook. "And that's another one gone," he whispered. "I suspect more than half his company are all under attainder of some sort in Thesreve."

I grimaced, remembering the summary justice in Thesreve—mostly having to do with public bonfires. Doing magic there was against the many, many laws.

"That's two, but I don't know how many might have arrived. They are all over the castle—"

"Where is the drunk runner?"

The angry voice stopped everyone in the kitchen. Hlanan stiffened and took a half-step in front of me, as if to shield me, but the newcomer's gaze passed over us, seeing only the aprons and yellow hats.

A burly fellow in military dress advanced into the room, complete to mailed jacket, with a broad belt around his middle holding both a sword and a long knife. Even his thick boots looked intimidating, his only affectation a carefully trimmed beard. "There's some snake of a scout or a runner mouthing off somewhere in this castle. If you see him, send for one of us," the man bawled, and I scowled at the basket I was holding rather than look at Hlanan.

"When's dinner?" the man snapped, and all the redheads turned out way.

"The tarts are due to come out of the oven," Hlanan said. "And we were just now discussing the possibility of a nut cake."

"We'll eat at the watch change," the man snarled. "See that it's ready!" He strode out, heels ringing like the drums of doom.

Hlanan looked around at the frightened gazes. "Good," he said in his soothing voice. "The tops are on those pies. What kind are they?"

"Cheese pies," I said proudly. "I told them how to make them."

"Let's get them into the ovens now that the tartlets are done. We'll serve those first, as cheese melts as quickly as the crust browns," Hlanan said. "Then we'll serve everything else as it finishes."

By then I was so hungry I was lightheaded. Faura detailed Deni to offload the tarts onto serving trays. I moved to help her, making four tarts vanish in eight gulps. That steadied me enough so that I didn't feel my head was about to float off my shoulders.

When I saw Hlanan blink rapidly as he stood between two tables, I picked up a couple more tarts and pressed them into his hand. "You have to eat something," I whispered. "All you've had today is whatever you drank in the wine closet."

"I know," he said, shutting his eyes. "We shouldn't. We might not have enough." But he ate them anyway, in two gulps.

Fam went off with his mother to check on the meats, which the blond spit boy was still lackadaisically tending, and I remembered my rice dish. Was it done yet? How long did rice take to cook, anyway?

Between the last time I'd seen it and now a vast change had

taken place. The rice had turned a strange color, reminding me of a summer thunderstorm before the first lightning strike. The rice grains surged and bubbled in slow gurgles, popping in craters that oozed and filled. An eye-watering smell rose from each pop.

I picked up the stirring spoon, dipped it, blew on the rice and then tasted it. My eyes bulged like those bubbles and began furiously watering as my tongue, mouth, and throat burst into flames. Or that's what it felt like.

What had I done? The rice had turned to mush. Tongue-burning mush! I gazed at that vast, heaving pot in dismay.

"It stinks."

I glanced up. Deni stood at my elbow, arms crossed exactly like her mother.

"It stinks," she stated, "like a sick skunk up and died in there, and 'twas seasoned by old boots. After a hunnert-day march."

It's supposed to smell like that? It'll smell better after it cooks? Before that steady, accusing gaze my lies dried right up.

"I am going to be a cook some day," Deni said. "Everybody loves food, and I will be a good cook. The best cook. *That* is one *mighty* stench, and 't looks worse." She pointed a freckled had accusingly at my burbling, heaving rice. "What kind of cook *are* you? We didn't even fry up the onions, and that's the best part of cheese pies, the smell of onions frying with the garlic."

I had been thinking rapidly. The truth might only get her into trouble if any of those invaders questioned her. And then get *us* into trouble.

"Do you want these invaders here?" I whispered.

Her frown turned to perplexity. "No!"

"The way I see it is, if we serve 'em good food, they'll want to stay."

"Oh-h-h." Her face cleared, and she grinned. "That's diff'rent."

"Sh-h-h-h, keep it a secret," I whispered.

In answer she picked another long wooden serving spoon from the rack beside the recessed fireplace, dipped it into the rice, and nibbled. Then shuddered. A lopsided smile. "It's *almost* tasty if you like hot spice and sweet from the berries at the same time."

"Then let's fix that," I suggested.

"I know!" She scampered off, and reappeared with a sizable

jug. She uncapped it, and the pungent odor of puckergrass soaked in vinegar walloped our noses. She poured. I stirred. It took both hands on that spoon to stir the dark green grass down into the mix. Brownish clots clung to the bottom of the spoon — the rice was burning!

I swung the pot out from the fire. That would have to do. Deni looked at the disgusting mess, heaving all over with suppressed laughter. I pushed one of the rolling tables over, fetched a stack of serving dishes, and together we ladled the rice into them. It looked...horrible.

"They'll take one glim and refuse to eat it," she whispered, tapping her eyes.

"So we mask the looks," I said. "How about cheese?" I'd seen several enormous cheese wheels. "Everything looks and tastes better with cheese."

Deni wiped her shiny face with the corner of her apron. "Sure as sun, that. I'll fetch the *old* cheese, the one that didn't turn out so good. If it melts on the top, it'll look pretty and no one will know until they bite in." Heaving silently with laughter again, she scurried away to fetch the cheese.

While Hlanan stirred the batter for nut cakes and Fam and his mother fixed the meat platters, Deni and I cut and laid thin slices of crackled old cheese over the steaming rice, and watched it melt into a lovely golden cap, hiding the weird-looking rice mush.

Clang! Clang Clang!

The redheads looked at each other. Faura said, "All the duke's fancy servers ran off. Up and took the ducal silver, too. You'll have to serve, Fam." She pointed at the oldest boy.

"N-n-n-ot m-m-m-e." The very idea seemed to make his stutter worse. He backed up, hands out as if pushing something away. "F-f-f-ootman." He thumped his scrawny chest. "Always f-f-f-follow. No t-t-talking."

"I'll help," I said. "And if anybody wants to talk, they can talk to me." Nobody was chasing me, for once, and maybe I could even overhear something for Hlanan.

"We'll tend the carts from outside the dining hall," Faura said, indicating Deni and Frandi. "After we fetch out the cheese pies."

"Thank you," Hlanan whispered to me as he quickly put

together his cakes in their pans.

While he finished setting up the nut cakes, Fam and Deni pulled the cheese pies from the oven. They looked golden and perfect, and smelled kind of oniony, but otherwise fine. In went the nut cakes.

Then Faura and the two younger children helped push the serving carts down the hall to a great double door, and formed into a line to pass Fam and me the platters. I left Fam to handle the big meat platters, as the smell rising off made my stomach lurch. I carried cheese pies on a tray.

We walked into dining hall, a long vaulted chamber decorated with tall tapestries, with two chandeliers hanging high over the long, empty table below the dais. The shorter table raised on a marble dais had already been in use, as it was covered with shoved-aside platters dirty with crumbs and congealed juices. The gathered commanders didn't seem to mind; several of them looked so drunk that they probably would not have notice if we'd served chicken feed in troughs.

Fam and I walked along the table, setting our serving dishes down.

Scarcely had we set down a serving dish before it was attacked by reaching spoons.

When the meats and the cheese pies had been delivered we returned to carry the rice and cabbage dishes in.

"Hey!" A huge man grabbed Fam by the front of his shirt. "These onions are *raw*!"

"Same here!"

"So's this one!"

The frightened boy looked my way. I said, "These are what the army eats in Liacz."

"Yes," Deni shrilled, poking her head in the open door. "They love that rice in Liacz!"

"Here, let's try that."

"It looks like a sick horse walked by, under this cheese."

"Smells like it, too!"

"Ah! Ah! Ah! My tongue! Gimme that ale!" A glare. "Are you trying to poison us?"

My heartbeat thundered. "It's a prize dish in Liacz," I said.

"They eat it by the cartload. They say," I added, getting an idea, "only the toughest get that down, and it makes them five times tougher."

"No wonder those boys are always fighting," someone muttered into his ale cup.

They fell on the meats.

Fam and I retreated, he looking at me fearfully. "M-m-m-aybe t-t-try southern r-r-recipes," he said as we rejoined the family.

Recipes? I thought as we pushed the carts back.

"Let's get the tarts to them," Faura muttered, giving me a strange look. Then she scowled at her daughter, who once again heaved in silent laughter like a boiling pot.

"*And* more ale," Frandi put in.

Hlanan had finished clearing off the prep table when we returned. All the redheads went off to fetch more bottles and jugs of drink. I sidled up to Hlanan. "What's a recipe? Fam says I should review southern recipes."

Hlanan stared at me. "You really don't know what a recipe is?"

"How should I? This is the first time I've been in a kitchen longer than it took to run through and steal something to eat."

"It's a list of ingredients, in specific amounts, with instructions on putting them together and how long to cook the dish."

"Oh, like the magic spells the Mage Council tried to teach!"

"Very much so. What did you use to make your rice dish?"

I told him how I'd begun, and he shook his head. "Didn't it occur to you to start over?"

"And waste food?" I asked, appalled. "My lies covered it all right. Deni thinks we have a plan. It's a very good idea, actually. We stink 'em out with horrible foods."

"They're far more likely to fall on us with all the wrath of disappointed hunger," he said, mopping absently at his apron. "Phew, there are few smells I hate worse than stale whiskey. I can't even smell your rice past my own reek."

I shrugged. "Have you a plan for your part?"

"I have." He pointed at the oven, as Faura led her troop past, each toting jugs and bottles. "I'm going to serve up the nut cakes with some lemon sauce I discovered untouched. If I mix a bit of cinnamon in it I can make a pretense of adjusting it to taste for each of them, and perhaps get some conversation going. Or listen to them, if I'm lucky enough to catch them talking of something substantive."

"Because no one ever notices servants."

"Right. The more I can learn about these fellows' intentions — what they say to each other, and what they think as individuals — the better chance I'll have with them one by one."

He went off to warm his sauce, watched anxiously by Faura.

This first quiet moment gave me a chance to breathe and to think about her and her family. Why hadn't they run the way Geric and his followers had? Because this was their home. I could hear the answer in Hlanan's voice.

There was that word *home* again. Yet another of the many things I did not understand, I thought uncomfortably before Fam pounded back in. "The tarts are all gone!"

A tall equerry appeared right behind him, glops of purple and green mush dripping off his ears, his face, and all down his battle tunic. "I was to tell you they're still hungry, and not to serve anything that tastes like the scrapings off the bottom of a bait bucket." He stamped out.

"Take the cakes out and I'll come round with the sauce," Hlanan said.

Frandi backed away, his fists under his chin. "No, no, I'm not going back, the way they're howling."

Faura pointed at Fam. "We'll take 'em. They smell good, these nut cakes."

Hlanan stood at one of the fires, a shallow pan set on a tripod thing over a fire as he stirred constantly, sniffing, tasting, then adding in pinches of cinnamon and other bits of spice. So that was how you did it!

I was going to comment when another of those magical tremors vibrated through me, as though a thousand invisible bees crawled up and down my bones.

I looked Hlanan's way, but he stirred rapidly, testing his sauce with a tiny spoon. If he felt it, it clearly didn't matter to him.

Fam and his mother had begun taking the cakes out of the oven. Frandi hopped about, fetching clean dishes to serve them on, and Deni watched Hlanan intently.

Since they were all busy I decided to investigate. Maybe I could learn something and surprise Hlanan!

I waited until Faura and her son rolled the cakes off to the dining hall, Hlanan following them with the sauce. Then I kicked off those horrible shoes and took off my apron and hat, as by then I was overheated enough to boil all on my own.

As soon as I stepped into the hallway, delightful cool air enveloped me. Breathing deeply, I walked aimlessly, unsure where I was going and what I was going to do when I got there. But I wanted to get away from the hot kitchen as much as I wanted to seek the source of that peculiar tickle of magic and then impress Hlanan with my discovery.

The lower hallways had been pretty well mucked up by muddy boots. Here and there furniture had been shoved aside or even overturned. Presently I found a marble stairway and paused, sniffing the air. I sensed magic above, so up I ran, then slowed when I found myself in another corridor. Most of the doors stood open. The sun had not quite set, the shadows revealing the angular shapes of furniture and lamps and cabinets tossed about as if impatient looters had been through, looking for small items to carry off.

I stopped in one room when a bigger-than-life painting caught my eye. I recognized Duchess Morith in that proud figure, probably painted when she was young. She wore a fancy rose and silver brocade gown with an underdress of pale green, and emeralds and diamonds, but it was difficult to make out more details than that as someone had used the painting for target practice. The canvas puckered all over with holes. I counted three right between her eyes.

I passed along.

The subtle buzz of magic drifted and faded, elusive as a scent on a mountain breeze. I wandered another floor into hallways decorated with statuary, the ceilings painted with stylized frames, stars, and birds. Carved doors stood open to rooms far more opulent, and surprisingly untouched, but then fine rugs and furnishings and tapestries were harder for light-fingered looters to bundle off. The heavy, stale air carried a whiff of familiar scent that instantly called Geric to mind. Of course. This had been his home.

I resisted the urge to hunt out his rooms in order to burgle them thoroughly, and pushed on until I reached the end. Here the hall debouched into a round stairwell leading up to the tower.

At the foot of the stairway something glittered. Gems! A jeweled armband, man sized, and on the step above, a couple of rings. I bent to pick them up, then stopped halfway in my stoop, my gaze landing on an exquisite gold necklet that lay on a step farther up. Clearly some thief had dropped loot on the way out.

I passed by the rings and the armband, drawn to the necklace of beautifully worked gold. It had been delicately etched to resemble the overlapping scales of a lizard or snake, in intricate pattern. Gold could not be sinuous, of course, but the artist managed to convey that effect.

Gold and beauty, beauty and gold.

I'd never been able to pass either.

I took another step. Then stopped.

I'd told Hlanan I'd stop stealing. He had never condemned me—never said anything at all—but I sensed that it bothered him. And I still carried several of Geric's jewels among my thief tools. Selling those in the right place would keep me comfortable for at least a season, maybe longer if I ended up alone again.

I didn't want to be alone again. That meant trying to live up to ideals I was not accustomed to, but instinctively knew were right. My fingers stretched out, hovering above the golden necklet, then I sighed. I didn't really need it, did I? And Hlanan would be so disappointed.

So I straightened up and it was then that I got that neck-hair lifting sense of being watched.

I backed to a wall and looked around. Sniffed. Listened. Until now I'd assumed the silence to be that neutrality peculiar to an empty series of rooms, but the notion that someone might be hiding somewhere filled the shadows with menace, and danger tensed my muscles.

I sidled along the wall to the corner, sniffing, listening, staring into every shadow.

Then a soft rustle, a step, a familiar scent—not the stale scent of empty rooms, but personal. Living.

"Geric."

I wasn't aware I'd spoken until he said, "Well met, thief."

I started, glaring at the top of the stairs. That was Geric, all right, coming down at a leisurely pace. He wore dark clothing, blending into the shadows except for the pale waves of his long hair.

"You said you were going away!" I exclaimed stupidly.

"I lied." His grin dared me to make anything of that.

"What I cannot determine," he drawled as he continued down the steps, "is if you are running Hlanan Vosaga or if he is running you. Or you're both being run by that despicable Ilyan Rajanas. At all events, His Royal Highness of Alezand is not here now."

"Running?"

"Is that the best you can do, Lhind the Spy? Pretend ignorance? I'm disappointed."

"Spy!" I exclaimed, and laughed. "Who would I spy for?"

"Whoever pays you most," he retorted.

This conversation made less sense with every word. I decided to ask my question, for Hlanan's sake, then I was done. "Was that you doing magic?" I asked, my heartbeat thundering. I poised to run.

"What do your Hrethan powers tell you?" he retorted, taking another step.

I backed away a step, keeping the same distance between us. I wasn't sure how much threat he was, given his recent wounds. At least I didn't see any throwing knives in his hands.

"Not much," I said. "That's what I came to find out." I eyed him. "Did you do something to Tir?"

"Dropped it with a stone spell. Entirely too interfering." He laughed, his manner changing. "And here I've been, trying to lift wards," he said. "Do you know anything about that? If you do, all these gems are yours." He flicked his fingers toward the stuff lying on the steps. "Earn your reward for once. See how you like it." He smiled.

I did not trust that smile. "I don't know anything about wards."

"You don't seem to know much of use at all outside of your shape change, and that's useless here, is it not?"

"I know enough to defend myself," I retorted. "I've got voice cast and mind thrust."

His eyes widened, but then he laughed again. "Your threats are as convincing as your lies. Here, why don't you make yourself useful. Pick these up for me and you can have half." He touched his shoulder. "I have trouble bending."

I could believe he had to be feeling those wounds still, though until now he had never made any reference to them. It felt odd — false, somehow, this strange shift from sarcasm to joviality, insult to affable. Confiding about the wounds. And who would give away precious gems to get them picked up?

"I don't want any jewels," I said loftily and backed away. It was time to let Hlanan know that Geric had returned. Maybe he could figure out this odd conversation.

"Come here," Geric snapped.

"No!" I ran.

Clang-g-g!

The bell at the front gate began to ring wildly, startling us both. Another bell farther away began to echo the tuneless cacophony.

I stumbled a step then caught my balance, my tail wrenching inside those wretched trousers of Nill's. I didn't stop until I reached the stairway; Geric might have been able to run me down before he and Rajanas had fought, but he wasn't fast now. I stopped at the landing, then jumped and kicked my way out of Nill's clothes, my crushed and wrinkled drape fluttering free.

I hopped onto the bannister and slid down on both feet, leaped to the bottom, and ran. When I looked back again, Geric was gone.

I fled down those long halls, caught a bannister and swung myself around to shoot me down the last, mud-slick hallway, then skidded into the kitchen. The heat was smothering. I threw the folds of my drape back over my shoulders and shoved my sleeves all the way up as Faura took one look at me and the crockery she held dropped with a crash.

Fam's voice cracked. "The c-c-court is filled with wuh, war-r-r, with *Ravens!*"

At first I thought he meant a swirl of black, cawing birds. Then I remembered the elite force of the empress.

Justeon was here! Only he hadn't commanded Ravens, had he?

"Where's Hluh—where's the cook?" I asked.

"In the dining hall serving out the cakes," Faura said, hands clasped tightly at her breast. "Ravens!" She uttered the word on a deep, outward breath. Then, "Children, to the cellar. We'd better hide and wait out whatever's going to happen."

Fam set aside the broom he'd picked up to sweep together the broken crockery, and walked away wordlessly.

Frandi moaned, "Aw, I want to see the Ravens!" His mother's answer was to take hold of his shoulder and hustle him away.

With a last worried look at me, Deni followed her mother in one direction while I pounded in the other.

I reached the dining hall and bolted through the open doors. One of the drunks bawled, "That there's a Hrethan! What're they doing here?"

"She's not blue," another stated in a slurred voice. "I thought they were blue."

"Grab her!" That was Geric, one hand clutching his shoulder as he stepped through a discreet door that opened directly onto the dais. As all the feasters swiveled to look at me, he shouted, "Take them both." He pointed at Hlanan.

Two big equerries (one with bits of purple rice still stuck to his outfit) leaped to take Hlanan's arms. I froze. What should I do? What should I do? My hand plunged under my tunic for my thief tools, but once again none of them were the least use here, even my liref. If I used the entire bag to put them all to sleep I wouldn't get out before breathing it too.

And that's when the big doors at the foot of the long table burst open, and the Ravens moved in with smooth efficiency.

I didn't hesitate. The Ravens were a whole lot safer than Dhes-Andis! I bolted for them and didn't stop until at least a dozen of them stood between me and the dais.

The Ravens halted, swords out, the back row behind me with arrows knocked. On the dais the commanders, drunk or not, had scrambled for their own weapons.

I glared from Geric to those holding Hlanan. If anyone dared try to hurt him, I'd...I'd...I quailed at the idea of using mind thrust. Not only was it dangerous to the target, it was also dangerous to me, a power I'd only used once, and it had taken me days to recover.

Voice cast I could use only if I knew someone's vocal harmonies, what I'd thought of as their range. Those holding Hlanan, no. Geric, yes, but to control someone for a few heartbeats was only useful if I gave a specific command. And it didn't last past a breath.

Still, I could try! I steadied myself, but lost my focus when Justeon marched in, chainmail jingling. "Lay down your arms," he ordered. "The castle is surrounded, and your camps are very shortly to be surrounded as well."

He caught sight of Geric, who said, "I am Geric Lendan, Prince of the Golden Circle, and Duke of Thann. This is my duchy. You have no rights here."

"Aranu Crown received a petition from the united guilds of Thann," Justeon said. "Claiming that you had abandoned them, and begging the empire to protect them from invaders."

"They are here by my leave," Geric said, his voice tight with anger. He made a visible effort and assumed a more courtly tone. "If you will surrender that Hrethan spy and thief, we will return your empire spy to you, and I will consider us quits. Withdraw peaceably, and there will be no further trouble."

"No," Hlanan said, wrenching at the hands holding him, but he was no match for two burly fellows. His cook hat fell off.

One of the commanders turned from one to the other and bawled, "The cook?" Another even more affronted back-and-forth stare. "The *cook* is the one who sent a third of our force running for home! He's the one busy driving a wedge between the rest of our command."

The drunks glared at Hlanan, a couple fingering their swords. "The cook was the one?"

"I'll dispatch him myself!"

"He's a spy for the empire," Geric said.

"Release him," Justeon called over their bluster. "Prince Geric, permit me to repeat: this castle is surrounded. Those forces who crossed the river from Keprima are being flanked at this moment. I believe it is the empire that will dictate terms, and those terms are direct orders from Aranu Crown—"

"Perhaps," Geric cut in, "this is the time to inform you that the forces you are so busily surrounding are only the decoy. There is a much larger force ready to be dispatched."

Justeon said, "You can be certain that the Empress has issued orders to all secondary garrisons to be prepared for such an eventuality."

Geric's forehead gleamed; his head tipped. And though the light was uncertain, as no one had lit the chandeliers overhead and the only illumination in the fast-vanishing day were the wildly streaming candles on the high table, I saw him pale.

"Before that," he said slowly, "but before that, Aranu Crown should know that in its retreat from Idaron Pass south to Keprima and then east, this army has been under orders to lay down certain talismans in every village and town."

I was about to shout LIAR! but Hlanan said in his reasonable voice, "How could you know that? You were with us until three days ago."

Geric gave him a distracted glance, and I had it. A horrible sensation shivered through all my nerves as I thought, *He's hearing voices.*

No, he's hearing HIS voice.

And so I said to Geric, "You can run."

I hated the fellow, and I knew he loathed me at least as much, but the pulse of urgency came out of a far greater fear and hate: the idea of Dhes-Andis in my mind.

Geric's chin lifted as he gazed across the heads of both sides. "Too late," he said in a low voice, almost a whisper, but it carried in that stone hall. "Years too late. Once he has you, you will never be free."

Hlanan's head snapped around, his lips parting, but Geric addressed Justeon. "If you want a demonstration, I am to inform you that His Imperial Serenity Emperor Jardis Dhes-Andis would like nothing more than to comply. The talismans are harmless unless the enchantment keyed to them is released. At that time they will spread neverquench flames everywhere they are placed—attics, basements, barns, barracks, dormitories. Mines, lumberyards, crowded streets, palaces. Tell your imperial mistress that I stand ready to release that enchantment, and this: she ought to know by now that when His Imperial Serenity bestirs himself to make a promise, he always carries it out. He has never yet made an empty threat."

Halfway through this speech Justeon took a round hand mirror from his belt pouch. From the faint greenish glow scintillating from it, and the care with which he handled it, I knew the mirror carried magic.

Justeon murmured softly, then laid the mirror gently on the floor and stepped back.

A starburst of magic spiraled up into millions of tiny specks of greenish light, then coalesced into a luminous image of the Empress, Aranu Crown, dressed in robes of state.

She spoke, her image seeming to gaze straight at Geric. "I have been until this moment conversing with my allies east and north of Sveran Djur. An invasion of this continent shall bring a united action against you, Jardis Dhes-Andis. And you should know that I, too, never make empty threats. Is that what you truly desire?"

Geric's head bent, then lifted. "His Imperial Serenity desires me to inform you that that game is yet to be played. At the moment, all he wishes is the return of his long-lost niece, the half-Hrethan you call Lhind. Apparently she holds importance to you, too?"

The Empress's image stilled. Then she crossed her arms, and uttered a bark of a laugh. "Hah! That urchin is nothing but trouble," the empress stated. "Even my fool of a scribe there, who demonstrates a lamentable tendency to adopt ill-conditioned pets, admits that she is a liar and a thief with no morals or manners. He is already in trouble for exceeding his orders. Keep him if you like."

The imperial hand waved dismissively at Hlanan as every word struck my heart with splinters of ice. Hlanan stared back at his mother, his profile pale and still as marble as the equerries gripped his arms.

Geric shrugged. "I've no orders concerning him." His tone changed. "And he did me signal service."

As Geric motioned for the equerries to free Hlanan, the Empress lifted her voice, every utterance cold and precise. "Take the thief and get you gone from my Kherval. Which," she added in an acid undertone, "is shortly to include Thann. Geric Lendan, you are declared foresworn, and as such are herewith stripped of title and holdings. Family Lendan will be summoned to hear this judgment...."

The Ravens had closed around me, and though I looked about wildly for any means of escape, I found none.

Without a glance at the Empress still sonorously pronouncing her decree, Geric advanced on me. I wasn't certain he even heard her as the Ravens closed in, permitting no escape. I poised for a leap, but the chandeliers hung out just of reach. And beyond the immediate circle of Ravens stood more with arrows still fitted to bows. They'd easily shoot me out of the air even if I could spring that high.

Hlanan tried to shove his way past the Ravens, but they fended him off easily. Sick with terror, I drew ready magic from all around me and fashioned it into the arrow of voice cast as Geric closed the distance. I drew in a breath, hurled the magic — and staggered in reaction as it splashed in coruscating fingers as if it had hit a wall.

So *that* was a ward.

I fumbled desperately for my bag of liref, though there were far too many of them to dose, as Geric blinked, staring at me in shock. "You do know voice cast," he murmured, faltering a step. He frowned at me as if trying to bring me into focus, but blinked rapidly. His fingers blurred. Quick as a heartbeat, greenish light flickered as something golden and sinuous snaked through the air and snapped around my neck.

Transfer magic wrenched me away from that place of desolation and betrayal.

Fifteen

I FELL TO MY knees, every muscle contracting. I wanted to be sick, but I couldn't catch enough breath for that. The reaction lasted only a few heartbeats, but it seemed eternal. Then my breath came in a shuddering gasp, leaving me trembling.

When the nausea receded enough to permit me to move my limbs, I tore at that necklet and pain, hotter than fire, sheered through my nerves.

I splatted on my face.

Once again I crowed for breath. For a second eternity — this one much longer — the struggle to breathe overwhelmed me. Gradually sight returned: shades of green in a worked pattern. Sensation: I lay on a soft carpet.

Sound: quiet laughter.

My poor, lacerated nerves chilled with recognition. Though I had only heard that voice mentally, I knew that resonant baritone. It belonged to Jardis Dhes-Andis, Emperor of Sveran Djur, Empire of a Thousand Islands.

My shoulder blades crawled as I forced my hands under me. Swaying with dizziness, I blinked away the blur in my vision.

Soothing green light resolved into pale-barked argan trees, lower branches gracefully espaliered in perfect symmetry and the upper branches pleached so that the silver leaves formed a canopy overhead, warmed by sunbeams slanting down through a domed ceiling of glass worked in arabesque patterns.

And below it, seated in an elegant wing-backed chair, a man. I scrubbed my grimy sleeve across my tear- and snot-smeared face, and my eyes met a pair of slanted eyes the same color and shape of my own, the light brown of mead in the sunlight.

The Emperor Jardis Dhes-Andis was very tall, or that might have been the effect of his layered robes. They were made of silk of a complicated weave threaded in white and gold that highlighted his golden skin, two of the panels ending in long golden tassels.

The only dark colors were the hint of a high-collared black shirt under all those layers—which framed something that glinted gold, and diamond, at his throat—and his black hair, worn long and tied back. He wore a thin golden coronet that dipped to a V between his brows.

My head swam when I tried to turn it, and I flopped onto my back. "Go ahead and kill me if you're going to," I croaked when memory crashed through the throbbing in my skull.

Much as my body hurt, betrayal hurt so much worse.

Again the laugh. "You are a pathetic object, are you not?"

Miserable in body, mind, and soul, I found enough sting in those words to mutter a retort, "Then send me back."

"After the trouble you've put me to? More than I have tolerated for most circumstances. That in itself was entertaining, to see how far I was willing to exert myself." Dhes-Andis's voice's tone shifted from warm and amused to dispassionate. "But I am convinced you will prove worth the effort."

"I'm not convinced of anything at all," I retorted, my voice croaking from the effects of the transfer magic, my gaze on those trees. As if not seeing him would make him go away. "You lied to me!"

He laughed again. "When? How?"

"You said you were my father, and you don't look much older than me." Whatever age that might be, I couldn't help thinking.

"There are seven years between us," he said, still sounding amused. "And you are the one who leaped to that curious conclusion. I merely let your assumption stand, if it would enable me to bring you home the faster."

"So that blond man in my memory, he's really my father? And the Blue Lady, my mother? Or was that another trick?"

"Rid your mind of those selfish fools who abandoned you and ran off. You are home again, and ahead of you is a new life, one worthy of your birth. Come along."

A soft thud—a cat hit the ground and leaped over me—then cloth whispered as Dhes-Andis rose to his feet.

My neck hairs prickled. I lay there angry and miserable, staring up at the trees. "Those fire things with the neverquench spell. That was real?"

"Oh yes. It would have made quite a spectacle, viewed from the mountains. Until the smoke obliterated it all, of course, and they summoned mages to douse it. After the cities and towns turned to dust. Get up, Elenderi."

"That's not my name," I snapped.

Fire-hot agony seared through me, far worse than mere transfer magic. Through it spoke that remorseless voice. "Long ago I lost my interest in witnessing the effects of pain. It's predictable, and too much of it robs the wits entirely, leaving the subject uselessly craven."

I gasped for breath, curling in a ball as the throbbing unstrung my muscles and turned my bones to water.

"But we discovered centuries ago that such correction is the purest as well as the most effective means of cauterizing that which is uncivilized in our natures. And you are uncivilized, are you not? Get to your feet and come along."

Somehow I found the strength to roll to my hands and knees. Trembling in every limb, I fumbled my feet under me. The throbbing began to fade, but its echo weakened me to a stunned dread. I straightened up, blinking pain tears away.

"Now."

It had been stupid to refuse to face him after that first quick look, as if he would vanish, and with him take away Aranu Crown's betrayal. I longed with all my strength to return to the Thann kitchens, Hlanan by my side working at his pastry and worrying at his plan to avert a war.

Before he stood in silence while his imperial mother flung me away as trash.

Anger flooded through me, as searing in its own way as Dhes-Andis's "pure correction." Anger enabled me to tighten my middle and raise my head so I could glare at my enemy. My stomach boiled with resentment and pain and fury and horror as he lifted his hand toward the door, his attitude best described as ironic patience.

He moved with a controlled, noiseless step, those long golden tassels swinging above his toes. His control called Rajanas to mind; a dip and a deft, graceful swipe of his train and he led the way out at a pace making it plain whatever else he did with his day besides torturing me, there was more to it than lolling around on a throne.

My strength and wits trickled back as I jogged awkwardly at his heels, the last of that lightning receding in decreasing throbs through my watery joints. I tried looking at my surroundings for any means of escape, taking in high vaulted ceiling of white marble veined with silver. Lancet arched windows divided into three panes gave onto a view of night sky.

"This will be your suite, Elenderi."

"My name is Lhind," I retorted, and when he glanced down at me, I sucked in my breath, shoulders to my ears, and braced.

He said, "I will tolerate waywardness as long as it amuses me, but two things I will not tolerate: insolence and lies. Understood?"

I glowered.

His voice softened. "Do you understand me?" He raised two fingers, twitched one, and heat flashed white-hot at my neck and seared through my nerves.

"Yes!" I squawked, dancing around on my toes and flapping my arms, though I knew the fire was magical, not real flame.

"An excellent start, Imperial Princess Elenderi." Each word was enunciated deliberately as the doors opened and silent servants stood to either side. "This was once your great-grandmother Lison's personal suite," Dhes-Andis said, taking no notice of the door-openers; I wondered if he would have walked nose first into one of those carved doors had not the servants known when to open them. And then what? Hours of torture?

My wits fled when The Imperial Enemy turned his palm outward. "Kal will be your steward."

Framed against a grand half-circle of tall lancet windows stood a dark-haired young man whose brown gaze was so familiar that once again my nerves sheered hot and then cold. *Not familiar, not,* my brain wailed; gratefully I noted his golden skin instead of brown, and his slanted eyes, and his long face with the pointed chin. I had never seen him before, ever. He, like the door-openers, wore a robe of muted gray pleated once in the front, high necked, though when he moved metal glinted above the collar.

Not familiar.

"Kal heads the staff who will see to your needs. He will also," Dhes-Andis's voice dropped a note into that amused detachment I had so distrusted during summer, "communicate my orders. Should you choose to ignore them, he and your staff shall feel the consequences of your actions. Responsibility," he measured the words, "comes with consequences, Your Imperial Serenity."

My breath hitched; the evil emperor swept out, the servants closing the door noiselessly behind him.

I turned quickly away from Kal, still shivering with reaction. Spy, I thought. He was there to spy on me.

That thought steadied me. It gave me a goal — resistance — and an enemy to outwit, to despise.

"If the Imperial Princess would honor us with any needs or wishes, it is our honor to obey," Kal said, bowing low.

He spoke Djuran, of course. I wanted to pretend I didn't understand it, but where would that get me? The Emperor of Evil knew I comprehended languages as soon as I heard them.

I scowled at the fine woven rug under my grimy bare toes. "I'm not an imperial princess," I said. "My name is Lhind. I like my name. I picked it myself."

Of course he didn't answer. And of course he'd be blabbing that to the imperial stinker as soon as he could. If that selfsame I. S. wasn't already earing in by some magical means. My scalp itched. My entire body itched as if invisible bugs crawled all over me.

I needed to retreat, to be alone. "Bath," I said.

Kal led me through an arched door to a tiled chamber that made Rajanas's splendid guest bath look like a tin tub at a dockside inn: an entire pool, shaped to look like something you'd find in nature, surrounded with more of those beautiful trees, their roots mysteriously tidied away below the tile, their branches trailing upward in graceful arcs so symmetrical and artistic they looked more like drawings than real trees. Fresh steaming water cascaded down a rocky incline covered with orchids whose blossoms represented every hue in the rainbow. In the opposite corner stood a beautiful porcelain stove, not as large as the one in the main room.

The door shut noiselessly behind me, felt in the stilling air currents.

I was alone.

Alone.

As if someone had gouged out my heart and slung a javelin of ice down my spine, I dropped to my knees, forearms pressed over my ribs. I choked on rib-shuddering sobs I could no more control than I could rip mountains up by the roots, or hurl this palace into the sky.

I don't know how long that lasted. It seemed an eternity. Every time I tried to get hold of myself my mind returned to the empress's words, to Hlanan standing there, shocked and silent while she threw me to the enemy.

When at last I got control of my breathing I lay in a damp, grimy, miserable ball, aware of the chuckle of running water nearby. I forced myself to sit up and shrug out of my filthy, rumpled drape, my thief tools falling to the floor in a soft thud. Feverishly I picked them up, looking around for a hiding place until it sank in that I was in far more trouble than these silly things would get me out of. I could knock those servants out there into slumber with the liref, use the lock picks (assuming the doors were even locked) but Dhes-Andis could lift a finger and smite me into witlessness through this horrible *thing* around my neck.

I dropped the bag of thief tools and knelt there, tugging and yanking at that golden choker until the burn-magic flashed.

I gave up, and slid into the warm water.

Physically it was bliss. But mind and heart still lay in smoking pieces. I floated on the water, my breath shaky as I gazed up through another small domed ceiling, the glass pieced in stylized orchid shapes.

I was alone, but for how long? I *had* to think!

Not about that betrayal. It hurt too much. The echoing flare in my nerves when I moved urged me to remember my immediate danger. The first thing to do was to get distance between me and that steward-who-was-not-familiar.

What was Hlanan doing?

I shut my eyes. That didn't matter anymore. Aranu Crown made that much really clear.

The instinct to physically get away—as if I could escape my thoughts—forced me out of that delightful bath. I shook all over, fluffing fuzz, hair, and tail.

I was going to put my grimy old drape back on, habit from spending most of my life changing my clothes once a year. But when I bent to pick it up, I spied a fluffy robe thing lying on a marble bench, and pulled that on instead. In my months away from concentrated grime I had come to like cleanliness if I could get it, and that drape *really* needed a cleaning frame. I swept it and the tools up, looked about, then remembered that staff I'd been threatened with. I set the thief tools down again.

Time to test the limits, I thought grimly, tugging the robe, which, made for someone larger, dragged behind me. I marched into the main room with its enormous bank of windows.

My gaze slid past Kal-who-was-*not*-familiar. Remembering the Emperor of Evil's threats about insolence, I said as politely as I could, "My drape can be taken away, as I don't see a cleaning frame, but the, ah, tools, I would like left alone."

Everybody bowed.

"As for me, I am very much afraid that the heat in this chamber is not tolerable for one of my kind. Would you please open all those windows?"

I'd framed a question, but Kal clearly did not hear one. He sprang to the windows one by one as if I'd uttered the direst of threats. At the current of icy air that rolled in, I hid a grin.

An enormous bedchamber opened off the main room, with its own curve of windows (now open). More of those perfectly trained trees grew under the bank of windows, opposite a huge canopied bed.

I condemned the bed with a point of my finger. "My kind only sleep in hammocks," I said as civilized as possible.

My grimy drape was born away in one direction. The bed was dismantled and more gray-clad servants came in with approximations of hammocks.

Apparently no one in the Empire of a Thousand Islands knew what a hammock was, or else "imperial" people did not lower themselves to such things: they offered me slung brocaded quilts and netted ropes of silk, all of which probably would have worked fine, but I sadly shook my head to each one.

I counted twelve silent servants moving about under Kal's watchful gaze as I stood near the windows in the dramatic currents of air and watched the suite dismantled a piece of furniture at a time.

The suite chilled in spite of the stove, which may have been fueled by magical Fire Sticks the way that most places (except Thesreve) do, but the cursed thing on my neck hummed with so much magic that I was not able to sense magic's presence or absence beyond it.

A new stream of servants entered with armloads of costly silken clothes. "I fear these stiff shoulder things will be uncomfortable...this is made for a much taller person...I cannot possibly wear that...there is no place for my tail...." I enjoyed finding fault with every single item.

At length the servants beetled off to hunt up more stuff and I withdrew to the alcove to the right of the bank of windows, where someone had laid out a repast on a low blackwood table inlaid with interlocked patterns of three in gold. A single silken cushion tasseled in gold sat on the floor below the table.

The windows had been judiciously opened there, too, in what seemed to be a tower room, judging by the circle of windows surrounding me. I stood where the currents of cold air roiled and snapped, fighting the warm air from the stove.

Hunger woke inside me, a ravening wolf. It seemed a thousand years had passed since I'd gobbled down those tarts. Hlanan's tarts—

I shut away the anguish and sat on the cushion, glaring at the thin porcelain bowls, in which someone had thoughtfully arranged a wide variety of nuts: scorched ones, fresh ones, and nuts candied and mashed into crisply baked bites. I did not know the names of many of them.

I loathed the idea that Dhes-Andis knew my food preferences. Geric could be thanked for that, mostly likely, I thought, hatred burning through me.

Or did Hrethan mostly eat nuts? That had been one of the many questions I had wanted to ask other Hrethan during my time in Erev-li-Erval. And now I knew why they had stayed away from me. Or I was kept from them, I thought bitterly, as Aranu Crown's contemptuous words echoed mercilessly in memory.

I munched defiantly as cold, sleety air blew steadily in, wet enough for me to feel the bite of ice. I fluffed out my fuzz, glad of the meal warming me from inside. When the hunger pangs abated, the memories flooded afresh, and in a futile attempt to escape them I slipped from the alcove, passed the servant standing outside it, and slipped into the great room, which was lit by its glowglobes on carved pedestals.

Since I was barefoot my steps made no noise; when I crossed the room I glimpsed an unobtrusive side alcove between the grand chamber and the bedroom. There in the shadows, Kal's profile caught my eye. He sat on a bench, eyes closed, head down, the skin below the short, thin sleeves of his tunic rough in the way of hairless people enduring bitter cold, his hands pressed tightly between his knees. His profile eloquent with misery.

Angry as I was with Aranu Crown I could not prevent myself from remembering what Hlanan had once said about servants and their powerlessness.

Kal might be a spy, but if he didn't do a good job as a spy, would he get a dose of that fiery pain?

Who is being evil now?

Flames of Rue, that was a nasty thought! I whirled around and moved to the first of the tall windows. The noise of my pulling the casement in roused Kal, who jumped up nearly flew to the window next to mine. "If the Imperial Princess desires the windows closed, she has only to express it and it is our honor to tend to it," he said, his voice strained. He was shivering.

"I'm sorry," I said. "It was stupid of me to demand they be opened. I'm angry. But you didn't put me here."

He gave me a worried glance and bowed low, empty hands away from his sides, his *not*-familiar eyes mercifully hidden. "As the Imperial Princess wishes." He turned to the windows and began shutting them far more swiftly than I could.

I looked outside for the first time. My fancy prison apparently stood on a precipice for a sheer drop fell away below. In the darkness the depth was impossible to guess. I leaned out—and warning heat tingled outward from that cursed necklet.

I yanked my head back inside. Then cautiously, slowly, leaned out again. The moment my head cleared the sill, the burn began to ignite. A ward, on the windows, to keep me corralled.

Scarcely had Kal finished shutting the windows up again when the inner door opened in the unobtrusive alcove. In came the stream of servants. Tired—ashamed, really—of my game, I accepted everything they brought and so I found myself settling into a net made of interwoven silken cords slung between two of the trees. The dressing room in the chamber between the bedroom and that bathroom now sported fabulous silks embroidered with stars, vines, and blossoms.

I sent the servants off to what I hoped would be a well-earned rest (after they made their report on the uncivilized half-Hrethan, I had no doubt), and once I was alone I opened a single window near the hammock.

I climbed into this new bed and stretched out, gently swinging.

That was the last night of unbroken sleep I was to get for a long time.

Sixteen

AND SO BEGAN MY life as an imperial prisoner—er, princess.

My prison was exquisitely elegant; nevertheless, this would be the hardest fight of my life.

That next morning I woke refreshed, swinging softly in a deliciously cool breeze. I opened my eyes to the hazy light of a cloudy dawn filtering between perfect leaves, light green underneath, silver on top—and memory tightened its shackles around my heart and mind as effectively as that thing around my neck.

I dug the heels of my hands into my eyes, longing with throat-choking intensity to slide back into sleep forever.

I had to find a way to escape.

That meant getting out of bed. I flipped out of my hammock and hit the floor. I landed soundlessly out of long habit, but here came one of the servants, a female around my age, with dark red hair and slanted blue eyes.

"His Imperial Serenity requests the honor of the Imperial Princess's presence at sunrise-trine."

My lips shaped the words, *How many of us will be tortured if I'm not there?* But I didn't. Guilt wrung me when I remembered my stupid gesture the previous night.

So all I said was, "What does 'sunrise-trine' mean?" I saw her about to define the words, and I added hastily, "I know the words aren't in Djuran."

"Sveranji, if it pleases the Imperial Princess," she whispered.

"Later I'll want to find out why you name times in another language, but for now, how do you measure time, whatever the language is?"

It turned out that the day was divided into three threes—sunrise-prime, sunrise-seconde, sunrise-trine, midday-prime, seconde, trine, and sunset-prime, seconde, and trine. Nighttime divisions were starrise, midnight, moonset—based on the movements of Little Moon, who always set before dawn, unlike Big Moon, who wandered about the sky in different places the year round.

Prime, seconde, and trine were the "hour" of Charas al Kherval. There, they divided the day and night into twelve hours each, something Thianra told me ancient ballads insist came with humans from other worlds beyond this one.

The Djuran hour was further broken into threes, their formal names prime-sand, seconde-sand, trine-sand, but among themselves the Djurans used shorter nicknames for various time measures. Pretty much as everybody does—for example, midnight among the dockside people in Thesreve is *cat-yowl*, and in Erev-li-Erval, second bell of the morning was always Rising—when the empress (may she fall into a vat of honey and ants find her) officially began her day, though Thianra said her mother was generally up long before dawn.

The serving maid explained with a constrained, hurried air that I saw mirrored in the others. Then I bathed. As I'd expected, my old drape was gone and with it the thief tools. So much for my authority, I thought. Dhes-Andis might be amusing himself with this princess pretense, but he was the one giving the orders.

So I pulled on the first of those new clothes that I laid my hands to. The staff clearly wanted to get me safely out the door.

The silks were woven in interlocking patterns that shimmered between white and silvery blue, or pale ivory and pale gold, or warm cream and the peachy glow of dawn, and other color combinations.

The over-robes all had long sleeves of the winged kind, the formal ones (with the most embroidery) ending in tassels.

In design, the unknown tailors had managed an interesting

adaptation of my drape, which is a sort of tunic that is paneled to permit my back hair to rise. Some drapes have sleeves, others don't; the main components are the open-backed tunic and the loose trousers that are also open at the back to permit the tail freedom. Over that one wears the secondary bit, a long rectangle of cloth that crosses over the front and is usually thrown back over the shoulders.

This rectangle was narrower than those I'd been introduced to in the Kherval, embroidered and tasseled at the ends. As soon as I attempted to cross it over me in front and throw the ends behind my shoulders, I saw in two sets of widened eyes that this was wrong.

"What is it?" I asked.

The maids, one maybe fifteen, turned to Kal—whose eyes still reminded me of someone I knew, but I *didn't* know anyone who looked the least like him, no! He bowed to me and said in the most neutral possible voice, "Our way is the...." He used a Sveranji word as he indicated a line from shoulder to foot.

So I was supposed to let them hang loose like a stole? For all I knew the Emperor of Evil was watching at that moment.

"Stole it is. Ready," I said rather louder than needed.

After another of those elaborate bows Kal asked, "Would the Imperial Princess desire to dine?"

No, I wanted to snap. My stomach boiled with nerves, but long habit—never turning down food when I could get it—overruled my fear of what lay in wait.

"What a luxury," I said, struggling to hide my apprehension, and the fact that I did not want to look at Kal if I could possibly help it. "I am used to eating once a day. If that."

I felt more looks exchanged behind me as I marched across the grand room to the dining alcove where once again I found a variety of fresh foods set out. Enough for ten people. But it was clear that it was all for me. It was equally clear that I was expected to dine in privacy, with a servant hovering outside in case I asked for something.

I piled bits from all the nut bowls on a plate with some wedges of citrus and munched as I walked to the bank of windows to peer out, now that I could actually see. My portion of this building did indeed perch at the edge of a precipice. To the south, a mountainous peninsula extended outward toward the horizon on which an enormous conical mountain rose, distinctive even in the haze of distance.

To the north and east, nothing but gray ocean on either side, under a lowering gray sky. To the west, tiny islands bumped up, bird-shaped specks swooping over the nearest.

A glance down hollowed my insides: oh, so high! If I could throw myself out that window, I could fly out over that water and join those far-away birds....

I moved to the window, halting at a pulse of remembered heat at my throat, and almost dropped my plate. I stood rigidly, fighting the urge to rip at that *thing* around my neck.

Instead I turned and yes, every one of them wore a silvery braided thing at their necks, barely visible above their plain gray tunic robes. "So we're all prisoners, is that it?" I asked bitterly as I flicked the snake thing above my collar bones with my free hand.

Expressions of puzzlement and consternation met my question.

Kal said with all the care that one might use before a dangerous animal, "I beg the Imperial Princess to understand that we all wear *fais*. How else are we to....?" The word he used translated in my head as *web*, but he used it as a verb.

I frowned. Before the previous summer I'd listened for surface thoughts without being aware that I was doing it. I'd always managed to pick up clues to what people meant by words or phrases. I fought the impulse to break that hard block I kept around my thoughts. Dhes-Andis might be waiting to pounce in the mental realm the way he had during summer. Now that I was a prisoner of the very person I had spent the two succeeding seasons resisting, I was more determined than ever to keep my thoughts behind a protective wall.

I touched the golden necklet. "So only mine is a torture instrument then?"

The word "torture" froze them as if I'd burned them with that evil spell. I stared at them, they stared at me, then they all bowed deeply, their faces hidden as Kal said, "Those given responsibility for correction are guardians, and above them the Imperial Chosen,

Your Imperial Serenity."

"Let me get this straight. You call that torture, where magical fire burns you alive, 'correction'?"

Nobody spoke. Either they were afraid of speaking, or else this conversation had no context. A distant bell chimed and once more they made that low, formal bow, their hands and shoulders tense.

I let out my breath in a whoosh. "I'm ready."

And once again I sensed relief signaling between them in minute motions of eye, turn of hand, relaxed breath.

Their relief intensified my apprehensions.

Kal had not issued any order that I heard, but the double doors, carved with fantastical birds and beasts intertwined with tripled knots of flowers, opened on a new servant in gray, a tall older woman.

"I beg the Imperial Princess to honor with her notice one Frei," Kal said. His quiet voice was low, his accent Djuran: I cherished every difference, but his familiarity kept striking me, again and again. "Frei shall have the honor of conducting the Imperial Princess to the Garden Chamber."

You mean the torture chamber, I thought as I followed Frei into the vaulted hall.

Less exhausted than I'd been the day before, less dazed by happenstance as well as transfer residue and pain, I took in details as we walked. Statuary sat in alcoves, sometimes individuals, sometimes figures in triples, asymmetrical and dramatic, leading the eye upward. Figures from history or ballad, that is, royal or heroes of other sorts?

The individuals all looked taller than actual people, imposing with complicated crowns. Royal, then. The statues wore long intricately carved panels from shoulder to feet that gave me a clue to at least one persistent style in Djuran wear. Those panels, or stoles, or whatever they were effectively divided the body into three parts.

As I passed under the unseeing eyes of a stern-looking bearded statue, I said, "Can you tell me what's meant by 'web'?" I pointed at her necklace — *fais*, I reminded myself.

Another of those inescapable bows and she said in a low, melodious voice, "If the Imperial Princess pleases, I shall do my best. At any time between our second and fourth years each Djuran is given his or her fais, and so we join our civilization."

"What does that mean?" And then it hit me. "You communicate with them?"

"Yes, Imperial Princess," she said.

"So it's not merely a torture device? Er, 'correction'?"

Frei's gaze flicked to me, her body tightening as if I'd flung a fire spell at her. But she didn't pause in her step as she said in that melodious singsong, "The Chosen honor us with correction to benefit civilization for all, Your Imperial Serenity, as do guardians for children."

I repeated those words over in my head. So this platitude meant that they tortured each other and called it civilization? No, guardians and Chosen did the torturing. And 'Chosen' was probably what Dhes-Andis and his sort called themselves.

One thing I'd learned from talk with Hlanan's half-sister Thianra during my months at Erev-li-Erval was that as far back in history as you went, no matter where you traveled, you found humans busy organizing themselves into hierarchies. Somebody was always at the top, whether they called themselves pirate captain, guild chief, head cook, or king. *Which is why I chose the bard's life,* she had said. *If I'm never to get away from hierarchies, at least let mine be determined by excellence in music.*

We approached a golden door twice the height of the tallest man. Gold flashed from the carving of a sun radiating outward as the door swung open.

Frei bowed low as another servant in the ubiquitous gray also bowed. They must be talking to each other somehow by their fais, I thought as I held my breath and stepped inside the room with all the trees. I hadn't heard them do it.

Two white cats scampered from tree to tree, distracting me. Another white cat perched on a low tree branch, tail twitching. Green eyes blinked at me. A black cat walked daintily over the patterned floor.

My hackles had stiffened. Not because of the cats; I made an effort to settle my hair, but even though danger tightened my middle and the anger and grief roiled in my mind like a thunderstorm about to strike, from somewhere a tiny flicker of humor hitched my breath when I recognized that my tail twitched behind me exactly like that cat's.

"Well done, Elenderi," came the hated voice, and there he was, approaching through the trees. "A step toward civilization!"

He paused. I braced myself to look at him, my shoulders tight. He wore white and gold, and yes, two long embroidered panels lay over the complicated folds of his robes, drawing the eye upward. As before, he wore a thin, graceful coronet of beaten gold over his blue-black hair.

"This way." He extended a hand as his long, embroidered sleeve moved gracefully, like a raptor folding its wing.

I fell back a step, an instinctive defensive reaction. His eyes narrowed.

Alarm burned through me, followed by anger. I was *not* going to cower. I recovered that step and folded my arms across my front, but my hair once again betrayed me by lifting all along my spine.

He swept his hand outward to gesture toward glass doors behind the trees. Servants in gray opened the two doors. Dhes-Andis walked by my side through these doors, as cold air billowed icily around us. I braced for anything, and found myself standing on a balcony overlooking a vast parade ground filled with people.

I blinked in astonishment at all those upturned faces in various hues of gold from brown to pale, blurred a little by the vapors of breathing the wintry air, as chiming bells rang a complication of triple chords from somewhere overhead.

Dhes-Andis didn't shout, but somehow his voice carried as he said, "Behold Her Imperial Serenity, Princess Elenderi, returned to Sveran Djur at long last!"

With a sough as if from a great wind, all those people dropped to their knees and touched their foreheads to the frozen ground.

I looked down in witless horror.

"Speak to them, Elenderi." Dhes-Andis's low murmur verged on laughter. "They await your words of wisdom."

Dislike curdled in me at his tone of soft mockery, but that only lasted a heartbeat. From his smile it was clear he expected me to be impressed. Maybe even pleased.

I could only shake my head, my hair swirling about me, the

ends roiling the way my innards roiled.

Dhes-Andis lifted his voice again. "Her Imperial Serenity is overcome by your loyalty and devotion. She wishes to give you, our loyal people, a festival day in her name."

A shout rang up the stone walls, reverberating through my skull and teeth and bones. I backed up a step and he let me retreat inside the Garden Chamber.

He followed me in, leaving all those hundreds—maybe a thousand or more—people outside in the frigid air, and stretched out his hand to one of the cats, who butted up against his fingers.

"You may take the remainder of the day to explore the imperial residence story," Dhes-Andis said, stroking the cat. "But when I have a moment to address the paucity of your education, you will promptly attend."

I was ready to run. I began a turn, then said, "Um, if I get lost...."

"You have only to speak Kal's name, and your desire."

"But I don't know how you do it," I said.

His brows lifted. "Do what?"

"This thing." I jerked my thumb at the fais around my throat. (I refused to think of it as mine.) "I gather everyone has one, but they also do something called web."

He said, "'Web' is the silent speech of servants, lest their noise disturb our reflections. You've only to speak. 'Kal, I am lost.' I presume you can manage that much?"

I bit my lips against a retort of equal sarcasm. I'd been around enough bullies and villains to suspect that that would constitute insolence (though of course *he* could be as sarcastic as he liked), and I felt morally certain that even when I did learn how to use the fais, it wouldn't come equipped with my own retaliatory torture spell.

I backed away—I couldn't get out of there fast enough—but before I reached the door, he said, "Elenderi."

I longed with every bone and feather to ignore him, to shout, "That is not my name!"

But I did neither. I forced myself to stop and turn.

"Before we meet again," he said in that measured voice, "see to it that Kal instructs you in the basics of etiquette."

Was that supposed to sting? It didn't. I didn't care a whit for his etiquette unless he threatened that magical fire. I reached the door, which a silent servant opened. As soon as it shut behind me, I let out my breath in relief and ran until I was well out of sight of those sun doors.

I found a stairway of pale mauve marble, but as soon as I set my foot on the first step, the fais flared hot. Magical ward, same as the windows in my suite.

I jumped back and ran, slowing when nothing more happened. So far I'd come along a single corridor with windows at my right. Though I was clearly confined to a single floor, it appeared to be vast. I did not want to get lost any more than I wanted to call for help. Were they listening to me at all times, was that how it worked? What a horrible idea!

So I explored the way I had in the past when alone in a forest or city. I began with a small square, making only right turns, and looked at all the landmarks, but instead of a distinctive clump of trees, I marked a statue of a woman with a triple crown on her head, and a long, pointed fais. Empress Triple Crown was where I first turned right.

I made my next right turn at an intersection of six arches, the floor tiled in marble pieces fitted around some stylized lettering. I could understand languages when I heard them, but I had to learn to read like anyone else. From one angle, the letters looked like the snap of a dragon's tail and an outstretched claw; as I passed to the right for my next turn, the lettering changed to a river below a crowned mountain.

Next turn, an age-softened statue of a man with a forked beard and a different kind of triple crown, sort of braided together. He wore what looked like it might have been a braided necklace, with some kind of stone at the end. Necklace or fais? I passed him and — I was not where I'd started.

So I cautiously tried two more corners, and there I found my starting point. All right. So this part of the building was six sided.

I ventured on, my attention snagging on jewel-toned hangings and stylized paintings in gold frames, mosaics, murals, statuary. All very different styles, but someone had placed them so that the eye moved naturally from one to the next.

My eyes were not the only sense busy. I strained to hear anyone—for I did not want to stumble into *him* by accident. But I saw no one. No servants. No guards.

The longer I walked alone, the uneasier I became. The palace in Erev-li-Erval had been filled with people. This place felt like a gigantic tomb, especially under that heavy gray cloud cover. Magical glowglobes glimmered in corners where light from the windows or overhead domes did not reach, but somehow that increased the sense that I was alone in this silent world of stone and metal and carved wood.

Alone, that is, except for the Evil Emperor.

Having completed a circuit around all six sides, I cautiously poked my head into rooms, listening first, and if I heard no sounds, peering to make certain *he* was not there.

I could not guess the purpose of most of those beautifully decorated rooms. I reached a very plain one with windows down one wall and spotted racks of various lengths of sticks arranged against the opposite wall. The sticks had been smoothed, with handsome handles at one end. Something for dancing? I reached toward one—and greenish magic crackled over it like lightning, flashing pain through my fingers right up my arm. I gasped and backed away rapidly.

This was not a ballroom.

I slunk out of there, not wanting to serve as target practice for anyone turning up looking for something to whack with those staves.

I hastened on, stopping when I reached a room full of musical instruments. I paused on my tiptoes, ready to run, though I had not seen or heard anyone.

I knew what caused my tension. All my life I'd struggled between adoration and loathing whenever I heard music. The loathing had followed the isolation and sadness I felt after the last notes of an entrancing melody faded into the air. Music was a lie, a false promise, a trick. And yet the yearning upwelling in my soul when I chanced upon great music—or heard echoes of it in dreams—never went away.

Thianra, Hlanan's sister, had devoted her life to music. She had tried to convince me that music inspired and united people.

I wondered what she might think about me now that her mother had thrown me to the enemy. Probably nothing at all. One thing I had learned (in fact, I had counted on in my eternal quest to remain invisible and unnoticed) was that we were never as interesting to others as we were to ourselves.

Unless, of course, we had the power to kill.

Intensely ambivalent, I ventured into the room and walked a slow circuit, looking on ancient instruments whose sounds I could not imagine, and on familiar ones. Beautiful instruments with inlaid gold threading and woodwork, old ones smoothed over the years by the touch of unknown hands, they were all there: woodwinds, strings, drums and cymbals and bells.

My circuit had begun in the direction away from the harp. But inexorably my feet brought me to the harp, a beautiful triple-coursed instrument with foot levers.

The music in my dreams that hurt the most had always been the shimmering sound of metal strings. Thianra had coaxed me to try a tiranthe, and once I'd easily mastered the idea of chords she'd loaned me that single-course harp that Prince Geric had thrown over the waterfall.

I hadn't even been able to master a single-course harp. It would be a travesty to touch with my clumsy paw this beautiful instrument. I moved close enough to see the fine carving along the neck depicting tiny bird-shapes chasing in and out of interwoven leaves and roses.

Birds? They looked like aidlars. Tir! My heart squeezed behind my ribs. Had Tir recovered from Prince Geric's stone spell?

The thought of Geric propelled me out of the room as if I could escape memory. I slunk back to my imperial prison cell, where Kal waited with his familiar gaze, which widened when I told him what the Evil Emperor had said.

I'm leaving out 'the Imperial Princess' and the 'if she will honor me' and all the rest of the formal speechifying that kept me as a third person, as if my imperial self was outside the room instead of standing right there in front of him. The basics of etiquette turned out to mean how to enter and leave rooms, in specific how to bow to emperors, which must be done every time I saw or left him. And there was not one bow. There were degrees of bows. The most formal one meant going down on your knees, and even putting your head to the ground the way those thousands of people had done on the freezing stone of that vast parade ground.

"Do I have to bang my head on the ground every time I lay my eyes on Emperor...." *Evil?* I managed to choke off the word, sensing that they would react with the same horror as they had to my mention of torture. And what if *he* was listening and struck at us all? But I couldn't help saying, "I'm afraid I'm going to laugh."

Kal's eyelids flashed up even more, but he said in that careful voice, "Only if His Imperial Serenity speaks in the aorist imperative. Or if you desire to present a petition. The Imperial Princess in the normal course of events would bow this way." He stood straight, head bent, straight arms at his sides, palms open and empty.

That was easy enough, not a lot different from how Hlanan's family had greeted one another, only they put their palms together in front of their hearts. It was the idea of bowing, of showing respect for someone I loathed with every breath, that made me squirm.

"Then there are the imperial cousins," Kal said.

"Cousins!" I squeaked in horror.

He bowed in the servants' manner. And in his mild, soft voice gave me to understand that there were indeed cousins among the select company who had the honor of attending upon the emperor in Icecrest Palace.

Imperial family of the first circle (Dhes-Andis and I) were all 'Your Imperial Serenity', the next layer of the Chosen were 'Most Noble,' and then mere 'the Noble.' And they all had specific bows, the latter a mere nod, hands inside one's sleeves, and a slight bob for the former. However, if I did not know anyone's specific rank, politesse dictated the safest course was to address them all as Most Noble.

They didn't seem to have dukes, barons, counts, archdukes, or any of the other titles I'd heard about in my travels. The fount of all glory, generosity, and grace (in one word, power) was the emperor; governorships were granted to those raised to Most Noble rank. Those only Noble weren't in charge of anything; they got their status from their birth, and I guess their prospective promotion either by earning a governorship or by marriage.

When both Kal and I were certain I had it all firmly in memory, he asked the Imperial P. if she would desire a repast. I said that she never turned down free food, and he departed noiselessly.

I retreated to one of the windows, which I opened. By careful testing, I discovered that I could sit on the sill with my toes hanging over the edge and my chin on my knees. In this way I could feel the bracing air and look out and down, pretending to freedom, without triggering the pain of those invisible bars.

For once the sky was at least partially clear, a long line of ragged clouds rolling away in the distance beyond one of the shark tooth islands.

It hurt as much as ever to think about Hlanan, but I knew I couldn't avoid it. I'd told him the very first day we were in Erev-li-Erval that I thought bowing and the rest of it was stupid. He'd replied that so was wearing clothing in summer and sitting at a table to eat—why didn't we fling ourselves on the ground and gobble at vegetables pulled directly from the soil?

"These manners are the outward markers of the social agreement we call society," he'd said. "If we all agree to honor one another through these forms we have a better chance of rubbing along with a semblance of grace as well as order, respect, and above all, peace. That is one of the marks of a good life."

"Good lives," I'd retorted, "would not require one to show respect toward evil princes like Geric. I would never bow to him. I don't respect him. It would be a lie, and you told me once that civilization means not lying."

"What you respect is the rank, not the person, if you bow formally," Thianra had said, gentle and patient as ever.

"But I don't respect rank either. Maybe I'd feel different if I'd been raised to it. But I think it's all silly."

I winced, remembering that I was supposedly a princess now. But back then, I'd had no idea such a threat was coming for me, and so I'd gone on to ask, "Do the Hrethan have hierarchies?"

"Yes," Hlanan had said. "However, you will have to talk to them about how they choose their ranks."

I ground my chin into my knees. I hadn't found that out

because the Hrethan had been elusive.

Now I knew why, thanks to Aranu Crown. In their eyes I was the next thing to an evil Djuran.

And to be fair—though it made me itch inside with impatience—from a distance, those spells I'd cast during summer (one that caused thunderstorms for an entire season) might look pretty evil. If you didn't know why I'd done it. Or that I hadn't known that it was Dhes-Andis teaching it to me. And I certainly hadn't had a clue about possible consequences.

So here I was, where Aranu Crown and those elusive Hrethan obviously thought I belonged. Alone again. And I couldn't even use magic to defend myself, so it would have to be my wits. Dhes-Andis's pretence that I was an imperial princess seemed more sinister than being thrown into a dungeon and threatened with terrible things, because threats and dungeons would have given me a clear target to hate. The only thing I could figure was that the Emperor of Evil was using all this pretense of civilization to fog my intent, if not my distrust.

I perched in the window stewing mentally until a pair of enormous, long-necked brown gryphs winged through the air outside maybe a hundred paces out over the water, an elaborate structure midway between a basket and a wheelless coach body suspended between them from fabulously carved harnesses glinting with gold. In it sat two females my age, who stared avidly at me under peaked hats as their basket swung gently. They were bundled up warmly, so all I saw were the two round faces.

Arcing high above them, the gryphs' heads bobbed gently as they flapped. The nearest eagle-beaked bird twitched her head minutely and I caught the gaze of a huge round eye, and swayed on my feet at the compelling sense of an image not-quite-seen, a voice just-below-audible.

I leaned dangerously out until my throat under the fais began to buzz and burn with magical warning as I watched the gryphs fly so beautifully in tandem, one's wings high as the other's swept low, weave and weave again.

I knew from my own flying that wings don't actually flap up and down, though it looks like that when one watches from human eyes. Wings move in a sort of triangle, which enabled this pair to braid the inside wings, in effect. My shoulder blades twitched as I tried to imagine gliding the inner wing through the air and scooping with the outside wing in order to keep from colliding with the other bird.

It wasn't natural flight, but it looked spectacular, as one of the females cast a last look behind at me before the gryphs and their passengers rounded a far tower, and vanished.

I swung my feet inside and said to Kal, who sat patiently on his bench awaiting my whim: "Who were those people in that thing in the air?"

After the usual bow that came before and after every single exchange, he informed the Imperial P. that she had glimpsed her first Chosen.

I retired not long after, and spent an uncomfortable night waking myself out of bad dreams about shattering walls and tunnels full of invaders. I'd jerk awake shivering and certain someone had attempted a magical attack.

When I finally gave up trying to sleep I retreated to the bath, and when I came out, I resolved that Lhind the Thief was not going back to that tree room to face Dhes-Andis. Instead, Lhind the Spy would go, masked in her false identity as Her Imperial Serenity, Princess Elenderi.

Seventeen

NEXT MORNING, SURE ENOUGH, the summons of doom came.

I picked out a pretty yellow outfit and I even essayed the silk slippers. The only thing I ignored was the headdress, a sort of tiara affair that dangled gems on the brow coming to a point over the nose, echoing the V of the fais. If my hair lifted suddenly, something I could control most of the time unless something shocked me, the headdress might go flying off somewhere. Wasn't certain how disastrous that might be.

Thus girded for the battle of wits, I took myself to the Garden Chamber. When I saw Dhes-Andis I made the sort of bow Princess Elenderi would make, and I did it with a flourish. May as well begin my masquerade right, I thought to myself.

Dhes-Andis sat in his wing chair that kind of resembled a stylized lily, two outward petals arching above the armrests, and the central one rising to an oval with that odd triple crown embroidered beneath. On a beautiful golden stand at the right-hand side of his chair sat a crystal, perfectly round, the size of a child's head. Three cats had joined him, one on his lap, one on the armrest, and one lying along the chair back to the right of the oval.

A wingchair had been set to face his, but on the floor below his dais. When he indicated with a nod in its direction that I was to sit down, I thought this would be easy, he was just going to talk at me. I had only to practice my Lhind the Spy mask and continue to seek an escape. Right?

Wrong again.

"An adequate first effort at civilized behavior," he said as he slowly stroked the cat on the armrest. Its eyes slitted, but otherwise it was silent.

His other hand made a subtle gesture too quick to catch. "Now, let us explore your skills. I've lifted the wards against your magic—"

It was instinct, really. Not my plan. But the moment I heard "lifted the wards," I focused on him, braced, and hurled a voice cast, because by now I knew that voice. I'd heard it in endless nightmares after those mental encounters the previous summer.

And he struck back without lifting a finger.

The voice cast splashed away harmlessly. I struggled to breathe. When the white lightning eased enough for me to get my shuddering ribs to expand, he said, "And one for stupidity."

He burned me again.

When I came out of that one I knew why he'd had the chair set, so I wouldn't fall flat on the ground again. That was not *civilized*.

"What have you just learned?" he said, still stroking the cat as if nothing had happened.

My mouth opened, but no sound came out. That's because I had enough wits left to choke off the first three or four responses I really wanted to make, all of which were absolutely guaranteed to net me another dose of his "correction."

His voice didn't lift in volume, but the consonants sharpened to precision. "What. Have. You. Learned, Elenderi?"

An echo of pain throbbed from my throat to my skull, and I flinched, slapping my hand to the cursed fais but of course I couldn't wrench the thing away from my neck. "That I can't do voice cast at you," I managed.

"Fast as you are, I am faster. As well as far your superior in skill," he said. "I expected you to challenge me, but I trust you have now learned the futility of that. Let us resume," the even, inexorable voice rolled over me. "What other magical skills do you possess?"

"None."

White lightning seared me.

"Answer my question, Elenderi."

"I can transform. To a bird. Only in the heights," I wheezed when I could speak again.

"That is an interesting variation, one we shall perhaps explore one day. Do not attempt a transformation. Warding transformation is one of the first controls laid on the fais. Human nature, being superior to every other form, suffices us. That is not to say that we might one day find a use for exceptions. But experiments may wait. What else?"

"I can understand any language."

"I already knew that. What other mental controls have you?"

I considered what to say—and he struck again.

"When you hesitate, you are contemplating another of your lies. I will not tolerate lies. You can speak mind to mind I already know, as I am certain you recollect."

"No. Yes," I said quickly. "I mean, I did not know I could do that until I took that whistle of Prince Geric's. I could hear, but I'd never tried sending my thoughts. Then I learned to make a wall inside my head. I have never broken it since."

"Let us essay that."

I hunched my shoulders, grimacing as I waited for another blast of pain-magic, but nothing happened. I cracked one eye to find his gaze not on me but on that crystal, in whose center glowed swirling color. When I tried to look at it I felt so dizzy I shut my eyes and hunched even tighter.

He was scrying. He didn't talk mind to mind the way I did, but he was very adept at scrying, that much I already knew. I could feel from the internal pressure around my thoughts that he was trying to reach past my mind barrier, but that had become such habit it was strong as steel. When he sat back, the sense of a vice squeezing my skull eased.

"We will explore that another time. What else?"

I swallowed, trying to get my voice—and my scattered wits—under control. "There's that fire spell. You taught me."

"Excellent. And?"

I cast an illusory replica of that fork-bearded statue with the triple crown, figuring that was neutral enough. "I call these shimmers."

"Do you know who this statue represents?"

"No."

"You will learn," Dhes-Andis said. "Suffice it to say that he was the first emperor who united this island, the Sveranji, with Djur, wherefrom came my ancestors and half of yours. What is a shimmer? I take it that is idiom for illusion?"

"It's what I called them when I was small. And that's all I know."

"No one has attempted to teach you magic?"

"Yes. But it was no use. I failed at the most elementary spells," I added, for the first time glad to have been a failure.

But he said, "Of course you failed at mage training. That's like trying to force a cataract through a reed-straw. I take it that fool of a scribe-mage attempted the traditional studies on you?"

I was caught. Though Aranu Crown had betrayed me, I found myself reluctant to tell Dhes-Andis anything about her court or mages. Just because she had gone from friend to enemy with one contemptuous dismissal, that didn't make Dhes-Andis my friend.

"Why the reluctance?" Dhes-Andis said, his eyes narrowing. "Ah. Of course. The occasion for your learning the fire spell was your desperate attempt to rescue that idiot, was it not? Was he your first pet, or were you his?"

If I hadn't still been exerting all my energy to stay upright as I recovered from those two magical shocks I might have blushed all the way to my ears. I was mostly relieved that he'd answered his own question, thereby saving me from having to talk about the Mage Council, or Erev-li-Erval.

Or who Hlanan really was. "Pet" indeed.

He smiled wryly. "Our first forays into that aspect of life are almost always with negligible people, but it's like anything else: one learns discernment as well as skill. That aside, anyone but an idiot would know that you must be trained as Hrethan are trained. So. I already know that you are capable of mastering high level spells, but as yet I have seen little evidence you have the discipline for control." He paused, studying me, and I tried to remember my Imperial Princess mask.

If he thought I'd protest that comment about discipline, well, he could wait forever.

"I ought to have foreseen this wrinkle," he said finally. "When we meet next, you will know whom that statue represents. At sunset seconde your cousins will meet you in the Chamber of Celestial Contemplation; it is time for your introduction to the Chosen, among whom number those of your principal family connections in residence here."

Somewhere in the distance a gentle bell toned, silvery and sweet. All three cats lifted their heads, looking off in one direction. I did, too, but saw nothing.

Dhes-Andis flicked the cat on the chair arm. "Go on."

The cats bounded to the floor, soft as snow and sinuous as water, vanishing among the trees somewhere. Only then I noticed I could not see the walls of the room. They were obscured by the trees, and maybe magic, as I could not bring anything beyond the trees into focus.

I realized belatedly that he had been talking to me, not the cats, and I got up, glad to get away, but sensed something wrong. My fur ruffled up my arm, then I remembered: Bow.

I bowed, my knees still watery, and tottered away as fast as I could. A servant appeared to open the door for me. As soon as it shut, I was alone. I got myself well away from line-of-sight of that chamber, then sank down onto the marble toes of the triple-crowned empress, wrapped my arms around my legs and my tail around my arms, and breathed until the shuddering stopped.

Stupid, I thought. Idiot. I knew what he was capable of. Why did I think this interview would be so easy?

Because I wasn't in a dungeon, of course. It seemed to amuse him to give me the outer trappings of power while making it clear that I had no power whatsoever.

Now what?

Cousins. I had no idea what to do about cousins. Other people had cousins. I did not know where to begin even thinking about the concept of a family.

A man's voice echoed down the marble halls. Was *he* on the prowl?

I got up and fled in the opposite direction, avoiding my room with Kal and the others always lurking to wait on me hand and foot. Watching.

I was not conscious of any destination, but somehow I fetched up at the music room, finding it deserted as before. I drifted in, soothed by that profound silence.

I made straight for the harp and reached for the middle note called True, and plucked it softly. The metal hummed, welling a rich shimmering sound that resonated sweetly through my still-throbbing nerves. Oh.

I spread my fingers to pluck its triad. All I'd managed to learn had been chord triads in what they called simple mode: first note of the chord its key. One-two-three, and I breathed deeply as soothing sound caressed my ears and reached all through me, cooling as rain after the scorch of a fire.

A carved bench sat beside the harp, with a fine, inviting cushion. I sat down and carefully toed the pedal so that the harp sat back against my knee and shoulder. As soon as I touched the strings, there was that sweet sensation again flowing through me in healing waves, and though my fingering on those simple practice harps in Erev-li-Erval had always been fumbling, somehow my fingers on this great, complicated harp knew their way as if guided —

I snatched my fingers away, instantly suspicious. I trusted *nothing* in this place, including a harp that might have magic on it to lure me in by making me feel good. For a time I sat there listening to my own heavy breathing as my tail swept this way and that. The soothing sense had faded, leaving...nothing.

No mysterious force compelled me. Nothing poked at my mental steel wall.

I half-rose, then sat down again. This time I tried with one finger. No mysterious magic flowed. I tried two fingers, then three, then five, and worked through the warm-up that Thianra had taught me. The sound shimmered around me like light on water. I could pull my fingers away and nothing happened beyond the ease with which I plucked chords.

Maybe the magic was inherent in the harp. If that was so it might be harmless, something beautiful that lazy Chosen could play and sound good. Comforted by that thought, I fingered my way through a couple of the simple songs I'd been taught.

It actually sounded good! Maybe this was the difference between indifferent practice instruments and great ones, I thought as I ran my fingers over the strings, reveling in the rich harmonies. Then—I was not really thinking—my fingers began to pick out another melody, familiar and yet not. I hate to use the word "haunting" because no ghosts howled around me or clanked chains, but the beauty was so oddly familiar, stirring deep feelings that I did not quite trust.

I yanked my hands away and wrung them as if some kind of slimy magic clung to them. Then I got up from the bench, the harp falling back into position with a thump and a discordant shimmer of sound.

One step, two, my shoulder blades crawling as I retreated.

When I got outside, I felt stupid. Nothing had happened to me. No evil enchantments lurked to ensnare me. It was just a music room.

Why should I scare myself with imaginings? I had enough real threat to face, like the prospect of the next session with Emperor Jardis Dhes-Andis.

Time for information.

I made my way back to the Princess Elenderi suite and braced myself for another dose of bowing and Imperial Princessing. When Kal came out of the servants' alcove, I told him what Dhes-Andis had said.

"How many cousins are there?" I asked. "I only saw two in that basket thing."

He began to tell me, but I was soon lost in the recitation of names. "Never mind," I said. "I think I'll do better when I see faces to put to the names."

Kal only bowed—as usual—but the deliberation of that bow made me wonder what I was missing.

And that reignited the sense of threat.

Eighteen

TIME WOUND INEXORABLY ON until one of the servants showed me the way to this new chamber, located on the floor beneath the one I'd explored. I'd faltered at the stairs, remembering that warning burn, but this time nothing happened. So the ward had been lifted at the stairs because I was expected to descend. That seemed evidence of a close watch kept on my movements, a thought that gave me that crawling sensation between my shoulder blades.

Down I went, finding even bigger rooms, with the vaulted ceilings and vast perimeters and marble and gilt and beautiful art, chambers designed to impress. Hlanan and Thianra had called the equivalent in Aranu Crown's palace state rooms. Here the marble was not smoothed into columns or pilasters, but had been carved into complicated tracery, alternating with walls of espaliered almond trees, many rooms under domes of glass. Some rooms were six sided, in fact most, though a lot of them had two parallel long walls that suggested ballrooms to me, a dais set in the alcove at the far end.

The one thing I never saw in any of these was refreshments. Court in Erev-li-Erval could be duller than watching ice melt, but you could always count on superlative feeds. Thianra had told me that some of the poorer nobles depended on courtly entertainments for their daily meals.

This Chamber of Celestial Contemplation sported a painted

night sky with stars added by magic so that they twinkled like the real thing. Magic moved the moons slowly, I noticed as the formal reception ground on with the speed of a glacier, making me wonder why they didn't simply build a gigantic glass dome and put down some mats so they could look up at the sky itself?

But I wasn't there to study the summer sky during winter. Seated on a low dais in one of those lily-petal chairs, I faced a semi-circle of the Dhes-Andis Chosen and they faced me.

Good things? Dhes-Andis was not there. And they were very pretty to look at. In fact I was considerably surprised to discover that Sveran Djur's nobles in their shimmer silks looked somehow more stylish and graceful than Erev-li-Erval's courtiers, who were not exactly lumbering ruffians in their velvet and lace.

Bad things? They looked exactly alike with their glossy black hair swooping back over the ears except for two long locks hanging down in front to dangle over those long tasseled stoles. These locks were either braided or decorated with gems (or both), and all wore the stylized broad shoulders and the paneled over-robes that suggested threes. They all wore thin gold bands on their brows that dipped in front, echoing the fais—most with tiny gems glittering against their brows.

"We are honored to welcome you at long last to your home, Your Imperial Serenity," said the tallest and handsomest of the men.

At least he said "you," I thought.

He began with himself—Darus—and turned to his right to introduce Amney, a beautiful young woman with a heart-shaped face and a striking outfit of black underneath, white over it, embroidered with holly.

"We welcome Your Imperial Serenity to Sveran Djur," she said in a sweet singsong.

"I thank you for your welcome, Most Noble," I said.

From there Darus progressed so swiftly that the flow of names and titles streamed past before I could commit either names or faces to memory. But the way he spoke gave me a pattern to copy and I got what little amusement I could in mimicking their slow, smooth speech as I thanked each one.

When the introduction finally ended a century later, Darus

said in his smooth, precise, musical voice (with about as much warmth as one of the icicles hanging outside the lancet windows), "We celebrate the welcome news that you have at last been found and brought home to us again, Your Imperial Serenity. Where have you dwelt?"

"In the eastern continent, Most Noble," I replied.

"From whom did you learn in that faraway place, Your Imperial Serenity?" one of the females asked.

"Many were my tutors, Most Noble," I replied in her exact tone.

They had to know that I'd been captured, that I'd been a thief on the run. Didn't they? If they wanted me to admit that I was uncivilized and ignorant they were going to wait as long as this interminable ritual seemed to be lasting. So I tried to deflect them with questions of my own: Where did they hail from (not a single name I recognized), was the weather typical for the season (I had no idea what the weather outside even was).

I'd already observed in Erev-li-Erval that courtly behavior meant stylized behavior, a control of voice and movement that reminded me of dancers on stage. Only not nearly as interesting to watch, which is how I came to be distracted by the ceiling until I began to wonder if they were being deliberately boring.

In desperation I distracted myself by oh-so-slowly lifting my head and spine hair to float around me, and my tail to curl and uncurl at my knee on one side. Two, then three, then five of them watched, their eyes following the undulations as if they, too, struggled to stay awake.

By the end of that reception I hadn't learned much more than I had known going in. We covered every exasperating aspect of snow and cold until at last one of the Chosen women who had been silent spoke up. "Might Your Imperial Serenity honor us with any questions? We should take great delight in introducing you to the world you were denied so long."

"Those basket things drawn by big brown gryphs," I said. "I would like very much to see one again."

I said it mostly to spark them, possibly find out if the two women I'd seen numbered among these here—and why they'd come.

A slight stir rustled among their silks. Quick looks darted before eyelids lowered, and that same woman (I noted that her hair had red highlights, even shades of very dark brown) said in a tone that almost revealed a hint of a speck of a modicum of emotion, "I trust you will honor us with your gracious pardon for disturbing your reflections, Your Imperial Serenity. If guilt is attributed, it must be acknowledged by myself and my sister, the Noble Ingras." A stylized gesture palm up toward the young woman sitting next to her.

"It did not disturb me at all, Most Noble," I said.

Ingras then spoke up, her voice higher. "In which case the honor would be mine and the Noble Pelan's if Your Imperial Serenity wished to view Icecrest from a royal float."

Icecrest. Hadn't someone at Erev-li-Erval referred once to Dhes-Andis's fortress on Ice Mountain? *Erev-li-Erval...Hlanan.*

I had to stop thinking about him. That part of my life was done.

That thought hurt so much I was glad when a distant bell chimed, and everyone looked at me expectantly. Experimentally I rose, and saw a subtle relief that the younger ones couldn't quite hide as they rose as a group and performed a formal bow.

I bowed to them, remembering the degree for Most Nobles. They bowed back in a manner that made it clear they expected me to leave first, so I did.

I was tired and nervy, looking forward to rest, but when I went to bed in my silken hammock I tumbled into anxious dreams of being lost in vast, echoing caverns, utterly alone as I tried to find the faint, familiar melody that haunted me.

I began to run in the dreams, panting with effort as I chased the music. I knew that song, it had once meant comfort and joy. It had had words, though I understood them not...I jerked awake, my heart thundering against my ribs, my mouth dry as I gasped for breath.

"Vandarus Andis," I whispered. I had not found out who he was!

Terror at what would await me if the Summons of Doom arrived in the morning and I was still ignorant drove me out of the hammock, though it was still dark.

I stumbled out of the room.

Someone, poor soul, obviously suffered the grim duty of sitting all night in that alcove, as immediately a woman said softly, "Does the Imperial Princess require anything?"

"Yes," I said, as her fingers slipped up to her fais and light sprang into being in the crystal globes supported in the silver holders along the walls. "How do I find out who Vandarus Andis was?"

Her eyes widened, then she hid her face in the usual bow. "He was the first great Andis emperor," she murmured, "honor be to his name. Much has been written about him in the royal archive."

"I don't think I know how to read your script," I said. "Is it different from that used in the Kherval?"

Her fingertips pressed to her lips on the word "Kherval" as if I'd spoken a forbidden word, but she only said (with the usual bow), "It would be my pleasure to read anything the Imperial Princess desires to hear."

I was ready to venture forth, but apparently it was not suitable to my prestige to go haring off in the middle of the night to the archive, so one of the hapless maids was presumably hauled out of bed to fetch a suitable book and read it to me.

As a storm battered the bank of windows, I listened to the ornate language rolling forth. If I hadn't spent those months at Erev-li-Erval I probably would have accepted the words as truth, or at least truth in the eyes of the Djurans: that Vandarus Andis had united the countless islands together under the Dragon banner, creating unity and peace at last.

He caused Icecrest to be built atop the ruins of the former Sveranji royal palace on Skyreach Mountain, symbol of order for all the united peoples to see, and there he dwelt in majesty, dispensing justice as he established the imperial line, and so on and so on.

In other words, courtly talk is lying? I'd said to Thianra one morning not long after my arrival in Erev-li-Erval, after listening to a courtly history recited at a function.

Thianra had replied seriously, *Courtly flattery, which my mother abominates, is lying. Court flatterers say what they think the empress wants to hear in order to get something.*

And these poets with all their pomposities about tradition and greatness?

She'd explained that the court poets and archivists did present the facts the way the monarch wanted them to be understood. Some were better at it than others, and Hlanan's father, an archivist by calling, had pointed out that nobody much reread the most blatant ones, but sought the records that hewed closer to the truth. And those were the types of records Aranu Crown gave her imprimatur.

Thianra had gone on to say, *Governments exist as long as they do when they represent order in the eyes of those governed. There are two faces to order.*

"I know," I'd said. "Rules and laws."

Well, everyone knowing what to expect from one another. But underlying that is the sense that order is rooted and secure, and that means tradition. That is a very powerful word, tradition.

Hot anger boiled inside me whenever I thought of Aranu Crown, but then I'd smack into memory of Hlanan or Thianra and fall into a morass of doubt and guilt.

The truth? Whenever I thought of Thianra I began to doubt myself. And I *hated* that. I'm my only ally, I'd say internally, and force my attention outward again.

In this case, from the long, poetic lacework of flattery I picked out the impression that Vandarus Andis had conquered Sveranji and plopped this gigantic palace on the highest mountain as a reminder to any who might have forgotten for a heartbeat who held the steel.

Or the fais, I thought, and waited until a pause in the flow of praise for his puissance to ask, "Was he the inventor of these things?" I touched my fais.

"We have always had fais, Imperial Princess," she said proudly.

The first chiming bell of the day rang. I flinched, half-expecting the summons of evil. Tired as I was, I dreaded it with a surge of boiling hatred inside me that killed my appetite for breakfast.

I bathed and dressed and fled, though I knew he could find me wherever I was. Once again I found myself at the music chamber. I stood for a time, my eyelids burning with exhaustion, and listened to the silence. Until that moment I had never thought about the quality of silence in different circumstances. Though no living thing besides myself walked in that room, it did not sound empty; I knew it for a fancy, but it seemed to me that music lay just beyond hearing, or as if all that had been played in this room had soaked into the walls, the way sunlight soaks into cloth and brightens it.

I dwelt against my will in the palace of an enemy, but this one room felt...I did not want to frame the word "safe." There was no safety until I got that fais off me and my self far from Sveran Djur.

But the music room seemed a pool of tranquility.

So why not play the harp?

I was too tired to resist. Sit, lean, lift and flex the hands. And once again my spirit bathed in the lovely shimmer of sound, perfectly tuned. My fingers moved nimbly the way they never had in Erev-li-Erval, but now seemed so right, so comforting as I began to pick out that plaintive melody that ran up and down the scales like the laughter of children.

The music flowed so easily, bringing up half-formed glimpses of delight—a butterfly—lilacs—the softness of fabric in the silvery blue of ice at dawn—a soft kiss on the tip of my nose—

I was an infant again. *Elenderi, my darling child.*

I recoiled so fast I did not even know I was out of the room until I found myself standing in the hall, shivering.

What evil attack is this? I thought desolately. Yet another insidious attempt to control my mind the way he could control my movements?

Mind locked down tighter than ever, I perforce returned to "my" suite. Where else had I to go?

As soon as I walked in, I discovered the entire circle of servants, who spread apart and bowed low.

Kal said, "If it pleases the Imperial Princess, a communication has just arrived from the Noble Pelan with an invitation to join her and her sister, the Noble Ingras, at their float." And a gesture toward the bank of windows.

I blinked, wondering what I was supposed to see in that broad expanse through which bright sunlight could be seen—oh. Sunshine! I was beginning to see how rare it was, but not what that meant.

My first thought was: Escape.

My second was: It can't be that easy.

But I would go anyway. The farther I got away from Dhes-Andis, the better I'd feel, even if it was a temporary respite.

One of the servants led me to the other side of the building, same floor. I guessed I was near the Garden Chamber with its balcony over that parade court, the way the morning sun blazed in through the tall windows and the dome overhead, almost blinding.

I shaded my eyes. Two heavily cloaked, hatted figures flowed toward me as if they rolled on wheels. They had to be Pelan and her sister Ingras, though the Chosen still all looked alike to me. The sisters performed bows so identical the sense of their being pressed from the same baking shape increased, and belatedly I remembered my own bow.

The shorter of the two gestured in a slow arc so that her sleeve barely shifted, and I turned to my left. My jaw dropped.

Beyond the archway the balcony extended in a hexagonal shape with some kind of platform or perch beneath it, on which three pairs of gryphs rested. Coach-baskets rested on the platform below the rail of the terrace, two very small, plain ones, harnessed to gray gryphs, and one elaborate coach-basket with fine gilding in graceful shapes, painted a cerulean blue to match the summer sky.

Imperial guards tended to the plain ones: tall, imposing warriors carrying wooden staves in baldrics in place of swords.

The sisters flowed in that peculiar scudding walk toward the fancy one, towing me along. Then everyone hitched to a stop as a wing-spread shadow passed between us and the sun; an immense gryph with iridescent violet feathers down its body glided down toward the perch before coming to rest and folding its wings.

A tall man slid off a fine gilt-edged pad on the bird's back, attached to the fais-like harness around its neck. The bird, though perched so that its back was level with our platform, still towered over our heads—taller than the two brown gryphs harnessed to the sisters' basket, or float, as they'd called it.

The bird turned a great dark eye in my direction. When my gaze met its unwinking gaze, my vision blurred and I wobbled as if the ground had shifted.

It was only an instant. And no one noticed because the sisters were busy bowing to the Chosen lord who'd ridden astride the great gryph. He wore fitted and quilted black riding clothes, actual trousers instead of the pleated wide pants that go under the paneled tunics, everything embroidered in crimson and gold, including his black gauntleted riding gloves.

He sent one glance my way from slanted eyes under brows so extravagantly steep his gaze seemed permanently ironic. His lips twitched in what might have been a smile, as he bowed elaborately in my direction, his long, shiny blue-black braid sliding over his shoulder briefly. Then he graced the sisters with a lesser bow.

And he walked away, no one having spoken.

"If Your Imperial Serenity will grace our float by choosing a place?" Ingras spoke, her high voice sweet and singsong.

I stepped in to find cushioned seats all around the float. I planted my imperial backside on a cushion at the far side of the basket so that I sat facing the birds. I curled my tail around me as the sisters entered and chose places across from me with their backs to the gryphs.

Pelan said, "If Your Imperial Serenity will pardon a trespass, would you care to wear a hat, or a thicker coat or cloak?"

"I don't get cold. Are hats required for a reason?"

They lifted their eyelids in brief surprise. "It is just that the winds can tangle one's hair to a painful degree." Ingras bowed with an air of faint apology, and I wondered if my question had been deemed uncouth.

"My hair doesn't tangle," I said, lifting it and snapping it before letting it settle around me. I had to laugh inside—my first, and too brief, bit of humor since my captivity—as their eyes lifted and watched, again in unnervingly matched echo.

They settled themselves with tiny twitches and pats to their thick cloaks, tugging their peaked hats securely. Delicate filigree netting at the back covered their long braided tails of hair.

One of them then flexed her gloved fingers in a gesture I would learn was part of their fais commands, touched what I'd assumed to be a decorative jewel on the rim of the basket between them and the birds, and I stared in surprise as magic flashed with scintillating green and the float slid gently off the platform into the air.

Even with the fais blurring my magic sense, I could feel powerful magic surging around me. Then the birds stretched out their necks, lifted their great wings, and leaped into the air. The silken cord neatly coiled at either side of the basket began to straighten, and on the second flap, pulled taut.

The float slid upward with a slight tug. The sisters looked at me expectantly, and I wondered if they were waiting for me to speak. I remembered the pretense of my superior rank (which made me wonder if they knew I was a prisoner), and said the first thing in my head that I figured would not get me into trouble if You Know Who was listening: "That fellow riding gryph-back. Do you ride the purple ones, and harness these brown or gray ones to the floats?"

"The great gryphs, the males with the violet feathers, are much rarer," Pelan said. "Their education presents a great challenge. Our brown hens, nearly as large, are quieter. The grays, smaller still, have like the browns long been egg-civilized. The great gryphs often do not survive past the first year in harness, in spite of very great care."

"The Most Noble Raifas caught and civilized his great gryph," Ingras finished. "And those are the rarest of all. When caught half-grown in the wild, they are faster even than the grays, and can fly longer distances. But they cannot fly in tandem."

By then the float had slid up the air until we glided away from the platform below.

Raifas had disappeared inside the building. "I don't remember him meeting him at the reception," I said, though I wasn't certain. They had all looked alike to me in a group; maybe those eyebrows weren't distinctive when surrounded by copies all more or less the same.

"He was not there. He surely had responsibilities at Ardam Pennon," Pelan said in that drifting voice.

"A pennon?" I asked. "Is that not a flag on a pole?" I turned my attention outward, aware that I did not like the sensation of being in the air without wings and a bird body. My stomach dropped in a peculiarly unpleasant way, and I gulped, hair and tail flashing outward to balance me. The sisters looked startled.

Then Pelan began to describe the empire in the same sort of cadence the servant had read that record, high-sounding language with a lot of greatness and so forth thrown in.

While she spoke I forced myself to look down. I knew the float was safe, or they wouldn't be sitting there so decorously. It swung very slowly and steadily, and I could feel the magic keeping it afloat as the gryphs drew it along.

We had progressed outward far enough so that I could see the whole of Icecrest Palace. Arches connected the towers of white marble in groups of three, suggesting a spiral upward. The highest tower flew a long banner with the dragon on it. The slanted roof was made in beautiful patterned tiles and dotted with small glass domes. These domes and the many lancet-arch windows threw back the sunlight in a glory of scintillation: they looked like cut gems from a distance. The palace's beauty and arrogance, crowning the rocky promontory, commanded the eye, a reminder of power.

Meanwhile, I listened to Pelan's soft, pleasing voice, sifting for the sense in all the courtly palaver. Pennons seems to be what anywhere else would be provinces, or dukedoms, or principalities, etc. I'd already learned from the Kherval that size did not always dictate rank. History had ways of creating kingdoms the size of a pimple, and baronies that took a week to ride across. And that didn't count the free cities that belonged to no one or the territories no one could claim.

So Sveran Djur was divided into pennons, and Nobles strove to attain the governance of these, becoming Most Nobles. The best of them got to inherit home pennons — apparently direct descent through families was desirable — but that wasn't guaranteed.

While I listened I looked down. The parade court extended in a broad circle, its far end opening to hundreds of steps winding downward to a city built into the west side of the mountain. The houses appeared to be constructed of white stone, the steep roofs covered with sparkling snow. The narrow streets angled in switchbacks and curves, with occasional widened terraces circled with espaliered trees, gray and winter-bare. People moved up and down the streets, tiny colorful dots in a city that looked like it had been made of sugar.

I lifted my gaze. A short distance away, to left and right, flew our escort, imperial guards pulled by the smaller, faster gray gryphs. Beyond lay the vast ocean, dotted with islands.

Beyond the city southward lay a long, narrow peninsula spined with mountains, as though a dragon had lain down in the water, hiding its head, its body represented by that huge conical peak in the hazy distance. Was that the origin of their dragon symbol, I wondered?

The float had lifted high enough so that we could see the ocean horizon in both directions. I knew I was high enough to transform, but when I drew a breath, flexing my back muscles in the way that presaged transformation, my neck burned warningly. Dhes-Andis had told the truth about *that*. "I hate this thing!" I burst out, clutching at the fais with my fingers.

The sisters jumped as if I'd slapped them. Pelan looked shocked, and Ingras wary. It was the first time I'd seen any difference in them besides the higher timbre of Ingras's voice.

"We could never exist without fais," Pelan said in that smooth, soft voice. "It is the gift of civilization. We use it every day to the betterment of life."

"You mean you torture people every day?" I asked. "How does that improve your life? It certainly doesn't for your victim, that I can promise."

Pelan paled, and Ingras blushed.

"You're speaking of correction?" Ingras asked at last. Pelan seemed unable to speak.

"If that's what you like to call it," I said. "But to me, torture is torture. Even if it doesn't leave a visible mark."

They looked at me as if I'd spewed the vilest language ever not heard in polite company. Or I spoke another language. Or I was insane. And though I had my steel mental wall (I checked it obsessively) somehow I could *feel* Dhes-Andis laughing as he peered into that scrying crystal.

"Never mind that," I said grimly, and to their visible relief, added, "All I see are very high mountains. Where is the farmland? Is that in the islands further south?"

"All our islands are mountainous, some with the dragonfire spouting to the sky," Pelan said. "As for farming, do you not see the terracing?"

Those terraces looked mighty small to be feeding cities of people, but I knew I was only seeing the extreme northern end of this island, and Sveran Djur was made up of a long archipelago here, and to the west, another cluster. And more.

"Though we have had droughts endangering our people," Ingras said. "But once we are united with the Ndai Islands, the dangers will lessen."

"Very true." Pelan seemed anxious to get past mention of droughts; she didn't seem to want to say anything that wasn't pleasant.

So I passed right on. "You said dragonfire. You mean the mountains that erupt in molten rock? Are there actual dragons inside them? The stories I've heard, real dragons long ago went out of the world."

Ingras spoke. "Our oldest ballads all talk of the fire creatures dwelling between worlds, but civilized people put little stock in songs and stories for children. Reaching the age of discretion implies sifting verifiable truth from entertainment. Pelan, see to the west: weather is coming. We must turn back."

"It was a good sunbloom," Pelan said a little sadly.

"Sunbloom?" I asked.

"Idiom for when the sun emerges for us."

From that I understood that the constant storms and gloom were common, and now I understood the purpose of that painted, magical sky in the Chamber of Celestial Contemplation. These Djurans scarcely ever saw the real stars.

Nineteen

WHEN DHES-ANDIS SUMMONED ME next, I assumed my Princess Elenderi mask, but defensively. He'd won the battle of wits. All I had was stealth.

I recited the history of Emperor Vandarus Andis as Chith had read it out. (I was beginning to learn the servants' names, though it was difficult to get past all that Imperial Princess talk to find the person behind the politesse.)

At the end, he said, "Very well recited. Do you have questions?"

I had plenty of them, but I stuck firmly to my mask. "No, Your Imperial Serenity," I lisped in a good mimicry of Pelan's voice.

His lips twitched, and I held my breath, but nothing happened.

He said, "I believe you still do not comprehend the civilized life, or how proximity to power can require commensurate understanding of pain until one truly comprehends one's limits. Correction is pure. The higher the rank, the greater the need for control. That and order are the fundaments of civilized life." He lifted his chin minutely, and the edge of his own fais gleamed golden above the deep blue of his collar, a hint of diamonds glittering. "Come."

He left his chair and walked to the balcony we had gone to before. Another blizzard howled outside, and I hoped that he hadn't forced all those people to trudge up those thousand steps to kneel on that parade ground again.

When he gestured to the window I stood on tiptoe and peered down, relieved to see it empty except for eddies of white swirling across the stones.

"No, this way. To the perch."

I turned my head and there was the balcony with the platform below it. Dark shapes humped above the railing, nearly obscured by falling snow: gryphs, with their heads tucked under their wings. In the center, a purple great gryph.

"Capturing and civilizing the great gryphs requires skill, patience, strength and wit. Those who are successful are more likely to win greater responsibility."

I knew then that I had guessed right. He had indeed been scrying me during my visit with the sisters, and further, he wanted me to know. Chills roughened the skin of my arms and that horrible fais seemed to tighten mercilessly, though I knew it was inert.

Memory of Dhes-Andis demonstrating his ability to communicate mentally whether one liked it or not, once he gained one's mental signature, still harrowed my dreams. It was the worst sort of violation, and as usual, I convulsively checked my mental steel wall. A brief image of Prince Geric's ravaged face there at the end hit me, and I wondered if he had actually tried to escape when he'd said he was going, and Dhes-Andis forced him back in order to lay that trap for me.

I swallowed, knowing I was expected to reply.

"Those golden collars. On the gryphs. Are those fais?" I asked.

"Of course," he replied. "All our beasts of burden wear them. Pets as well. Animals are protected thereby. Would you like a great gryph of your own? I possess two who are beautifully trained, and perfectly safe to ride."

"I'd rather fly myself," I said, and immediately I sensed that it was the wrong answer. I didn't see any reaction, but I was becoming acutely aware of any change in his breathing, a flicker of eyelash, a subtle alteration of note in his voice, any sign before the lightning struck.

It did not strike now, but he led the way back to the chairs, saying—with that warning note impossible to describe, except in the way my flesh crawled in anticipation of pain—"Let us begin with your fire spell. I desire you to focus, and set fire to a target I have had prepared...."

Warning flared through me, almost as painful as the so-called correction. "Target?"

He looked amused as one of the cats leaped up onto the arm of his chair, leaned out and polished its head against the scrying crystal. "A bundle of hay. It sits in one of the empty harvest barns. Have you ever used a scry stone before?"

"No."

"I don't know if Hrethan use them in the same manner we do, but you are not fully Hrethan, so we can experiment with your abilities and limitations...."

Setting fire to hay, I thought, seemed harmless enough. Certainly harmless to me, considering the alternative. And maybe I could keep him busy too long to attempt the scry stone.

※

By nightfall my eyes burned with tiredness.

Did I sleep well? No. Once again that melody haunted me and I turned restlessly, my mind chasing it through memory until I jerked awake, gasping for breath. How had I ever thought I had liked it? But I *had*. Once.

Toward morning exhaustion overcame even memories and haunted melodies, and I slept like a rock for too short a while, waking when light filtered in the windows. I always woke at first light, and here was another day of captivity closing inexorably around me.

As soon as my feet hit the floor, quiet as I was, one of the servants emerged from their alcove. They had to have some kind of warning magic. The idea of twelve people whose days were spent anticipating my whims, and could be punished for my perceived transgressions, weighed on my spirit, increasing my sense of powerlessness. Contemplating how much they must secretly hate me drove me once more to the music room.

As soon as I saw the harp, my fingers tingled. All right. I'd let myself play, but at the first sign of any suspicious mind invasion I'd smash the harp to splinters, I thought savagely as I sat and ran my fingers over the strings.

As always, perfectly in tune. My fingers plucked out that melody, beautiful, soothing, comfortingly familiar in a way that brought gentle imaginings, and best of all, no voices. Oh, a sense of the *sound* of voices, but not what they said: loving, comforting, one blue face and one pale with light-colored long hair...windharps on high mountain peaks...tiny star-shaped flowers in a translucent bowl that caught sun shafts from outside a window, so that it seemed to be full of light.

I tried to reach it, my hands falling short....

My hands.

My small, fat hands.

This was a memory from before I could talk, before I could walk.

Once again I pulled my fingers away from the harp. My skin roughened, my fuzz fluffing and my hair flashing straight up, then curling in around me protectively. I wanted to run, but equally strong was my desire to remain, and recapture what I had thought lost forever.

It had to be a trick, I thought, backing away. It did not feel like anything Dhes-Andis would do, or even think of, but there I was a prisoner in his citadel, and I could not trust anything.

I didn't even trust *trust*, I thought as I stalked away, scowling at old Vandarus as I passed. Trust *always* betrayed you, that much I'd learned from Hlanan's beloved empire.

"Your Imperial Serenity."

It was a man's voice. But not Emperor Evil's.

I halted, back to a wall, and gazed up a forest green silk tunic embroidered with stylized mulberries and cranes to Most Noble eyebrows.

"My abject apologies for missing introduction to Your Imperial Serenity," he said, bowing.

"It's fine," I replied at random, too distracted to practice my courtly mimicry. "I still can't tell anyone apart. You're Raifas, right? The Most Noble of Ardam Pennon?"

He bowed again. "I am honored by Your Imperial Serenity's notice."

I struggled to pull my Princess Elenderi mask together, in spite of my raw emotions and the tiredness nearly overwhelming me. Another dull conversation of courtly nothings was only slightly better than another Dhes-Andis interview.

Raifas said, "There is no sun, and likely none expected, but the snow has lifted for a time. And I am told you are not afraid of winter weather. Would you enjoy a ride?"

"You mean on a gryph?" I asked, surprised.

"This way." He flashed a grin. It might have been a challenge — disbelief — I didn't care. The chance to get away pulled at me so strongly I whirled and started off in the direction of his lifted hand.

He uttered a soft laugh as he took a quick step to catch up. "I see that I am to take deed for word."

"Why talk?" I said. "You're just going to do more bowing and Your Imperial Serenitying. I'd rather get away —" Fiercely I caught myself. *Mask!* "Away into the sky to enjoy the wind."

As we started down the steps, he said, "If you desire to set aside the privileges of honorifics, what would you prefer to be called?"

My name is Lhind shaped my lips — I drew breath to say it — then I thought, Why let any of them see my true nature? There are those who believe that knowing a true name can result in magery, but I never believed that. Perhaps in some sense it was true. Not the name itself having power, but giving someone the key to your private citadel of mind and heart who should never be let within.

My name is Hlanan Vosaga.

Oh, *how* memory can hurt! I tried to breathe out the heartache as my thoughts flickered faster than a heartbeat through the vivid memories: when he first spoke his name, to our travel alone up the central valley, and then to his admitting who he was. "Hlanan Vosaga" had told me nothing whatsoever about his true self. That I had had to learn on my own.

Names were merely names. But Princess Elenderi was my mask.

I paused on the step, swept a bow, and said, "Elenderi will do, Most Noble."

"May I return the favor? The simplicity of Raifas is refreshing."

As soon as we got out the door the wind hit hard, bitingly cold, even for me. I fluffed my fuzz, snapped hair and tail around me, and breathed in, instinct permitting enough of my bird nature to let the cold flow over me and away.

Servants waited on the perch balcony, leaning into the gusts. Raifas stripped off his long green-paneled tunic, revealing his thick quilted riding jacket beneath made tight to his body, and equally tight trousers tucked into solid boots. With a deliberate movement he slung the tunic to one side, where the wind tried to take it. But one of the servants sprang forth to catch it and began carefully folding it with his back to the wind.

"His Imperial Serenity has graciously offered Andisla for you to ride," Raifas shouted against the wind. Andisla: *Little Andis*, my mind promptly translated. "He is safer by far than my Firebird, though not as fast."

We approached the two immense purple gryphs, one with a harness and saddle far finer than that on the other.

He offered a hand to me as if I needed a lift. I sprang up easily into the air, somersaulting in the wind before landing on my toes on the gryph's back. I laughed as his brows shot to his hairline and then settled into the saddle, ignoring the stirrups in favor of sitting cross-legged.

He set his foot to Firebird's stirrup and vaulted into his saddle, then said over his shoulder, "I suggest you grip with your knees. The launch is stronger than you might expect."

"I'll be fine," I said, though I was wondering, what if I fell off?

I left the thought there, choking the cold curdle of despair. No. I refused to throw myself off. Escape I would, but not into death, because then Dhes-Andis would win. He was trying to destroy Lhind while making her into this pretend princess, and that was the surest way of accomplishing the first.

A sudden bounce and lurch, and we plummeted down as Andisla spread his wings. Then we leveled out and banked at a steep slant.

Because my entire body knew to muscle and bone how to fly, I leaned as the bird leaned, so exhilarated I laughed, the wind taking the sound in a stream.

Ahead, Raifas looked back once, and his lip curled in challenge. He touched the beautiful golden harness—greenish magical light flashed—and Firebird cried out harshly and dove toward the gray water far below. Andisla followed, which answered the question forming in my mind about guidance. Raifas led on Firebird and Andisla followed. I would not be able to guide the gryph away. Of course. Or I never would have been permitted that ride.

So I'd enjoy the semblance of freedom, and I leaned into Andisla's neck, the wind so strong I slitted my eyes. Down we sped until we neared the white crests of the waves, then with a snap of wings the gryphs leveled out and skimmed over the water, occasionally smashing through icy spray. Then up, and so began a dance between sky and water, weaving with the wind.

I could have ridden the wind forever, but snow arrived on a gust. It thickened with the rising gale, and I could feel Andisla beginning to labor under me.

I bent low, wondering if it made any difference. I felt the slightest easement in Andisla, so I pressed myself against his neck.

Veering near, Raifas shouted over the flurries whirling between us, "You in danger?"

"No!" I screeched, the wind ripping away my high voice. "I think this gryph is tired."

"They're quite strong," he countered, swooping overhead. "But we can return if you like."

"Yes." Maybe they were strong, but they didn't fly for choice in this weather, especially when the snow was so sticky. It was beginning to clump up over the gryph's fais, along the harness, and over the saddle as well as the edge of Andisla's wings. I tried to kick and brush away what I could reach until the wind almost took me, and so I pressed in tight again.

By the time the gryphs returned to the palace they were definitely struggling. Their wings had built up glistening globs of white, rimed with ice. Andisla landed heavily, shuddering a shower of clotted snow.

I felt as if I wore a harness, as if that fais encircled my neck instead of the gryph's neck. An impulse seized me. After all that practice with the straw in the barn, why not try something useful? I steadied myself against the low railing, concentrated, and whispered the fire spell as I brushed warmth over the bird to melt the icy snow.

Andisla snapped his wings out, fluffed his feathers, and his head came up and around. He let out a thin cry that I felt as the gryph version of "Ah-h-h-h."

Raifas had bent into the wind and was already crossing the terrace toward the door into the palace. A thickening curtain of icy snow rendered him into a silhouette. Firebird wriggled and shook as attendants scurried out from the snow-obscured aviary to attend to the birds.

Perhaps they had a way to get that ice off the gryphs, but I still used my spell to free Firebird of his load. Then I scudded after Raifas and left the bird-tenders to do whatever it was they did.

As soon as we passed inside the doors I shook myself, fluffing my fuzz and snapping snow from my hair. The waiting servant handed Raifas his green silk robe, which he pulled over his riding clothes. Then he stood a couple paces away, arms crossed and head canted as I finished fluffing myself free of snow and ice.

I stopped as soon as I noticed.

He spoke. "Elenderi, may I ask how you knew the weather was turning to ice? Is this an innate knowledge?"

"I didn't," I said. "Did you not feel the gryphs laboring?"

"Firebird is stronger than a mere wind. The ride is the better when he strives and triumphs," he said, and then added, "You very nearly caught up once or twice. The egg-civilized are never as fast as the wild, but your riding was superlative. You must have been riding since childhood."

I spread my hands in their manner, palm out. "That was my first."

This time the eyebrows didn't shoot quite so high, but he gave me a speculative look, as if he didn't believe me. Not that I cared if he did or not. I wasn't going to talk about my flying. Let him think I lied like a rug. After all, I'd spent a lifetime doing just that!

"Do you care to ride again?" he asked finally.

"Yes," I said, with the first enthusiasm I'd felt since I'd been wrenched into Sveran Djur.

He smiled. "If the storm lifts long enough and the wind is favorable, we could reach Ardam Pennon. Does that prospect interest you?"

"Certainly."

"Your Imperial Serenity." A new voice.

Ingras approached, her steps so tiny it seemed as if she floated, or rolled on wheels. Seeing my gaze, she halted and performed her most formal bow. "I beg forgiveness for my rude interruption. Most Noble, yours as well."

They both gave me expectant glances, and I remembered that as the supposed senior in rank it was my prerogative to accept the interruption, or to end the conversation.

"Were you looking for me?" I asked.

"My sister desired me to request the honor of your company for an informal poetry reading," she said, looking from him to me.

Raifas's smile was not a grin. Barely even a smile, and yet he seemed on the verge of laughter. I saw nothing amusing in the invitation, and then Ingras said in the most formal manner, "Your Imperial Serenity, my sister and I would be honored if you would consider us as guides any time you wish to educate, ah, to acquaint yourself with our ways."

"I believe I may fairly say that the entire family would be honored by any questions you wish to ask," Raifas said, and this time I recognized irony.

I was missing some other undercurrent. I knew it though I could not identify it. So I backed up a step, remembered the exasperating bows, and said, "Another time?"

And I fled. Halfway up the marble stairs I faltered. The idea of being closed in that suite with all those servants waiting for me to give them orders brought me to a stop. The music room? The way my heart surged scared me. I didn't trust anything there, did not dare to.

But I could get educated in order to defend myself, could I not? And I'd had an offer for exactly that.

So I retraced my steps, running on my silent bare feet, just to discover the way to the perch balcony empty. I recollected the direction Ingras had come from and sped that way, shoulders hunched lest I run into an invisible wall and get burned.

Six sides, lots of angled corners. I heard their voices before I saw anyone.

Ingras, with her tiny steps, must have arrived directly before me, for I heard Pelan say, "She comes not? And we went to all this trouble!"

The first real, normal expression I'd ever heard in her voice.

Ingras replied, "She ran off like some wild creature. Really, what is His Imperial Serenity thinking?"

Pelan exclaimed, "Do you think he is thinking of getting an heir with her?"

"Impossible," Ingras replied firmly. And as I sagged against the wall in relief, "When he would burn any of his consorts for daring to have a child? No. Amney is certain he wants her for some other purpose in spite of his whim about calling her a princess."

Pelan said, "Then he will marry her off to the empire's advantage, the same as all the rest of us. Was Raifas there?"

"He was, and Pelan, in spite of his avowal to Darus last night that he would comply with the minimum degree of welcome toward that boorish Hrethan, I heard Raifas offer to take her out again, and to Ardam, yet...."

The voices had been fading. At that point Ingras's voice became a murmur in which individual words could not be distinguished. I could have turned the corner to follow and eavesdrop more, except why? I'd learned enough to think about!

Once again I ran for my suite, but this time it was not a retreat. It had been something of a relief to hear Pelan's and Ingras's real voices instead of that unnervingly smooth, expressionless courtly intonation that they considered so civilized. But Ingras's opinion of me was so different from her behavior that I lost any interest in asking her for guidance.

So far, the only ones who hadn't seemed to lie to me (I reserved judgment about Dhes-Andis, whatever he claimed) were the servants.

When I got there, I had my questions ordered in my mind. Kal and Tay, young man and older woman, came out of the alcove.

"What does egg-civilized mean?" I asked when the bowing rigmarole was over.

Tay flicked a glance at Kal, who returned her look with a minute nod: though she was the elder, he was staff leader.

Tay said, "It is both an idiom and a specific, Imperial Princess.

LHIND THE SPY

The specific meaning is to give a newly hatched or born creature a fais upon birth, to begin civilization at once."

"Civilization means like training a horse?"

They glanced at one another, then Tay bowed. "I believe so, Imperial Princess, though we do not have horses on this island. But we know what they are. Other animals and birds are civilized in much the same way."

"And so the idiom?"

"It is a term for the diligent parent or guardian," Tay said. "Whose vigilant correction guides the child to learn in gentle increments. Thus the child is permitted to go into company at a young age."

"Correction, you say? With a fais?" I asked in horror.

She studied me with a mirrored horror, and then (if I skip all the bowing and the careful third person formality owed to my non-existent serenity) said, "We *all* were raised with fais. Before anyone is given responsibility, we understand the consequences of influence."

"What does that mean?"

"I served in the nursery in my young years," Tay said. "One learns the art of proper correction by practicing on oneself." She demonstrated by smacking two fingers smartly inside her wrist, then touching her fais.

Fascinated, I saw a tiny flash of green on the inside of her wrist.

"So it doesn't hurt any more than that?" I asked in total disbelief.

By now they were all there, and every single one of them bowed and assured me that no, the correction was no more than that.

"When do you start doing it?"

"Why, as soon as a child begins to walk," said she, and indicated the stove. "We all know it is warm in winter, but we also know that to touch it would be to burn our hands. How did we learn? A tiny slap away from the stove on curious fingers is a far better deterrent than permitting the child to burn tender flesh, is it not?"

"The guardian must be responsible for both himself and the

child," Kal said. "We are all educated in civilized behavior from the time we first crawl. And if a child has been born among the Chosen, education in responsibility equally begins early."

That caused a fresh cascade of questions, but an imperial minion arrived with a summons to you know where.

At once they bustled around me, switching out my rumpled, still-damp outfit for a fresh formal one embroidered over with tiny lilies and rosebuds.

Then off I went, hurrying to the timing of my thudding heart, my throat echoing with remembered pain.

I nearly stumbled over one of the white cats, same color as the marble floor, and risked a moment to bend down to apologize as I dared not reach mentally. I held out a finger. The cat's tail went straight up, except for an interrogative hook at the end as it advanced daintily, sniffed then permitted me to scratch its head. It began to wind around my ankle. Two more pats while the minion waited and I straightened up, feeling the urgency in that quiet stare. If correction was so gentle, why that anxious gaze?

No, there was definitely something missing there, I thought as the door minions tended those big double doors so that I did not have to defile my fingers.

Twenty

I BRACED FOR ANOTHER harrowing session, but Dhes-Andis said only, "The perch tenders reported your gesture with magic, apparently to the benefit of the great gryphs."

"It still makes me dizzy," I said, "but I can do it."

"I think practice to a better purpose than burning straw might be useful," he replied, taking me by surprise. "You probably know that the stoves here use Fire Sticks, made the same way the world over: young mages sit outside in spring and summer, repeating the spell to draw and store sun warmth in the Sticks. It is regrettably tedious work, something that most mages have to endure for their first year or two of study. I suggest you go through the palace and renew the magic on the Fire Sticks."

"If I do, will not the mages be put out of work?" I asked.

"On the contrary, they would be grateful beyond measure. The spell is simple. There is no need to perform it endlessly except that it must be done. So it is given to beginners to discipline them. But discipline can be learnt as well in other ways. The skill to call and control fire is rarer. If you can draw and store your fire in the form of warmth in those Sticks, mage students will be free to turn their efforts to other uses."

Such as making whatever it was you threatened to ignite back in Thann? I thought.

I didn't ask it, though I despised myself for my cowardice. And the answer was obvious anyway. If he wanted that spell done it would get done, whether or not Fire Sticks got made.

He added with his smile that looked so benign, "And I will remind you that effort is always rewarded. Go experiment. See what you can achieve."

I didn't even try to hide my relief. There was no reason to refuse—no one would be hurt or harmed.

I began in my suite, where I could make mistakes and not be distracted by watchers other than the people I knew already had to watch me.

It took me a couple of days of frustrating experiments in tiny bursts, for I did not want to risk cracking the porcelain of the stove if I lost control of the withering stream of fire, or reducing the enameled Fire Sticks to ash. This spell's dangers I'd learned the summer before, and had nearly destroyed myself and half of Fara Bay in the doing.

I retreated a couple of times to the music room, which I found comforting in a frightening situation that kept me restless and tossing at night no matter how tired I was.

By the second day I found myself falling asleep if I sat and closed my eyes. It was in the state between waking and sleep after one of these inadvertent snoozes that I found myself sensing magic beyond the continual "hum" of the fais.

That meant I could evaluate the Fire Sticks's stored magic, perceiving how many of the repeated spells gathering sun warmth still remained. It was like counting a stack of sheets of paper. I didn't have to frame those cumbersome repeated spells into one hypothetical sheet of paper at a time. I shaped my fire magic by curling my thumb and forefinger in a tiny circle no bigger than a pin-hole and drawing it through by force of mind. Using the pin-hole as a way of controlling the magic, I sent a steady but thin stream of fire magic into the Fire Sticks until they pulsed green in the mental plane: enough.

They glowed full of magic, safely releasing the warmth through the framing spell, which I had managed not to destroy. They would probably last at least a year, maybe more, before needing more magic.

My breath still shuddered in my chest. That spell always cost. But I was sitting cross-legged on the ground, so I pressed my hands to the floor on either side of me, and kept my eyes shut until the swimming sensation passed.

Then I moved to the little stove in the bath. The magic in those Fire Sticks was far more diminished. Whoosh! Sit. Recover.

Then to the stove in the bedroom, and in the two sitting rooms that I never used, one formal and one extremely formal.

When I was done, I said to Kal, "Do you have a stove in whatever space you have beyond that alcove?"

He bowed very low, then said, "The Imperial Princess honors us with her question, but there is no need to bestir herself. Our needs are seen to by the royal steward."

I said, "But someone still has to do the work to bespell your Fire Sticks, do they not? Why not me when I can do it faster? The emperor asked me to practice," I added, and sure enough, mention of Dhes-Andis got them hopping.

Well. Not hopping. Djurans don't hop. But they permitted me beyond the limit of their little alcove, which was built to be unobtrusive.

I was relieved to discover a spacious six-sided room beyond: spacious, plaster instead of marble, lit by glowglobes. It also had a small dome overhead to permit what sunlight there was. Plain doors opened off all six sides into small bedchambers.

An equally plain stove had been built in the center of the room. An old woman sat by it, embroidering intertwined vines full of blossoms onto a length of silk.

I sat cross-legged on the floor, concentrated, and renewed their stove. When I'd recovered, I said, "Do you have stoves in your rooms?"

Kal—with a lot of embarrassed circumlocution—gave me to understand that the rooms were very small as they spent no time in them beyond sleeping, at which time they opened them to the main room to catch the heat flow.

They all stood around with their hands together, watching me. I became aware that I had crossed some kind of invisible boundary, and there were no rules for the situation. Rather than make them uncomfortable, I scrambled to my feet and retreated to the grand suite of fancy rooms suitable for one imperial princess.

I had done what I'd been asked and no one was hurt. It was

even helpful. And I'd enjoyed myself.

Without further examining my motivations, as a four-day blizzard pounded the palace walls and windows, I moved from chamber to chamber to renew the Fire Sticks. If a door opened to me, and not all of them did, I went inside.

At no time did the fais stop me, so I learned something of the life of the palace. Those upper floors, spread between the highest three towers, made up the imperial residence—which had been an inner wing in Erev-li-Erval, with its own gardens. No garden here, except those carefully tended and trained trees in some rooms. I didn't think about how they dealt with the roots when there were floors beneath, but it would be important later.

At first I moved with trepidation, dreading a stumble into Dhes-Andis's lair. Horrid thought! But I avoided going near the golden doors with rampant dragons carved amid stylized flames. Those had to be his personal suite.

That brought the question: why didn't *he* go around once a year and renew the Fire Sticks himself? Those many layers testified to laborious spellcasting of the sort beginners did. He could save them days of labor, but I wasn't going to ask. I was happy enough to avoid him, though his presence began to shape itself around me in odd ways. Like that room with all the weapons. Late one morning I passed it and heard the murmur of his voice inside—and here were two of his guards on duty, and a faint trace of his scent in the air.

It was not at all an unpleasant scent, rather the opposite, complex yet subtle. In fact, anywhere else I would have liked it, but my nerves recognized it before I did, flashing an echo of burn, and I sped away as if I'd been caught stealing.

So he went there to use those weapons. But I already knew that Sveran-Djur civilization was capable of astoundingly, flagrantly non-peaceful behavior.

At the other end of the floor several cats decided to follow me, so quiet at first I didn't notice. I crouched down, scratching and petting heads, under chins, over backs. The cats rubbed cheeks against my hand and humped backs into my fingers, as all cats do, except they were so silent, like ghost cats.

They followed me the rest of the way on that floor, but stopped at the stairway. I had to laugh at the feline vanguard along the top stair, tails raised like banners, then I ran down.

Below this floor lay state rooms, and the floor below that comprised the guest suites where stayed the Chosen. Almost all those doors were shut, save two large spaces whose purpose I could not guess. I renewed the stoves there, then ran down another set of stairs.

Here I found the largest part of the palace by a significant margin. The building was still marble, but bare of decorative carving and art, the vaulted corridors opening to a bewildering warren of connecting suites used by the administration of the empire. Three floors of it. I spent the larger part of my days there, and though I encountered what must have been hundreds of Djurans, alike in their black hair and similar robes, who bowed like sheaves of wheat in the wind whenever my eye fell on them, then faded back. No one spoke to me.

I found that unsettling, to be visibly invisible—so very much the opposite of my experience in life so far—but I stuck to my task.

An even more bewildering warren below that belonged to the servants who did all the work of maintaining that beautiful palace. Here the people wore the familiar gray linen but had different colors of hair, including a surprising number of fair-haired folk. So servants did not dye their hair black, or could not?

No one to answer that. And I didn't dare ask lest it somehow be interpreted as uncivilized.

The blizzard ended the day before I finished my Fire Stick renewal. During that time no one disturbed me, but on the last day it became apparent that Dhes-Andis had kept a close eye on my progress, because I had scarcely finished the last room and was facing the long climb up the stairs to the top again when I was summoned.

I ran all the way up, turning right instead of left.

"Well done," Dhes-Andis said when I arrived breathless. "I wondered how far you would go to please me."

Please him! I bent my head in a quick bow to hide my horror. I had not done that to please him. Had I?

"What did you learn?" he went on.

I braced myself inwardly, doing my best to smooth my

expression. "I learned how to sense the magic remaining on the Fire Sticks, then I learned how to limit the magic like this." I demonstrated my pin-hole with finger and thumb. "By the time I reached the lower floors, I could picture my finger and thumb here." I tapped my forehead. "And do the spell that way."

"Excellent. And as I promised you success is always rewarded. You have done a superlative job. What would you ask?"

Stop burning me with fais magic? But I knew he would only laugh, or chide me, and I'd get yet another lecture about civilization. "I already have more stuff in that suite than I've ever had in my life. I don't need more."

"You will learn to appreciate fine things. For now, I trust you will enjoy a broader boundary, say to the city?"

A semblance of freedom, like a leashed pet, I thought bitterly as I gave him My Imperial Serenity's best bow.

And out I went before he could change his mind, straight to the stairs. I had to get away, though I knew that escape was relative. He could spy on me through his scry crystal any time he pleased, thanks to this horrible, choking fais. But a semblance of escape was better than nothing, and I had to think. The idea that I might have been motivated to please him was so...so insidious! But I knew that underneath all my other excuses — it needed doing, it was good practice, people needed it — there had to be some truth.

I hated that thought so much I ran down the stairs as if escaping my own magical fire.

When I reached the lowest terrace, which opened onto that giant parade ground, I found the stones swept clean of snow. A servant approached to ask if I wished for a cart, indicating a decorated one or two person carriage on wheels, harnessed to a pair of creatures I'd never seen before, somewhat like a long-necked bird, but with a lizard's head, and reddish scaled skin except on its round body, which was feathered in brown. They balanced on two long, spindly legs with three long toes, and they had two tiny front arms folded in against their bodies below golden fais attached to the harness.

Their heads moved lizard-quick, one eye then the other looking my way. When I met the gaze of the foremost, I got that blurry, heady feeling, as if the ground were unsteady, and I looked away. "That's all right, thanks," I said. "I would enjoy the walk."

"As the Imperial Princess desires."

I turned my back on the low bow, and crossed the parade ground toward the broad stairway at the other end.

The urge to escape intensified my itch to be moving, after all that enforced enclosure. I stood at the top of the steps that had been carved in switchbacks down the mountain, with little curved stone benches at every turn. I leaped down the steps, five at a time, happy to be in the air again.

Oh, the urge to transform was so strong! I tried to assuage it by ever longer leaps, hair and tail flashing out to balance me, until I dared the long leap from one switchback to that below it, my feet stinging when I smacked to the stone. The sting subsided so I did it again, and again, somersaulting through the air, and finally practicing wide-armed dives, head over heels before landing.

Exhilarated in spite of my awareness that freedom was only pretense, I reached the street long before I was ready to.

Until then I had not given a thought to my appearance among the mostly dark-haired, golden or bronze-skinned Djurans. All my life I had hidden my differences, striving to blend in without notice. I was used to being invisible in any crowd. But the first people I encountered stared before quickly turning away.

It couldn't be helped. Either I went back up to hide or ventured on and got stared at. And if so, what were they going to do?

Yes, what *were* they going to do? Were they going to hate me after that appalling business when their emperor made them trudge all the way up the mountain to stand in the icy air, just for me to make an appearance for about the space of three breaths?

The first thing I became aware of was music. Threes were so important that I was not surprised to hear triple beats, but when I passed down the narrow street between high-piled snowbanks, above which peeked steep-roofed houses, I heard syncopated rhythms in ravishing chords. Instead of threes in four-beat measures I heard five counts, ONE-two-three-FOUR-five.

Though the sun hid behind a solid bank of white cloud, rendering the wintry air extra bitter, everybody seemed to be out and about after those days of blizzard. People of all ages walked about on peg-bottomed clogs. Here, as in the lower levels of the palace, people had a variety of hair colors, mostly dark, but with a few fair heads here or there.

They talked and smiled, carrying baskets or pushing or pulling little carts, but no one seemed to be worried about pickpockets or thieves. I saw coins glinting in baskets, right out in the open. That never would have happened in Fara Bay, or anywhere on Thesreve's coast.

I could feel those quick, curious glances, but no one approached me, just as in the lower layers of the palace. People either backed away to let me pass or flowed around me at least a pace away, eyes averted. They acted as if I were invisible, but my life had depending for too long on my remaining undetected for me not to know the difference between people pretending not to notice me and actually not noticing me.

The houses differed from those of the continent not in the steep roofs, common in all mountainy areas I'd ever seen, but in the eave edging of smooth curves. All the houses had this edging, large and small. Pale stone formed walls and stairs and street alike, the sameness broken by patterned tiles on the roofs. Touches of color appeared in windows, especially in the upper stories, behind which potted flowers grew.

Here and there people had tunneled ice-blue arches through the snowbanks. I paused when I spotted a half-collapsed archway in an enormous snowdrift where an avalanche had obviously fallen from farther up the mountain. People squeezed in and out one at a time, some sliding on the glassy smooth ice, which seemed to be too deep for their clog pegs to penetrate.

I stepped around a clump of ice. When the crowd thinned I held my breath, aimed through the mental pin-hole and flash! The entire drift melted in a pleasing hiss, hot water streaming away to run off the lower zigzag.

I hurried away, pausing at another burst of music in entrancing rhythm. What was going on in those houses? Not all could be inns offering entertainment! Who would be traveling in this weather?

At the end of that street before the downward curve to the next switchback, the houses tucked into the bend had windows that enabled me to look down inside. The upper rooms appeared to be empty, but in a lower, gold-lit room I glimpsed a circle of people weaving silk as a trio of musicians played while they worked.

This reminded me of Thesreve in summer, when at sundown musicians played on balconies for the entire street to hear and everybody would toss them a coin, however small in value. Only in Thesreve, windows and doors stood open to vent the heat. Many preferred to work or visit during the long twilight once the heat had begun to wane.

In those days sometimes when the music could not be resisted, I'd danced on rooftops where no one could see me. The Djurans' entrancing melodies tingled my toes, but I was too self-conscious to want to dance in that icy street with all those sideways glances.

I'd almost reached the first turning when the splash of quick footsteps behind me caused me to whirl around. A small boy ran toward me, short silky red hair swinging at each step. Then he faltered, one hand brushing over his scarf-swathed throat. He swayed, and when he saw my gaze, his mouth rounded, and he dropped to his knees—splash!—and banged his forehead on the ground.

"Don't do that," I exclaimed, springing forward at the same time a fair-haired man hurried up, throwing anxious glances left and right and bobbing apologetically.

"Mor," he said when he reached the boy, his voice low and anxious. And to me, "I beg forgiveness of the Imperial Princess, and request her pardon for my son, who is still learning civilized behavior." Splash! He too went to his knees and bowed down.

"Please get up. It's so cold," I said, and to the child, "Did you want to talk to me, Mor?"

The little boy looked up. He couldn't have been more than three. "You have a tail," he ventured in his piping little voice.

I laughed, and swished it from side to side.

"I want a tail," he stated.

"Mor," the man said in an agonized undertone, and reached to take the boy's hand.

The boy looked back at me, forehead puckered. "Make it go?" His fat little hand lifted toward what I'd taken to be an extra high snowbank between two shops. It almost blocked a smaller, older house set back a ways. From the looks of it, they'd tried to make a tunnel, but it had caved in.

The man said apologetically, "My son noticed from the window above my shop the magic the Imperial Princess made that melted the snow." His hand indicated the cobbler's sign halfway up the street. "It is our most earnest hope that the Imperial Princess would be merciful and forgive his curiosity."

"He wants me to melt that snowdrift?"

The man dropped to his knees again. "It is nothing, Imperial Princess," he said to the ground; distracted, I noticed that his hair, like those of many others around me, was clipped short at collar length.

I groaned, and he looked up, startled out of his "civilization."

"I am new to Sveran Djur," I said carefully, nerves prickling. The Evil Emperor had to be watching me, probably hooting with amusement. (If he was annoyed, I'd feel it.) "If the snow needs melting, I can easily make that happen. If my doing so doesn't break a rule of civilization—" I barely got that word out. "That I don't yet know."

"We would never presume," he began, and paused, as if searching for the correct words in a situation never before encountered.

So the Chosen didn't walk about talking to non-Chosen people. They stayed in the skies, either in the palace or in their floats.

I said, "If I melt that snow, it won't cause a problem below, will it?" My eyes tracked the water's likely path, and I made a discovery. "Oh."

Now that I could look down at that house tucked into the switchback curve, I saw that what I'd taken to be curved eave decorations were rain gutters.

By now the spell was easy enough to perform, and it took me only a few steadying breaths to recover. As little Mor watched, I melted the snowbank with a greenish flash, and we all watched as the steaming water gurgled and chuckled in a stream across the street past our feet, dropping into a gutter at the side of the road and then falling from roof to balcony to fence to street in beautifully arranged cascades that had to have evolved over centuries.

Mor gave a crow of laughter.

"Did you like that?" I asked him, and when he waved his arms in a semblance of that palms-to-the-side gesture of assent used by adults, I found another awkward snow bank on the next turn and flashed that one, too.

When I recovered, my shoulder blades crawled. I turned to find a huge semi-circle of people. At my gaze, they bent like grass in the wind, knees hitting the pavement. They had to hate that. Clearly there was no regular interaction between Chosen and people, and I wondered why Dhes-Andis had given me permission to explore. To discover how isolated I was? To tempt me to do something that would get me burned?

My gaze flicked back to Mor, and I remembered that little falter. Obviously I'd seen a correction, but it couldn't have been much more than a quick sting unless these folk were made of steel.

"Does anyone else want their snowbank melted?" I asked.

The adults didn't move but another child, a spindle-legged girl, pointed silently at a dirty pile of snow backed up covering the windows of a shop. An adult hissed, and the girl flinched slightly then dropped to her knees.

"I like doing this," I said into the icy air, hoping it made a difference.

I flashed the girl's pile of snow and did it three more times along the lower street, as some people followed at a cautious distance, and others faded away. At one point I heard a wavering elderly female voice from a window overhead: "Why, it's the Empress's day come again, may her memory be blessed. She used to walk among us...."

"Mother, come inside and close the window! You'll be heard."

I could feel the resistance of habit and of expectation in them, and I knew I was not going to overcome it.

Mindful of tiring myself when I had the long climb ahead, I turned back. Mor and his father were still there, so I smiled down at him.

"Farewell, Mor," I said to the little boy.

His father's finger tugged at his hand. The child obediently mimicked the adults and my heart dropped right along with those little knees, hitting the icy ground.

Twenty-one

As soon as I was safely out of sight of the townspeople, I began running up the steps, and then leaping. Though it was a long way up, it felt good to leap again, even when my heart began thumping and I became short of breath.

As I ran I thought about how good it felt to please little Mor, though I hated the idea of exerting myself to please Jardis Dhes-Andis. In each case I had done something that I thought useful and good, but the little boy had no power to demand and to punish if I denied him. He had the freedom to ask, I had the freedom to answer. In pleasing Dhes-Andis, I felt as if I lost ground in the invisible battle between us.

I was breathless when I reached the palace again, my mood pensive. It worsened to bleak when I arrived at my suite to an invitation from another of the Chosen.

I recollected what I'd overheard from Ingras, who'd told the truth only when I wasn't around to hear it. She'd made it very clear that these invitations were not prompted by any friendly or welcoming emotions. They'd been ordered.

I considered refusing, but I knew what the result would be: another visit to the Garden Chamber. I would do anything to avoid that, especially as the outcome was easy to predict. If their emperor was ordering his Chosen to pretend to welcome me, then I was expected to be there. And boring as it was, what else was I going to do, sit in that suite with twelve servants standing around waiting for orders?

On my way to the formal chamber I was startled when one of the black cats chased a white one across my path. The first turned and faced the other, humping up. They met, teeth showed, and they batted at each other. When I took a step toward them they separated, running off with tails in angry bends. The weird thing was, neither had made a sound.

The room for this prospective reading featured a low platform running around its perimeter. Refreshments? I wondered hopefully. Though I wasn't hungry, eating would give me something to do.

No. I discovered that we sat on cushions around that low platform, each with our own tiny table containing gold-nibbed pens, three colors of ink, and squares of rice paper. We faced inward, where the readers came out to perform.

My place was on the slightly higher platform at the far end, next to an empty cushion so beautiful with its pure gold tassels and the dragon embroidered I knew it was intended for Dhes-Andis's imperial backside. I sat on the silver-tasseled cushion next to it, grateful that he was lurking somewhere else.

At my right sat the sisters. They greeted me with sedate courtly effusions that I recognized now as empty courtly palaver. Maybe I could still ask them questions. Just not about anything that had to do with me.

"I went into the town today," I said.

Pelan's brows lifted minutely in surprise. Ingras's lips tightened the measure of a hair. I was beginning to see past the mask, and noted that they did not look at all alike: Pelan's hair had those warm reddish highlights and her cheeks were round. Ingras's hair was a dead blue-black — I sensed the magic — her chin square.

"If you would honor me with your expertise," I said, striving to mimic their smooth singsong, "would you tell me what those creatures are attached to the rolling carts?"

"Lizardrakes, Your Imperial Serenity," Pelan said. "I understand they are rare outside of our islands, but they are common here. Very difficult to find outside of ours bred from the egg."

The first reader came out then and the conversation perforce ended.

The readings were long, intricate poems with internal rhymes in interchanging threes, about history I didn't know. In Erev-li-Erval the courtiers express their pleasure by tapping fingers lightly against palms. Here, it was a low, musical "Ah-h-h."

If the listeners were so moved, they wrote extemporaneous (or so it seemed) poetry in response, and one by one stood to read their responses, again to that sigh of approval.

Naturally I had nothing to say even if I had known their alphabet. Therefore, as the readings went on I studied the others, trying to find individuality under the courtly masks. I spotted Darus, the tallest, his profile severe. No Raifas. I would have recognized those eyebrows again, the blade cheekbones, the ironic curve of his lips.

At my left—on the other side of the emperor's empty cushion—sat Amney, who was easily the most beautiful of them all. Either she paid the fantastic price in gold and time to have a mage permanently dye the roots of each hair follicle so it would forever grow out black, or she'd inherited the color they prized most. She had the delicate widows peak above a heart-shaped face that, according to their art, they most prized. Her long-lashed eyes were so dark a brown they looked black, and her gestures were neat, graceful without being fussy or fluttery or too studied.

Her outer robe shimmered in pale blue with silvery tones, the embroidery not symmetrical. As she dipped her pen and wrote her commentary in superb writing, I studied the exquisite figures on their embroidery; the design began at the lower left and worked slantwise upward across her front in green arabesques meant to suggest rose stalks, complete with thorns. Lower down, the stalks attenuated into rosebuds of pale pink, but these opened out gradually to full-blown roses of mauve on the inner sleeves. You only saw those when she gestured, which had the effect of a bouquet of roses presented and then whisked away.

After each reading she read out her commentary, and fell into a kind of academic duel with one of the men. His writing was even more convolutedly ornate than hers. Then others took their turns.

I didn't catch how they did it, but they decided that the Most

Noble Artist's commentary on one poem and Amney's on another were worthy. I got the impression that their papers would be added to the book where those poems were kept.

Then at last it was over. Amney rose and glanced down at my empty paper, her face as expressive as a doll's. She dipped her head gracefully, the tiny chimes dangling from her forelocks tinkling faintly, then said, "Your Imperial Serenity. I wish to give a reception in your honor. If you have a preference for the form?"

"Yes," I said. "Music. Do you have dancing in Sveran Djur?"

Her face was utterly composed as she bowed again, but behind her Darus waited, and I caught the barest flicker of expression before he saw my gaze and smoothed his face.

"Our dances," Amney said in her soft, musical voice, "are regrettably complicated."

"I enjoy watching people dance," I replied, trying to sound civilized.

"Would it please you to gather in the Chamber of Lilacs at starrise prime tomorrow, Your Serenity?"

"It would please me very much, Most Noble," I replied.

She bowed. I bowed.

On my way back to my lair, I reflected on that hint of expression I'd seen in Darus. Disdain, derision. We'd never spoken outside of that reception. While I had thoroughly convinced myself I did not care what any Djuran thought of me, still, why? Because I didn't know how to write in Djuran? Maybe I'd misread him, though I was fairly certain that whatever was going on behind that courtly mask wasn't friendly feelings.

I walked on, determined to dismiss him as another Prince Geric, and veered in the direction of the music room to play the harp and shake off my uneasy mood. As always, my fingers flexed into expertise as soon as I touched the strings, and within a few chords the warmth of sunrise glowed up my hands to my arms, to my heart, soul, and mind, bringing comforting memories.

I played out song after song, no longer questioning how I knew them. It was enough that I could play them, one beautiful melody after another.

Finally I sighed and began the long trudge back to my suite, tiredness weighing me down so much that my tail flapped against the back of my silken trousers.

When I got there, I sensed a subtle change in the atmosphere. Food awaited me, as always, and no one spoke first, again as always.

By now I knew I was expected to eat alone. Before I entered the alcove, I said, "Tomorrow there's a dance given by the Most Noble Amney at starrise prime. Should I wear something different than what I've been wearing?"

Kal turned to Chith, who glanced at Tay, all faster than a single heartbeat, then Chith said tentatively, "Perhaps the Imperial Princess might wish to wear the butterfly robe?"

"What is that?" I asked.

Another exchange of looks, then Chith bowed herself out of the room into the alcove, and to my surprise returned with the very old woman I'd seen sewing. In triumph she spread her hands, watered silk hanging from her fingers like a shower of stars. The rich, muted glisten of this silk bespoke a weave I'd rarely seen. Over that shade of white, silver, pewter, and the faintest hint of blue had been embroidered butterflies with fantastic gold and black patterns, the lower end of their wings trailing in a such a way that when the silk billowed, it looked as if the butterflies pulsed their wings.

The winged sleeves were scalloped in graceful arcs, each with a tiny silken tassel.

"This was...left," the woman whispered. "Folded away by those of us who made it. We think that it should be offered to the Imperial Princess."

The beauty of the robe, the complete silence of everybody there, all added up to some story that they weren't telling. Great, I thought. Another secret. Just what I need. But those expressions of hope could be no more denied than the beauty of that embroidered silk.

"That butterfly robe is exquisite. I will wear it tomorrow," I said.

Everybody bowed.

"We will finish restoring it for the Imperial Princess," Tay said.

"It looks perfect to me."

With extreme circumlocution and many more bows they gave

me to know that the finishing was not perfect, and this robe must be perfect. We all retired, I to look for the first time at the workmanship on these silken clothes that, beautiful as they were, symbolized everything wrong in my life. No hem visible. Inner and outer layers had been joined and turned inward by some kind of tiny stitching I had no name for. Every detail was exact, right down to the weave.

I doused the light and so commenced another restless night of music-laced dreams underscored by an urgency that translated into my chasing butterflies that receded as fast as I ran.

I woke with the little boy Mor on my mind. No, it was his father, and the way he had apologized right and left to his neighbors.

After I got ready for the day I said to Kal, "Are there thieves here?"

He was so startled that for a moment he forgot all the bowing. "Thieves, Your Imperial Serenity?" he repeated with a glance at the walls as if he expected thieves to leap from the windows or crawl out from behind the porcelain stove.

"In the town," I said. "People carried their coins in the open."

"Such a tendency to take what does not belong to one must be corrected early, Your Imperial Serenity," Kal said earnestly.

Back to the fais again.

"What kind of magic is in fais?" I asked. "I know you can communicate with yours, and you mentioned some being able to correct children. What else are they used for?"

"If the Imperial Princess will forgive me, I would point out that imperial fais can do those things and much more." His hand gestured briefly toward my throat.

"I have an imperial fais?" I stared in blank surprise. My assumption had been that Dhes-Andis had Geric Lendan slap a punitive one on me, with that transfer spell loaded on it.

"The imperial fais is the most difficult to make, Your Imperial Serenity. From the birth of an imperial child the mages begin adding the necessary magic in advance of the child gaining responsibility."

"You mean someone was busy making this thing since I was born?"

"The Imperial Princess is correct."

"But mine doesn't tor...uh, correct, does it? Does it do anything?" *Besides ward me from escape?*

Another flicker of surprise, then with the usual long circumlocution required by imperial etiquette I learned that the fais spells were so shaped that first a child would touch fingers to it — one, two, three, four — or tap, or brush, for certain specific responses to specific people. Once they learned it, they only had to think the taps or brushes for it to respond. In a limited way it was a bit like how I was learning to shape my magic.

Kal taught me various signs and signals, including correction. When I experimented with a tap and his fais sign, he blinked. He had no reaction — for him this was apparently life as usual — but I was astonished that my fais hadn't been warded in that regard, the way it warded me from transforming.

As soon as Kal was done, I withdrew to my bedroom and experimented on myself. I found within two tries (one briefly excruciating) that yes, I had the power of correction. Since I did not believe anything Dhes-Andis did was accidental, the import seemed sinister in the extreme.

I remembered him encouraging me to blast Prince Geric and his minions with fire, when first he taught me that spell as I stood on the rooftops at Fara Bay trying to find a way to rescue Hlanan. I was certain that I was warded against actually attacking Dhes-Andis (witness his response to my desperate attempt to use voice cast against him), though apparently he was quite willing to permit me to experiment with "correction" on others.

This thought I found so disturbing I reacted in my usual way: I ran.

Humans have two ways of dealing with threat, danger, disturbances — fight or flight. My way has always been flight, for preference. Even when I have to fight, I use what I can to interfere with the attacker so that I can escape.

I had to get away now. Fill my mind with something else. I had a free day ahead of me (unless I got the Call of Doom) before that dance, so I decided to visit the town again and see if I could discern ordinary people using fais for something besides correction.

But when I reached the parade court, I found a cluster of beautifully dressed Chosen waiting as lizardrake carts were brought.

As soon as they saw me they bowed, their pretty chiming voices uttering words of welcome. Ingras and Pelan being among them, I suspected how much truth lay behind that welcome and was going to pass on by when they clamored for me to join them.

They could call another cart — they would be honored — I must see Venar's home on Seaforth Mountain, for it was even older than Icecrest. It was the prospect of getting away as well as seeing something new that changed my mind.

I didn't perceive how they decided who would get into which of the two carts, partly because of the usual bowing and stylized hand gesturing, but also because I was intrigued by my first close view of a lizardrake. The closest pair gazed past us as if they did not really see us. It was not at all like meeting the eyes of the great gryphs, but it disturbed me in a different way.

I was glad to find myself in the first cart with Venar, who close up seemed about forty, her eyes lined at the corners. Naisan, the one male of the group, appeared to be a young cousin or nephew not much older than Nill back in Alezand. Naisan sat backward with Venar so that I could face forward. They might not have felt any more friendly toward me than Ingras, but at least I hadn't heard them say anything nasty, and so we whiled the ride in nothing-talk (prettily done, of course) as the cart progressed onto the windswept ridge above the town.

The road was made of close-fit stone. Midway between the mountains the ridge had broken centuries before and had been spanned with a spectacular bridge that afforded a view down into a tumbled chasm that was now full of icicles on both sides. I wondered what it would look like when the waters melted; the thought of still being a prisoner in spring and summer chilled me more thoroughly than the frigid air.

When we'd crossed the bridge, the road led up in switchbacks to a round building of pale stone with the familiar lancet windows, their edges blurred by hundreds of years of wind.

Except for those familiar windows and the pale stone (juts of which could be seen scattered here and there on rocky cliffs and ridges) this building was altogether different than the palace, profoundly simpler, sturdy as if bracing against the eternal icy winds. Built by the Sveranji, Seaforth had been known as Kribinsi, as Skyreach had once been Vesjin. "But that was the old language, before we became civilized."

Venar took me around the walls, which gave a full circle view of the island: Icecrest towering skyward at the north end, dominating land, sea, and sky, and in the south, the great conical mountain brooding hazily in the distance down the spine of the long peninsula. Below to the west, the town I'd begun to explore, and on the east side, a harbor, with a fleet of warships riding bare-poled in the bay. On the slopes above the bay, more terracing for farming.

Inside, my attention caught on the trees. These were not trained into exact symmetry as were those in the palace, but permitted to grow as they would, reaching up to touch their leaves against the high glass dome above.

This semblance of forest caused me to ask, "Where are the roots?"

Venar's smile and lifted hands answered before she said, "An ancient mystery. These inside gardens were popular long before the island united into the present empire."

Shortly thereafter it became apparent that a sizable storm was on its way, so we climbed back into the carts and headed back over the ridge as the winds began to rise, moaning warningly over the escarpments.

Brief, dramatic rays of golden sunlight lanced across the sea, lighting the tops of the waves in gray-green and striking the eastern side of the palace so that it glowed like an ice carving. It was breathtakingly beautiful, and evanescent: by the time we reached the parade ground, the oncoming storm had doused what was left of the light and even I shivered, wishing I'd thought to get a cloak.

Scarcely had I stepped inside when a servant said that His Imperial Serenity awaited me.

Fear made me fast. I reached the Garden Lair to find him surrounded by cats. He appeared to be in a benign mood; he said he was pleased to see me consorting with my relations, encouraged me to enjoy the dance in my honor, then said, "We will explore the fire spell further, but let us essay a different direction, equally useful. You know how to infuse an object such as a Fire Stick with heat. I want you to attempt to remove the heat from water."

If it had been anyone else, I would have said, "Just put it outside!"

But the mere thought of joking with him made my nerves flare with alarm. I knew I would never trust him, and as he indicated a waiting pail of steaming water, it occurred to me that he did not trust me either. Once again I wondered how long I would be a prisoner—how long I would last as *me*.

Or what I would be turned into.

At first I could not concentrate. Again and again he made me send heat into the water, and then pull it out again, until I began again with my thumb and forefinger pin-hole. Clumsy and obvious as it was, it worked.

I was light-headed from the effort when he finally released me, after praising me for my effort as well as my success. Relief I could live with; the treacherous sense of pleasure I squashed hard as I wobbled back to my lair to a dinner of parched almonds, nut cakes, cheese, and some preserved berries.

Then it was time to get ready.

I, who love to dance, had been to only five aristocratic balls in Erev-li-Erval, at which the dancing was done in patterns of circle or line, at so sedate a pace that I'd felt I was walking rather than dancing.

Much more fun had been a festival dance during my brief stint as a theater illusion mage, before I'd fallen violently in love with a handsome rotter who collected hearts as conveniences. I'd been frightened when one of the stage managers tried to get me to "Do that on stage"—it was then that I learned that not everybody had the light step of a person half-bird. Not that I knew then that I was half-bird.

More fun than that had been the village and town dances I'd

seen—and sometimes slipped into if it was crowded enough—throughout the kingdoms I'd wandered. A month or so before I met Hlanan I'd sneaked into a wild wedding among dock folk in Tu Jhan so that I could raid the refreshments table and perhaps thieve something against future meals. But I'd had so much fun flinging myself into the whirl that I couldn't bring myself to rob them, and I'd ended up whirling on my toes as people clapped around me, laughing and cheering. I'd laughed and cheered because—even if for barely a sand-glass of time—I belonged.

I expected that this dance was going to fall under the stiffly boring court category, and so my expectations were low when I slipped on the cool, slithery silk of the midnight blue under-robe, and then the gorgeous butterfly robe. Last, the dancing slippers I'd never worn. Actual diamonds winked and glittered along the tops of the slippers.

Amney greeted me at the door, even more beautiful than the last time I'd seen her, dressed in palest blue and pure white, with gold embroidery in delicately rendered snowflakes. She conducted me to a dais, where I was seated on the second finest cushion, the emperor's sitting empty as usual. I was placed at his right. Everything with the outward signs of honor, but she turned away immediately to engage Raifas in conversation.

The guests arrived in a sedate stream, each crossing the room to bow to me and utter a formal greeting before moving on to talk to each other. Raifas arrived with two fellows whose names I'd forgotten, and right on their heels, Ingras and Pelan.

Darus arrived and, like the others, approached to greet me first. After the usual formal palaver I had to test that impression from earlier, and led with a question meant to show that I was not completely ignorant. "Darus," I said. "Are you named for Vandarus Andis?"

"Obliquely, Your Imperial Serenity." He bowed and moved away.

Amney stepped between us and gestured with her fingers in a little circle, her voice sweet. "The old forms were triple-syllables. Everything was done in threes back then. These days those long names are considered pretentious, and more syllables than three vulgar in their ostentation."

Like Elenderi?

"There is elegance in simplicity," she said in that silver-sweet voice. "The Chosen confine themselves to two, which is enough to differentiate from those who serve, who from long tradition are given personal names of one syllable." She bowed and smiled as if she hadn't just called me pretentious, vulgar, and ostentatious, and added winsomely, "We shall begin if you will honor us with your august favor."

I bowed. She turned away and joined her friends. Musicians hidden among the complication of vaulting overhead struck up with sweet woodwinds, cymbals, and then strings. Everything appeared to be centered around me, a hollow mockery of an honor because it was very clear that they all knew what to do, and I was left to sit and watch.

And Amney, with her smiling insults, had arranged it all deliberately.

Not that I cared what they thought of me. I hated them all, and their emperor the worst of them.

The courtiers began forming up into triangles of pairs, except for Pelan. I wondered if she was the lowest ranking of the bunch as she scudded my way, looking dutiful rather than pleased when she said, "It would be my honor to explain the Shadow Dance to you, Your Imperial Serenity. It is our oldest, its origin actually lost in time. The Chosen have begun formal dances with it since the empire was first made...."

As she spoke, the musical prelude gave way to syncopated triplets, counterpoint rhythms marked by little hand drums and clashing cymbals. Pelan might have meant well. At least she'd never been rude, but her painstaking description of the twirls, step-two-threes and robe-flaring hops faded from my notice when I saw the pattern. The dance was a millennia-old galliard, only with six steps instead of five. The couples in threes met and parted, tassel-kicked and posed, whirled and leaped, changing partners all around the triangles as they mirrored each other.

Then they stopped, turned, and when the musicians shifted half a step up minor to major they began again in reverse. That was not at all like the courtly galliard I'd seen in Charas al Kherval.

The Shadow dance was actually two dances, in mirror. The sixes wove in and out, in and out, exchanging places so that the triangles formed a large triangle that moved to all cardinal points before returning to the place they started, at which time the musicians took the melody up half a chord and began again a little faster. As Pelan counted out the beats that I began to anticipate, the entire dance, turnabout-and-shadow, wove through a third round before it finally ended.

They bowed and talked, and I was left with this odd sense that something was missing. But none of them seemed to think so.

Pelan bowed to me, asked if I were satisfied in a way that I suspected she hoped would be answered with a yes. The moment I assented she scudded off to join the next dance, and so sat alone in the place of honor utterly ignored as they danced and flirted and smiled and talked, always in that graceful studied stylish motion and tone.

As that dance ended and another began, and another, the sick sensation inside me began to kindle into anger. I sat there with a knot of rage behind my ribs as I mentally caressed that fais and imagined striking the supercilious hauteur from Darus with a lightning bolt of pain. Then I imagined the poisonously sweet Amney lying on the floor like a crushed insect after a jolt of white heat to the midsection.

One by one I thought them all to the floor in smoking, quivering ruin as I stepped past in my beautiful butterfly robe that should be dancing right now to that tantalizing waterfall of triplets.

I came so very close: If one of them dared come up to insult me in those pretty words and gestures, maybe I'd even do it, ha ha.

But they ignored me until the music at last came to an end, they all bowed low to me. Oh yes. I had to leave first. Quivering with humiliation I bowed, walked out, and retreated to my solitary existence, surrounded by twelve silent servants.

And sleep evaded me, as mercilessly and inexorably as ever. I tossed and turned, until my mind slipped into that half-dream state in which that old harp melody played over and over, and as the dream world slowly formed around me, a blue figure emerged, sighing, *"Oh, Elenn, my heart's dear, you are not alone. But the dream realm is chancy, even dangerous. You must go to the harp."*

"*The harp?*" I repeated, and the reminder of something real dissolved the dream around me.

I lost the dream, and the voice, but an image lingered past my waking: that small blue figure, a silver-haired babe on her lap as she sat at the harp carved with birds.

Twenty-two

I LAY THERE CLAMMY and trembling, that image so intense it had to be more than mere dream fancy.

I nearly swung out of my hammock, but fell back, remembering that my least movement alerted the duty servant. Who probably reported to Dhes-Andis. Most of what I did was innocuous enough, but I had a feeling a midnight trip to the music room wouldn't be seen that way.

I considered that. My fear had been that the harp's peculiar effect on me was a sneaky plot by Dhes-Andis. In which case, he would want me to go there and play the music.

Elenn...Eh-LENN, a soft exhalation, almost a sigh, tenderly caressing.

I knew that sound, somewhere way back in memory, before I could speak. Elenn...*Lhind.*

For the first time I let myself consider that the Blue Lady was no figment of my imagination, or a contrivance of evil. Then of course my mind swung the other way, questioning my impressions, throwing up horrors of *what if?*

I had gone so long without anyone to trust except myself — until I met Hlanan, and, well, I had all-too painful memories of how *that* had turned out.

The hour was more advanced than I had thought. Dawn began to lift the darkness at the window. By the time I rose, bathed, dressed, and ate breakfast, long squares of rare sunlight painted the floor from the east windows in the dining alcove.

I said airily, "I am going to practice music," and traipsed sedately to the music room. By the time I got there, my fingers began to tremble in anticipation.

As always as soon as I touched the harp, my hands knew what to do. I closed my eyes. Being so tired, I found it easier than ever to sink into the images evoked by the music.

And there she was again, as if seen in the reflection of water.

Elenderi, she said. *You can hear me mind to mind. I laid wards over this harp to protect us both. It is far less dangerous if we meet only here, while you are touching it, until you learn to speak mind to mind.* And again I saw the image of the blue lady with the baby on her lap, and the harp glittering with magic.

No, I cried. *HE will be waiting to get me.*

Memory floated up: Dhes-Andis's mental contact when I was aboard the pirate ship, and worse, his invasive presence in the mental realm after I left Rajanas's principality. Before I learned to shut him out with my mental wall.

You can keep him out and limit your focus, she said.

I can?

It is much the same way you have been learning to control your magic. Concentrate on whom you wish to hear in the mental realm, and confine your focus only to that person. But until you master it, the greater the distance, the more chance you can be scryed by adepts like Jardis. It is far safer, until you become more skilled, to make your attempts strictly in proximity.

I can use my pin-hole? I was so surprised I slipped right out of the connection.

Or maybe it was a sound: I opened my eyes, startled to discover one of the palace servants stood there, waiting.

After the bows and apologies and formal palaver about the Imperial Princess, she gave me a nerve-chilling shock: His Imperial Serenity desired my presence in the Garden Chamber.

Did he know? Had he heard?

Terror sped me along, my neck throbbing in anticipation, but when I got there I found Dhes-Andis and Raifas awaiting me, the latter wearing his embroidered black riding clothes.

"Elenderi," said Dhes-Andis, "I am told you enjoyed riding the great gryph. As you no doubt are aware, we are experiencing that rarity, an entirely empty sky. The Most Noble Raifas intends to travel to Ardam Pennon to see to certain duties there, and has offered to take you with him that you might widen your experience of your homeland."

He wasn't asking, he was telling. But I was so relieved about the harp, the blue Hrethan, and above all the chance to get away that I bowed in gratitude.

And he clearly didn't expect me to say anything as he added, "Andisla is being fitted with the travel harness. Have your staff prepare what you need for later transfer."

Raifas said, "Your Imperial Serenity, if I may be permitted to make a suggestion, we shall be flying at a high altitude, where the currents are stronger. It can be quite cold."

"I'll fetch a wrap," I said.

I took proper formal leave then beetled back to my suite, where I told Kal what was going to happen. "Since I don't know what I will need, anything you pack will be fine." Then I got to the important question. "I know this might sound funny, but I don't know where I was born. Was it here?"

Kal bowed low enough to hide his face. When he straightened, his expression had masked as bland as any Chosen. "I am told the Imperial Princess was born in Icecrest. If she requires corroboration, that I am unable to provide. I was in training then, as a child. But I believe Brin was in imperial service," naming the old woman who sewed the fine embroidery.

"May I go in and ask?"

He bowed again and as I looked at the glossy top of his head I had a sense that he was hiding his face as he said, "The staff is here to serve the Imperial Princess."

I felt the pressure of expectation. I couldn't take too long, but I had to know.

I walked through the dark alcove into their big common room and there sat Brin, working at embroidering white cherry blossoms and deep red rose buds on silk the color of pewter.

"Brin, was I born here?"

She set aside her sewing to rise with difficulty. "The Imperial Princess was indeed born in this palace, though not in this suite, which belonged to the Empress Lison, blessed be her memory." The way Brin said the words, they did not feel like mere rote.

"And then? What happened then?"

"I beg pardon of the Imperial Princess for my inadequate answer, but I was not present to see."

I looked from her to Kal, whose gaze remained on her. The other servants had stilled, and I sensed that I had stumbled into fraught territory. Maybe they didn't know. Or maybe they couldn't tell me.

I longed to get back to the harp — to get answers to the questions proliferating in my head — but I could feel the Emperor of Evil waiting for me to get my fuzzy imperial hide to that perch balcony. I'd wondered all my life why I'd been abandoned at an early age — according to Dhes-Andis, by selfish, careless parents. Maybe that was true as he saw it, but that didn't make it *my* truth. I could wait a little longer

When I got there, Raifas waved off the waiting servants and indicated the enormous gryph. He gave me a challenging smile, and said low-voiced, "Think you can ride fast? If so, we might reach Mount Dragon by nightfall."

Mount Dragon! I leaped up to the saddle, my warm cloak spreading over the gryph's back. I hoped it wouldn't be uncivilized to ask the story behind that name.

Andisla and Firebird surged into the air and away we climbed, circling up on lazy currents until the island lay below like a toy with a sugar-statue of a palace atop a pinnacle.

I felt the change when the gryphs found their current. They stretched out their long necks, powerful wings whipping forward, down, and up until we shot into the streaming wind. The cold air forced my eyes to slits, yet it exhilarated my racing blood, and when I glanced at Raifas, his teeth showed in a brief, slashing grin.

The whistle and moan of the wind rendered conversation impossible. Good. I had too many questions buzzing through my mind like maddeningly insistent flies.

So I settled myself firmly against Andisla's broad back, the great wing-muscles working below my arms, and attempted to make a mental pin-hole through which to reach the gryph's mind. Not to other humans. Even without the threat of Dhes-Andis catching me, I had always shied away from that. People's minds are too much like noisy cities at noon. Animals' minds are so different, not crowding mine with words, but with image and the impressions of other senses.

I concentrated on Andisla, for the longest time without any success. I was so afraid of letting my shield slip for an instant, lest Dhes-Andis strike. And even when I did make tiny tries, each left me so dizzy that I pressed my forehead against the bird's feathery back until the vertigo died away.

But as the long day wore past, I tried intermittently, using image to frame my inquiry, then connecting the images, so to speak, until I gained a blurry sense of the scene ahead. That was the source of the vertigo: what the bird saw imposing over what I saw, only our eyes comprehend so differently.

Andisla's focus was on flying, but beyond that, all I gained was a kind of foggy blur that I was too tired, too stressed, and too distracted to understand.

Meanwhile, down the white-blanketed spine of the dragon we flew, the trees sparsely scattered over the jutting cliffs and chasms of bare rock under its thick load of snow. We passed terraced towns and villages tucked here and there on slopes, always where the infrequent sun traveled most.

As the day began to wane the once-hazy and distant conical mountain seemed to grow, spreading in vast, slanting expanses out to the coast. These long slopes formed the Pennons, Ardam (meaning East in Djuran) Pennon on one side, and Hindam (meaning West) on the far side.

The gryphs glided downward, wings outspread. I tried another pin-hole, and sensed Andisla's tiredness and hunger.

The Ardam side of Mount Dragon had a town set above a great, curving harbor, the two connected by the familiar switchback roads.

On a prominent lower peak, with the harbor below and the great fire mountain above, sat a three-towered castle a lot like Seaforth, the tallest tower over the gate and two at the back corners of the square walls.

The birds landed with jolting steps in the broad central square, and servants ran out to take charge as Raifas trod toward the archway leading inside the main tower.

We walked past a magnificent indoor tree at which he did not cast a glance as he said, "If you're half as sharp-set as I, you'll want to dine before taking a tour." And paused, looking at me expectantly.

So glad was I to dispense with the eternal courtly ritual — both tedious and false — that I assented cheerfully.

Those winged brows of his lifted, but he didn't speak as he flicked three fingers at the gray-clad young man who'd appeared. Court behavior between us was thankfully absent, but I sensed he wouldn't talk informally before the servants.

Raifas's staff flowed quietly away through shaded alcoves as their Most Noble led me upstairs while loosening the lacing on his tight black jacket. When we reached an upper room warmed by a fine stove, he shrugged off the jacket and slung it over a bench by the door, and a young servant appeared carrying a long silk robe over one arm. Raifas pulled it over his loose-sleeved shirt, his fais glinting, plain gold in an interlocked weave, at his throat.

"Do you want to rid yourself of that shroud?" he asked, indicating my cape.

I surrendered it to the waiting servant as Raifas said, "You have something against jackets?"

"My hair and tail do," I said, fluffing both around me.

He chuckled. "You've never used a comb, I gather."

"Never."

The servants bore away the winter clothing as I turned to take in the enormous lancet windows. They afforded a circular view, visible from a pair of low tables with cushions before them.

A stream of servants appeared bearing trays which they set down on both tables, then flowed noiselessly out again. Raifas sat on one cushion, and used the round, shallow spoon to eat from each dish.

I picked up the spoon by mine, turning it over. Thianra and Hlanan had taught me how to manage eating utensils, which were different from this little spoon. I knew what to do with it, but I much prefer eating with my fingers as I have my entire life.

However, the dishes before me smelled of meats. I turned my head.

"Nothing here to your taste, O Imperial Princess?" Raifas asked.

"It's not taste. It's what happens inside. I never ate meat even when I was a starveling rat in alleys."

He set down his silver spoon and regarded me under those winged brows. "Never eat meat? But half of you is half of us." He spread his fingers, touching himself on his chest.

"Nevertheless."

"We'll have to fix that."

"There is nothing to fix," I said.

He snapped his fingers at the open door and a servant appeared. "The Imperial Princess will list her preferred menu." And to me, "I trust your delicate tastes are not *too* rarified. I feel obliged to point out that this is winter."

"I don't know how rare nuts, fruits, and the like are." And I listed my preferences before finishing up with things I could eat if I had to.

"Cheese," Raifas said, pouncing on an item halfway down my list. "I can safely promise you excellent goat cheese. It's a specialty on this particular part of the island, made finer by the grasses the goats eat."

Very soon I had some of it (and he was right) plus a small variety of nuts and dried berries.

"You will have more by tomorrow," he promised, and then said, "If we do not waken to a blizzard, I'll give you a tour of the harbor. You can see my fleet in its winter quarters below."

I glanced through the window at the forest of bare poles moving up and down on the deep blue sea, barely visible in the fading light.

"And if we do waken to a blizzard?" I asked.

"We can still visit the mouth of the fire mountain. It's only a short flight."

"Won't the gryphs need rest? Or do you have others?"

"Firebird is as yet my only," he said. "You don't seem to appreciate that he is the work of five years." Raifas made a dismissive gesture. "The egg-civilized are more common, but expensive, dull, and therefore useless for my plans."

"Plans?"

"I'll explain once we've seen the harbor and explored inside Mount Dragon," he said. "Easier. Unless you've knowledge of fleet strategy and tactics?"

"Don't know a thing about that," I said. *And care even less.* While I was ready enough to give answers to questions, I did not trust him enough to offer my opinions, except on things like food and clothes and the like. As always I feared Dhes-Andis and his scrying crystal, and of course even if the Evil Emperor was busy with other things, he might be expecting a report. Because there had to be a reason I was here besides getting to ride a gryph and touring the island.

The warmth and food so weighted my eyelids that I fought yawn after yawn, and barely had we finished when Raifas said with considerable amusement, "I have pennon affairs to see to if you'd like to retire."

"Yes," I said, and upstairs we slogged to another tower room where they had slung a hammock, more evidence of silent communication.

Raifas waited at the door, and when I turned away to look out the windows into the darkness, he said wryly, "I'll wish you good rest, then." Then I heard his swft footsteps descending the stair.

I was beyond question, even beyond worry. My first instinct was to try to reach the Blue Lady through a pin-hole in my mental shield, but I remembered what she had said about distance, danger, and control.

I was far too tired to even pretend I had control. But distance? The thought of Dhes-Andis lurking at a physical remove at the other end of the island was so comforting that I sank into sleep, and for the first time since my arrival in Sveran Djur, I passed an unbroken—and dreamless—night.

Twenty-three

I WOKE TO BLEAK light through the many windows, affording a view of an uneasy sky with two layers of clouds: thin white high above, and lower down, a marching army of brooding gray.

The chamber otherwise gave me a sense of great age, enhanced by time-blurred painted carvings up under the ceiling, of winged cats and horses and lizards bowing to each other in pairs, wings uplifted at a graceful angle. As if they were about to begin to play, or to dance.

I craned my neck, finding aidlars and eagles, lizardrakes with hands outstretched to touch palm to palm, yeth hounds and wolves bowed in canine play, one paw forward. It was so old the paint had all but worn away, but I liked this carving better than anything I'd seen yet in Sveran Djur.

However I could not lie there all day.

With a good sleep behind me, memory marched as inexorable as those clouds. My birth—my mother having lived in the palace—the harp magic—the mental shield—my experiments with magic—fais, the town, the servants....

. . . And conversations. *Then he will marry her off to advantage, the same as the rest of us.*

That jolted me right out of the hammock.

I froze at the circle of windows and gazed over the gray seas at the slow undulation of the warships' bare masts as they rode the rising waves.

One: the threat so far was only speculative gossip.

Two: I was a long way from Icecrest.

I breathed out the tension. Time to get ready for the day. The bath adjacent was a modest affair with a stone sink and a pitcher of water to tip into it. A Fire Stick lay nearby, but I used my magic to heat the sink water to steaming.

When I was refreshed, I turned to the trunk that had been transferred by magic. I put on the first thing packed on top and ran downstairs to search for Raifas.

At the bottom level I found myself in the entry hall with the gigantic tree. I had to stop and look up at it. So beautiful! The urge to try my mental pin-hole again prompted me to shut my eyes and reach carefully. A sense of infinitely slow movement and awareness of the distant sun and deep rootedness pulled me down and down, until far in the distance I became vaguely aware of a slow, booming thrum...thrum...thrum....

Noise — wind — violent shivering through branches...I soared upward and gasped, my knees buckling. Hard hands on my arms kept me upright, and I squinted in bewilderment into Raifas's face as he frowned at me, worry and perplexity plain to see.

"What happened?"

"Happened?" I repeated as I got my feet under me again. "Nothing."

"Nothing? I thought someone dropped a stone spell on you. When you didn't come down for breakfast, or call for a servant, I sent someone after you — to discover you'd been standing there all morning."

I stared witlessly back at him, my mind floundering. What could I say?

"Is this some Hrethan thing?" he asked.

Grateful for the respite, I said, "Yes. My pardon." I looked down. "This tree. It has roots in the ground, does it not? It isn't one of those where the roots are...invisible?"

His perplexity altered to relief, then impatience. "Yes. This part of the castle was built around the old tree, I'm told." He smiled at me. "This entire building was originally a meeting and trading place between the Sveranji and your people. At least they called them Snow Folk, and they looked pretty much like you according to some of the old artwork nobody has gotten rid of. Lived in the trees, back when there *were* trees all over these mountains, not just the mulberry plantations on the south and west-facing slopes as now. Here, let's get some breakfast into you. Then we're off. The gryphs have been harnessed and ready since sunrise trine, and the wind is rising."

Even though I had no appetite—I was too wobbly, though recovering fast—I was glad of the respite. As I sat down to nut cakes, cheese, and more dried fruit, my mind began to recover. I had connected with a tree, whose sense of time and life is so very different. That distant boom had to be my heart slowing down to a dangerous degree.

All right, then. No more tree contacts. But (I exulted) I'd done it!

Raifas had dressed again in his black outfit with the dragon embroidery. A quiet servant waited nearby with my cloak, which I took with a word of thanks that set off the inescapable bowing. Out we walked, me looking at the time-blurred carving of knotted patterns in the stonework surrounding the arched doors. I slid my fingers over the carvings, trying to imagine the long-ago hands that had worked to shape the stone, and I wondered what the artisan had thought—if she, or he, had shared a vision of the building with the tile layers and the others who had made the place. Or had they been constrained by fais—had their work come at the cost of sorrow and anger and pain?

The birds awaited us. I leaped onto Andisla and felt in the way the bird rocked slightly under the impact that he could fly, but was not as springy as the day previous. I wanted to say something, but I would have to explain my concern, and I was not ready to share my faltering new skill with anyone as yet.

As he'd said, the flight was relatively short. The birds flapped hard into the rising wind, soaring upwards, then circling to use the wind effectively before angling on the tumbling currents of hot air rising to meet the cold winter winds.

"Hold on," Raifas shouted as Firebird screamed. "This is the rough part!" Greenish magical fire scintillated around the gryph as Firebird screamed again, flapping and veering downward. Andisla followed as if on a string, straight into a roiling turmoil of vapors and smoke.

My eyes stung and my vision blurred with shadowy shapes diving and rising. I squinted into the whorls, unconsciously reaching through that pin-hole in my mental wall — and the shadows brightened to scaled, spike-backed, bat-winged creatures of wildly different sizes and shapes, their eyes glowing as brightly as the fire beating far below. But they were half-invisible: I could see the rock plainly through them.

Somewhere Firebird shrieked, and because I was listening in the mental realm I felt the green lightning strike him with stunning pain. I gulped, flinching, and nearly fell off Andisla, who jolted, wings juddering.

I reached mentally for Firebird, who struggled wildly against pain and fear. My entire body flashed with chill when I looked through the gryph's mind to the vast shape stirring down below in the heart of the fire.

Another flash of white-pain rocked me backward, and I gasped, blinking sightlessly into the smoke as Andisla struggled upward, bursting into the cold air.

"There you are!" Raifas shouted, pale with worry. "Thought you fell!"

I barely heard him over the hiss and seethe and roar of wind and molten rock. The shadows vanished in the smoke, and I coughed as the gryphs sailed up into cold, clean air, then drifted slowly down the slope to the castle courtyard.

I slid off Andisla, dizzy, headachy, totally confused. Alarm still shivered through me at the awareness of that ruby-scaled creature as big as an island who dwelt in that space between the surging boiling rock...and where was that?

"Elenderi!"

I blinked up into Raifas's face.

"I thought you fell into the pit. I couldn't see you at all," he said, eyes narrowed. "Until I pulled the beasts up. You fell backward between Andisla's wings, is that it?"

"Backward," I repeated witlessly.

"I should probably have waited," he admitted. "I really wanted to show you my idea, but for some reason Firebird fought the descent like a fledgling, which caused Andisla uncertainty.

And when you nearly vanished...." He shook his head. "My pardon for putting you in danger. We shall wait a day. How are you feeling? Do you need to recruit yourself, or are you able to tour the flagship?" He looked down as tiny snowflakes drifted to touch his shoulders and hair. "It is an easy ride. We need not exert ourselves. I doubt the snow will worsen. The sky looks the same clear to the horizon and the lizardrakes will do all the work."

As he spoke, servants had begun leading the two gryphs away.

I don't know why I tipped my head back. Partly because my neck ached and my eyes still stung, but perhaps a residue of mental connection remained because once again my gaze was caught by that great gryph eye, and hot rage blasted me nearly off my feet.

I stepped back, then steadied myself against the rail. Raifas did not see. He had turned his attention to the harnessed sleigh approaching, drawn by three pairs of lizardrakes.

He stretched out a hand to me in invitation. Numbly I followed, my mind wailing wordlessly. Too much, too fast. I craved a chance to sit, to breathe.

The creatures began to pull the sleigh at a spanking pace along the ancient road zigzagging down the mountain. Raifas took the reins himself, which kept him busy enough for me to shut my eyes and try to sort out the turmoil inside my head. Did they know about that immense creature in the fire world?

Fire world. Slowly I began to sift the impressions. The dragon—if it was a dragon—that majestic immanence dwelt between the fire rock and wherever-it-was...I had no words. I opened my eyes, my awareness still heightened by my encounter with the tree.

Around me, snow. To the left, the gray-green sea as the sleigh's runners hissed down the icy road. Before us, three pairs of bird heads on skinny necks bobbing as the lizardrakes ran. But the middle creature on the right bore a shadow. I tried to blink it away, then remembered a blurrier shadow on the first lizardrake I'd ever seen.

This shadow sharpened into a human shape. Was I seeing ghosts now? The human shape moved with the lizardrake in the manner of a true shadow. Ghosts, all songs and records insist, drifted or lurked about on their own.

Images and impressions began fitting into a semblance of coherence like pieces of a puzzle: the roots of the trees, even the odd, blurring shapes around some of the creatures.

The puzzle was by no means complete, but I sensed that all these things were related. However, the instinct to keep silent surpassed all until I understood more, such as why Firebird was so angry and what those shadows might be, and how this other world fit with Sveran Djur as I was beginning to comprehend it.

Gradually I became aware that Raifas was addressing comments to me as we descended toward the wharf. He didn't talk all the time — he was busy guiding the sleigh — but I gained the impression that he spent his winters attending on the emperor and working at pennon affairs, and spring was when he departed with the East Fleet.

"Do you like ocean travel?" he asked presently.

"I've only been on two vessels," I said, "a yacht and a trader."

I wondered how much to say about being forced aboard Ilyan Rajanas's yacht, or more importantly, the trader when Hlanan, Kee, and I had been trying to escape Prince Geric by sailing from Fara Bay. Until Lendan brought pirate ships to chase us — with Dhes-Andis's full cooperation.

Looking back, I could see how I had stupidly, ignorantly piqued Dhes-Andis's interest, thereby putting a lot of other people in danger. He had some sort of connection with Prince Geric, yet he'd been quite willing to throw away Geric's life in order to test me.

I wondered if Prince Geric had ever been in Sveran Djur.

Raifas guided the sleigh down the last curve of the road, and the sleigh began bumping along the icy quay, recalling my attention to my surroundings.

Servants ran down a long pier from the mightiest of the warships as Raifas guided the sleigh to a stop. We climbed out and servants took charge of the lizardrakes; I glanced back at the one with the shadow. Yes, I could see a distinctly human silhouette with bowed head as the creature plodded away.

I skipped to catch up with Raifas, who led me down the pier to a ramp gently heaving on the sea, its high end connected to the warship.

From the castle up the mountain all these ships had looked like toys. Warships were different from traders, which in my experience had looked rather like barrels with a pointy end, slow because they sat heavy in the water with their holds full of goods. These warships lay long and lean, their masts raked back, the better to brace into strong winds.

Djuran warships were the fastest and best-made on the seas, Raifas began telling me as we mounted the ramp. Because of the protection magic worked into each piece of wood as it is laid down, from keelson to the trucks holding up the upper masts, some of these vessels were more than five hundred years old.

I wondered if that was where the forests had gone as Raifas conducted me along the companionway, affording us a clear view fore and aft—which admittedly was beautiful. Tripled patterns carved everywhere, the lovely inward slanted windows at the back end (stern, he corrected me), the gentle slope from the captain's deck back of the wheel to the foredeck, it was all lovely, except that storage place below the crew-deck, where swords, lances, knives and other steel weapons were stored, along with barrels of arrows and bows ready to be strung.

"Much faster on deep waters than Shinjan galleys," he said as we made our way back up the ladder. "Their galleys maneuver well in light airs. Better than ours when there is no wind." He waved his hand up at the masts as we walked to the bow, which looked out to sea. "But if necessary we can get out sweeps, and while their slaves can row far faster than our sailors, at what a cost! A man is not going to row at strength while his back is raw with festering wounds, if you will pardon the crudity." His mouth crimpled with disgust.

He turned away, leaving the subject of Shinjan slaves to the wintry air, and explained how Djuran warships could keep that narrow, lean look by a long history of transferred supplies from shore. But those supplies were difficult to get when harvests were scarce, and thus Sveran Djur ever sought to unite with kingdoms not primarily made of rock.

"Would you like to climb aloft?" He turned his hand toward the complication of ropes binding the masts to each side.

"The snow is coming down harder," I said. "How much would we see?"

He looked up, then out. "Probably little," he admitted with a rueful curve of his lips. "I confess I wanted to demonstrate my skills. I was sent to sea at ten and every year since, summer has found me on the water. First learning to sail, then to command." He pointed at the warehouse on the quay at the other end of the pier. "I know you can put sunlight into Fire Sticks, and someone mentioned your having cleared snow off the streets in town. Can you clear that roof?"

I peered doubtfully at it. The roof lay at a farther distance than I'd tried yet, and it was also a vast affair, whereas I had worked hard to confine my fire magic to small targets. "I don't think I can," I said.

"Ah, probably as well you haven't the magical reach."

"Why?"

"I had an idea about your using your fire magic against enemy ships, but my understanding is that magic is unreliable in warfare, once the surprise is gone. What one mage comes up with, another can ward."

I had been thinking that my difficulty was with using too *much* fire. I still got that danger-grip at the back of my neck when I remembered how very close I had come to losing control on the rooftop in Fara Bay. But I did not want to explain that now. One vow I meant to keep was never again to send fire against ships the way I had against those pirates.

Raifas moved on and I followed him, glad to have the subject dropped.

The command cabin was that space with the pretty windows across the stern, under the captain's deck. Like the ship itself, this cabin was clean and elegant in design and fittings, dominated opposite the row of windows by an embroidered dragon tapestry edged with golden knotwork in threes. Neat shelves held books and scrolls. Fine cushions surrounded a low table bolted to the deck, above which swung golden lamps overhead. Against the curve of the bulkheads someone had affixed beautifully rendered maps.

The fleet, he explained as we sat down, had only winter crews, a scarce handful coming out by weekly rotations to keep the ships clean and damage free. Most of the crew lived in various hamlets, villages, and towns in the pennon.

On the flagship the winter crew included a cook and ensigns to see to it the stove warmed the cabin, and to serve the food as well, as Raifas often visited. They brought me a fruit preserve compote, nut bread, and cheese.

Once we'd been served, Raifas said, "Have you any questions?"

I nodded. "Did you ever meet Prince Geric Lendan?"

Up went the slanted brows. His lips began to shape the word No—and I was distracted by the curve of his lips—when he sat back, brow furrowed. "Wait. Was he one of the princes?"

"Princes?"

"One of Emperor Ifan's cadre of princes studying magic with Cousin Jardis. I recollect first glimpsing them some twenty, twenty-five years ago."

"He would have been not much more than a toddler then," I said doubtfully. "Or five at most."

"We were all small, and they were not all the same age. Uncle Ifan brought them in over the years, I'm told, but we scarcely ever saw them when we visited court, which admittedly was only twice a year. They lived in a private house, where dwelt the unfaised."

"They didn't have fais?" I asked. That would explain the bone whistle that I'd stolen from Geric, which was the cause of Dhes-Andis finding me. I had not known it was a magical device to facilitate mind-to-mind communication.

Raifas flashed his grin. "I know very little about magic. But my understanding was, these princes were to be sent home to bring their kingdoms into unity with the Djuran Empire. Our mages would not risk the fais being meddled with by foreign mages." He spread his hands. "Except for one or two—among whom might very well have been your Prince Geric Lendan—they were pretty much gone by the time Shinja attacked us and Emperor Ifan died in the Battle of Athaniaz Island."

"He's not my Prince Geric," I said.

Raifas laughed. "Then why do you ask?"

"Because I think he was taught magic here, and I wondered by whom."

"Likeliest either Emperor Ifan or Cousin Jardis. The service mages are sequestered far away, with their own palace. We never see them. They rarely come to the imperial island, except as summoned by Cousin Jardis."

"Here's another question," I said, wanting to get away from the subject of the Evil Emperor. "My understanding is that Emperor Vandarus Andis unified Sveran Djur. What does that mean? This island isn't Djur, so either they invited someone else's ruler, or he conquered it. Which is it?"

"Does it matter, as long as there is peace?"

"But if he conquered it, there wasn't peace when he was doing it."

"You simplify these matters to absurdity. What if unrest and violence existed before he came? From everything I have learned, the Sveranji existed in ignorance. Union brought the civilization we enjoy today. It is the same civilization Ndai will enjoy, for when I am Prince of Ndai, I will govern as well as I do in Ardam Pennon. Do not take my words as idle self-praise," he added, head tipping to the side as he studied my expression. "I will show you over the island if you like. You may see for yourself."

"So you're going to be attacking Ndai?"

"How much do you know about Ndai?"

"Nothing," I had to say.

"I can point you to evidence that they squabble with the continent east of them, especially Damatras, who fights with everyone. They squabble among themselves, their nobles against the mages. Nothing new. You can find wars all over the world, breaking out on the slightest pretext. In Sveran Djur we have no war."

I remembered those threatened fires, the mercenary army, and while I was still angry with Aranu Crown, I remembered how hard Hlanan had worked to save lives, and I said, "That's because you take it to other people."

"Union is seldom easy," he said with the steady gaze of total conviction. "But afterward, I assure you, there is peace."

"When everybody gets a fais."

"Precisely."

More pieces of the puzzle, I thought as we finished up. It was getting dark by then, and Raifas said, "I hate magic transfer, but the storm is worsening. I'll have the lizardrakes sent to the harbor barn."

His gaze diffused: fais communication. I was seeing it done, though I still could not manage much more than short communications with Kal. Apparently one needed a lifetime to learn to web.

"Can you magic transfer with fais?" I asked when he looked up again.

He looked surprised at that. "Of course. You have to touch it, but the spell is easy enough. It's recovering that's hard." And demonstrated what I was to do.

It was my turn to be surprised when it actually worked.

As always, it jolted us as if we'd leaped off a tower. He went off to change, so I braced myself, held my breath, and pictured the Destination at Rajanas's castle in Alezand—but the instant I assembled the inner picture of that Destination, white lightning caused my knees to buckle.

As I picked myself up off the tiles, gulping for breath, I knew my transfers were limited to the imperial island. I was still on a leash.

Raifas returned in flowing robes without the stiff shoulder things. His robe was not folded in the tight V, but worn loose so that his shirt was visible beneath, open at the throat, his golden fais framed by a long fringed silk scarf in blue hanging over the outer robe.

"So, tomorrow," he said. "I gather you would not be impressed by a journey down the Emperor's Road with outriders, everyone summoned to line the sides and bow?"

"I would not," I said.

"There are many among the Chosen who crave that very thing. Why are you different?"

"Because I know what those bowing are really thinking."

He laughed. "You can scry their minds?"

"No. But I spent a lot of time among people who do the bowing, and I heard what they said."

"In Sveran Djur?" he retorted skeptically.

"No," I had to admit.

"You will find things very different here. We do not have crime or insurrection, covert or overt. Come along. I promised to show you the music chamber, and I should do that before I forget." He led the way up age-smoothed pale stone stairs to a round room in one of the other towers.

The room was not large, but contained several stringed instruments, and some wooden ones set on a side table.

"Go on," he said.

I hated the idea of playing in front of someone else. I moved to the harp and ran my fingers along it. "Needs tuning," I said, aware that my fingers did not move with the facility they did when I played my mother's harp. *Mother's harp.* My heart rapped against my ribs with my longing to play it again. But I had no desire to be under the same roof with Jardis Dhes-Andis before I had to. "I am not very good at it," I added when I became aware I'd let a silence build. "I am a mere beginner."

"That is not what I've been told," he replied. "Perhaps you Hrethan are overly modest? But if you do not want to play you certainly needn't. Truth to tell, I can take or leave music, except as an adjunct to dancing."

"Ah, I love to dance," I exclaimed.

He had started out, but turned around to regard me with one brow more steeply aslant than the other. "You do? But not Djuran dances, I take it?"

"If you mean the other night, I wasn't asked."

"Your Imperial Serenity," he retorted with one of those formal, sleeve-sweeping bows, "you have only to walk out into the middle of the room and they will all reform the dance around you. And if you want a different sort of dance, you speak up. That is what being an imperial princess means."

"And won't they hate me even more," I retorted right back.

Both brows went up. "You mocked their prestige by performing beginning mage magic down in the bowels of the palace where the scrubbers and cleaners live, and then went out to clear snow that the laborers had missed, and yet you seem astonished at their circumspection."

Circumspection? I snorted. "I did something useful. Further, when I cleared snow in the town, I overheard an old woman say that this was just like the old days with some empress."

"Some empress," he repeated slowly. "Would that be Lison, your great-grandmother?"

"I did not know I had a great-grandmother until very recently," I said stiffly. "I don't know anyone's name. The idea of a family isn't real to me yet."

He led the way downstairs again, saying in a more courtly voice, "Her Imperial Serenity Lison—my great-grandmother as well—was much beloved by the people, all the old relatives say. Though her reign was not impressive in the political sense. She apparently felt it was our duty to tighten sashes during bad harvests and long winters, and to beg and plead for allies when Shinja threatened. In any case, at the height of the troubles she walked out the windows of her chamber of contemplation, leaving Emperor Ifan to take up the triple crown and raise the islands to deal with the Shinjans."

We sat down in the comfortable room with all the windows, snow beating against the night-dark glass. "But we have ranged over a number of subjects as fast as a hawk can fly. If you will permit me to go back a few, why did you wear a robe embroidered with butterflies and yet refuse to dance?"

"I told you why I didn't dance. What's the significance of butterflies? I wore what the servants gave me. I thought it was pretty."

"You thought it was pretty," he repeated as he poured blue wine into two goblets. "Of course it was. That robe must have cost the equivalent of two fully equipped warships. Maybe more. You did not understand the conversation of weave, the color, and the symbols?"

"Symbols?" I sipped the wine, a kind I had learned was rare and expensive. It tasted like liquid gold. "So the spiky thorns and thistles on Amney's robes every time I see her are more than chance decoration?"

Raifas poured more wine for me and then for himself as he said, "I am almost tempted not to answer, but it's probably best. What do you think thorns and spikes signify?"

"Things that tear and make you bleed."

He grimaced briefly. "By choice we avoid such ugliness. Thorns warn one to be wary around roses, yes?"

"So that is a warning to me, am I right? It surely wouldn't be meant as warning to the Ev — to the emperor."

"I would not hazard any suppositions about her relationship with Cousin Jardis. At least out loud," he admitted with one of those flashing smiles. "I will say that defying either of them has its cost."

"Why? I never did anything to her — no, I don't even care why." I wanted to escape, not to gossip. I gulped down half my blue wine in an effort to obliterate the sneaking conviction I would never escape.

"I will say only this, Amney is ambitious. And whether or not it is actually true, she regards you as an obstacle in her path."

"Then she's got thorns in the head," I muttered, the wine burning like liquid gold down to my deepest places. "Tell me what other things the embroidery symbolizes."

"Messages lie in color and shade, and whether figures flow left to right or reverse, but one can begin with dragons, the Djuran symbol, which is usually taken as...."

I let a lot of the rest of what he said flow by, knowing I would never remember it all, because everything took on conditional meanings according to the knots in edging, and so on, and then it changed again according to what event you wore the thing to, and who the host was. Empire politics, personal politics. That much I knew from listening to talk about the court at Erev-li-Erval. In that sense, probably every royal or imperial court is the same: unspoken messages are a game that the rich and stylish play among themselves. I could never hope to compete even if I wanted to.

When he was done, I pointed out that the clothes I wore had probably been left-overs from other people, hastily remade to accommodate my spine hair and tail. And that was fine. The silks could symbolize whatever they wanted to.

I had finished my wine by then. Feeling that pleasant, heady warmth, I assented to more as I said, "About dragons. Is your dragon banner in honor of the dragon in the fire mountain?"

"What dragon?" he asked. "Are you speaking symbolically of

the burning rock, or are you referring to old folk tales?"

I blinked at him, so astonished I didn't know what to say.

He went on about dragon symbolism—power and beauty, awe, intelligence, and majesty, and from there he went on into the majesty of Djuran history, but by then I wasn't listening so much as watching his lips.

And then he was sitting next to me rather than across from me, and I leaned toward him, liking how he was a little flushed from wine, the light reflecting in his slanted eyes as he gazed back at me. Not clear: I tried to blink away the shadow, or double vision, but his proximity only sharpened the blur into the gaze of a raptor.

The wine, the warmth, muffled what might have been surprise. All I thought was, of course he is part bird. Did he know it?

The wine had kindled an insistent warmth in me that I had thought forever gone, and my gaze blinked away the subtle raptor shadow to appreciate the clean line of his shoulder under the flattering sea-colored silk, the outline of his chest under the folds of the long blue scarf. His well-shaped hands, nails neatly trimmed.

"Is that it?" I asked, my lips pleasantly numb, as another puzzle piece locked into place. But giddy as I was, wariness was far older, and rather than comment on his bird shape outright I said tentatively, "The Sveranji. They were shape changers?"

"Long ago." His brows lifted in mild surprise, then he smiled. "But we put animal natures behind us when we grasped civilization. And our fais help us keep them there."

"I'm part bird," I said.

He ran a finger up my wrist to my elbow over the tiny feathers of my fuzz. I shivered, but not from cold as I breathed in the warm, garden-fragrant sweetness of attraction.

"It's miraculously soft," he observed in a low voice that rumbled in his chest. "You're part Hrethan. And part imperial Dhes-Andis. We might say the laws of hierarchy are different for you."

I shivered again.

"Elenderi?" he asked, and stroked his forefinger down my cheek to my neck, and to my collarbone. Then his fingers spread and lightly rested on my shoulder.

"You're talking to Princess Elenderi," I muttered. And not to Lhind, about whom he never asked.

A scorching image, raptors tumbling through the sky wing over wing, talons locked....

"Princess Elenderi," he murmured. "Bewitching combination of contradictions."

Contradictions.

And an errant memory: Hlanan's voice as he watched Tir soaring against the sunlight, *Aidlars mate for life.*

I did not know why that thought came. Didn't care. After the betrayals and fears and anguish of the past days, in this moment I simply wanted to be kissed. And here was the first Djuran I actually liked; his arm enclosed me and his perfumed hair slid soft as silk against my cheek.

But we put animal natures behind us when we grasped civilization, he'd said. He was ready to kiss Princess Elenderi, the mask. Not Lhind the half-bird.

Here was no meeting of minds.

With Hlanan I had found and cherished a meeting of minds. He wasn't handsome like Raifas. He didn't fly boldly on gryph back, but oh, who else in the world could I sit down beside and tell my every thought without weighing the consequences or anticipating effect? Who had listened with all his attention as if every word I said mattered, not to political necessity but to *him*?

And he was gone forever. Tears of anger burned. I couldn't have Hlanan. I ought to grab this pleasure, ephemeral as I knew it to be, because why not?

But there was Hlanan's image interposing itself, and I stiffened in the grip of those warm, strong arms, and turned my face away from those kissable lips.

"Elenderi?" he asked, dropping his hands.

"Good night." My throat hurt. My eyes stung. I got out of there and upstairs to the guest chamber, where I threw open the windows to the storm. And howled curses at Aranu Crown and the unfair world.

Twenty-four

With morning (and a lack of wine sloshing in my brain) came clarity. My emotions were ambivalent about what had nearly happened the night before, equal parts regret and relief. Maybe there'd be another chance, maybe not. I didn't even know how I felt about that.

So I would think about something else.

I got up, shut the windows, and melted the snow that had scudded up against the walls, but my nerves chilled when I considered the two newest pieces of the puzzle.

One: that vast ruby-scaled shape not quite in the molten rock. From what Raifas said we would be visiting it again, so perhaps I would discover more.

The other puzzle-piece was those shadows, human shadows attached to lizardrakes, in the same way that Raifas carried a raptor shadow. If Raifas's "civilization" meant that offspring had lost their ability to transform, what had happened to the lizardrakes with human shadows?

The only thing I could think of was that their fais had locked them into lizardrake form, so they mated with other lizardrakes, and their offspring had lost the ability to transform before the fais was even put on them. Or had they chosen to give up their human shape and stay lizardrakes?

I changed and descended to the dining room, where I found Raifas talking to a scribe and a couple of servants. At my appearance the latter three bowed themselves out and closed the door.

Raifas greeted me, making no reference to what had almost happened the night before. As I settled down in my place, I said, "Are we going to the fire mountain?"

The words had scarcely gone from my lips into the air when I sensed a shift around me. It is difficult to explain: not the same as those shadows, or yet the connection with the tree, though the sensitivity that had awakened in me after my communion with the tree had not faded.

This sense was akin to the shadow figure sense, only I mentally perceived myself enclosed in glass as an amber eye regarded me. A heartbeat later I knew what it was: Dhes-Andis scrying.

"The gryphs are being harnessed now," Raifas said. "We have only to breakfast, and we can leave."

The glass bowl and the eye winked into non-existence. The sense of pressure around my head eased.

All right. This might be a new skill, but now I understood that Dhes-Andis was not watching all the time. Further, I would know when he was. That meant I could practice my pin-hole in the mental realm when his attention was away.

We got ready to go.

The flight up the mountain might have been faster if the wind had not blustered mercilessly from over the ocean, icy with sleet. I crouched down on Andisla's back, glad of my thick cloak. Mere cold I did not mind, but no warm-blooded creature likes icy wetness.

So for most of the flight I concentrated on hanging on, though I did briefly practice my pin-hole contact on Andisla, to find pretty much the same blurred focus as before, as if the gryph's mind existed behind glass.

Then we reached the vapors, and the real fight began: wind, cold, heat, and through it, Firebird struggling with all his strength against the storm, vapors, fear, and the inescapable coercion of the fais. I reached for his mind and recoiled from his fury underscored by agony. The intensity of his emotions seemed scarcely contained by the magical boundary that in Andisla felt thick as glass. I broke the connection, perilously dizzy.

Raifas's will (and fais) predominated. Firebird broke through the underside of the cloud of vapors and smoke, followed by Andisla. They glided in tight circles through the rising fumes and hot air above the glowing molten rock glowing with the glory of a smoldering sun below.

The birds lit on a shelf of cooled rock, Firebird dancing back and forth, occasionally letting forth a weird cry, echoed by Andisla.

I gazed down in fascination at the whirling, diving dance of fire-bright forms. Glowing, evanescent lizardrakes predominated, their arms busy with tasks instead of folded in awkwardly against their bodies, though I could not see their purpose as they faded in and out of my vision.

Other winged creatures winkled in and out, too brief to descry with any clarity, but far below, or beyond, lay that vasty ruby-scaled deepness. As I reached mentally I sensed a great stirring, as if alien eyes sought to meet mine.

Terrified lest my mind burn in that eerie fire, I closed my mental shield tight—and Firebird let loose a long, mournful howl. As Andisla began to echo it, greenish magic flickered over the decorative fais around the bird's neck and the cry choked off.

Raifas leaned toward me, the glow reflecting in his enormous pupils. "Is this not splendid?" Before I could form any kind of answer, he indicated the surging mass of boiling rock below. "Now, here's our purpose. Think you there is any way to fetch this up for the gryphs to carry? Is it magical, or physical, or both?"

"That is why we are here?" I called back.

"Yes. As I said. My idea for my fleet. Look about you. Is there a way to fetch and preserve the melted rock long enough to use its fire at sea?"

I looked around, but not at ways to bucket up the boiling rock. His raptor shadow-self either was not strong enough for him to recognize the half-seen denizens in the strange red glow below, or he shut them out as irrelevant.

I blinked, aware of my feathers singeing in the withering heat; I flexed my scalp and spine, winding my hair and tail into ropes, and drew the cloak around myself.

Firebird danced again, and again Raifas flashed the fais magic.

I winced at how much it hurt the bird, an echo of my own fais pain, which in turn caused Andisla to dance nervously on the perch.

"Seen enough?" Raifas called.

"Yes."

He sat back, and Firebird launched toward the dimly lit hole above, half-veiled by vapors and smoke. Andisla followed, as always.

Another jolting ride through the zone of hot vapors fighting icy winds, and then we burst into the sky and the weather, which at least had turned from sleet to snow.

When we reached the castle again, and a warm room with hot spiced wine to drink, Raifas said, "What did you see, Elenderi?"

"What was I supposed to see?" I asked.

He spread his hands. "You are half-Hrethan, which I am told means you are neither wholly the one or the other. Moreover, events have caused you to be now learning the skills you ought to have been taught from childhood. And that includes whatever skills you have inherited. Am I correct?"

"Yes," I said, unable to repeat the word "correct." I didn't think I could ever say it again without a shudder.

"Your kind, that is, the Snow Folk, who I am given to understand are kin to Hrethan, used to cluster on this mountain, according to both written records and endless fanciful ballads and tales. Hrethan and firedrake, Snow Folk and Fire Dragon. There is more than a suggestion that magic and material mixed."

"And so?" Did he sense that other world after all? I wavered, tempted to ask.

"Is it not obvious?" He leaned toward me, no mask, his enthusiasm open. "I know that magic alone is seldom useful in ship to ship conflict. But if you saw a way to combine them both so that I could drop molten rock onto enemy ships and set them aflame, a protracted struggle might be reduced to one or two examples and then surrender to the inevitable."

"So you want the molten rock for war."

"We think of it as defense, but you are correct."

"To be carried by Firebird?"

"I am in the process of educating him in that direction, but the idea is to build a force of gryphs. Train them the way I've trained him. If we could make use of the gryphs to carry molten rock, I'd find a way to broaden the aft decks of our ships to enable gryphs to perch and launch. But I would still need to keep the molten rock sufficiently fired. And that's why I asked about magic." He drank spiced wine, and set his cup down. "Not to your taste?"

I had not drunk any. I needed to reflect and had no desire for wine haze. I lifted the cup and pretended to sip, to avoid answering.

"If you cannot think of anything immediately," Raifas said quite kindly, "I understand. Your skills are new. Your education only beginning. I wished to show you the possibility, that you might consider it as you learn more. And I have my part as well. It took an entire autumn five years ago to hunt down a male great gryph, get him into fais, and keep him alive long enough to train. Firebird was my fourth try, my success."

Success? That angry, desperate bird was a *success*?

"As it happens, I enjoy the hunt and the battle of wills. Human subduing beast. The natural order. And the egg-civilized are not capable of the speed and maneuverability that we need for the fleet. They are too slow, too amiable. And unfortunately too easily shot out of the sky by an enemy with a powerful longbow. So my plan would required time to catch and train the gryphs in evasive flight — as you and I experienced on your first journey — before we could train them to carry and drop the molten rock on command. It is not going to happen overnight."

He smiled and gestured toward the window. "The snow is worsening, so we shall have to postpone your tour of the pennon. And I must see to some pressing matters. I invite you to visit the music chamber — you know where it is — or indeed, anywhere else you wish to explore. There is a library in the floor above the music chamber, if you would like to peruse local archives."

His manner, so kind and practical after his extraordinary request and explanation, left me without words as another puzzle piece slowly resolved and locked inexorably into place.

In spite of Ingras's words — and Raifas's readiness to engage in flirtation the previous evening, if I had wanted it — it was clear that this was no courtship. Oh, maybe Dhes-Andis was still thinking of marriage between Raifas and me. I did not know. I had no idea how such things were arranged here.

But Raifas did not see me in that regard, except maybe for idle diversion if I had agreed. He wanted me as a *weapon*.

———◆◆◆———

Two more days I stayed, during which we took that tour.

Everywhere I saw what he wanted me to see, and what might even have existed: contented people busy with their labors among their pretty steep-roofed houses, their snow-covered terracing awaiting spring planting, and the blossoming of the neatly ordered silk trees where once wild forest had grown. The fais-controlled lizardrakes and goats and other animals were never anything but quiet and obedient.

How long would I have gone before understanding that the oddness I'd been aware of was that the palace cats had no voices, had I not seen those quiet animals? Or heard Firebird's anguished cries choked off by a lightning bolt of correction?

Oh, yes, Firebird. The last day, as we readied to return to Icecrest, I tried to reach Firebird through my pin-hole to encounter a blast of hatred. It was mostly aimed at Raifas, but there was plenty left for all two-legs.

Overwhelming impulse caused me to ask, "May I ride Firebird back?"

Raifas hesitated, and then bowed. If there was irony in the turn of his wrist, I ignored it. The Imperial Princess Had Spoken, and right in front of the waiting servants. "No one else has successfully ridden him, as he is still undergoing education," he began, but by then I was on Firebird's back.

"Ah, yes," he said, and this time the irony was out front, no mask, along with appreciation. "Lead on, O Imperial Princess." He laughed as he vaulted onto Andisla's harness pad.

Firebird wasn't happy with me, either, but took off in a leap, and flapped hard into the air. Once we reached the gliding currents, I settled myself, shut my eyes, checked for scrying (none), and then reached for the great gryph.

No words here. I thought words at him anyway, because that's what humans do, but I hoped even if the bird was only hearing *bibblebibblebibble* in the mental realm, I wanted my emotions to carry as I said, *I will try to free you. If there is a way, I will find it.*

Firebird gave a long cry.

Raifas yelled, "Tap the harness on the acanthus carving to dissuade that noise."

"It hurts them," I shouted back.

"Only until they learn," he called with his usual careless cheer. "We all had to learn when we were small."

"Is that why the palace cats are so silent?"

"No one likes yowling," he responded. "They have excellent lives. No need for screeching."

"Every creature deserves a voice," I said, but under my breath.

I can't say how much of my words reached Firebird. The emotions that reached me were so difficult for me to comprehend except for the ones all creatures share, like anger and fear of pain. But this much I got: Firebird did not believe me in the same way I was beginning to not believe me.

By the time we reached Icecrest my emotions were bleak as the winter around us. I was lying to myself now, I thought as I slid off the harness to the beautifully paved stones of the perch balcony. There was no escape.

I leaned my head against the bird's neck, thinking: *I'm sorry. I'm sorry*, my pity divided between us both.

The only thing I wanted was to run to that harp. Hope is all I have left, I was thinking as Raifas said something or other in the polite court mode. If hope died, I would.

We bowed to one another—formal court mode resumed—and he gave me a slight, mocking grin as if we shared a joke. But we didn't. The possibility of friendship, still less anything closer, had vanished when he talked so casually about the battle of wills, and the prospect of extending what he had done to Firebird to more great gryphs.

I tried to speak as I had, and to smile back, as I did not want to seem different. Still before we parted he gave me a narrow-eyed, questioning glance, but then came an imperial servant to conduct me to Dhes-Andis, and the yoke of fear tightened around me once again.

I needed to concentrate on my mask. Inside, Lhind the Thief, outside the empty shell of Princess Elenderi.

The servant opened the door to the Garden Chamber, and as I passed inside my neck tightened in the familiar stress. I'd had several blissful days away from all the bowing and the fear. My respite was over.

I performed the Princess Elenderi bow, noticing several silent cats sitting about.

Dhes-Andis said, "Sit down, Elenderi. Give me your impressions of Ardam Pennon."

I practiced my court voice as I said what I thought he wanted to hear: fine buildings, handsome castle, vast fleet in the harbor.

He listened in silence, nothing to be read in his face, one hand slowly stroking a slit-eyed cat. When I ran out of superlatives, he said, "And your real impression?" When I opened my mouth, he said slowly, "Uttering inanities is a form of lying."

The implied warning flared my nerves, and I couldn't help jumping. Then came the anger and hate. I stilled myself. "I don't know enough. Everything was snowy."

"Did you practice your magic?"

"Yes. That is, I melted snow. I forgot to try taking warmth out of something, and creating ice."

"We will assay that momentarily. Did the Most Noble Raifas explain his new idea for a tactical defense?"

Wasn't attacking Ndai an *offense?* I held my breath lest the thought somehow leak out either past my mental shield (locked hard as it was) or in my demeanor. "Yes, he did. But I don't see how molten rock could be taken out of the mountain and carried out to sea."

"You did not consider transporting it from the mountain to a designated receptacle?"

"I don't understand transfer magic at all," I said. "It hurts when I transfer. I never thought about objects."

"We shall assay that, too. But I desire you to take your mind back to Mount Dragon. Did you experience any alteration in your awareness or your magical skills?"

My instinct to hide what I had seen was so strong that I said quickly, "All I noticed was how hot it was. How much it stinks! I don't know which hurt worse, my eyes or my lungs."

"Enough." He raised a hand. "Apparently your Hrethan blood does not extend to recognizing what used to be a place of power for the Snow Folk, who are doubtless part of your heritage. It could be that with more education you will awaken new skills of which you are as yet unaware—and likewise it is possible that the legends in the old records are mere story. The Sveranji were uncivilized in so many regards. Mixing truth and poetic hyperbole being one."

I struggled so hard not to show my emotions that his eyes narrowed. "What is it? If you have a question, ask it. There is no fault in awareness of one's own ignorance."

"I was wondering, of what use would be any skills I'd find in the middle of a mountain of stinky molten rock?"

"Ah, discussion of strategy assumes awareness. When you demonstrate a commensurate degree of skill and focus, you will be enlightened. As well as rewarded with freedom and responsibility. Raifas," he added, "is ambitious, and his loyalty to the good of the empire has been consistently demonstrated. His reward will be rank and power."

"He told me he would become Prince of Ndai, if he conquered it," I said.

Dhes-Andis didn't flicker at the word conquer. "And so he shall. I am convinced he will govern that fractious group of islands far better than their idiosyncratic witch-queen could ever hope to, and bring the benefit to us. Come. Let us see what you can do."

He seemed pleased at how well I managed fire, and how easily I adapted that to taking heat out of something. I turned a bucket of boiling water to ice, and then took the heat out of a roll sitting on a plate.

When he asked me to remove the heat from a rootling in a small pot, I said, "Won't it kill the plant? This is not like a stone spell, which slows down life."

"Do you object to killing the equivalent of a weed that someone would pull out of her vegetable garden?"

I allowed as how that would not bother me, but still queasiness lurched in my middle when the magic snapped greenish and the plant shattered at a tick of his fingernail against it. His subsequent praise worsened my sense that I had lost some kind of contest, and I was glad when he dismissed me at last—with a reminder that the Chosen had put forward several entertainments which they hoped I would grace.

Sure they did, I thought as I escaped. They hoped I would grace it about as much as they hoped for a knock on the head.

I returned to the Princess Elenderi suite because I did not want to be seen rushing straight to the music room. There they all were, bowing like wheat in the wind, and the choking sense of falsity tightened another notch.

When Kal straightened, that familiarity in his face struck me anew, and this time I recognized what I had failed to see, or couldn't bear to see: how much his eyes were shaped like mine.

Not that they were completely the same. Far more strongly, the shape of his eyes and the line of his jaw resembled that of Emperor Jardis Dhes-Andis.

I had begun to like Kal until then, but that thought was so horrible that I could scarcely wait to get out of there.

And so uncertain had I become that even though I had been eager to return to the harp, when I sat down at last—mindful of what Raifas had said so carelessly, about my supposed skill being overheard, which meant I was being listened to at the very least—I yawned and stretched and shook my fingers, worried as always that the magic on the harp was some kind of nefarious trap.

As soon as I touched the harp strings the magically caused skill flowed back, and with it the loving warmth that caused my breath to hitch in my chest. I had forgotten the depth of that love, had begun to diminish and to question it.

In spite of my doubts and distrust, she was there.

And though my thought had been wordless, still came an answer: *I will always be here, sleeping and waking, until you are safe. I sensed you had gone away from Skyreach Mountain?*

Ardam Pennon, I answered, with quick images that were half-inadvertent.

The equally wordless flow of comfort flowed from her, carrying enough of regret and sorrow that I cried out mournfully, *I nearly seduced Raifas, I am so lonely.*

That is a normal human response, she said, a trickle of humor sparkling in the colors of warmth, and I thought I breathed in a faint scent of rose. *The problem comes in mistaking one kind of love for another.*

Still, I will not make that error again. I lost my attraction for him when I discovered —

And I halted, the mental wall shuttering. I still couldn't trust that I wasn't being tricked, that Dhes-Andis wasn't using this truly insidious method to control me from inside out.

So I put forth a cautious question: *Why would Dhes-Andis ask me about the fire mountain?*

Before our cousins the Snow Folk fled to Summer Islands long ago, they lived on the mountaintops among the Sveranji. But as the Djurans advanced northwards, they used their fais magic to force the Sveranji shape-changers into their beast shapes, and took their homes and isles.

And the mountain? I asked.

It is the gateway to a sister world where their other shapes dwelt, one of great magic. The reason Danis and I left Sveran Djur was because he discovered his half-brother Jardis desires access to that gate in order to fais the great drake there, who is said to be thousands of years old, and possessed of powerful magic. Such as immortality.

Another puzzle piece locked into place, and with its appearance fell away the last of my distrust. *Mother*, I said, for the first time.

Twenty-five

SHE DID NOT RESPOND in words. Maybe she couldn't. But the overwhelming flow of love, without condition or expectation, choked me up so much my hands fell away from the strings.

I was not alone.

Pelan stood within arm's reach, wiping away tears, and at her shoulder, Ilhas, a young fellow of maybe twenty.

I gulped back my own tears, fighting against the vertigo of change in focus, and squashing down the questions I wanted so badly to ask. But I'd find my mother again, I reminded myself. I had to protect the connection.

The two bowed deeply, I bowed back, and Pelan said impulsively (for a Chosen), "I beg Your Imperial Serenity's pardon for my presumption, but oh, why have you not played to us? You are so skilled, and these melodies! So refined, so elevating to the higher senses! That lament you were just now performing was so very beautiful. Is it Hrethan music?"

"Yes," I said, though I had no idea. Only a scrap of melody lingered in my mind, expressive of longing. "I play merely as recreation and contemplation," I said to end the dangerous subject, and glanced up at Ilhas. "Why are you here?"

"If you will forgive me, Your Imperial Serenity, I would remind you that this is the hour Ilhas and I always come here."

So the room wasn't completely abandoned, as I'd first thought. I'd never encountered them because I had mostly come first thing in the morning.

"Well, then," I said, determined to shift attention away from me and my supposed skills. "I love to listen. May I remain, or do you also play for your own contemplation?"

"I would be honored to play to Your Imperial Serenity," Ilhas said with genuine-sounding emotion behind the courtly cadence.

"As would I," Pelan put in.

I moved away from my place, and held my breath as Pelan self-consciously took my place and touched her fingers to the harp. But she clearly felt nothing unusual, and ran her hands along the strings to warm up her fingers as Ilhas took up a woodwind.

And so the two commenced a duet. I sat on a nearby cushion, my hands together in the prescribed form, and while Pelan pricked and strummed with far more skill than I had with ordinary instruments, though not half as well as Thianra, I sifted the Blue Lady's...*Mother's*...words.

First and most formidable, that about the ancient dragon who dwelt in that place in and yet not in the molten rock of Mount Dragon. An ageless and magical being, it was the reason I'd been sent to Ardam Pennon. Those questions on my return made it clear that the Evil Emperor had an interest extending beyond the possibility of scooping lava to throw at other ships.

Raifas was not the only one who wanted me as a weapon.

Another puzzle piece slid into place. A big one, one of the biggest, but I still did not have it all yet.

I tried to fight back the rush of fear and anxiety by reasserting my mask. I had to remember that I was Lhind the Spy, and though I had a few tricks, I knew nothing at all of mysterious mountains.

The two finished their song. Before they began another they talked a little about Djuran music: imperial triads, songs of the seasons, traditions.

Apparently it was acceptable for Chosen to perform for one another in trios—one on strings, one on winds, and one maintaining the counterpoint on either cymbals or sticks or little hand drums—but Pelan and Ilhas had not found a third. I suspected it was because they ranked lowest in the Chosen hierarchy. If Amney or Darus (or Raifas, who had admitted his indifference to music) had taken up an instrument, there would be trio concerts every day, and this room would be in constant use.

When the time chimes rang in the distance we parted with mutual bows, and they said they hoped to be honored by my presence at the Most Noble Darus's dance.

What dance?

Chith was waiting to recite a list of invitations. Some were for excursions in floats to this or that island if we were graced with a sunbloom, but the preponderance were for dances. As I counted them up—one for every night for several days—I thought, Raifas has been talking.

So it was in a belligerent spirit that I got ready for the first dance. Remembering what Raifas had said about symbols, for the first time I looked at the clothing in my wardrobe, sorting for embroidery, weave, and color messages.

I wanted to choose the spikiest spikes, except I didn't have any. Anyway it seemed a bad idea to suddenly declare war on them through their symbols. Everybody knew Princess Elenderi for an ignorant boor.

The boor didn't matter. The ignorance was going, but I didn't want them to know that. I passed over the beautiful butterfly one—I still didn't know what those signified—and chose white-silver silk with crimson poppies and gray-blue long-legged cranes in flight.

This dance began exactly the way Amney's dance had, only the smiling host who led me to the place of honor was Darus, Amney looking on with an icy pretense at a smile in the background.

I sat alone on the same cushion on the same platform in the same lonely place of honor—and no sooner had I carefully disposed my train and my sleeves than that flicker of pressure on my skull presaged the glass-bowl-and-eye sense of scrying. I kept my mental shield locked hard as arrivals minced forward to bow to me, again exactly as they had before, including Raifas. Then once again the scry-eye was gone. Dhes-Andis had been checking in, probably while having more fun elsewhere.

I bowed back to Raifas, formal and unsmiling. He gave me one of those assessing looks, then was distracted when Ingras approached him and began talking in a voice too low for me to overhear.

And — as before — the musicians in the gallery above began the prelude to the Shadow Dance.

The Chosen began their careful advance-and-retreat according to rank and politesse as they sorted themselves into groups of three pairs.

Step-two-three, turn-two-three, mirror left, mirror right, bow....

The dancers began to trip gracefully through the intricate pattern, the left-hand person mirroring the right-hand, and the meaning of the Shadow Dance locked another puzzle piece into place.

This had been a Sveranji dance, taken by the conquerors, who mirrored themselves. By so doing they had subsumed the true meaning, the celebration of human and other shape.

Though this appropriation and change had taken place centuries ago, a swelling of anger burned and bubbled inside of me as hot as any molten rock.

You have only to walk into the middle of them....

The music already had my shoulders twitching and my toes bunching up. I can't sing, or draw, or truly play an instrument — in fact I'm not very skilled at much — but I can dance.

And I could see the true pattern.

As the first of the three repetitions wound toward its end, all triangles coming back to their starting place, I slid off my cushion, and hair and tail clouding — if you're going to do something that's probably a stupid idea, do it with style — I glided off the dais toward the center of the room.

The musicians faltered a single beat, then repeated the prelude.

I glimpsed Raifas laughing for half a heartbeat before he smoothed his face into courtly aloofness; I turned away and stopped in the middle of the room, my right hand out. I didn't even look, though my heartbeat thundered.

With a reluctance that I could feel through my bones all the way to my back teeth, Darus slowly stepped up next to me and bowed low. Everybody else, with a hiss of silks and a shuffle of expensive embroidered dancing slippers, also bowed and reformed into new pairs.

And the dance commenced. Each of the three evolutions had two parts, the first representing the human, which now enabled me to be certain of the steps. When we had stepped, leaped, and twirled round all the points of all the triangles, it was time for the second part: the shadow. The others merely turned to go back the other way, but I lifted my arms out like wings, spread my tail to suggest tail feathers, and added height to my leaps, whirling in the air with my wings wide.

I could feel the startled gazes but I kept on, making pecking motions instead of bows.

"Oh," Vian said softly to Ingras, her partner. "The princess is being a bird! How sublime!"

Ilhas began strutting like a rooster, which caused a muffled laugh, but he never missed a step or turn, and smiled triumphantly until Amney gave him a freezing stare when they briefly met hands-high. His fun faded and he stiffened into obedient hauteur.

I leaped even higher, spinning three times in the air on the last notes. When I landed, the Chosen (with the expected exceptions) uttered their soft, cooing sigh.

Third evolution.

Human again. I began watching them carefully, for the first time not seeing them as faceless as a set of rice-paper dolls. Yes, out of those Chosen present, seven had shadows, though most of them were so faded that it was difficult to recognize what shape they had once had. Except for the eighth, whose shadow was so sharp I was surprised I had never noticed. Because I had ignored him as much as I could.

When the time drew nigh for the mirror dance, I pointed at Voyas, who had the clearest of the seven muted shadows, and said, "You are a leopard."

His eyelids flashed up. *Yes*, I thought. *Have you lived as a leopard in your dreams? Is he in your nature?* He rolled his shoulders and stepped out with a hint of a prowl that caught the eye.

I used my supposed rank and pointed to the rest of my half-dozen: "You, a lillend, you, a hippogryph, you a minotaur, you a lamiar, you a sphinx, you a yeth-hound." None of them reacted; they clearly did not recognize their animal natures, perhaps too thinned over the generations, or too buried in dreams to ever be acknowledged.

And I came face to face with my partner, the eighth, whose courtly mask showed no expression besides a faint upper-lip crimp of contempt, but whose ophidian-eyed wolf-shadow glared in teeth-bared hatred.

"Wolf," I said to Darus. "You are a wolf."

His gaze widened in a flash of anger, then narrowed into suspicion, and it was then that I remembered my danger.

"Oh, what am I?" Pelan asked. "Please, Your Imperial Serenity...."

"A dove," I said, glad to turn away, and I began choosing at random to hide my blunder. Swiftly I handed out birds and beasts, and when I came to Amney, whose mouth smiled mockingly, I said, "Eagle." And though the mockery remained, she lifted her chin in the briefest instant of satisfaction that at least I had given her a bird considered noble.

She turned away, mocking and yet still graceful in her swoops and dives, her sleeve tassels streaming, and those who must always follow mimicked her with not-quite-hidden zeal.

Then I came face to face with Raifas, and my alarm flared again. "Centaur," I said, and he laughed a little as he stepped away.

And so, for the first time in centuries, the animals danced in mirror image to the humans—except for Darus, who stalked through the dance with cold precision, his wolf up-hackled at his back, though no one could see it but I; and Raifas, who danced as he always did, neither mocking, pretending, or affronted. To him, complacent in his human superiority, it was all a joke.

Yet around him hippogryph pawed, and eagle soared with a flash of peach-colored wings, leopard prowled, dove fluttered, and fingers sparked tiny greenish stars when hand met hand, building a heady effervescence that somehow brought out the horns in brighter tones, the strings hummed in a shimmer of sound, the cymbals rang in entrancing patterns.

At first I thought the shift in my perception due to the dizziness caused by my spinning so often, after not having danced wildly in too many months to count. But the shadow vision dissolved the walls, so that the stars beyond the never-ending storms shone down and magic glistened through the chamber.

And in the distance Firebird bugled, echoed more indistinctly by four other great gryphs, the brown gryphs, and higher, the grays, finally, almost indistinct, the tiny voices of the lizardrakes....

And the cats.

Then the last notes died away, and silence fell, inside and out. Partners smiled at one another, eyes bright, cheeks flushed. For a few heartbeats we all shared the giddiness of joy.

No, not all. Amney was the first to stiffen into courtly grace, her expression masked; Raifas bowed to her and she bowed back, exquisite in their civilization. Darus lifted a hand to signal another dance, and the joy sank under courtly hauteur. It was then that I felt another scry, a longer one, as everyone moved in stylized order as if whatever had happened never had.

The musicians altered their style, commencing a technically complicated pavane that required sedately intricate steps.

Darus faced me, as blank as a statue, and I felt his unspoken challenge. I said—as I suspected I was supposed to—"I do not know the steps to this dance."

He bowed, turned to another partner, and I retreated to my cushion, the last vestige of joy doused by the time My Imperial Seat landed on the cushion. I was not at all certain what had almost happened during that Shadow Dance, but this much I knew: I had to be careful. I had almost revealed my ability to see those animal shadows, and to an enemy.

Twenty-six

BACK TO COURT TEDIUM for the remainder of the night. Now that I'd seen Darus's vigilant wolf, I couldn't stop seeing it instead of the tall, handsome courtier wearing four layers of green, cream, yellow, and gold silk folded into a sharp V below his fais, which glinted between the stiffly embroidered collar points at his throat. His fais did not have a diamond, I noted when he passed me by dipping into one of those exquisitely icy bows. The only one with diamonds belonged to Jardis Dhes-Andis. I still did not know if the diamonds had magical properties or were mere imperial decoration.

After ten eternities, the evening finally ended. I left first, as before.

The next morning, I said loudly to Kal and the staff, "The music was so fine last night that I am inspired to resume my music studies. I shall retire to play the harp."

There, I thought. Let whoever had to report my doings repeat that.

But scarcely had I consumed half a piece of nut bread when I sensed a sharp alertness in Tay, who had brought me fresh peach tarts, and Kal and Chith waiting in the larger room. Fais communication? They began fading back as if some kind of storm approached below the horizon.

The double doors opened to the hands of imperial guards, and in walked his emperorship, Jardis Dhes-Andis.

My nerves flashed painfully as I jolted to my feet and gave him his emperor bow.

His manner was at its most benign as he indicated my never-used formal chamber. With a running flash of pale silver silk sleeve complementing the deep violet panels of his stole, he settled in a quick, graceful movement on the principal cushion. Out of all my roiling fears, a single breath of relief trickled through me as I recognized no shadow about him. At least I didn't have to not notice it.

I sat opposite him. He waved off servants and guards with a slight lift of his forefinger, and the door shut on us, leaving us alone.

He said, "I understand you introduced a change into our oldest imperial dance."

I said, "It seemed like it might be fun. No one told me I couldn't."

"It is not their place to deny your whims. As I am certain you are by now aware. What gave you the notion to change the dance?"

His manner appeared so benign except for that unblinking amber gaze, and yet in my new perception I sensed the dragon wings of death beating slowly around me. It had nothing to do with the physical realm—it was not *his* dragon, that is, he had no shadow, but I sensed it as ineluctably as I had the walls dissolving to that canopy of stars during the Shadow Dance.

I dared not tell the truth—

And white lightning burned me to ash, then left me a quivering puddle.

The wings pressed close around me as I sobbed for breath.

"It grieves me to be required to repeat the obvious," he said without any sign of emotion. "That was for your hesitation, which could only be due to your concocting some lie, and this is for stupidity."

The universe ripped me into tiny components of pain.

Slowly, inexorably, they coalesced. My wits had scattered so badly I could not find my name, or even my self—though my first desperate thought was to scrabble for my mental shield. As Hlanan had promised, once I made it solid, the unconsciousness of sleep would not permit its alteration.

Memory rebuilt awareness, a flutter of images connecting on some deeper level I was not yet able to perceive. But one image lingered: my guest room at Ardam Pennon.

"Why," Dhes-Andis said, "did you disrupt the dance in a way that has been described as deliberately uncivilized by two witnesses?"

I gulped for breath. Sat upright, though I had to clasp my hands on my knees to keep me there. "At Raifas's castle, there is a carving all around the ceiling in the guest chamber. Winged lions and hippogryphs and aidlars bowing to their partners," I said. "After looking at it each morning when I woke, the fancy stayed with me. It came into my head when the dance began."

"Ah." The wings lifted, hovering. "I have seen that chamber. Why did you not tell me when I asked?"

"Because it was impulse," I said, thumbing away the tears that burned my eyes. "The dance, I mean. I didn't think about it, it just came to me as a fun idea. Because of the fancy I from looking at the c-carvings," I almost said *animals,* and caught myself. My verbal stumble passed because my voice was already so unsteady.

"Did you hear the cats yowling?" he asked.

"Cats?" I repeated witlessly, and he took that for surprise that cats should be yowling, rather than surprise that he would bring up the animals' strange response. I shook my head slowly, then said, "Animals hear things that humans don't, even when there aren't musicians playing. Maybe there was some noise from down the cliffs, or in the wind."

"They will learn decorous behavior again," he said, but the tension in his shoulders eased minutely, and so did his breathing. It occurred to me that he had never once touched me, but I was conscious of every subtle change in him. If he ever did, it would surely slay me.

Two heartbeats, three. Then he said, "We began adversely, I am aware. In an effort to mitigate that, outside of the necessity of your education, my intent was to leave you free to become acquainted with the Chosen. In particular your family, and without my presence. But it seems to have been less successful than I had expected. We shall change that."

I was already so wrung out that I guess the fresh suffusion of horror didn't show.

He went on in a reasonable tone, "Your gesture was perhaps well-meant, but childish and ignorant. You must not mock the oldest and most revered of court rituals."

"I wasn't...." I flinched at his glance, my fingers pawing at the fais. I yanked my hand down.

"Mocking?" he asked, watching my hand. "It was not, perhaps, your intent, but the effect was the same."

That was two uses of *perhaps*. Both flashed my nerves with warning.

"But this is to revert to unpleasant subjects. I told you that success and effort are always rewarded, an advantage I never had. I want to reward you. I like rewarding you. Yet you ask for nothing." He bent his head a little closer, and I had to tense every muscle to keep from scrambling backward. "What do you want, Elenderi?"

"My freedom." It was out before I could stop it. At the narrowing of his eyes I gulped in a breath, and no amount of control could keep me from flinching, my shoulders hunching tight under my ears, both my hands tense lest I give in and yank futilely at that horrible fais.

"You *have* freedom." He opened his hands. "Within reasonable limits. Even if I were fool enough to send you back to stealing your next meal, do you really believe Aranu or that interfering Magic Council would permit you to run about, now that they know what you are capable of?"

"No," I had to admit.

"You existed for years with no discipline or responsibility. You knew nothing else. But it has left you stunted, in all important ways still as unruly and ignorant as a child, with a child's preoccupation with its own whim. I wanted you to discover the talents you should have been training all along, but perhaps it is time to begin your education in a more systematic manner. Come."

Of course I must come.

He took me down to the governmental level, which I'd been through before on my Fire Stick hunt. No matter how busy people were, they dropped to their knees, heads bent—except for the Chosen, who stopped what they were doing, took three steps back and made the formal court bow.

I didn't comprehend half of the stream of explanation as we walked from department to department. One thing was clear: all important decisions were made by the emperor. Everyone else was there to gather, to sort, to facilitate dividing matters into piles from urgent to trivial. He called that responsibility, and I could see that he believed it, but the lesson to me was that he held all the power.

Only one incident is worth recording, when we entered the Chamber of Wisdom. There Darus sat with two other Chosen on a dais.

When they saw us everything stopped and all bowed. My gaze snapped to Darus's wolf, which gave me a hackle-risen, noiseless snarl, though he stood with hands out and head decorously bent.

"This," Dhes-Andis said, "is where the Most Noble learn to listen, evaluate, and summarize with discernment and precision, so that I may swiftly reach judgment. They serve here for at least a year, more often three, before being considered eligible for pennon stewardship." He lifted a hand and the room's occupants returned to what they were doing—or pretended to, as every ear was cocked our way.

Before we passed out of the room Dhes-Andis said to me, "I shall expect you to begin attendance here."

The door shut behind us, but not before I felt the wolf's wrath like a blow to my already pain-tender spirit.

<hr />

My knees had turned to water by the time we finished that very long tour in demonstration of the steely strength of Sveran Djur's pyramid of power.

The last chamber contained maps with magical lights and markers twinkling over them, some moving minutely.

Dhes-Andis took me to one, a set of small islands not far from a continent I had never heard of: he named off the kingdoms of the continent, and I vaguely recognized Damatras among them.

"Ndai." He spoke the words with distaste as he flicked the

islands. "Run by a family of witches whose control over squabbling natives is non-existent. They can squander months arguing and hollering at one another while nothing is efficiently managed. The world's most excellent rice grows there—enough to guarantee comfortable winters for half my islands—and an uncounted variety of fruits grown year round. Civilization can only benefit such wretched disorder."

When at last he let me go, he said in that benign voice, "I am told that tonight's entertainment is specially selected for you, a superlative rendition of one of our most famous plays. Tomorrow," he added, "you shall begin lessons with the scry stone."

That meant no time for the music room. The chiming bells forced me back to bathe and get into formal silk robes. I knew I would never be able to convince anyone that I was not ignorant, and I supposed many saw me as emotionally stunted. In fact, I knew that myself: I'd never had the kind of relationships everyone else grows up with.

But as I shook out my hair and tail, one thing I was convinced of. I knew that Jardis Dhes-Andis did not believe he was lying, and yet what he said was not the truth.

When I arrived at the chamber for the evening's frivolities, the Most Noble Venar of Seaforth Pennon gave me an imperial welcome, but I was conducted to the second most important cushion.

That was all the warning I had before *he* appeared, resplendent in midnight blue and gold.

I had to sit next to him as a long play unfolded full of stylized gesture and innuendo that everyone but me laughed at, and historical reference that elicited the *Ah!* of approval from all except me.

Through it I sat trying not to give in to the nearly overmastering wish to tear that horrible weight from my throat. A hundred eternities dragged by before that play finally drew to a close, with me no more enlightened about its point than I'd been at the beginning.

He bent his head and said in a low voice audible only to me, though on the periphery I could see covert glances our way, "You were entirely lost."

I copied their courtly gesture, turning my forefingers out in assent.

He said, "I will send a scroll for you to study. You ought to know the principal events in our history."

He rose. The rest of us rose. The courtiers' silks rustled like a breeze through ferns as all bowed low until he had left the room. When his imperial guards closed the door, I took my leave, the bows for me not as deep, but the silence as profound.

My shoulder blades crawled until the doors shut behind me, and I forced myself to keep from running to the music room. It was late. I'd be noticed. Inside my mental wall I howled at the injustice; I resolved to go first thing in the morning.

My dreams that night were all about trying to fly, but hard as I flapped my wings, I could not get off the ground because I was moored by a golden rope to a collar round my neck.

I woke to a stormy morning. As soon as I'd swallowed my breakfast, I made my way to the music room. And oh, she was there the moment I touched the strings; my fingers began to pluck out melodies I scarcely heard as I opened my memory to her.

Sorrow and comfort flooded back in a tide of sweetness and balm, then she said, *I have much to say and we know there's little time to say it. First, you must not believe ill of Ndai. I have been there, and witnessed councils that are noisy, people coming and going as they wish because they all understand that negotiation and compromise are of primary importance. Laws and justice are reached by consensus.*

I knew it, I thought in triumph. *His truth is not everyone's truth.*

I salute you for comprehending that, my dearest. Reaching consensus is a long process, and not everyone comes away entirely content with the decision, but do you see the underlying freedom there? The principal is choice rather than constraint.

I shaped words in my mind. *The fais forces compliance. And yet nobody seems to see it that way.*

She said, *They grow up used to the fais, which are very useful in so many other ways. And the surface life of Sveran Djur does seem quiet and civilized, a matter of great pride. Finally, when you know no other way, you accept as normal what you see around you.*

And that led me to the question that had been bothering me

ever since I had begun to accept that she might be my mother: *How did you end up here anyway? Were you a prisoner, too?*

Empress Lison wanted better relations with other lands, and Crown Prince Ifan paid lip service to her desires, though he had different goals. His son Danis was sent on a tour, the idea being to contract a royal marriage that would bring peace and alliance. We met in Ndai, and became friends, and then more than friends. The Empress encouraged him to bring me back even though I have no political importance. Ifan again had his own reason for hailing this idea.

With the words flowed images: the empress, a tall, smiling figure with a high, thoughtful brow and slanted amber eyes; an older court of mostly unfamiliar faces; the imperial heir, Ifan, who looked a lot like Jardis but also like Darus in his chiseled handsomeness, his mask marble-hard.

Yes, you see what I did not at first. I had so little experience of courts, and none of Djurans. I was so very young! Ifan, who Lison believed was a model son, was teaching his Cadre of Princes in secret, which on the surface was presented as a model for future world peace and cooperation, but was truly intended for one purpose: the gaining of power.

Images flowed of dances, float parties, tours, everyone beautiful and smiling, but central of all Danis, my father. His smile, especially when my mother met him face to face, was real, very much like his imperial grandmother's.

Danis's mother had been a fair-haired princess from another land, one where the royal family were reputed to hand down certain gifts such as mind-talk and an affinity for magic. She could not adjust to life in Sveran Djur, and so it was said that she returned home after Danis's birth, but there were whispers that Ifan made her vanish.

Jardis's mother was a very ambitious courtier of impressive degree, also chosen for inherited gifts. In addition Ifan consorted with carefully chosen women from among those who serve, again selecting for possible inherited talents.

I thought of Kal, and his resemblance to the emperor. *Was he one of those?*

Yes. Those with gifts were sent to the mage training, and those without stayed to become part of the imperial household.

So Kal really is my uncle?

The imperial family would be aghast at the idea. He might even be made to vanish if you so much as hint. Place is rigid in Sveran Djur. They see that as order.

Oh, you don't need to warn me, I thought swallowing convulsively, my throat moving under the hated fais. *Does Kal know who he is?*

I know not, Mother replied. *Time ebbs, and this communication is difficult to sustain, my darling. Let me finish swiftly before you are interrupted again, for your danger is far greater than mine.*

She continued. *The year we gained the empress's consent to marry, two of the Cadre of Princes died under mysterious circumstances, and another pair of the princes went home wielding dark magic to disastrous effect. We scarcely ever saw Jardis. He was very much under his father's control, which was reputed to be strict and unrelenting.*

No one saw the confrontation between Lison and Ifan. All we know is that she either cast herself or was cast from the window in her Chamber of Contemplation, after which Ifan emerged with her diamond fais, and had the diamonds transferred to his own. They are reputed to contain enormous power.

The images flowed fast: Danis's shock at his mother's death, people walking in fear as Ifan's enemies at court vanished. Jardis seemed to be the model son as he reached his middle teens, obedient to his father in all things, but Mother sensed the same dark wings I did.

Ifan agreed to our wedding, with the proviso that if any children revealed magical potential, he would train them.

Who trained him, if he was so different from the empress? I asked.

I know not that answer. The Djuran mages are so secretive! We could not determine whether Ifan controlled them or they him. Danis would once have consented without a thought, as that is the Djuran way, but he shared my fears. He was forced to agree, but we promised one another that if our child displayed the least talent we would find a way to hide it — or we would leave the empire altogether.

And that is what came to pass. Your talents were there almost at birth; you cast illusions of the palace kittens in your crib before you crawled. We did our best to hide you from Ifan, who was busy with his wars, but a servant betrayed us.

We discovered it when Ifan suddenly invited us to a fais ceremony, not only for you but for myself. This was entirely against tradition, yet all court was to be there. You see I wore no fais, as I had been an honored guest of the empress, with my own magic; I had adopted a golden necklet to appear in harmony with court. As for you, children were never given their fais until they could walk and talk. You had scarcely begun sitting upright.

He wanted to get a yoke on us, I thought with morose satisfaction.

So we feared. We also knew Ifan never brooked defiance. Danis managed to slip to the lower levels to get us servants' robes. I spent a night and a day laying the enchantment upon this harp, keyed upon you. For the only thing that kept you quiet and smiling through teething and other complaints of infancy was music, in particular, harp music. And I was deathly afraid he would prevail.

Then came the memory images: my father's harrowed looks as his fingers pressed to his fais. My mother's blue hands spreading gently over his head as she reversed the spell that made his hair fashionably black.

My mother had shrouded herself and me in illusion, so that all anyone saw was a blond servant with another nondescript one, and they used the servants' byways to get to the stable annex where they stored the floats.

And there my mother called birds to her—ordinary birds willing to help. Under rainy night skies she and my father climbed into a float, and activated its magic that kept it in the air. That made it easy for a flock of small birds to draw it unseen from the palace, whose lights were soon doused by the curtain of rain.

Their absence was not noticed until the next morning. They knew because Ifan struck through Danis's fais.

For three days and nights, as a succession of birds drew the float across the ocean toward the Kherval and eventually the mountains far north, my mother had to stay awake, her hands pressed to my father's fais to keep that "correction" spell from killing him. Three days and nights without sleep, as my father did his best to care for me in the float. They had only the food he had been able to glean hidden in a basket, rain water to drink, and no clothes to change to, but at least it was summer.

My mother knew when Ifan went away to rest because Jardis took his place. Young as he was, he had been well taught in fais "correction"—which came as no surprise to me.

Our goal was to reach the heights far north of the Kherval where my people dwelt, but he commenced magic attacks that I had to ward. I could not call for help as my strength was failing, but the aidlars who found us flew to get aid.

Finally Ifan found a way to strike through a binding enchantment. I tried to ward it, but I was too weak, and fell unconscious; the float tangled in trees as the birds had fled. I lay as one stunned, and Danis was nearly killed. You vanished completely.

When I woke my kin had arrived, and had been forced to change Danis to a bird to confound the binding. They admitted in sorrow that you were nowhere to be found. We had to assume he had either taken you or killed you. I do not know to this day what happened to you.

I don't remember, either, I responded. *So my father is a bird? Can he transform back?*

He cannot transform at all. It is not in his nature. Elenn, you must remember that even those with dual natures must spend time in both, or gradually the other is lost. By the time we figured out how to break Ifan's ward, your father had been too long in the bird shape. He is a prince among aidlars, but he is forever aidlar.

Does he know one named Tir?

Yes! Tir is the one who discovered you, though it took time to put you together with my missing daughter.

Is Tir all right? Geric said he used a stone spell.

Again came the wordless warmth and comfort, along with the words, *Tir recovered, and flew north to us.*

And so I was alone until I did an illusion before the wrong person. And stole from another wrong person, I thought bitterly. *You don't have to pretend. I had already figured out that the Hrethan rejected me and the Mage Council didn't trust me. That in fact I was next thing to a prisoner at the court of Erev-li-Erval, though I didn't know it.*

My darling child, the Hrethan have very little influence in lowland governments. They did share the Magic Council's determination to discover if you were truly the missing Elenderi. There are many dual-natured people in the world. And secondly, they wanted to learn how much influence the Djurans had over you, because the news of your possible identity was coupled with the report that your powers were awakening as a result of contact over the mental realm with Jardis.

I wanted—needed—time to think about that, but we both felt

the pressure of time. *They didn't let you come to Erev-li-Erval? Because they weren't sure who I was?*

By the time I found out, you were already gone. We are very isolated in our mountain reaches, and your father and I had been away.

Can I learn to ward a fais? I thought to her, but any answer splintered into ice shards at the interruption of a voice of a servant, anxiously begging pardon, but His Imperial Serenity awaited me.

Twenty-seven

I WAS LATE!

I stared witlessly at the servant, my lips moving but no sound coming forth. Everything I'd just learned—it all had to be hidden. Anxiously I fought to recover my Princess Elenderi mask.

As we walked along the silent, gleaming marble halls, I struggled to separate out all the roiling emotions of discovery, grief, and longing, and steady myself. I am me, I thought. My father, once human, was now a bird. My mother had risked her life to save me. I could be as strong. I *would* be as strong. Princess Elenderi is a role, and I'm secretly a Hrethan spy.

When we reached the Garden Chamber, and I saw those silent cats running about, it was anger that finally steadied me. No, the cats did not appear to be hurt—they were sleek, well fed, and content. But it still seemed wrong to force them to give up their voices merely because cats' noises are unmelodic.

Despite all my efforts to bolster myself, my heartbeat galloped against my ribs when I saw the emperor. I had kept him waiting. This could only be bad.

And yet he greeted me with that benign voice I so distrusted, and bade me sit down. "It appears," he said, "you have an affinity for music?"

"It is the only thing I'm good at, Your Imperial Serenity," I said, making an effort to keep my voice steady. "I beg pardon for keeping you waiting. I got lost in playing ballads."

"So I am told. You may address me as Jardis," he said suddenly. "When we are alone. My father always required the extremity of formality, as if either of us ever forgot who held the power. I want for us to study magic together for the benefit of Sveran Djur."

My mouth had fallen open. I shut it. I bowed again, because it enabled me to hide my face. *Something* had changed after that dance when the beasts sang. I could sense that he was hiding his reasons, but I had no idea what they might be.

"If you are that enamored of harp playing," he said, "we shall have a harp specially made for you. And any other instrument you desire. Do you want more music? Perhaps a tutor?"

A tutor would know how badly I play! To hide my dismay I said quickly, "Perhaps later, when I haven't so much to learn?"

"A wise decision. Your education must come first. I said I would send suitable records from the archive for you to study."

"I don't have your alphabet."

"Kal will write it out for you. Our language is written as it sounds. You will master it quickly enough, and really, you ought to be literate. See to it after we are finished here. We shall begin with transfer magic...."

If I'd had any doubt that he wanted something specific from me, it would have ended when he dropped the subject of transfer magic as soon as it became clear that I had no inborn skill. After all that talk about educating me, he had no interest in coaching me through the very complicated, precise magic of transfer.

So then it was time for the scry stone. I shut my mental wall so hard that when I looked into the thing I only saw myself staring back, except strangely, not mirror image, but opposite: if I reached my left hand, in the stone, the crosswise hand lifted, not the one opposite my left in the way of mirrors. Trying to blink the image into clarity made me so dizzy that I had to clutch at the chair arms to keep myself from falling.

I suspect my complexion turned convincingly green because he watched narrow-eyed, then sat back with an irritated expression. But no question.

"I suspect I have gone about this the wrong way," he said. "Your ability with the fire spell before we even met gave me hopes that your talents would be equally easily discovered and trained. We need to find a way for you to break that mental lock. It is not natural, and it closes you off from so much potential."

I swallowed convulsively, unable to breathe.

"We shall begin with the fundamentals. But first I want an exact accounting of all your magical knowledge. How you discovered it, when, and what you did. Take a day to think back so that when next we meet you can give me a detailed, coherent summary."

The bell rang, which eased the immediate threat: he had somewhere else to be, so he sent me away. I escaped, but with an intensifying sense of impending doom.

I wanted so badly to escape to the music room, but I didn't dare. I loathed the need to be so very careful in everything I did — and yet it never quite seemed to be enough.

One thing for certain: I *must* not draw attention to the harp. My mother would not communicate with him if he touched it, but surely he would know that a great deal of magic had been overlaid on it. Maybe he could even determine by whom, I didn't know.

I had a free hour. Hating the place, the situation, and my own profound ignorance of magic, I prowled around in a circle, then made my way outside. The blizzard was too strong even for me. Yet I so resisted the idea of going back inside, though I knew I should, I wandered to the other end of the balcony perch and found my way to the aviary where the birds were housed.

The mild air inside the aviary and the complexities of scent were strange yet comforting. I snuffed them in as aviary servants looked at me in surprise, then bowed and backed out of my way.

I wandered aimlessly until I found Firebird, who had settled into the stall, head tucked under his wing. At my approach he lifted his head, his singe eye regarding me with dulled pain.

A servant appeared at my shoulder, waiting for orders, I guess. "Is this great gryph ill?" I asked.

"No, Your Imperial Serenity. The Most Noble took him out for training earlier this morning."

The word *why* nearly burst out of me, but I knew no servant would answer. And I knew why. Raifas was working on making the great gryph into a warrior bird for his ships. And there was nothing I could do; Firebird seemed to intuit my uselessness, turned his face away and tucked his head under the other wing

I passed by, sick with regret and boiling, furious helplessness. So wrong, and what could I do? I couldn't even help myself!

I kept moving. That wall contained the biggest stalls, each occupied by a great gryph. Andisla slept in the next stall, head under the opposite wing, and did not stir at the sound of my footsteps. The third lifted his head.

I sucked in an inadvertent breath when I saw a shadow glimmering around the shape of the bird. It's difficult to explain, as great gryphs are so enormous, and humans are human-sized, but I made out enough of a human outline to hazard a guess that this great gryph might be the offspring of a dual-natured person.

His curiosity about me registered in a ruffling of feathers between his eyes, a soft, rumbling noise in his throat, and his nose slits widened as he brought his head down toward me to take in my scent. Mindful of the waiting, watching servant, I reached to lay a hand between the bird's eyes and stroked the feathers above the nubbly golden area where his beak joined to his head. "Bee-yoo-tiful bird," I crooned inanely as I made a pin-hole and thought: *Can you hear me?*

Hear two-leg.

Even though the thought was faint, as if shouted from beyond glass, my heart leaped with joy. For less than a breath. Then came the doubt. So what if I could hear their minds. What good did that do for either of us?

But communication felt so good, and so did the fact that my guess was right, that the ones in fairly recent descent from a dual-natured person could perceive and form words.

Are you happy?

As soon as I thought it I knew it was stupid. But enough emotions of my own must have shaped the thought for the gryph to get the concept. To me flowed images and emotions of superficial mild contentment: nest and food and time for mating, but underneath, way underneath like a grotto under the surface of the world, a sense of melancholy. But then came a more disturbing thought, attended with perplexity and under it sorrow: a mental picture of Firebird and the word: *Dies.*

With that an echo of sharp longing, and an image of diving into oblivion. I knew this did not come from the gryph under my hand. It must be a thought from Firebird, either communicated mind to mind or perhaps in their own cries, shaped with smell and image.

Then another sharp word: *Free*, and the wide sky, the sense of wings outstretched, sun on one's back, so vivid an image and visceral a sensation that my back muscles bunched and I swayed on my feet and had to steady myself.

I understood. Denied freedom, Firebird welcomed death. Or maybe he hoped to be dead soon. Either way wrenched me with anguish and guilt and anger. I lifted my hand, tempted to promise what I could not possibly deliver, yet another human betrayal of their kind.

When I had steadied myself, I discovered not one but three servants lined up waiting for orders, the question implied in their gazes igniting warning through my nerves. Of course whatever I did here would be reported. And I did not want any Djuran knowing that I could communicate with the gryphs even in so limited a form.

"I love their soft feathers," I said, trying to sound cheerful. "The Emp—His Imperial Serenity said that I might have a gryph of my own. Or a float. I am trying to decide which."

The servants bowed, their expressions smoothing out. Now my movements made sense. I was given to understand through the usual circumlocution that the great gryphs were not used to pull floats, except for the emperor, and then they flew harnessed three in a row. Only the hens did well in tandem flying, as their wings were shorter, and they fouled much less often.

I followed the servants to where the brown gryphs nested. One of these also had a shadow, much dimmer than that of the great gryph. I went from one stall to the next, asking questions of the servants about floats, gryphs, and how the Chosen learned to guide the birds as I made my way to the brown gryph with the shadow.

As with the two others, she let me stroke her head, and I put my question again, since the great gryph had provided an answer. From her a wave of emotions with the images of small gryph beaks poking through brown shells, and a thought in clear, distinct words: *I want them free.* Under that, memory of former clutches taken away from her and reappearing as half-grown birds with green-glowing harnesses around their necks, their minds unreachable.

I had learned something about gryphs, at the cost of feeling even more helpless and useless. To hide my distress I forced out a couple more questions to the servants about how floats were decorated, and how long one could fly. I didn't listen to a word of the answers, just waited as I steadied myself, then thanked them and departed.

Step, step, step. I had to *make* myself avoid the music room and return to my pretty cell, where the promised books waited.

Kal had already written out the alphabet for me, more evidence of the constant unseen and unheard communication, as if I needed it. I settled into my hammock and did my best.

Jardis was right. The alphabet was easy enough to learn, though reading was slow going at first, as I worked to get it into memory.

Time passed, and the courtly enumeration of emperors, empresses, and their accomplishments piled up in my head like beads, without ever forming a pattern that made sense to me, much less a whole. Still, I made myself go back and back until I had committed to memory a sizable list of names.

By that time the sun had set, and it was time to dine and then get ready for whatever dull and covertly insulting courtly delight awaited me. I longed to refuse, but I knew that I'd be asked why. It was safer to go and sit with my own thoughts while I was ignored.

Without much enthusiasm I went to the dining alcove, where as always I found a fine meal waiting. As I sat down, a thought occurred, and I said to Kal, who hovered outside the door as always, "Do Djurans ever eat at state dinners?"

"State dinners?" he repeated (I'm not adding on all the rigamarole).

"Yes. Like they have in other places. Big long table. A lot of courses brought in one by one...."

His widening eyes caused me to falter to a stop.

"I guess they don't have state dinners here," I said.

"The Chosen always eat alone," he said. "Or at most with someone with whom they are intimate." He looked away the way people do when embarrassed.

I wanted to ask if he ate alone, but the thought that he would have to answer a personal question that embarrassed him shut me up. I really didn't know anything about the servants' lives. I'd seen their chambers, but not what went on there. And who knew, maybe they had places the Chosen never saw.

I hoped so.

I picked up my goblet and sipped the water that I preferred to their wines. Then I blinked. "Did you add herbs to this water?"

"I added nothing to the Imperial Princess's water that she did not request," he said formally.

I understood that I had insulted him—or complained, which was worse.

"It doesn't taste bad," I hastened to say. "Just a bit odd, a kind of oily almost-sweetness. Perhaps some kind of seed fell in the jug." I set the goblet down and reached for some hothouse grapes. Kal took the water away at once.

My appetite, never very good since my arrival in Sveran Djur, had entirely vanished. I was so tired. More than tired. Dispirited, glum. I castigated myself mentally. One more Princess Elenderi appearance, and I would be done for the night. And in the morning, my harp. I got up and crossed to the wardrobe, falling into reverie, but then I pulled my thoughts up short.

Must not even think about the harp, I scolded myself as I permitted Chith to twitch my stole and folds into place.

She gave me a startled look, and I blinked at her. "Did I say that out loud?"

"Yes, Your Imperial Serenity," she whispered.

"I must be more fatigued than I thought," I said. "Tired and bored. Ulp! Time to be quiet now. Thanks, Chith. You're free now, or as free as you get. Which is more than I get...ugh! Now I'm whining."

I shut my mouth, pressing my lips together. Oh, was I weary! Talking mind to mind with those gryphs had worn me out. No, no, don't think about that, think about sleep soon, after this tedious poetry session with a select audience, was that how Kal had worded it when he spoke the invitation?

I reached the chamber, a small, very formal six-sided room decorated in white raw silk hangings embroidered with scenes of spring. The Most Noble Nial met me with a low bow and led me to one of those cushions with a low table, pen, ink, and very expensive rice paper. The tables — only four — had been set in a square.

"...Pardon, Your Imperial Serenity?"

"Rice-paper, very fine," I said, then belatedly recognized I'd spoken in Elras, Hlanan's home language. That was odd. And would get me into trouble! My wits were really wandering.

Once again I compressed my lips, thankful when she moved away to greet Darus and Amney, who had arrived together.

"And we are all gathered," Nial said, hands together. "Let us commence, if you will, Your Imperial Serenity. We thought to offer you an evening of our most famous poetry."

"Most famous or most boring?" I asked, and tried to suppress a hiccough of laughter. Oops! Once again I'd spoken in Elras. I found that hilarious, and clapped my hand over my mouth as I snickered.

"Your pardon, Your Imperial Serenity. I misheard," Nial said, obviously perplexed.

Amney and Darus had taken their seats, he with a small, smug smile at her before they noticed me staring. They smoothed their expressions into twin court masks.

I enunciated in Djuran, "You only speak one language? Oh, I must not call that ignorant. That is rude. I would not be rude in any of the nine languages I speak."

I turned to that superior Amney to see how she took that, ha ha, to surprise a wide-eyed glance toward Darus. She murmured, "I thought—"

Darus made a quick movement with two fingers as he turned to me. "Now, *Princess* Elenderi," he said in distinct tones. "You will hear and obey."

"I will what?" I retorted, crossing my arms. Or tried to cross my arms. One wrist bumped into the other, and I rocked on my cushion. "Ulp."

"You will cease your encroachments on imperial prerogative."

"I doan' wantcher imperial prerogative," I retorted, and

Amney gave Darus a quick glance.

His tone sharpened. "You will refuse the great gryphs that are not yours to take."

"I will set them —"

On the word *free*, the doors opened to the hands of imperial guards, and Jardis Dhes-Andis entered, tassels swinging.

Darus and Amney both looked as if someone had shocked them with lightning bolts before they folded deep in bows. Nial stepped back a pace, bowed to the deepest degree, swaying as if she intended to drop to her knees. "Your Imperial Serenity —"

"I see you did not actually expect me," Jardis said, sounding amused as he gestured toward my cushion alone on the dais. "It is true I seldom attend poetry readings, though you all faithfully invite me. But I aim to reform. A reading for such a select group must surely furnish a superlative list." He made a slight nod in my direction. "I look forward to your opinion, Elenderi."

I knew I must bow, but my joints seemed curiously unhinged. I tried to get up and fell forward, knocking the ink bottle over so that it rattled in a circle. "Ugh," I said in Elras. "I dunno what's wrong with me. I wouldn't want to make a foo a' myself here, whuh, with the ones't hate me mosh." My lips felt numb, and I bit them. "Mosssst."

Nial whispered, "I beg pardon, Your Imperial Serenity. Did you address me?"

"No." I swallowed as Jardis took the place where Nial should have sat as hostess and stared at me with a frown between his brows.

I muttered, "Djuran. Not Elras. No you haven't insulted me. But I know. Thass all right. Interloper, thass me, if only you knew, but I won't say anything, annnn-ything, in front of those two, right there, for they are sure to make it even worse, yes, *you* Amney, with your un-civ-il-ized four shyllabubbles. Lemme tell *you*. I hadda nuth-ing to do with choosing my name! I uh-SHOOR you I wudda stobbed it if I coulda, and I kinda did...."

Somewhere far, far beneath the splashy, out-of-control surface of my mind I wailed with fear. What was happening to me?

"Elenderi," Dhes-Andis said sharply.

"Don't burn me, I dunno why I got so, wuh-wha...I better not try annnn...." *anymore mind communication,* I wanted to say, but now my jaw wouldn't work.

The last thing I saw was the most surprising sight of all: none other than Kal slipping alone into the room and throwing himself face down flat on the floor at the emperor's feet. "The Imperial Princess has been poisoned," Kal said desolately. "And I failed to catch it. I deserve death."

"Nooooo...." I moaned.

Klonk! My forehead hit the table.

<hr>

I woke when my stomach summarily chose to part with its contents.

When *that* was over, I lay groaning, my head pounding fit to crack my skull. The rest of me shivered like a jelly in a high wind.

"Your Imperial Serenity...try to sip this. It will help...." Tay's hand cradled the back of my skull, but that gentle grip might as well have been an ice pick.

"Ow-ow-ow-ow."

Something pressed insistently against my lower lip and a fresh scent like spring grass in the rain wafted into my face. I sipped, then gulped, and oh, bliss, the pain began to recede. I began to slide into sleep but then I heard a new voice. "Elenderi, waken. For a moment."

It was *his* voice. Alarm caused me to gasp and I sat up, clutching at my throat. My head swam and I fell back again, blinking blurrily up.

Jardis bent over me, Tay's anxious face floating blurrily behind.

"Elenderi, it is for you to decide Kal's fate. He neglected to assure the safety of your comestibles."

"No," I croaked. "I heard. He came. Warning."

"Yes, he investigated and reported to me at once, as you saw, though breaking every rule of decorum. In a situation of extremity—and, as it happens, before the perpetrator of your afflicttion. But we shall address that anon. What is your judgment on Kal?"

"Don'. Unnersand."

"You were poisoned. It is part of his duty to taste of everything to determine its safety. Though granted, it has been ten years since anyone has attempted so dire a trespass. Many among the staff have come to assume safety when not given orders to the contrary."

"Why. Should. He. Get poison. Meant for me?"

"We shall have to discourse upon the fundamentals, but I see your struggle to speak, and I gather you are in favor of clemency. So shall it be. Rest until tomorrow. I will require your presence in the Chamber of Engagement at sunrise seconde."

He moved away and my eyes closed. On a sigh of relief I fell into sleep.

Twice I dreamed, and both times I sought the Blue Lady — and in the seeking, remembered danger, which jolted me back out of the dream world into a sluggish, headachy wakefulness. Frustrated, I fell back to sleep, and did not waken until the next day, when thirst forced me up through the layers of scattered image, memory, and voice. All that vanished like mist when I opened my eyes.

Fear and anxiety, underscored by the smoldering of anger, got me out of bed, though my arms and legs felt loose and unstrung. But the more I moved the faster that feeling faded. A hot bath chased the remainder of the lassitude away. My body had recovered. But my mind?

When I sat down to breakfast Kal was there as always, though pale and subdued, his eyes ringed with dark skin.

I said, "I hope you didn't get tortured. Corrected." I sighed, prickling with ire. "No, it's torture, no matter what anyone calls it." My rising wrath died down when his face shuttered as effectively as any courtier's.

"There was no chastisement, much as it was deserved, Your Imperial Serenity."

"I still don't quite understand what happened, except that I will wager anything Darus and Amney were part of it. But if I was the target, I don't see why you should be poisoned instead."

"It is my duty, Your Imperial Serenity."

"I just don't *see* that. Oh, I understand about hierarchies. But it seems to me for it to be truly just, everyone willingly falls into their role by *choice*. I'm here by someone else's will."

"It is your duty," he said gently. "Your Imperial Serenity."

I gave up. Of course I was not going to be able to change anyone's mind. I didn't have the wit, the skill, or the knowledge, and in spite of all that bowing and imperial this-and-that I certainly did not have the power.

Feeling thoroughly squashed, I said, "What is the Chamber of Engagement?"

Turned out it was that long room with the staves in racks. On my way there I sensed a tension and stillness in the air though I'd be hard put to define how I knew, since the halls were as empty as ever.

The bells of sunrise seconde tanged sweetly twice in the distance as two imperial guards opened the doors for me. My neck hairs lifted. I was used to flitting about these halls in the morning when no one was about.

Inside, a male figure knelt at the far end of the room, palms turned up on his thighs. When I recognized that handsome profile as Darus's, I backed hastily toward the door again—and was nearly knocked flat as the doors opened once more.

I jumped back inside as Jardis entered, wearing black, gold, and a framing edge of white. The black over-robe had been embroidered with a dragon rampant.

Behind him glided two more of his imperial guards.

I remembered my bow and performed it hastily, keeping my head low because the tension in the room simmered like that molten rock deep under Mount Dragon, and with an equal sense of threat.

"Your Imperial Serenity," Jardis said, and it seemed to me he enunciated each word with deliberate emphasis. "You were poisoned by the Most Noble Darus. It therefore your prerogative to execute justice as you will."

"Why did you do it?" I burst out.

Darus's beautifully chiseled chin lifted, but his gaze went straight to Jardis, who lifted two fingers slightly.

The servants bowed themselves out and shut the door.

"Darus?" I knew that tone of voice, deceptively gentle, but with pain hovering very, very near. My nerves flashed, though for once I was not the target. *Yet.* "It is already a capital offense, for in striking at Princess Elenderi, you are striking at me."

"No. Never that." Darus's hands tightened into fists on his thighs, then flexed and flattened in an effort of will that I could feel. "It is unconscionable, after generations of work and will to master the beast natures, just to blur our blood with *that*." He sent me a look of acute revulsion. "Ilhas prates all over of her beauty, Pelan mimics her dancing, Raifas—*Raifas!*—professes himself ready to marry her if you don't want her yourself, and look at her. No civilization—she'd be a bird now if she could."

Jardis smiled. "Is that true, Elenderi?"

"Yes," I admitted. "About the bird," I added quickly. "I don't know anything about the rest of it. And I don't want to be married."

Jardis shook with silent laughter. "Of course civilization is not to be expected of one lost to us all these years. A fact of which I took great care to inform my family, and the Chosen. What you do not comprehend, Darus, because you never studied magic, is that the Hrethan, though they do not appear to have attained the high degree of civilization that we enjoy, are very powerful. In some ways, I suspect, far more powerful than our particular form of humanity, though much of their culture remains hidden. But I have studied their influence on world events, which you, apparently, have not. Civilization can be taught. Inherited power cannot be taught, and must be governed."

He turned to me. "The veris seed is well known for certain properties, one of which is to render those who take it suggestible for a time. It is used by healers to help those who wish to overcome some habit that they haven't the will or the ability to master, such as fear of thunderstorms, or biting nails. Many times the suggestion, under influence of veris, will help the weak to master ill-conditioned habits."

His voice hardened subtly, and I saw my own flinch echoed in the tightening along Darus's shoulders. "The dose you were given was some fifty times the customary. I gather Darus thought that compounding the dose would render you amenable to his orders. What were those to be, Darus? An assassination attempt against me?"

"No, Your Imperial Serenity."

"Then you hoped merely that she would humiliate herself for the entertainment of you and your chief confidante? Amney is on her way to Djur Pennon, where she shall serve under its governor, my elder-cousin the Most Noble Theris, as scribe for five years. With full fais control in Theris's capable, if severe, hands. In that time I trust Amney will reflect upon the wisdom of choosing to follow stupidity and short-sightedness."

Darus flushed.

"Humiliation, Elenderi, is a vulgar tactic. If you choose to submit Darus to one of the many vulgarities used by foreigners, I approve the elegant symmetry of such justice."

He held out his hand to me.

When I hesitated, he gave me that amused smile that never reached his eyes. "Do you want him beaten with a club? Or flogged? What is it they do to traitors on the continent?" Darus's face blanched with shock as Jardis went on. "Or would you prefer to administer justice yourself? Go ahead. This would be a perfect opportunity to practice your mind thrust." And when Darus flinched, Jardis's smile broadened, showing the edges of his teeth. "Did you not know? Elenderi could kill you with a thought if she so desired. But Elenderi, I want him to live. And learn. As you have done. So perhaps correction is the appropriate response. Go ahead. Waiting doesn't make it easier," he added.

My fingers drifted up to my collarbones, but didn't touch the hated fais. I stared at Darus, who stared back. In spite of his court mask I could see in the flinch of his eyes and in the subtle downturn of his mouth that he felt as sick and miserable as ever I had.

I pictured him green with pain, whooping for breath the way I'd done so many times. I could do it. I was expected to do it. And I would so *enjoy* it.

It was that fierce expectation of pleasure that stayed my hand. Though my mother was not at all present in my mind, I could imagine her sorrow at the prospect. For all Jardis's claim to a superior civilization, I knew even in the brief acquaintance we had had so far that my mother would never willingly hurt another.

But she had never been tortured. Or thrown to her enemies as worthless. I was angry at Charas al Kherval's empress, court, mages, and laws, but....

But. I couldn't articulate the objection, though the anger simmering and smoldering underneath my thoughts shot up in gouting flames. I wanted to blast Darus, but after I did, what then?

I'd do it again.

And it would be easier each time I did it. Lying and stealing had certainly become easier, as had dancing, and leaping, and flying....

"No," I said.

Jardis lifted his brows. "Why not?"

I glanced at Darus, and sure enough there was the contempt I expected to see. He thought I was afraid.

I wanted so very badly to say *Because it's not civilized.* "I just can't."

"You are still learning our customs and laws. Part of your learning is to witness the consequences of all actions when you are in a position of power. Observe now."

He lifted his hand toward the long wall opposite the rack of staves, then turned to Darus. But instead of blasting him with fais torture, he spoke. "As your rude and offensive action against Princess Elenderi was in truth a challenge to me, I shall answer the challenge in traditional mode. Choose your wand and make ready."

Darus rose slowly to his feet, his jaw hardening. Both men moved right hands to the silken ties tucked behind the outer flap of their over-robes. Jardis dropped his robe behind him without a glance. Darus laid his with a quick gesture over one of the far racks. Then off came the plain silk robe beneath, Jardis's red edged with gold, Darus's pale green edged with dark green. I had no idea what these colors symbolized, except that Jardis's looked militant.

One more robe on Jardis's part, and they stood in white silk, loose-sleeved shirts and flowing dark trousers tucked into boots.

They moved to the rack and chose staves, which looked pretty much like wooden swords only with thin blades. Magic snapped over them in faint green scintillation.

Then they moved to the center of the room, each bowed, and they attacked.

It was kind of like a sword fight and kind of not. As they wielded the stick with delicate precision, another puzzle-piece snapped into place: the Chosen go out of their way not to distort their faces and movements. They eat in private. They flirt in private. The empress in committing suicide (or in being murdered) dove into the sea from a thousand paces above. And this fight was not conducted in flesh-tearing, bruise-raising thwacks and thuds, but in fast, stylized movements resulting in light taps that obviously hurt at least as much as the worst fais-torture. It was pretty to look at, but obviously painful to be in.

I know as little about sword fighting as I do about writing poetry, but I am certain I saw the moment Darus decided he had nothing more to lose, for he whirled that stick in and made every effort to strike Jardis where it would hurt most.

I wondered what would happen if he actually won, but there was no winning in this situation. Jardis could call his guards in through his fais and they would hammer Darus flat. In any case Jardis blocked with well-honed skill, even I could see that. When Darus's strikes slowed, Jardis began returning strikes, half of which Darus blocked. But each time Jardis connected, Darus hid his reaction a fraction less well until he'd received enough that he could not keep himself from stiffening, his eyes flashing wide, then dazed.

Wrist. Knee. Shoulder. Each tap coruscated greenish, and I have to confess that in the beginning every time Darus got hit my heart gave an angry leap of joy. I didn't care if Jardis got it or not, I only wanted Darus to get what he deserved.

He did. Again, and again, until my angry joy vanished and I began closing my eyes each time the inexorable sword-stick touched some part of Darus, who swayed on his feet.

Finally—it seemed forever—came three sharp raps: one on either side of his jaw, then in the middle of his chest.

Darus's stick dropped, his body stiffened, and he fell on his face, sobbing for breath. "Mercy," he cried. "Mercy."

Jardis smiled my way. "Elenderi?"

"No more," I whispered, sickened.

"Kneel, Darus," Jardis said, and when Darus had struggled to his knees, Jardis actually used the aorist imperative for the first time in my hearing. "You shall return to your Chosen duty by evening. Except that you shall not attend the Chamber of Wisdom. You shall strive to earn that privilege again."

Darus, breathing harshly, bowed forward until his forehead touched the floor.

"Go."

Darus rose with painful slowness as the door opened and Jardis's four guards streamed in. Jardis held out the sword stick, which one took, as two others picked up the fallen robes. Those were swiftly slid up his arms and smoothed into place in quick motions, the ties fashioned, and except for a couple of blue-black hairs that had come loose and curved over his brow, you would never know he'd been whacking the Rue out of Darus moments before.

Darus fumbled at his robes, shaking badly, until Jardis lifted a forefinger and a servant hastened to his aid.

"Come, Your Imperial Serenity," Jardis said to me.

The extreme formality after that deadly tension required the same from me. I jerked a bow to Darus, oblivious though he appeared to be, and the imperial bow to Jardis. Now that I was used to it, I actually preferred this bow because I could hide my face for a heartbeat or two as I steadied my breathing. I straightened up as he started walking, and I bustled to keep pace.

Outside in the corridor, he smiled—a real smile that reached his eyes as he said, "I'd forgotten the pleasure of intent. I am so accustomed to the passionless obligation of daily exercise."

I scurried along with a sick sensation in my middle, longing for escape. But there was no escape, there would *never* be any escape.

"The Chosen have disappointed me. I relied on them to perceive...ah, if not the breadth of my vision for the benefit of the empire, at least I expected them to possess the wit to understand that I have vision. I spent too much time in private study. It is necessary, and in private pleasure, which is indulgence. It is time to reign as well as to rule. I will not be my father," he added in that hard voice that always presaged pain for me. "Expecting compliance without rewarding it, and only exerting himself when he was displeased."

He walked straight toward the golden doors of the Garden

Chamber without a pause, and sure enough they opened from the inside. I took a moment to appreciate the smooth, silent compliance of the staff as Jardis walked and talked without rewarding them. But their entire lives were exertions in remaining unperceived.

He indicated we sit. "Perhaps we ought to try veris as an experiment." And at the shock I could not hide, "Oh, I would never poison you. But I marked the effect the herb had on you, which was not quite the same effect as is usual. That might be your Hrethan side: perhaps a mild dose will enable you to unlock that mental block that keeps you from reaching the mental plane again. I know you have the capability. That is where we met."

He seemed to think that funny. I could not hide my horror, and so when his amusement began to alter to question, I said, "The very thought of it makes me ill. I was *very* sick."

"Ah, yes. We shall wait until the memory is less raw. There are other exercises, specifically with the scry stone, that may prove to be as useful. I can see you are still recovering from the effects, and I have all the affairs to attend to that I postponed during my investigation, which I conducted myself. Tonight Vian desires to recover her honor with another poetry reading. You must be there to lend her grace. Recover your strength so that you may enjoy it."

With nothing truthful to say to any of that, I felt that a bow would be a good answer.

But he must have seen something in my face, for he said, "It is finished. I am not my father; I will not put all your staff and the entire kitchen to death as a warning. In any case, it proved to be a conspiracy of two. Darus used his authority to send the kitchen runner on a useless errand to fetch him new slippers so that he could enter the veris into the clean dishes being carried to your suite. Vian's mortification was entirely due to her having accepted without question Amney's assurance that I would not attend. So she had not ordered a place set for me." He lifted his hand in dismissal.

I got out of there, my single thought to escape to the music room. Which I did....

When I sat down, the music came readily to my fingers.

But my mother was not there.

Twenty-eight

NOR WAS SHE THE next day. Or the one after that.

So far, I'd had various experiences that I had thought the worst yet, but here was the darkest of the dark, and it was all inside me.

On the surface, things could not have been better. The Chosen were assiduously polite to me. Ilhas was more than polite. I think he was hoping to be invited to dinner, which I'd finally figured out was to the Chosen a step toward flirtation.

He wasn't the only one. I was scrupulously polite to Raifas at concerts and play readings when he singled me out for a compliment or question, but I never made any gesture toward him. And I turned down his invitation to return to Ardam Pennon again—his wishes were straight-forward enough, but I knew if Jardis let me have that relative freedom, it was only because he would scry me when we flew to Mount Dragon. I dared not go back.

In any case I was more interested in visiting Raifas's great gryph, which never failed to make me feel terrible. I needed that, for reasons I'll get to.

Pelan—without the scornful influence of her sister now that Amney was gone—became more friendly. She was friendly with everybody. It was her natural state, like Hlanan's, and don't think that reminder didn't hurt.

Which brings me to below-the-surface.

First, the pain of abandonment. Three more times I tried the harp, but it hurt so much to hear silence beyond the music that I stopped going altogether. I will skip over recording the agonizing through nights about why my mother had turned away from me. Of course I deserved it, because Princess Elenderi was a lie being honed into a weapon and Lhind was merely a thief. Who could blame her for not wanting either of them?

Second, Darus continued to attend Chosen entertainments as always. He was meticulously courteous, but I could feel his hatred, far, *far* more intensely than his previous dismissive disdain.

And third, Emperor Jardis Dhes-Andis kept his promise to be more involved. He was there at every evening court gathering, and made time for me every morning for magic lessons and to test me on what I had read of the history of Sveran Djur. And I found myself doing my utmost in order to avoid the pain of correction.

I felt genuine relief when each session was over, because at no time did I trust him not to attack me. And yet the relief sometimes mixed with gratitude after his words of genuine praise. Sometimes the gratitude was closer to pleasure when he talked about art and the highest striving of the human mind. Once I even found myself lying in my hammock midway between wakefulness and sleep, thinking ahead of his reaction once I mastered the mental control for snapping heat from air.

That jolted me awake. I punished myself by getting up to memorize another load of courtly records about the greatness of Sveran Djur until I reflected that studying the doings of emperors was something Princess Elenderi would do.

I loathed myself for that. I knew very well that pleasing Jardis meant Princess Elenderi gained another measure of control over my identity, a measure Lhind lost.

And so I was drawn to the aviary to visit the gryphs. These were not happy communications, as I said. Images and emotions streamed from the birds, expressing pain, longing, grief. The best I could get from them was the glassed-in sense of indifference caused by long-established control. Yet I could not stay away. Their distress was real, was true. It was also emblematic of my own imprisonment, and I wanted—no, I *needed* to find a way for them to be free.

Because, the chill whisper in my mind insisted, I would never be free.

When the weather permitted, I stole down the mountain into the town. Though it was nearly always cloudy, the snow storms had begun to mix with rain. I didn't mind rain as long as I remembered to wear linen when I wandered about listening to the music of the silk spinners.

Sometimes I practiced my magic by clearing slushy snow, and once I was followed by a shy group of children. I kicked and stomped water into the air, and flashed the heat out of it so that it fell in tinkling ice shards. They loved that.

Before the end of midday trine I always bounded back up the mountain by pushing myself to my limits, because then all I had to think about was reaching the next platform, and then the next step.

Finally, there were the magic lessons.

I'd learned that spells and wards were like recipes — you gather the ingredients, mix for a given time, bake for a given time, then you get a result. An enchantment was a combination of spells or wards, like first baking bread, then cooking meat, then grinding and combining a sauce, and finally assembling them all as the ingredients for a spectacular dish which in turn had to be mixed and baked for a given time.

I began to perceive the thousands of green layers of magic on my fais, interlocked into complicated knots of enchantments. I could not descry how to unlock them. As the days crawled by, the deeper became my conviction that I would never break it.

Then came the day it all changed.

———✦———

It began with another scrying lesson. Jardis demanded I try for a short time at the beginning of each lesson. One day he said, "We are making progress. Let me see if magic will break the impasse."

I nearly passed out from the effort of holding hard to my mental wall.

He said impatiently, "This is a waste of time. Elenderi, we must experiment with veris." And at my reaction, "You will not taste it at all. Recollect that you were given enough to dose half the palace. So, to your studies. Whence comes the Dhes in our name?"

I recited obediently, "Prince Shimosar Dhes from the West

Kingdom of the Shinja Empire, in marriage treaty with Imperial Princess Dannay Andis, who became empress ten years later."

"It is the only time we have ever crossed blood with Shinja," Jardis said. "Though the peace treaty did not hold past the next generation, the prince embraced our civilization entirely. You will enjoy his travel journal through the empire of his day."

He talked on, and I tried to listen, but the old dread gnawed at me with renewed fervor. I knew what would happen with the veris, and next time I would not have the relative safety of dropping unconscious from too high a dose.

When he released me I could not go escape to the town as a violent thunderstorm rattled the windows, and I could hear the distress of the birds in the aviary.

In desperation I wandered back to the music room to find Pelan there. Once again, I'd forgotten the midday trine practice hour.

Though this time it was Pelan alone. She greeted me with genuine pleasure, and when I refused to play—I could not risk having an audience to my grief if my mother was still absent, or my joy and perhaps inattention to my surroundings if she was there—Pelan leaped to the idea that I had come to listen to her. I dared not deny it.

So I sat there looking at the harp that I could not touch as she plunked her way through endless Djuran triplets. And when she was done she asked me questions about the beautiful pieces I played—would I teach her—where did I learn them.

I answered randomly, and when she begged me to give a concert I turned her down. "The Chosen despise foreign things. That means they will think foreign music uncivilized."

"Oh, Your Imperial Serenity, I assure you they do not. Ilhas has talked much about your exquisite music, and everyone wants to hear it."

I could not prevent a bitter laugh. "Everyone like Darus, Amney, and their followers?"

Pelan flushed. She was kindly, and even sincere, and here I was blasting her with angry sarcasm. I said, "I beg pardon. I didn't mean to...." *Snarl*, I wanted to say, but the closest word in Djuran was *growl-of-beasts*. And anything having to do with beasts was vulgar.

She lowered her gaze. "I beg you to understand that Amney is very ambitious. She...always got what she set her sights on."

"What could I possibly have done to get in the way of her ambition? I scarcely ever saw her."

Pelan's eyes widened. "She was courting the emperor before you returned to us. She is so beautiful, so graceful. And there you were, as beautiful and graceful, some even thought you moreso. Until then, you see, she had always been first and best. And then you were granted so many private interviews with him. He used to be among us often. As now. But when you came—"

She hesitated, and I almost laughed, though it strangled in my throat. "Go on, say it. But when I came?"

"Once you arrived we never saw him, and it was said that you were granted private interviews whenever you desired."

I nearly laughed out loud. "Is that what it looked like?" I stopped. I knew I was not being scryed, but I had no idea if Pelan's mind might be scryed at another time. I dared not tell her the truth, that her emperor's intent was to turn me into a fais-controlled weapon. Like a human great gryph, harnessed to his will and whim. I settled on, "My imperial interviews are magic lessons. Anyway, we are related by blood."

She lifted a shoulder, the tiny pearls in her headdress trembling on her forehead. "Only through one side, not both—that is, the imperial brothers had different mothers. One-sided cousin-aunt-uncle marriages are common in the imperial line, to keep the blood pure, though in alternating generations lest it weaken."

"I thought he had consorts," I said cautiously, remembering her gossip with her sister.

"Oh of course, but we are discussing imperial *marriage*."

"Then there is no love in marriage?"

She gazed at me with an expression difficult to interpret. "I think—I believe—I am not certain. The ballads and even records will say different things. And I am not part of the imperial family, Your Imperial Serenity." She bowed in place. "But it seems to me that they will take love if they can get it. There are many reasons for imperial marriages."

I don't know what she saw in my face, but she lowered her

gaze and leaned toward me to whisper, "Our emperor at least is handsome. And fastidious. He dances and converses well, and there have been no adverse rumors about him from those he consorts with privately. As my mother warned me against the old emperor when I first came to court, the year before he died in the Shinjan War. He was a glutton, and...." She gestured down her body, glancing away as if she couldn't bring herself to say the word *slovenly*. "And cruel."

Cruel? I thought. And you think Jardis Dhes-Andis isn't? But hard on that thought memory intruded: me standing there looking at Darus and coming so close to obliterating him with fais "correction." Then my angry pleasure in Jardis whacking him into extreme pain instead.

I wondered if that was how Jardis started, a childhood of angry pain, after which he became the giver. Who was going to tell an emperor it was not justified?

That made me wonder about the circumstances of Emperor Ifan's death on some faraway island.

Pelan straightened, her voice returning to a more normal courtly cadence. "To resume. Amney would settle for no less than the triple crown, and there you were that night of your first dance, wearing an imperial courting robe."

"I was?"

She put a finger to her lip. "The silver butterfly robe you wore."

I remembered asking Raifas about the symbolism of butterflies, and now it registered that he had not actually answered me.

"The butterflies with long trailing trains, the silver and white — surely you knew that those butterflies signify willingness for courtship, and the silver is imperial?"

"I didn't know that at all," I said. "The staff gave that robe to me to wear. One said it had been left behind, or something like that. I thought it was an expensive cast-off that I ought to get use out of, considering how much labor went into it."

"Such a robe would be cherished for generations, and only brought out for special occasions." Her brow furrowed. "It might have been your mother's. She lived here, you know, before she married Prince Danis and went into exile."

"Do you know what happened?"

She looked away, and I knew before she said anything that asking about it was probably considered vulgar. Or dangerous.

"I was born that year, so I don't know the details," she said in a low, apologetic tone, bowing slightly in place.

"So with the butterfly robe. The servants wanted to get me into trouble by bringing up old...problems?"

"Oh, never. The opposite, surely — a great honor — but do you really permit them to choose your robes?"

"Most of the time. I did not grow up knowing what all the symbols mean."

"Oh, I would be glad to tell you anything you wish to know. Though some things have changed in meaning even in the short time I have lived in Icecrest. Amney has always been the leader of fashion, and...."

She went on about Amney in a tone difficult for me to define. It wasn't a malicious tone. More vindicated, somehow, which made me wonder if Amney had been the one to push Pelan to the lowest rung in their hierarchy.

At any rate, she talked about Amney, fashion, and symbols until the bell rang signifying the end of afternoon. That meant it was time to withdraw for dinner and then to get ready for that night's dance, which Pelan was hosting with her sister.

We parted, me forcing a smile with my thanks for her enlightening talk. It was not her fault that all her words closed the prison bars around me that much tighter.

When the time came, I went off to the dance.

In honor of the Union festival day, instead of relying on the magical glow globes for lighting, they had set out hundreds of candles in crystal and mirror holders. The effect was quite beautiful as we paced sedately through the Shadow Dance, no one more controlled than I, with Jardis Dhes-Andis as my partner. We touched for the first time, his hand cool, clasp brief and not at all demanding. But all I could think of was him wielding that stick so artfully until Darus collapsed to the ground.

Though nothing untoward happened that evening, Pelan's gossip heightened my anxiety to such a pitch that I could not sleep that night. My brain prowled from one imagined horror to another; never had I felt so alone.

When I finally slipped into sleep, it was to a landscape of tumbled rock and pits of smoke with flames shooting up. The air shimmered with magical scintillation, the deep green of impending storm.

And through it glided — the Blue Lady.

Elenderi my darling, she said, holding out her hands.

Surprise — joy — sorrow rushed through me with such violence that I plunged out of the dreamscape into wakefulness, lunging upright. My hammock swayed as I gasped for breath.

And...of course I could not get back to sleep.

I pitched and turned, and in desperation finally slipped to the floor, but I had scarcely made it to my doorway when the duty servant appeared, her voice a little hoarse. "Your Imperial Serenity requires something?"

"I was thirsty," I lied, and then was forced to drink water I didn't want, fetched by someone who would rather have been sleeping. Because an imperial princess did not sneak around at night without raising question.

The next morning I hastened through breakfast in hopes I could get to the music room before being summoned to magic studies.

And when I got there, though every other instrument lay untouched, the harp was gone.

Something was wrong. I could feel it.

For the first time in days — weeks — the sun streamed through the long palace windows, illuminating the marble to warm translucence and painting the statues with a golden light that made them seem alive.

When I was summoned to the chamber of perfectly trained trees, cats, and fear, I found Jardis in a benevolent mood. "It appears," he said, "that you have won a genuine admirer in Third-Cousin Pelan. She has arranged a surprise for you at midday seconde, so we will have to cut your lessons short as I have affairs to tend to. At midday trine you will commence attending the

Chamber of Wisdom."

"But I...."

"You need not speak. Listen. Learn. That will be far more useful than your entertaining the silk-weavers down below. I understand that you enjoy practicing your magic in that way, but your future is not going to be squandered doing minor magics for those who serve."

Another escape denied. Though the fais had never changed size, the sense that it choked me was so strong that it took all my strength not to wind my fingers in it and either yank it free or cut my fingers to ribbons.

But I didn't. Again I gripped myself and forced my focus to the lesson of the day, which were the properties of wood. With especial reference to its destruction.

When at last the lesson was done it felt as if someone had wound a band of metal around my brow like the coronet Jardis wore, only mine was inexorably tightening.

He let me go, saying we would meet again in the Rose Chamber for Pelan's concert. Instead of retiring for the midday meal, which I didn't think I could eat, I could not resist making my way to the aviary.

But this time I heard a familiar voice: Darus.

". . . Visits my Stormwing? Does she also do this with Firebird, or is it only my great gryph?" he asked, his courtly cadence sharpened.

"Most Noble, her Imperial Serenity visits them all, but only to scratch their heads and pet them. If I may be permitted, they seem to favor it."

"I am not interested in what birds think," he retorted haughtily. "Carry on."

I backed away and fled, hastily examining memory of my visits for any sign that could reveal my mental conversations. Sick with worry, I wondered if this was yet another thing I would be denied. But surely Darus would not go complaining to Jardis, considering what had happened.

No, it merely gave him another thing to detest me for.

I sped back to the west side of the residence floor. The music room was empty, the harp still missing.

I returned to my suite and prowled restlessly along the windows, gazing out at the sparkling sea. It hurt so badly to watch those distant waves far below, the azure water reflecting the serene blue of the sky. *Serene.* So many words had become tarnished: serene, civilization, order, even peace.

And yet I could not get away. To escape pain I suppressed my inner truth; I was afraid to speak as once I had done so easily; I was not smart enough, or wise enough, to see my way out of being bound in silken ribbons until Lhind was smothered to death and Princess Elenderi took her place, weapon of Sveran Djur and imperial consort of Jardis Dhes-Andis.

Because all that seemed real, that is, inescapable, was power.

My eyes burned. Midday prime had reached its second sand, and here was Kal patiently waiting for me to take the midday meal. It lay in the fine porcelain dishes, good food that was hard to come by so far into winter. Everything I liked. Probably tested against poison.

And yet my stomach had closed. My throat ached too much to swallow.

"Your Imperial Serenity I beg your forgiveness, but I must observe that you would do well to eat and regain your strength," Kal said in a gentle tone. "Your well-being is our chief concern."

And I was not well. But food would not fix what was wrong with me.

I shut my jaw tightly against a retort. That was another thing I hated, that furnace of anger ready to burn brightly inside me. When would I surrender and strike out because I could?

My eyes stung. I ground them against my shoulder, despising my self-pity. How useless!

I forced a couple of hazelnuts past my lips, crunched them, and got them down with a wash of water. Then I found myself prowling back and forth along the circle of windows in my tower dining room as I studied sky and sea, and far out near one of the islands the white sails of a vessel, its details too distant to make out.

I wished myself aboard it with the fishers, Djuran or not, and then turned away, disgusted at the awareness that my self-pity had become maudlin.

The ting of sand trine rang. Mealtime was over. Midday seconde was nigh. Grateful for that respite, I got ready for Pelan's concert. At least no one would attack me there.

I made my way to the room of rose marble where select concerts or readings were customarily held. And there was the harp in the center of the room.

I let out a quiet breath. I should have guessed; I was disgusted with myself. With what else was Pelan going to give a concert?

Pelan greeted me with genuine pleasure as she conducted me to the dais where two cushions sat. Then she sedately fussed over her performance cushion, the harp, and her stole until the doors opened to the hands of imperial guards and Jardis arrived, impressive in gold-embroidered black silk.

He took his seat beside me, the air stirring with a trace of his herb-scented soap. *Fastidious*, Pelan had said. I locked my muscles hard against a shiver as Pelan sat to the harp, and began.

She played three complicated pieces, then was joined by Ilhas in three duets. We applauded, and I thought, a sand and a half to go before I would be expected at that Chamber of Wisdom after which more interminable courtly affairs.

But then Pelan approached me, dropped to her knees and said, "Your Imperial Serenity, here are all friends, people who appreciate music. Any kind. I ascertained that myself. I beg you to give us the same joy I tried to gift you, though I cannot play nearly as well."

I stared at her, fury and fear boiling up with white heat to a painful degree.

"Go ahead, Elenderi. I promise, no one is here to do anything but take pleasure in whatever music you choose to give us," Jardis said.

Witlessly I gazed at him, excuses streaming through my mind and out again. The others could not question, but he could. And every excuse would bring me perilously near my single most precious secret. Because my mother had not abandoned me, however brief was our contact.

That reminder steadied me enough to enable me to rise and take my place at the harp. I had to trust that if she was there again she would understand why I must shut her out quickly.

I sat, pulled the harp to me, touched the strings, and out came music.

And there she was.

Fear lanced through me and I prepared to shut her out, but she, experienced at a lifetime of communication in the realm of the mind, saw in a flash what I could not tell her and arrowed a single thought to me: *Be ready: He comes.*

Then she was gone.

He? Who was that? I nearly opened my mind again, but I had to look Jardis's way, and caught that watchful gaze that always flared through my nerves. He couldn't have seen anything wrong. My eyes had been closed no more than two breaths. What was I playing? I had fallen into a habit of letting the music guide my hands without my hearing myself as I listened in the mental realm.

The song was indeed beautiful. Passionate, powerful. And familiar.

Oh, joy. Under the four-chord harmonies lay the original melody of the Shadow Dance.

This had to be ancient Snow Folk music.

I had not finished the piece when Jardis got that distant look that meant some kind of contact. When the song ended, I pulled my fingers quickly away from the strings, then flexed them.

Jardis waited as the others signified approval, then said, "Truly, if anything your talent was understated. And I am surprised at your knowledge of Hrethan music, but we can discuss where you learned it later. At this moment I suspect your presence will the more quickly resolve a...puzzle."

My first reaction was of course a fresh gout of fear.

The guards opened the doors and I followed Jardis to the perch balcony, of all unexpected places. We reached it as a plain float drawn by the imperial guard's fast grays settled into place. Several Chosen—those not invited to Pelan's concert—were also there, either having just disembarked from their floats or about to set out to enjoy the sunbloom. Both Darus' and Raifas's great gryphs stood harnessed and ready as the imperial guard stepped past them, drawing a shorter figure between them, then knocking him to his knees.

It was Hlanan.

Twenty-nine

BEFORE I COULD THINK I burst out, "What are you doing here?"

I only realized I'd spoken in Djuran when Hlanan winced, then responded in the same language, heavily accented, "I be come, bring...." He paused, drawing a sodden sleeve across his face. He was completely drenched.

He knelt there damply between the tall imperial guards as Jardis frowned then said, "You're familiar." And in flawless Elras, "Ah. It's the failed scribe. Or was it a failed mage? You may answer Her Imperial Serenity in your own tongue: what *are* you doing here?"

Hlanan lifted a hand to wipe his straggling hair off his forehead. "I came to find Lhind. To see if she was safe. And I brought a message. But my boat capsized off the coast."

"As you see, the person you were ignorant enough to call 'Lhind' has returned home to her proper rank in life." And to me, "He is yours to dispose of as you will. We can throw him back into the ocean. Or set a servant's fais to him and you can put him to work. Or keep him as a pet."

He looked and sounded benign but I sensed him watching — not quite suspicious, but wary.

"Seems a little late to wonder about my safety," I said to Hlanan, my shock having given way to the ready anger, after all this time of silence and abandonment. My hair flexed overhead, and my tail lashed. I did not even try to control them. "Seeing as it was the Empress of Charas al Kherval who made it clear I was trash well rid of."

"But you and I were once friends," he returned, his gaze steady. "Remember the bard Thianra? She counted you a friend too. Wrote you a letter. I brought it. Here it is." He pulled a little scroll from his tunic, rather damp.

Jardis lifted a finger. A guard twitched the letter from Hlanan's grip and took it to the emperor, who looked up. "It has magic on it."

"Against a wetting by rain, I assume," Hlanan said. "I agreed to carry it. I didn't write it."

Jardis broke the seal, ran his eyes down it, and shrugged. "It seems a great deal of effort to send a letter about harp music."

Thianra was one of my true regrets. I never believed she would turn her back on me. "She taught me to play," I said.

"Ah, truly admirable, if your recent performance is a result of her tutelage."

"May I read it?"

Jardis handed the scroll to me, and I felt the weight of his gaze as I took it.

A sudden boom in the distance, like a single thunderclap, startled everyone to stillness.

The birds were the first to react, going wild. Firebird began clawing at his neck in a frenzy of desperation, rending terrible furrows in his flesh around the fais. Feathers whirled madly in the air around him.

Then the cold breeze vanished before a surge of hot wind that smelled of burnt rock, so strong it nearly blew us off the balcony. People cried out, civilization forgotten as clothing and hair snapped, and bodies staggered toward the walls and the thousand-pace drop below.

"Look!" Raifas shouted, pointing.

On the southern horizon a black cloud smeared the horizon, hiding Mount Dragon. Through the smoke appeared a crimson glow. Rapidly it swelled in size, and thunder in an impossibly regular cadence like the beating of a moon-sized drum struck the air, causing the ground and the stone of the palace to thrum and rattle.

Another thundering WHOMP and the red swell resolved into a vast dragon, ruby scales fire-bright in the sun, throwing the island from Seaforth to Icecrest into shadow as it flew overhead. Stone rumbled underfoot.

We all stared, witless. *He comes.* "Flames of Rue," I whispered. Mother had not meant Hlanan—she'd meant the dragon!

I turned to Hlanan, who had scrambled to his feet. He pointed insistently at the letter with one hand as with the other he gestured in sign language, *Touch-fais! Touch-fais!*

That was the magic I sensed, a single very powerful enchantment bound together by Hrethan magic. No wonder Jardis had not sensed the extent of it.

I brought the paper toward my neck, but in raising my eyes caught sight of Firebird bleeding as he fought to free himself or die. One moment of violent inner turmoil, and my meaningless, worthless life resolved into purpose.

I knew what I must do.

I leaped over the perch wall and slapped the paper to Firebird's fais. Magic flashed. The great gryph stiffened, feathers ruffling up.

You are free, I said mind to mind.

He threw up his head to shriek a high, ear-rending cry, then snapped his head around. He leaped toward Raifas, claws extended.

Raifas clapped his hand to his fais, but there was no controlling the great gryph now. He stood his ground as Firebird screeched and dove down toward him.

Jardis muttered, fire glowing about his hands.

Flee, before he kills you, I thought at the bird as I threw my own fireball to meet Jardis's. The two fireballs exploded, momentarily blinding the humans.

Firebird recoiled in a mad flapping of wings, then leaped to the next perch, where sat Stormwing, Darus's great gryph. Firebird's head darted at Stormwing's neck and snap-snap! The powerful sword-edged beak broke the harness-fais, which fell to the ground.

The two great gryphs turned to their fellows, wings beating, claws scraping, beaks snapping as they broke fais after fais. Humans, Chosen, guards, and servants alike could only back away, completely unprepared for unfaised, infuriated birds. Jardis gave me one white-lipped look, then raised his hands, green glowing around his fingers. I clapped my hands, and sucked all the fire out of the air between us. A shower of ice shards tinkled musically to the ground. Then BOOM!

Another surge of hot wind, from the north this time. Tumultuous wing-beats thundered: the dragon had banked, glided in a circle, and flew directly toward us as if he intended to knock the towers into gravel.

Many ducked. Jardis stood alone, his furious gaze going from me to the dragon. Around us people crouched as the dragon glided so low that the topmost tower appeared to scrape his belly. Then THA-DUMP! Immense wings beat once, the towers swayed, and every lancet window in the palace shattered.

Chosen stumbled for the doors over the trembling, cracking ground as glass rained down from above.

Behind us the gryphs rose in a beating of wings. Not all of them took to the sky. Andisla cried out, then settled back. Half the hens vanished, several grays, and a flock of lizardrakes—freed from their fais by a hen whose human shadow stood out sharply for those who could see it—followed after her, their stubby wings humming in a blur. They rose over the wall and glided down to skim over the water far below.

"*She* did this." Oblivious to glass cuts bleeding on his forehead and hands, Darus pointed at me, his voice thick with hatred. "I *knew* she was talking somehow with the gryphs."

Jardis's head turned sharply, his hair flying in the wind. "Is this true, Elenderi?"

There was no use in lying, or masking. Though the fais still bound me, the birds' freedom made everything worthwhile, even death. And in dying I would be free enough to speak true. "Yes," I cried out. "Yes! I talk to the birds mind to mind, and yes I freed them because they should be able to choose! Everybody should have the freedom to choose!"

I looked away from Darus's bleak triumph and Jardis's white-lipped fury to Hlanan, who stared back aghast. "That fais spell worked only the once," he said in the language of Alezand, his tone every bit as anguished as anything I had felt since I was taken prisoner.

I threw Thianra's letter to the wind. "Go," I said to Hlanan as Jardis motioned his guards to flank me — as yet he had no interest in Hlanan, and he would never harm the prestige of the Chosen by striking me through the fais in public. He wanted to get me in private where he could annihilate me at his pleasure.

"While you can," I said to Hlanan as I leaped over the guards' heads, somersaulting to land on the wall. *"Go!"*

Hlanan uttered a low cry, wiped his eyes, then transferred away. His guards looked around wildly. Jardis ignored them both as he addressed me, his voice controlled though I could feel his fury. "Why would you betray us, Elenderi? You have here all the benefits of civilization."

"Yet no freedom," I replied, giddy with the pleasure of speaking the truth. Though I knew what was to come. "Every creature should have its voice. Even cats."

"A piece of irrational sentimentality that disappoints me to hear you utter," he retorted.

I shook my head, my hair flaring around me. "Even when I was hungriest, chased by mage-burners in Thesreve, wearing stolen clothes a year at a time, I was free in body, mind, and spirit." And because it felt so *good* to shed all the secrets, though my life was measured in heartbeats, I pin-holed my mind and reached for his. *I choose freedom.*

The shock of realization in his face began to change to the anger that I had inherited — that we both shared. But I did not wait for him to retaliate.

The fais ward would do it for him.

I flung my arms wide, and fell backward off the wall, hoping I would hit the sea before he could do the complicated magic to effect a transfer.

The wall ward hit me with all the force of the burning sun and I fell end over end, locked in pain so fierce I could not even breathe.

Until the jolt of talons cut into my arms.

My body sagged between those gripping claws. I knew I bled, but the pain was already so great my mind could not comprehend anything more than a massive purple feathered bird breast above my head. Then the cool, smooth hardness of a beak slid along my throat, and snap!

The pain vanished as the golden snake of the fais tumbled glittering down and down—then vanished in Jardis's transfer spell, where it probably lay broken on the rug in the Garden Room.

Magic, Jardis had said repeatedly—echoing what the Mage Council teacher had drilled into us what seemed a thousand years ago—must be precise. The fais, with all its many complexities, had never been warded against the beak of a great gryph breaking it.

As the last of the burn wrung out of my nerves, red-hot pain throbbed from both my arms where the claws cut my flesh.

I can fly, I thought at Firebird.

He let me go. I fell through the air, drawing it deep into my lungs, then spread my arms and transformed. My Djuran silks floated away toward the sea as I flitted upward, suffused with so fierce a joy my heart expanded in my chest.

Firebird bugled a long, triumphant cry, banked, and flew upward into the sky then and away after the ruby dragon.

I tried pin-holing Hlanan, but either my bird shape interfered or he could not hear me in the mental realm.

However someone else saw me. "Lhind!"

I knew that bird squawk! I pin-holed the aidlar: *Tir?*

Came a mental image: a yacht, under full sail, as seen from above.

Looking inward for directions at the same time I flew made me dizzy, and I faltered in the air, then shut my mind to concentrate on my flying. I couldn't do both.

But Tir could. The moment I found a lifting current to ride, a white shape sailed down from above, banked, and there was Tir, ruby eye cocked. I lifted my wings to follow.

The two of us soared upward and away from Icecrest, tall and beautiful on its mighty promontory. I spied a lone figure in black and gold standing on the Garden Chamber balcony, watching me break for freedom.

Then I turned my tail feathers to Sveran Djur, and flew out over the open sea.

Thirty

FROM ABOVE, I RECOGNIZED the clean lines of Ilyan Rajanas's yacht. Tir drifted down toward its deck, where Hlanan stood with a blanket wrapped around him.

Tir creeled and Hlanan whirled around. Even from the heights I could see his distraught expression, which changed to wonder when he peered up against the sun at two birds.

If I'd had a mouth instead of a beak, I would have gaped when I recognized who stood with Hlanan. *Geric Lendan?*

Unfortunately, as soon as I had descended to a certain height my transformation threw me back into human form and I plunged into the sea with a mighty splash. At once the cuts in my arms stung from the brine.

I sort-of knew how to swim. Paddling my arms and pumping my legs, I rode the waves that had looked so small from above, but from water level appeared as high as a mountain. As I concentrated on keeping my head up—the weight of my sodden hair and tail pulling me downward—the yacht's crew got a boat over, Hlanan and a couple of sailors dropped down into it, and they began rowing toward me.

Tir, who had been circling overhead, gave another cry. I felt a bump mentally, and pin-holed as I blinked up at the aidlar. *I go.* With the words came an image of snowy peaks and gray, silver, and white birds.

Tir flapped off, then the boat came alongside me and a hand

appeared over the side. After some tugging I flopped onto the bottom of the boat. I shook myself, a quick hard snap of hair and tail that shed seawater in all directions. The others looked away to avoid getting a face full of brine, and when they turned back, my hair cloaked me.

"Lhind," Hlanan said tentatively, his face shocked as he took in the blood mixed with brine trickling down my arms.

"You're here." I lunged at him and locked my arms around him, blanket and all. The urge to scream and howl was so strong I thought I would shatter into smoking pieces. I gulped, clenched my fists, and said tightly, "I thought you...." My throat closed. I clawed at it, though no fais was there.

"Abandoned you without a thought?" He hugged me back, but when I made those convulsive scrabbles at my neck, he let me go. "You're bleeding. And thin as a twig. Didn't they feed you?"

"Sumptuously. But I couldn't eat," I said, my throat closing again. I pawed at it, breathing out once I'd reassured myself that yes, the fais was still gone. But it still felt like an iron ring encircled my throat. "And these are from the great gryph who saved me." I touched my arms gingerly, the claw gouges stinging fiercely.

"Here," he said, a tremor of laughter in his voice. "Though you look very fetching wearing nothing but that silver hair, I think you need this blanket more than I do."

I accepted the blanket because it contained his warmth, and his scent, and I discovered that I had been violently shuddering. We sat side by side in silence, me with my eyes shut as I fought to control my breathing. The sailors pulled the last few strokes to close with the yacht.

We bumped up on the side of the yacht, and I roused when Prince Geric peered over, ruddy hair streaming.

My anger flashed. "What is *he* doing here? I won't get in that yacht with him there!"

Hlanan winced at the shrill fury in my voice. "He helped us," he said. "Guided us to Sveran Djur. And this island."

"Jardis Dhes-Andis can't scry me anymore, thief," Prince Geric called down. "We're both safe enough right now from his magical reach, but I wouldn't trust how long we'll go unnoticed out here if we don't sail soon."

I remembered looking out my window at what I'd taken to be a fishing boat almost hidden beyond one of the islands on the west side. "Right," I said, the fury fading and exhaustion closing around me.

We were soon on deck and sailing in the lee of the island directly away from the peninsula crowned by Icecrest at its northern peak. I stayed on deck until I saw the dragon spine sink safely below the horizon, and when I turned away, found that my knees had gone watery.

Hlanan took me below and hunted up bandages and clothes for me. A cleaning frame got rid of the salt, and I was soon bandaged, dressed, and dry. We sat in one of the little guest cabins, where once I had spied on him talking me over with Rajanas. "I don't know where to start, except with an apology," he said at last.

Anger surged up. I clenched my jaw, then tipped my head backward toward Icecrest. "How did you get caught by the imperial guards?"

"I didn't." He gazed down at his hands, then up at me. "Ever since you vanished I've been reading and listening to anything I can find about Sveran Djur. The most often repeated information was that anyone who went to the main islands never returned. Diplomats and traders all thought they were captured and killed. So you can imagine how adamantly everyone in Erev-li-Erval tried to talk me out of going after you."

"They probably weren't killed. Why waste a perfectly good slave when you can slap a fais on them and force them to work?" I said bitterly.

"Yes. So Geric said. Though he couldn't tell me much more about fais than that servants wore one kind and their masters another. He finally told me something of his years here, but he'd had no fais. The previous emperor and the present one had wards on him."

I nodded. No surprise there.

Hlanan said, "He brought us here in the lee of that island. Though there is a very wide-ranging patrol out on the seas looking for enemy fleets, the weather until today has been so bad we were able to slip by them."

He paused to study me, question puckering his brow. And worry.

"Go on," I said.

"Last night I took the skiff by myself. It has a sail. Unfortunately I don't know how to beach one successfully. It crashed on a rock. Some roaming guards plucked me out of the surf, and when I gave them my carefully memorized Djuran speech about looking for you, they put me in that flying basket. You know the rest."

"But—why you? If Jardis knew who you were...."

"I hoped that he didn't," Hlanan said, with the straight, true gaze I remembered so well. "In any case, I couldn't ask anyone else to face the danger for me."

Oh, Hlanan! My throat began to close up again, but anger got there first, and I said caustically—even with my eyes stinging with tears—"How very *unemperorly* of you. I hope your mother doesn't try you for treason."

He held out his hands, and I laid my rage-stiff fingers in his. "Lhind," he said, and I could feel his regret and sorrow. And I could hear his question on the mental realm.

I shut my mental wall tight, remembering that last stupid gesture at Jardis. I knew in my bones that he would keep trying to scry me.

"I can't talk about it. Not now," I said. "After your mother told him to take me, I never thought I would see you again." My voice tightened once more and I made another swipe at my bare neck. "Does she know you're here?"

"Lhind, I came because I wanted to. You know I have freedom within certain limits, those being that I can do nothing that will hurt the empire. Speaking up that day in Thann would have hurt the empire. Didn't you see? Dhes-Andis was ready to hold you hostage against an entire empire if he thought he could. My mother had to convince him otherwise, and she had to make the decision fast. She said that she tried to speak so outrageously— throwing in some insults about me—that you would know it for expedience."

"I knew it for truth," I said. "Every word she said about me, I mean. It was the last truth I heard. Until now." And when he winced, I relented. "All right, the Djurans didn't all lie. That is, they believe what they say is true. Mostly," I muttered, thinking of Amney's poisonous pretense at civility.

I straightened up. "Hlanan, this much is true, I'm broken. I lived a lie all this time, hiding my identity just as I did when I was Lhind the Thief, only the new lie was Princess Elenderi, and it was taking me over bit by bit. I thought even my mother abandoned me at the end there, and you know what? I couldn't blame her."

Hlanan recaptured my hand again, his brown gaze warm and steady. "There are a lot of people who would argue with that condemnation. Thianra for one. She was pretty wild when she found out what happened. I've rarely heard her raise her voice, but after we got back to Erev-li-Erval she lit into my mother, reminding her first off why she would never have considered becoming heir. She was so furious about Aranu Crown surrendering you that she threatened to leave Erev-li-Erval and never return." He paused and shook his head.

I gave a watery smile, easily picturing Thianra taking on the formidable empress.

"As for your mother, she would never have told you, but once she found out you had been taken to Sveran Djur she had to take to her bed in hopes you might discover that harp she'd enchanted. It was the only way she could be ready at any hour, and to be able to sustain the connection."

"I did not know that. She didn't tell me."

"The Hrethan are exceptionally powerful with mind skills, but even they cannot maintain long distance contacts and go about daily lives. She only flew down from her mountain heights because the Snow Folk contacted the Hrethan to warn them that the dragon was going to rise. Lady Eleth went to the Hrethan for the fais spell to be put into a form that one of us could use, and then it took her a week to fly to Erev-li-Erval. She dared not use transfer magic."

So that was why I'd lost her contact. "Why did that dragon rise?"

"No one knows. Except that they are all convinced it has something to do with you."

"Me?"

Hlanan nodded. "The subject has been you for this past week.

Month. More, really. Confused you might be. Angry, too, and have every right. But worthless you are not."

"The Mage Council certainly thought so. I didn't figure out how they kept me in a kind of cage of ignorance until I had to live in a similar cage up at Icecrest."

"That's because no one knows what to do about you," he said seriously. "You appeared so suddenly. With inherited powers possessed by very few. Untrained, but still powerful. And hunted by the Emperor of Sveran Djur."

I sighed.

"Granted, he is not as terrifying as his father, but Jardis Dhes-Andis is ruthless in getting what he wants. Little as I know about military things, I do understand military strategy in a general sense, and even I have seen that he has designs on the Kherval. But his immediate goal is Ndai, which he could use as a staging point to invade one of the richest continents in the world."

"Here's what's strange," I said. "He thinks he's doing the right thing for the empire. And because he holds all the power, nobody can argue with him. Those fais things...." I clawed convulsively at my neck again. "How did you break it?"

"I didn't. Your mother brought the spell for breaking it. You have to realize that a lot of what I'm telling you I only just recently found out myself."

"My mother told you?"

"By scrying," he said. "I set sail as soon as the word came about that dragon rising. I was busy concocting this elaborate plan of pretending to be a fisherman blown off course until a few days ago when my mother got the mages to scry me and explain about your mother, who had just arrived in Erev-li-Erval. It was they who put together the plan with that enchanted note of Thianra's."

"So your mother knew about it?"

"It was all done on her orders. I learned that the Hrethan had studied your father's fais for a long time after his transformation. They succeeded in breaking its control, but kept the knowledge put away in case it was ever needed. You know they do not interfere in political affairs. The moreso since your mother's disastrous journey to Sveran Djur."

Which had resulted in me, I thought sourly. Disaster indeed.

He went on. "Lady Eleth explained that because of the nature of the magic it must be put in a form that could be physically carried, without raising Djuran suspicions. Otherwise a Hrethan would have to be present to touch the fais and complete the spell. Their magic, as you are probably aware, is different."

"I've figured that much out. So your mother really allowed you to sail to Sveran Djur to rescue me?"

"She had no say in the matter." Hlanan looked grim. "I told her if she wanted an heir who would always choose political necessity above everything else, to look to Justeon. She's still angry with him for nearly launching an all-out war." He slid his fingers between mine and gripped our hands together. "It's always going to be this way, Lhind. What I need is not always going to come before what the empire needs. But I won't forget. I have to find a way to compromise."

I sighed, all my anger leaking out though I felt it below the surface, ready to boil up again. "I've been learning about power and what it does to people. In a way it's as bad as pain. They both distort."

"They can distort," Hlanan said. "That is, I will never argue in favor of pain as coercion, the way the Lady Eleth described the fais when she scryed me. Pain can teach, the way we learn to walk. We fall down, get up, and walk better. Many suffer, and surmount it. Life deals blows, and we try to recover, and make things better for all. Power can be used in that sense. I believe it. I have to believe it. That's the principle on which I've predicated my entire life. But pain used to control people...Lady Eleth said that most Djurans seem content, at least on the surface. But if the Djurans ever do rise against their rulers, it's going to be worse than what happened with those great gryphs on that terrace."

I gazed back at him, free at last to speak my mind—oh, a richness better than gold and silk and bowing—but I couldn't find any words. Instead I thought of Darus's bitter wrath, Raifas's careless conviction of Djuran superiority, Amney's calculating ambition. And shook my head.

"You don't have to say anything." He smiled ruefully. "Maybe there is no real answer. We're both tired. I set out at midnight when Big Moon came up, after the storm blew away, because of the way the tides go. I'm half-asleep on my feet. Oh! I smell hot buns baking. Shall we eat? Wasn't that dragon astonishing?"

"I saw him in the fire mountain," I said.

"You did?" He had half-risen, but fell onto the bench again, eyes wide. "Lhind, that is even more amazing, especially considering I grew up with all the records insisting that dragons were long gone from the world. How could he get out of a mountain?"

"I don't know. But there's this shadow world, kind of. I can see it. In our world, but not quite."

He whistled.

"What?"

"Remember what I said about abilities?"

I grimaced. "Let's not talk about my abilities. Or empires. Or dragons. So how did Prince Geric break Jardis's wards?"

"Jardis." Hlanan repeated the word voicelessly, his expression difficult to interpret. Then he cleared his throat and gripped my hands again. "Geric was abandoned after he fulfilled his promise to capture you. Your mother broke the remaining ward a few days ago when she scryed us. Hrethans know more about scrying and the mental realm than any of *our* mages."

I nodded, hoping that when we met at last, she would teach me. But I would not let myself think about that. Yet.

"Go on."

"Not much more to say. Prince Geric felt badly after you were taken, in his own way. There was no reason for him to offer to help me. We haven't exactly been friends. But he did, though there was a risk for him as well."

"What's going to happen with him?"

"There are three or four princesses and duchesses who all want to court him, beginning with Kressanthe of Meshrec." Hlanan gave me a comical grimace.

"Ugh! They deserve each other."

He laughed, shaking his head. "He's already had one terrible wife. In any case, I suspect he will do very well now that he is truly free of Djuran wards. Though he lost Thann, he does have Duchess Morith's personal fortune, and Ilyan Rajanas promised him that if he actually helped us get you safely, he could have the yacht. Ilyan highly approved my rescue idea, by the way. Offered the yacht as transportation."

"I hope whichever princess or duchess ends up with Geric is both strong and smart," I said, letting go the last of my anger toward him. Much as I disliked him, I knew how horrendous it must have been to labor under that ward, an invisible fais. And he'd borne it for years, not mere months.

A knock at the cabin door was followed by a muffled shout. "Scribe Vosaga, there's eats in the wardroom."

"Shall we?"

Hlanan opened the door and we joined Prince Geric in the cramped wardroom, where the grizzled yacht captain, Hucharwe, sat at the head of the table.

"Well, thief," Prince Geric said, eyebrows lifted. They looked oddly straight after all those winged brows. Like my own, like my own. "Did you enjoy Djuran-style tutoring?"

"Like a kick from an angry mule," I retorted.

His lip curled. "Sounds like nothing's changed. Drink some wine," he said, as the captain passed the bottle. "You probably need it. I know I always did, after I left their Imperial Serenities."

———◆———

We could have transferred at any time, of course. But Hlanan left that decision to me. We spent a couple of quiet days on the ocean, sailing steadily northeast. When a roaring early-spring storm caught up with us, causing the yacht to climb kelp-veined waves as high as the masthead, I told Hlanan it was time.

Leaving Prince Geric to his new yacht, we transferred to Erev-li-Erval, which I had thought I would never see again. Within moments after our recovery from the transfer magic a tiny blue woman in a floaty drape ran into the Destination chamber, hair whorling about her head in fascinating patterns, her arms wide.

"Oh my love," she cried, her voice like bells, no, like the prettiest birdsong, no, *better.*

"I can't sing," I mumbled into her shoulder as I flung myself into her clasp—I'd had more human contact in the last couple days than all that time in my silken prison, and yet I was still starved for love and touch.

"Oh, Elenderi, my darling child, neither could your father," she whispered into my hair, trembling between laughter and tears.

"And I don't know how to be part of a family," I said, all the old fears welling up. "I don't really even know what love is. That horrid Maita said that love conquers all, when she was ready to sacrifice Hlanan for his blood. And trust? I don't believe it exists."

"Do you feel my love? And my trust?" She lifted her head and regarded me, her deep blue eyes somehow open as the sea and sky, and equally full of a light that I perceived in the mental realm. I felt the strength of her unconditional devotion, intensified by her years of yearning and searching, warm as those currents of air high above the ground, only deeper, higher—ineffable.

"Yes," I whispered, and she touched her forehead to mine.

"Then here is where we begin. One breath at a time, one day at a time. Love is one of the simplest of what we call the Mysteries, and yet the strongest, like air: the greatest treasure cannot buy it nor the smartest thief steal it nor the most powerful emperor command it. And like air, it freely fills to capacity whatever is open to it. Everything else will come when you are ready. When you choose."

For a heartbeat the anger leeched out of me, but then it was there again, a molten pool of hot, destructive rock all of my own. "Won't the Hrethan object to that? They left me here alone, you know. Before Prince Geric grabbed me. One thing about trust I am certain of—they sure didn't trust me."

Mother said, "They were confused and afraid. They will make themselves plain, for that was one of my demands during that time I was talking to them, when you could not reach me. They wish to make amends, but we shall proceed as you choose. And perhaps, one day, when you say you are ready, we shall transform and fly to the heights to meet your father."

I drew a breath. And another. She was right. One breath at a time, one decision at a time. I was free to choose. *Free?* I wasn't truly free. Even standing there in the middle of Aranu Crown's citadel with my mother's arms around me, I could feel Jardis Dhes-Andis out there. I would never be completely free while we were both in the same world.

But right now I was free enough.

"All right," I said, sighing the tension out. "I can do that."

She lifted her head, glanced aside, and then gave me a wistful smile. "We are requested to come before the Empress, who is waiting. Can you compass that, my darling Elenderi?"

"One thing I've learned in this last year is, the world can be falling apart but you Do Not Keep Imperial Types Waiting."

She laughed softly, a sound like lark song, and tucked her hand through my arm. Hlanan stood a little distance away. When we reached him, he said, "Ready?"

"Yes," I said, and he opened the tall door himself.

I remembered that quiet room overlooking the cascade.

A stout woman of sixty-some years, her dark hair shot with gray, Aranu Crown regarded me under straight brows. "I'm glad you're safe," she said. "And I want to thank you for keeping secret what you probably could have been justified in revealing, given our last encounter. I trust my son explained my dilemma?"

"Yes," I said, reflexively giving her the Djuran imperial bow.

I saw a subtle reaction in them all, then the Empress waved toward the circle of comfortable chairs. "Sit. And tell us, who are you now? Elenderi of Sveran Djur or Lhind of nowhere?"

I was about to reject the name Elenderi, but I couldn't, quite — not after hearing the tender way my mother pronounced it. Amney had despised it as Hrethan and foreign, and I was not about to accept *her* judgment. And like it or not, Princess Elenderi as I'd lived her these past weeks was part of me, in the same way Lhind had been...part of me.

"I don't know," I said.

"Fair enough. I believe you've earned the right to find it out in your own way. But I feel obliged to warn you that there are a lot of people, some of them very powerful indeed, interested in what you decide. And a few of them—I think I need mention no names—might not wait to find out. And," she drew a deep breath, "there is the matter of an ancient dragon named Rue."

Rue? All my life I'd exclaimed *Flames of Rue*, though I had never known where the expression came from. My neck hairs curled. "That dragon had nothing to do with me," I said quickly. "I mean, I never had any contact with him. I just saw him when I visited his mountain."

She grunted. "That's not quite the way Hlanan explains it. That dragon stooped, or as near as, on Skyreach Mountain, blasting out all the windows. Even if the dragon did not contact you, he saw fit to rise. After centuries. *Centuries*, child. I think you are going to have to learn not only what you can do, and figure out who you are, but what place you want to take in the world. Because I hope you can see that returning to running around as a thief disguised as an urchin is not a reliable future."

Hlanan shot her a look and she raised her hands. "I'm done, I'm done. I felt I ought to put that much forward for you to consider."

"Then I'm not a prisoner? I'm free to...do what I want?"

The Empress uttered a dry laugh. "At this point I doubt that any of us could hold you, if you were truly determined. Lady Eleth, may I request you to wait a moment?"

I jumped up, glad to escape, though there was no sense of threat or rancor. In either of us, I was glad to discover. My resentment against her had dissipated.

Hlanan and I walked out into the quiet hall. Hlanan put his arm around me and I leaned into him, sighing.

"Thianra is waiting impatiently," he murmured.

"I want to see her, too. I thought about her. A lot," I said.

"We shall have this evening. Including your mother, of course. And tomorrow, I very much fear that the Mage Council is going to insist on an interview at least, and then, of course, the Hrethan ambassadors are going to be arriving to apologize for various lapses, after which your mother will probably want to whisk you away altogether. For you should not be kept from meeting your father."

"You're telling me what I already know because...." I stopped and faced him. "You're leading up to something horrid?" I clutched at my throat.

His gaze flicked from my fingers — which I yanked down — to my face as he shook his head. "No, no. Maybe I ought to wait. It's too early."

"But that just makes me more worried."

He sighed and drew me into one of the bay windows, through which the warm early-spring sun embraced us both. "Here it is, then. Aranu Crown has confided to me that she wants to step down within a few years. Points out that the best emperors and empresses did. Her father, Aulin the Ugly, kept putting it off—and she had to undo the damage of his last years of rule. Her goal is to hand over a successful, peaceful empire to her successor, which might very well be me, and live the remainder of her life in the world again."

"Oh."

He glanced outside into the garden, where the trees showed fuzzy green, ready to burst into leaf. "I thought you ought to keep that in mind. I don't have any idea what's going to happen in the world. Including Sveran Djur. I have to laugh at myself when I remember swearing to you in my arrogant ignorance that I would one day find a way to bring down Jardis Dhes-Andis."

"It seemed easier when he was the Evil Emperor of stories and songs? You just find the right spell, he vanishes in defeat, and everybody celebrates?"

"Exactly." He grinned, then sobered. "The Djurans might not be ready to break such a long-established culture, but on the other hand, what one beak can snap—and was seen to snap—another can, in another way."

I was about to retort that I didn't care what happened to the Djurans, but I thought of Pelan, and Kal, and Mor. No, it really wasn't simple.

Hlanan's thoughts seemed to parallel mine, as they often had. "One thing I am certain of, we had better learn more about that Shadow Dance. Dhes-Andis's reaction was as telling as the magic you glimpsed, and the animals' responses."

"I've been thinking about that," I said.

"Which brings us to you." He held my hands in a light grip, in case I needed to break free. "And me. We never had time to figure out where we were going before complications like dragons and mysterious powers and angry emperors." He glanced toward the window and back. "I planned this better in my head. I meant to say that I'll wait while you figure things out. You know the demands on my life. You are as important to me as any of them."

I leaned against him, my head tucked against his collar bones, his steady heartbeat under my ear. "I think that is the perfect place to start."

About Book View Café

Book View Café Publishing Cooperative is an author-owned cooperative of over fifty professional writers, publishing in a variety of genres such as fantasy, romance, mystery, and science fiction.

BVC authors include *New York Times* and *USA Today* bestsellers; Nebula, Hugo, and Philip K. Dick Award winners; World Fantasy Award, Campbell Award, and RITA Award nominees; and winners and nominees of many other publishing awards.

Since its debut in 2008, BVC has gained a reputation for producing high-quality e-books, and is now bringing that same quality to its print editions.

CPSIA information can be obtained
at www.ICGtesting.com
Printed in the USA
LVOW12s0222150917
548806LV00001B/113/P